BY EASTERN WINDOWS

A Biographical Novel

GRETTA CURRAN BROWNE

88

EIGHTY-EIGHT PUBLICATIONS

Dedicated in loving memory of two very special young angels now in Heaven

My beautiful niece

SUSAN AYEE

Who was born in a British military hospital in the East, and died young in the West.

And my nephew

RONAN BROWNE

A wonderful young man who loved the sea, his young wife Linda, his parents Richard and Maíre, and all of his family.

Panis Angelicus

ISBN: 978-0-9572310-8-5

Cover Design: E & A Creative Designs / The Cover Collection.

Eighty-Eight Publications
2 Spencer Avenue
London N13 4TR

Author's Note

Although presented here as a novel, and cloaked in the style of fiction, this story is true one based on the private letters, diaries and documents of Lachlan Macquarie, Elizabeth Campbell, and many of the other people involved.

For providing me with copies from microfilm of relevant documents from the Macquarie Papers, I am deeply grateful to the Mitchell Library in Sydney, as well as to the Archives Authority of New South Wales.

And my very special thanks to Andrew Southern in Australia.

PROLOGUE

Isle of Mull
Scotland 1787

The rising sun appeared like a huge golden ball hanging low in the sky, streaking its rays down the valley, dazzling the eyes of Donald Macquarie as he stood in the sheep field and squinted towards the ridge of the eastern hill where, just a few moments earlier, a young man had appeared and now stood outlined in the morning sunshine.

Donald stared at him, disbelieving, watching as the young man stood motionless, gazing around him as if observing every detail of the landscape. He was tall, and wore no hat, his sun-streaked hair glinting in the sun But it was the clothes he wore that made Donald's heart pound in his chest – he was wearing the scarlet jacket of an officer of the line.

Donald felt a sudden quaking of excitement. For the past ten years all his memories had been of a fifteen-year-old boy, not of a grown man, but the young officer on the ridge... He watched as the soldier continued his journey down the road that led to the farm, walking with a steady step and carrying a leather holdall in his hand. And only then – when he was absolutely certain that the oncoming soldier was his younger brother, did Donald suddenly abandon his watch and spring into an excited run.

'Lockie!'

Lieutenant Lachlan Macquarie smiled as Donald reached him and crushed him into a fierce hug. He dropped his bag and hugged Donald just as strongly, laughing his delight. 'Ah Donnie ... man, it's good to see you again.'

Donald's chest was still heaving with the power of his excitement, words only finding utterance after a number of long breaths. 'Ye've come back, Lachlan, ye've come back!'

`Aye, I have, but you knew that I would, Donald.'

'I didna know, Lachlan, I didna know anything! I feared never to see you again!' Donald pointed back at the field. 'Ask the sheep, they know what I feared.'

Lachlan felt his throat tighten and that old pain returning – that dull pain of pity he had always felt for his older brother. Donald was now twenty-nine-years old, a man whom their father had always described as 'the bonniest lad in all Scotland,' but a lad who would always have the mental age of an innocent child.

From as far back as Lachlan could remember, Donald had worked the farm quietly and diligently and had always seemed bewildered when the cruel children of Mull shouted to him that he was 'No` the full shilling!' He lived a solitary life, close to his mother, and Lachlan had been the baby brother that Donald had petted and loved and helped to bring up. But now it was Lachlan who was the man.

'Mother will be over the moon when she sees you!' Donald snatched up the holdall. 'Come on, Lachlan, I canna wait to see her face when ye walk in!'

In the large, neatly kept kitchen of the farmhouse, Mrs Macquarie was sitting by the fire knitting, the needles moving at a rapid pace, her back to the door.

'Hello, Mother.'

She turned ... her eyes widening as she stared at the red coated young officer who stood smiling at her, as disbelieving of his actual presence as Donald had been earlier.

'Lachlan!' she finally breathed. 'Oh, praise God ...'

Donald could not contain his excitement when he saw the expression on his mother's face, rubbing his hands with pleasure as she threw down her knitting and rose to welcome Lachlan with a joyous hug.

Mrs Macquarie drew back, holding her youngest son at arm's length, her eyes gazing over him in wonderment – so changed from the fifteen-year-old boy she had last seen. And by! – So handsome now! He looked tall and fit and strong, and even his hair had changed to a sun-streaked light brown, no longer as blond as corn. Only his eyes remained the same, those smiling brown eyes that always reminded her of her dead husband. Her son, a man now, and back from America at last.

'To think ...' she said finally, 'that you're now twenty-five. Oh, son ... what a shock! When did ye get in?'

'Last night...' Donald had his arms around Lachlan, hugging him again. 'I sailed over from Oban on the late ferry then stopped off to spend the night at Uncle Murdoch's house before setting out this morning.'

'What? Ye came all the way from Lochbuy this morning? Did ye get a lift or did ye walk? Have ye had any breakfast?'

'No, I left hours before breakfast. I wanted an early start for my very long walk.'

'Then sit yourself down while I cook ye some breakfast,' she ordered. 'You too, Donald, come and sit down with your brother.'

Donald sat down at the table next to Lachlan, giggling irrepressibly at the delicious joy and surprise of it all.

By evening time the farmhouse at Oskamull was packed with relatives come to greet the returned soldier. Mrs Macquarie watched Lachlan with secret pride as he sat surrounded by a group of admiring cousins. She listened to the tales of his travels and the friends he had made.

Lachlan was not the only fifteen-year-old who had left home to join the scarlet battalions crossing the Atlantic to fight in the American Revolution. A year – they had all thought they would be coming back home in a year – but the war had lasted seven years, the Americans had proved unbeatable, and now the rule of George the Third had been replaced by the rule of George Washington.

In his ten years away, she learned, he had served with the 89th Regiment in Canada, then in the second battalion of the 71st in New York, finally shipping out from America with the 71st, not for home, but a further two years service in Jamaica.

'Jamaica?' she asked curiously. 'Where is that now?'

Lachlan smiled. 'Where it has always been, Mother, on the other side of the world.'

Three mornings later, Lachlan returned to his uncle's estate at Lochbuy, strolling easily down the path through the long green lawns and up the steps to the front door of the huge Georgian grey-stone house.

Murdoch Maclaine had almost finished his breakfast when Lachlan was shown in to the dining room.

'You sent for me?' Lachlan looked questioningly at his uncle, a broad and solid man of forty-six years who was still a bachelor and always wore a fraught expression on his face.

'Sit in,' Murdoch ordered, pointing to a chair. 'Take some tea.' He pushed a white china cup and saucer towards Lachlan and beckoned for the maid to pour. When she had done so, he waved a hand in dismissal and watched her flurry out, then sat back and gazed gravely at Lachlan.

'You do *know* why I sent for you, don't ye, lad?'

'No, not yet.' Lachlan tasted his tea.

'We need to discuss your debts.'

'What debts?' Lachlan frowned. 'I have no debts.'

Murdoch could not restrain a smile of gentle reproach. 'Is that right now? No debts? Well, let's you and me talk some more and I'll refresh your memory.'

Lachlan listened in absolute silence while his uncle did all the talking, reminding him of the great debt Lachlan owed to him, and without which Lachlan could never have succeeded in becoming an officer of any rank in the British Army. But he *had* become an officer, and he *had* earned an officer's *pay* along with it – and all thanks to his very generous uncle, Murdoch Maclaine.

Lachlan finally understood, but Murdoch held up a hand and talked on. 'I'm a practical man, Lachlan, and I had no intention to be cruel, no, but when your father died so young and left my sister a widow, I just didna have the money to waste on any education for Donald. What good would it have done, eh? But I did spend a great deal on *your* education in Edinburgh. And as I say, I'm a practical man, so I trust I can now reap some profit from that investment.'

'Profit?'

'Aye, profit – by you becoming my estate manager, now that you're back and full-grown. I'll be handing over to you complete control of all papers of business relating to Lochbuy. You were always a genius with figures, so now I'll be putting into your hands the books and accounts and all the responsibility for the collection of rents from the tenants, the payment of wages, all of it.'

Lachlan sat back in his chair, a sardonic expression on his

face as he eyed his uncle. 'And there was me ...' he said wryly, 'all these years, thinking your decision to educate me was due to family love and consideration for your widowed sister.'

Murdoch helped himself to more bread and flourished his knife over the butter. 'I'll pay you a wage of course. And you'll still have some time to help Donald at your own place. Should be easy for a strong young soldier like you. So now – I have a visitor arriving shortly, and before she arrives I need to know if you intend to honour your debt by agreeing to sort out my accounts and become my estate manager?'

Lachlan pushed back his chair and stood up to leave. 'No,' he said quietly. 'I'm sorry you were so quick to make your plans for me, Murdoch, but I'll decide my own future and my own employment.'

Murdoch stopped chewing and stared. 'You're not refusing me now?'

Lachlan nodded. 'Aye, I am.'

Outraged, Murdoch swallowed the food in his mouth and blurted, 'Listen, me laddie, you were nothing more than a harum-scarum youngster when I paid to have ye sent to school and educated. Good money I paid out, but I'm not the Bank of Scotland. I expected some return long before this. I didn't expect ye to go running off to America. But now that you're back, ten years later, you surely must give some repayment to the business that supported you in those early years – and that was *me* and *this* estate of Lochbuy!'

With a sudden sense of fairness, as well as deep resentment, Lachlan realised that he did owe something to Murdoch and the estate of Lochbuy – but neither was getting the rest of his life in return for five years of schooling.

6

'The money you paid for my education I will repay you, one day, as soon as I possibly can,' Lachlan said finally, 'every penny of it. I know the exact amount because you've written and told me often enough.'

'Repay it? One day? Some day?' Murdoch sat back in his chair. 'Och, that's an easy thing for any man to say. I wish I could say it to my bank!'

'I'll not run the estate for you,' Lachlan said determinedly, 'but I will help you out for a time, a short time, until I get some other paid employment.' He looked steadily at Murdoch. 'Now that's my offer, take it or leave it.'

Murdoch Maclaine was canny enough to know it was the best offer he would get this day, but given time, he was sure he would be able to talk Lachlan round to his way of thinking.

Damn and blast, Murdoch thought angrily, why had he not married sooner? He needed a *son*, a few sons to run this estate. In the meantime he needed his nephew to sort out his accounts and collect the rents. When it came to money, he held no trust for strangers.

Murdoch sighed and stood up from his chair, holding his hand out. 'Well, there it is, laddie, there it is – your offer and my acceptance. Give me your hand and we'll shake on it.'

Lachlan hesitated for a moment, and then took his uncle's hand. 'Part time, for a short time, agreed?'

'Agreed ... aye, agreed.' Murdoch shook his nephew's hand vigorously, not meaning a word of it. 'Now, I'll need you to start as soon as tomorrow. No point in wasting time, not with a big estate like this to run – and *me* with a marriage to arrange! Did I tell you the cook was leaving?'

On the morning ferry from Oban to Mull, Elizabeth Campbell lost her hat while throwing biscuits to the gulls, but she didn't care – she was more bored than she feared she would be, and tired out from listening to her older sister Margaret prattling on about the man she hoped to marry, Murdoch Maclaine of Lochbuy.

Elizabeth couldn't see the attraction at all. Murdoch Maclaine had visited their home in Airds on the mainland quite a few times now, and on each occasion he had struck Elizabeth as being very plain, very boring, and very old.

'That's because you're only thirteen,' Margaret had responded good-naturedly. 'A man of forty-six is not old at all.'

'But *you* are only *nineteen!*' Elizabeth had replied. 'And you're pretty while he's plain, and you're funny while he's dull. How can you be in love with him?'

'Love? Oh, that's all blah and nonsense,' Margaret had sniffed. 'Papa told me that and I'm inclined to trust Papa in all things, as *you* should too. And you should also hold your tongue instead of lying about me being pretty, because you know I'm not. I'm roly-poly fat with a face as round as the sun itself.'

'No, you're just a wee bit plump' Elizabeth had insisted, although in truth Margaret had always been round and robust, displaying not only a disparity in age between the two sisters, but also in their looks. Margaret was tidily comfortable under her matronly bun of black hair, whereas Elizabeth was long-legged and skinny with a mane of copper-gold hair that hung round her shoulders in a mass of unruly curls.

Elizabeth had enough of the screeching gulls, left the deck, and returned to her seat next to her sister.

'You *do* know, Margaret,' she said, continuing their conversation, 'that Papa doesn't know *everything*. He just wants you to marry Murdoch Maclaine because he's the Laird of Lochbuy and has lots of money.'

'And a fine thing it will be for a girl like me to become the *mistress* of an estate like Lochbuy,' Margaret said happily. 'And Papa says the house is very big, almost baronial'

Elizabeth gave up the fight and sat back as Margaret prattled on about the benefits of marrying Murdoch Maclaine, parroting their father's every word about how *lucky* Margaret was, as plain as she was, as uneducated as she was, to have the chance of rising to the position of becoming the 'Mistress' of an estate like Lochbuy....

The ferry was approaching the dock, and now the two sisters stood in readiness for their first visit to the Isle of Mull, so that Margaret could take a look at the estate that may become her future home.

The coach journey from the Ferry Port across the countryside to Lochbuy had been pleasant for Elizabeth Campbell, banishing most of her boredom. She had not expected the island of Mull to be so beautiful, so lushly green.

'There it is!' Margaret's head had been stuck out the carriage window for over ten minutes and now she cried in triumph. 'Oh, look – look at it, Elizabeth! Mr Maclaine's house!'

Elizabeth stuck her head out and looked ... in size the house was indeed big, and must have contained at least twenty rooms ... clearly the home of a Laird.

'Here we are then,' Margaret's voice was high with excitement. 'And here is dear Mr Maclaine coming down the steps to greet us!'

When Elizabeth stepped down from the carriage she still thought Murdoch Maclaine just impossible to like, and despite her bests efforts she could manage no more than a sullen response to his greeting.

`She's only thirteen,' Margaret said quickly to Murdoch by way of excuse, `still learning her manners.'

Elizabeth did not hear Murdoch's reply because a young man had come through the open front door and was running down the steps towards them. He was tall and slender and agile, his light-brown hair flying gallantly behind the collar of his brown fitted jacket.

Elizabeth stared at him, spellbound. His sudden appearance was like sunshine on a winter's day, a young man in an old world, handsome and full of life and health – and when he smiled at her, Elizabeth's young heart jumped with an emotion she had never before experienced.

Murdoch had already started the introductions to Margaret. '... My sister's son, and my new estate manager – educated from the age of nine and the expense of it all paid for by me.'

Finally, briefly, almost as an afterthought, Murdoch introduced Elizabeth to his nephew, but Elizabeth was incapable of any response. While she stared up at him mutely with wide eyes, he smiled at her again, almost tenderly, as if deciding she must be a shy and simple child, then he quickly moved on, repeating both his welcome and apologies to her sister, in a hurry to leave.

In the days and weeks that followed, Elizabeth began to see Murdoch's nephew frequently on the estate, simply because she spent every moment of her days searching him out ... then standing in the shadows watching him like an unseen ghost.

She once followed him as he meandered through the gardens at the back of the house, concealing her presence by moving stealthily and hiding behind bushes, her blue eyes watching his every move. He paused in his strolling and leant with a melancholy grace against a tree, lost in his own thoughts, moving his gaze upwards to a row of windows on the top floor of the house. In her mind and eyes, misted by adolescent romance, he looked like a soulful Romeo waiting for his Juliet to appear at one of those windows.

Elizabeth was filled with an unfathomable longing, and in the days and weeks that followed her desire to see him as often as possible developed into an intense obsession. She craved to speak to him, to have a proper conversation with him, but following his arrival in the afternoons he never seemed to stop working, usually in the library, and he had never once accepted Murdoch's invitation to stay for dinner, always eager to be off.

So Elizabeth had no choice but to spend each evening sitting at the table in silence as Murdoch and Margaret prattled endlessly about the plans for their wedding, whilst she gazed wistfully out of the window, her eyes focused on the darkening trees and the last limpid light of day, wishing for time to fly until the next afternoon when she hoped she might see him again.

And she always did, she made sure of it. In fact, she made sure that they were always encountering each other, here, there and everywhere, and although he never delayed at length to speak to her, he always smiled and greeted her politely before moving on.

She began to love that smile, and hated the catastrophic day when Margaret told her it was time to leave Mull to return to their home on the mainland. They had spent a full two months on the estate of Lochbuy during which time Margaret had got to know all of the house-servants and many of the land-tenants, and they in turn seemed happy enough with their future mistress.

Home seemed bleak in comparison. Elizabeth had always enjoyed life on their small estate at Airds, the beautiful gardens and the comfortable house, but now she wandered around it in lost loneliness, obsessed in her thoughts of a young man who had once been a soldier.

An eternity later, although in reality only a month, when Margaret announced that they would be returning to Mull, Elizabeth squealed with delight.

Margaret beamed. 'I'm so glad that you like Murdoch now.'

'Oh, I do, I do,' Elizabeth lied passionately. 'I like him very well now.'

'And do you still believe he is too old for me?'

'No, not a bit!' insisted Elizabeth, conscious that her own hero was twenty-four and therefore eleven years older than she was. 'Who cares about a difference in age at the end of it,' she said excitedly. 'It's the man that counts, Margaret, the man!'

'I agree,' Margaret replied, 'but the man is never as important as the home he provides, nor the children that follow him. Mama told me that and I was always inclined to trust Mama about such things.'

'When do we leave?' Elizabeth asked impatiently.

`Soon,' Margaret beamed again. `The wedding is to take place in four weeks time, in the drawing-room at Lochbuy.'

Although more than three months had passed since his return to Mull, Mrs Macquarie was filled with worry. She watched as Lachlan kept himself busy at work and also managed to enjoy an active social life in the evenings with his friends and cousins, but she knew he was not happy. What he needed was some true contentment in his life to help him settle down here at home. What he needed was a wife.

She decided to wait until Sunday to broach the subject, because Sunday was the only day he did not have to ride over to Lochbuy.

On Sunday she waited until Donald had gone down to the shore's edge to do a bit of fishing, then turned her eyes apprehensively to Lachlan. He was sitting at the table, head bent, writing steadily and quickly over a thick sheet of paper. She watched his intent, handsome face, wondering to whom he was writing the letter and marvelling that he could write with such ease. She herself could not read nor write a word. All she had ever been taught was every method needed to cook and run a household.

'Lachlan,' she said finally.

'Aye,' he replied, but kept on writing.

'I was thinking ... you do know, don't ye, Lachlan, that ye are now twenty-five years old?'

'Of course I know.'

'So mebbe it's time you started thinking of a wife. Is there no young lassie, out of all the lasses you're friendly with, that's maybe taken your fancy?'

He stopped writing, but remained silent for so long she

wondered if he had heard her.

'Lachlan, did ye hear me speaking to ye now?'

He had heard her, but her question merely depressed him. She still did not understand that he had changed, that he had travelled far beyond Mull's horizons and had seen new parts of the world and lived through experiences that she would be unable even to imagine. The island of Mull was too small for him now. He could not settle here, not yet, not until he was older, much older. The world out there was big and wondrous and strange, and he craved to see more of it, be a part of it.

Yet he knew that to his mother the world was just some place 'out there' beyond the islands and the ocean, and as removed from her needs and understanding as the sky and all of its stars.

He laid down his pen, knowing that even if he had wished to stay here, and settle here, he could not ... and now he must tell her why. He turned his head to look at her, and this time his mother's voice was almost pleading. 'Surely there must be some young lassie that's taken your fancy?'

'No,' he deliberately kept his voice gentle, 'but, Mother, if there was someone, and I did wish to marry, how would we live?'

'Live?' She blinked in puzzlement. 'What do ye mean?'

'This small farm can barely sustain the three of us. It's only the money I earn at Lochbuy that's keeping us going. For the past four months I've been working at Lochbuy as well as managing the accounts of this farm here – but despite what you and Murdoch say about my skill with figures, I can't work *magic*. I can't produce money from a box that is empty. Mother, you do realise that you don't have a penny to your name?'

'Not a penny, I know, I know,' she said guiltily. 'But it's no' my fault, Lachlan! The last few years were hard years for Scotland. Everyone suffered badly. Everyone fell into bad debt.' She looked at him defensively. 'At least I didna do that – fall into debt.'

'Only because of the money I sent home from my Army pay.'

'Aye, oh aye,' she agreed, 'only for that coming regularly I wouldna have been able to manage at all.'

He sat silent for a long moment, looking at her hopelessly. 'Mother, can't you see there is no future here for me. No future here for any of us ... unless I go away again.'

She jerked on her seat in alarm. 'No, son, no – there's no need for ye to go away again. I couldna bear it ... could ye not ask Murdoch to pay ye more money?'

'I wouldn't ask Murdoch for anything,' he said grimly. 'And anyway,' he shrugged, 'Murdoch is in debt up to his neck. It took me only a few days of sorting through his estate papers to realise that. He's just about keeping his chin above the water. None of his accounting figures make any sense, yet he wants me to "balance" his books in any which way I can – cook them, fry them, lose them – just enough to satisfy the tax inspector, you understand? His financial situation is dire and if things get any worse, he will have to sell Lochbuy.'

'Sell Lochbuy?' His mother frowned prodigiously. Before her marriage she had been a Maclaine and had been born and raised on the Maclaine's family estate of Lochbuy. As the oldest child the estate should have fallen to her, but no, the law forbade her to inherit it because she was only a woman, and so it had gone to Murdoch, the son and legal heir. And now Murdoch was running the estate badly, wasting all of its income, constantly blabbing about the pittance he had spent on Lachlan's education and now he was clawing it back as a debt – whilst she had spent all her married and widowed years living on a farm rented from the Duke of Argyll.

'Murdoch already has a huge mortgage on Lochbuy,' said Lachlan, 'but from next week, he will have two huge mortgages on it.'

'Two huge mortgages! From who?'

'The Duke of Argyll.'

'The Duke of Argyll?' Mrs Macquarie tutted angrily. 'By, that man must own half of Mull now. And he must be fair rich from all the rent we've paid him on this place.'

'I've told you about the mortgages,' Lachlan said, 'simply to help you understand why no financial help is to be sought from Murdoch ... and why I've decided to write this letter ... to the War Office in London.'

Mrs Macquarie fussed with her apron and struggled with the blast of her emotions. 'So that's it ... ye want to leave us again ... and go back to the Army.'

'It's the only way,' he said honestly. 'The only way I can continue to support you and Donald. The only way I can continue to pay the rent on this farm each quarter day. I have no other choice but to go away and earn enough money to send back to you regularly.'

'And ... to get that money,' she faltered miserably, 'I must lose my youngest son again?'

'No, to get that money means that you will be able to keep on taking care of *Donald*, without fear or worry. We *both* will.'

She saw, dimly, that Donald had come into the kitchen,

carrying a box of rich green cabbages he had grown from seeds to full heads, the triumph and delight in his innocent eyes touching her heart to the core as he held them out for her approval.

'Aye,' she said huskily, smiling at him, 'aye, ye did well, Donald.'

A moment later she looked at Lachlan and nodded resignedly, giving her agreement. If his going away provided the rent to keep her dear Donald safe and happy on this farm, then so be it.

The following morning Lachlan made the long ride over the hills to the town of Tobermory to post his letter to London. He did not expect a speedy reply, but he received one three weeks later, offering him a lieutenant's commission in a new Scottish regiment which was being raised to serve in India.

'It will be known as the 77th,' Lachlan told his mother, his eyes on the letter. 'I'm ordered to report to Colonel Balfour in London as soon as possible and be ready to depart for Bombay on the sixteenth.'

'That soon?'

He looked at her, apologetically. 'Aye, that soon.' He folded the letter. 'I'll have to send a letter over to Murdoch informing him of the reason for my sudden departure. I wonder how he'll take it?'

'Badly.' His mother nodded positively. 'He'll be ranting and raging for a week.'

Lachlan smiled. 'Aye, I suppose he will.'

He had no smile later that evening when he saw Donald's tears. Poor Donald just could not understand why Lachlan had to go away again. His eyes filled up with more tears as he implored Lachlan to tell him why he had to go.

'Why, though, *why?*'

Lachlan looked helplessly at his brother. 'It's a matter of necessity, Donald. It's a job I have to do. Nothing more than that, just a job of work that will take me away for a while.'

'So *when* will ye be coming back then?'

Lachlan did not know.

'But I *will* come back, Donald, I promise. Wherever I go, I'll always come back to Scotland. You know that, don't you?'

Donald looked unsure. 'Is India as far away as America?' he asked.

'No,' Lachlan lied.

'Not nearly ten years away?'

'No, just a few months on a ship.'

It was three days before Jamie McTavish arrived at Lochbuy to deliver Lachlan's letter, only minutes after Murdoch and the Campbell family had sat down to luncheon, the day before the wedding.

Murdoch was so upset by the letter he glared at Margaret. 'I don't believe it! He's gone – again! Gone back to soldiering! Only it's a *heathen* land he's gone to this time. All the way to *India* no less!'

Elizabeth's face turned as pale as paper. She drew in her breath and realised the only place she wanted to be was upstairs in the privacy of her room and she ran to it, throwing herself down on the bed and crying noisily like a small child.

Margaret entered the room, full of concern. 'What's brought this on? I can't have you puffing and reddening up your eyes with all this bawling – and you to be bridesmaid at my wedding tomorrow!'

In the pain of her heartbreak, Elizabeth could not stop herself from sobbing out to Margaret the truth of her loss.

'Oh, my wee hennie ...' Margaret crooned. 'What you felt was nothing more than a girlish fancy. It'll be gone in a week.'

'No. I loved him, I truly loved him!'

'Love? Oh, that's all blah and nonsense!' Margaret sniffed. 'You should know that by now, I've told you often enough.'

Elizabeth did not answer, too engulfed in sobbing to argue. All she knew for certain was that her first true love affair had come to a bitter, *bitter* end.

PART ONE

INDIA

Where the hedges drop pink rose-petals,
And the bulbul sings love songs in Persian,
And the Sahib lives in a little white house
In a garden, which is almost, home.

ONE

The heat was unbearable. The marching feet of the men sent up clouds of dust, columns of soldiers in scarlet coats soaked with sweat, marching monotonously while their officers sat elegantly astride their mounts.

The march ended on a hill about fifteen hundred yards from Fort Avery, one of the enemy's crucial positions defended by a large garrison and a few small cannon. From the distance the soldiers could hear the screaming commentary of the enraged enemy as they watched the oncoming British.

The soldiers halted and formed into line. Immediately they were pounded with cannon balls that had no hope of reaching a distance of fifteen hundred yards. From the fort walls the enemy then sent out gunpowder rockets, but all fell too short.

General Sir Robert Abercromby surveyed the battle-ground before him and then looked up at the sun. It was after three o'clock, the sun had past its zenith, and only a few hours of daylight left. He turned to his staff officers. `Well, gentlemen, we are somewhat late, we have missed tiffin, so I think we should console ourselves with an early dinner.'

The General and his staff retired to the shade and accepted drinks from their servants while keeping an occasional eye on the enemy through their spyglasses. A large white tent was erected, a table unfolded, a white linen cloth draped over it. The silver and crystal were unpacked, bottles of Madeira uncorked, and the general and his staff sat back in preparation for a long campaign conference over an even longer dinner.

Except for the piquet lines, the rest of the soldiers were thankful enough to be given a stand-easy and drank thirstily from their water flasks.

Lachlan had flopped down under the shade of a tree beside Lieutenant Grant, who sat for a moment looking around him bleakly. 'Why the hell did we ever come to this place anyway?'

Lachlan removed his hat and wiped the sweat from his hair. 'Because we wanted to be soldiers, Edward, part of the great British Army.'

Grant shrugged. 'Well, intrepid daredevil I may be, but I never thought I'd be expected to get involved in anything so extreme as an all-out battle.' After another doleful moment, Grant sighed. 'I thought we were certain of a very cushy life here in India.'

Cushy? For the past two years Lachlan had found life in India *unbearably* cushy, utterly dull and monotonous. Apart from the regular drills and parades and afternoons spent in language lessons with a native *Munshi* in order to learn Hindustani, there was little else for an officer to do. And with little to do, military life had lapsed into an endless round of regimental dinners and socialising.

As for India itself, the 77th had quickly discovered that India was a mish-mash of territories ruled by different governments; parts of the sub-continent were ruled separately by the British and Dutch, and the remainder by princes and maharajas of the Hindu, Mohammedan, and Afghan dynasties – the latter three always being at war with each other.

At least, that's how it was, until three weeks ago, when

Tipu Sultan, the maharaja of Mysore, declared war on the British, threatening to reduce Madras and Bombay to ashes and drive every red-coated *Angrezi* out of India.

'The impertinent bugger is clearly begging to be pole-axed!' Lord Cornwallis, Governor-General of British India, had responded to Tipu Sultan's threat with fury. And now here the British Army were, in Cananore, before Fort Avery, preparing for battle with Prince Ali Rajah, a staunch ally of Tipu, who had *also* declared war on the British.

The enemy ceased its bombardment, clearly bewildered by the British who were blithely ignoring their cannon-fire and preparing to dine. Tents were being pitched on the hilltop while coolies and servants rushed around preparing cooking fires.

As evening approached, Lachlan received a summons to report to the tent of his commanding officer.

'Sir?' Lachlan saluted Colonel Balfour, a blue-eyed, fair-skinned man of robust build and a pleasant face that suggested a kind and genial disposition.

'Ah, Lieutenant Macquarie!' Balfour smiled warmly. He greeted all his junior officers as if they were his adopted sons. 'A hot and busy day before us tomorrow, my boy.'

'Yes, sir.'

'However, we do have to sort out a few problems beforehand,' Balfour said in a low voice, as if confiding a great secret. 'General Abercromby would dearly like to destroy the enemy's fort around dawn, but he is of the opinion that from fifteen hundred yards our fire is sure to fall short. Would you agree?'

Lachlan agreed. 'Even the eighteen-pounders would need to be at least four hundred yards nearer to the fort.'

Colonel Balfour beamed. He had expected that answer,

but pretended surprise. 'Why! – That's exactly the distance Major Jones suggested! How *very* astute of you, Lieutenant!'

It was something any junior officer would know, but Balfour raised a palm to Lachlan's protest. 'You are absolutely right, dear boy, bang on, just as I knew you would be, at least four hundred yards nearer! Major Jones was just as specific.'

Lachlan stemmed a sigh. Whenever Balfour was in a state of such sweet flattery it was best to remain silent.

'We shall, of course, need to detail a number of working parties to attend to it...'

Balfour paused to swat irritably at a fly near his face, and with that gesture Lachlan suddenly realised why he had been summoned, because he knew all of Balfour's tricks. For all his pretended geniality, Colonel Balfour had the skill of a scorpion. He always started with a smile and flattery, paused to swat a fly ... then dished out the dirty work.

And sure enough, minutes later, Colonel Balfour was pulling off his scarlet jacket in preparation for a rest while Lachlan left the tent to form a working party which would spend the night building a battery for the guns, four hundred yards closer to the enemy's fort.

A detachment from 5th Company collected their tools and began to move down the valley, but with every few yards they marched forward, the enemy sent out musket fire in their direction.

Private McKenzie, a big strong Jock who had enlisted simply to get drink, and had never experienced being under fire, nearly jumped out of his skin. '*Bluidy hell!* The buggers are firing at us, sir! At *us!*'

Lachlan looked at him wryly. 'So what did you expect

them to do, McKenzie – wave to us in greeting!'

'But, sir – we canna be expected to work wi' bullets flying towards us!'

Lachlan called a halt to the march and turned to face the men: dealing with new recruits on the ground was always hard, but they had signed up as soldiers and so must learn to think and act like soldiers.

He decided to shift their minds away from the dangers of India and focus their concentration on the land they all loved.

'This may be India,' he said gravely, 'but this is also the British Army. And not only are you soldiers of the British Army, you are also *Scottish* soldiers. So although Colonel Balfour says that you all look as if you only enlisted to get drink, I know that is not true.'

A number of the men glanced uneasily at each other, because they *had* only enlisted to get drink – a soldier's daily ration of a third of a pint of rum, to be exact, and for no other reason. A fact Lachlan was well aware of.

'And General Abercrombie may say that you all appear to be the worst picture of men, the absolute scum of Scotland's earth,' he continued, 'but I know that's also not true. So here's what I want you to do – I want you to prove them wrong! Show them what fine men you truly are. Do your families and your homeland proud. Show the generals who have brought us here that you are not Scotland's scum – but Scotland's best!'

The men cheered, animated and rallied, and seconds later they were marching forcefully down the valley as if the musket-fire in the distance caused them no fear. On reaching the site designated for the batteries they energetically threw themselves into the task of shovelling earth into sandbags.

It was hard and filthy work and by midnight the emplacements were only half completed, their progress hampered by the darkness. Private McKenzie could not restrain another complaint. 'Heck, sir, the night's as dark as a rajah's arse.'

As if in reply, a succession of shots suddenly cracked through the night – one of the Indian sepoys standing on sentry duty dropped like a sandbag. Lachlan swiftly drew out his pistol and ran forward, firing into the darkness at the unseen enemy snipers who could be heard shuffling away through the undergrowth.

'McKenzie's been hit!' someone shouted.

'I've been het!' McKenzie cried in astonishment. 'I've been het!'

Lachlan turned to see the big Scotsman half-lying on the ground with a hand over his heart. He rushed back and knelt down beside the soldier. 'Let me see.'

He lifted the big-knuckled hand covering the area of McKenzie's breastbone and peered curiously. 'There's no blood.'

'Wha'?' McKenzie began pawing his chest. He stared at Lachlan in horror. 'Ma bescets!' he yelled in outrage. 'The buggers have smashed ma bescets!'

The rest of the men grinned with relief. The worst that had happened to McKenzie was a dud musket ball had broken the biscuits he carried in a leather bag inside his tunic.

McKenzie pulled out the small leather bag which hung from a string around his neck and which contained all his worldly wealth. He uptilted it morosely and watched the crumbling biscuit pieces fall on to his palm

'Hell's teeth,' he said sadly. 'I was savin' them bescets to have later wi' ma tae.'

'You're unhurt so look lively!' Lachlan snapped. 'And from now on, McKenzie, you are forbidden to speak without my permission to do so. In short – keep that bloody blaring gob of yours shut.'

Lachlan turned his attention to the sepoy sentry who had been wounded. He instructed two of the men to carry him back to the camp.

'Permission to speak, sir!' McKenzie called out.

Lachlan swiftly returned to where McKenzie was still lying and smacked him hard on the back of his head. 'Permission denied, you bloody idiot!' he snapped in a loud whisper. 'Do you want your voice to mark you as a target? Now get back to work – in bloody silence.'

*

Just before dawn the battery was finished. An hour after dawn a bombardment of cannon balls from a line of eighteen-pounders crashed against the walls of Fort Avery, informing the enemy that the British had finished breakfast and were now ready for business.

The Fort gates opened, a surge of shock troops charged out screaming vengeance, only to be met by a line of free-riding cavalry waving sabres who sent them screaming back to the safety of their fort.

By noon the front walls of Fort Avery had been severely damaged, the gates were breached, and the scarlet lines swept forward. By dusk the inhabitants of the Fort were stacking their arms in surrender.

Having worked through the night and fought through the

day, Lieutenant Macquarie and his men were glad of the rest. Many of them were inspecting and comparing their wounds. 'We didna do a bad job, did we, sir!' McKenzie shouted.

Lachlan allowed the big Scotsman a small smile. 'You did very well.'

'Is that a fact now, is that a fact?' McKenzie murmured, then stood in a silence of his own heroic emotions.

'But remember, McKenzie, this is just the beginning. Our real battle will be at Mysore, with the army of Tipu Sultan.'

'Eh? Wha'?' McKenzie jerked round. 'Ye mean we're not done, sir? Ye mean we have to do it all *again!*'

''Fraid so.' Lachlan offered McKenzie a cynical glance. 'But with you in our ranks, McKenzie, with all your bulk and brawn and that blathering blaring voice of yours, I'm sure the Sultan's troops will flee at the first sight and sound of you.'

McKenzie's face twitched in a spasm of surprised joy. 'Ye reckon? So why do ye always place me at the back then, sir?'

'Just saving the worst till last,' Lachlan replied sarcastically, mounting his horse.

After a long pause, McKenzie's suddenly gushed, 'Och, sweet Jesus! Ye mean like a hidden weapon that's kept back to take 'em by surprise?'

His words were ignored as Lachlan rode off and another soldier ambled up to McKenzie, saying scathingly, 'So what's he been saying to ye now? Our fine young officer. Didna we prove to him that none of us are cowards?'

McKenzie turned his head and replied coolly, 'Our fine young officer is a gentleman which ye ain't. He knows what needs to be done which ye don't. And wha' he just told me in private – in *private* mind – is none of your bluidy business.'

*

The marching resumed, day after day, over wild stretches of land towards the Indian hills. The soldiers sweltered in the heat. Teams of oxen pulled the cannons and sturdy elephants carried the baggage and tents. After ten days they were ready to make their way up the treacherous jungle pass to the head of the Poodicherum Ghaut. The ascent was ten miles high and dangerously steep, almost up a precipice, a task made worse by the falling of rain.

At first the men were refreshed by the rain but it quickly proved worse than the heat as they found themselves plodding in mud. The artillery train came to a halt, bogged in the slough.

Lachlan received a summons from his commanding officer. Colonel Balfour greeted him grimly. 'Ah, Lieutenant Macquarie. What say you about these mud slopes, eh?'

'Our progress will be slow, sir. The wheels and guns will continue to get bogged down no matter how many times we pull them clear.'

'Quite so, quite so.' Balfour hesitated, there was a reason of course for the summons, but he always considered it only fair to compliment an officer in some way before making him miserable. 'Efficient work you and the men did building the batteries,' he said. 'Major Jones's guns were perfectly positioned and right on time. Good show.'

'Just doing our duty, sir.'

'Ah yes, duty. The First Commandment for all soldiers. Duty is what makes us push on when we long to turn back. And we, poor dutiful souls, must push on through all this ruddy mud...' Balfour sighed bleakly. 'So, Lieutenant, my orders are to command you to take six subalterns and one hundred men to build a road over the mud to make it easier for the artillery train and stores to be hauled up the Pass.'

'Build ... a *road*?'

'Not you personally, Lieutenant, no indeed no! Your men will do the actual work. All you will have to do is instruct and supervise them.'

Lachlan recovered from his shock, staring angrily at Balfour. 'But the *men,* sir ... the men are half-dead with exhaustion.'

Balfour's eyes also flashed anger. 'Our dead we bury immediately and respectfully, but those soldiers who are alive and can still walk – we keep working! Now set to it, Lieutenant, as soon as you can.'

At daybreak Lachlan and his men were already out, cutting down trees and laying a timber road, mile by mile, over which the guns were hauled. Some days the going was so tough only two miles could be covered. Each night Lachlan wearily splashed through the mud of the camp into the dryness of the tent he shared with Dr Anderson, falling down in sleep in his hammock without removing his scarlet coat.

The timber road finally reached the head of the Poodicherum Ghaut, overlooking Tipu Sultan's country of Mysore; one of the most beautiful parts of India that Lachlan had ever seen, saturated with groves of orange trees and lush green gardens throughout the wide-ranging plains. It had taken them three months of marching and numerous halts before they at last joined with Lord Cornwallis's troops in one great army outside Seringaptam.

The first attack would be a night attack, Cornwallis

decided. Surrounding the walls and storming the city was the first business he wanted done. The men waited in the darkness and while they did, Private McKenzie took it upon himself to instruct his comrades.

'Now listen lads, ye'll all be doin' Scotland proud when ye go out there fightin' like soldiers! Like real soldiers, like proper soldiers! An' remember – I'll be reet behind ye!'

A hard whack on the back of his head by a pistol butt sent McKenzie staggering forward in mid-sentence. `You stupid sod!' Lachlan hissed furiously. `Does that big gob of yours never shut?'

'But, sir ...' McKenzie steadied himself and rubbed the back of his head in puzzlement. 'I was only – '

'Only marking our spot for every murderous skirmisher hiding out there in the groves.' Lachlan quickly pointed the pistol at McKenzie's head and the sound of the hammer being cocked made the big man freeze. 'If you ever put my men in such danger again, McKenzie, I swear I'll not hesitate to blow your brains out. Is that clear?'

'Aye, sir,' McKenzie stuttered, `clear as d-daylight.'

'Now back into line!'

'Aye, s-sir,' McKenzie mumbled, but seemed unable to move.

'So do it!' Lachlan lowered the gun and holstered it as Lieutenant Grant and an ensign approached him.

'Dispatches have been going back and forth between Cornwallis and Tipu,' Grant told him quietly. 'It seems the sultan is not too happy at the sight of all the Indian regiments of the British Army gathered at his threshold. The latest news is that he has decided to call a halt to all hostilities and enter into a Peace Treaty with the British.'

'Until the next time he gets in a bad mood?' Lachlan

asked cynically.

'Probably,' Grant agreed, 'but all the signs now are that the big battle will not be fought this night or even this year. Still, the fat old darling is obviously as good a strategist as Cornwallis – knows not only when to fight, but when *not* to fight.'

Throughout the night and the following day the troops remained in their positions while inside the sultan's palace Lord Cornwallis and his staff negotiated the terms of the treaty, which was that Tipu would relinquish control of at least half of his dominions, as well as contributing three million rupees towards the expense of the war that he had started.

Tipu Sultan readily signed the Peace Treaty and then sent down to his vast treasury and paid over the three million rupees demanded.

'We will meet again,' he said coldly to Lord Cornwallis.

Cornwallis nodded. 'I have no doubt that we will.'

'You red-coated *Angrezi* will not always win the battles here in India.'

'Perhaps not,' Cornwallis replied curtly, removing the hat from under his arm and placing it on his head. 'But I think we can agree that the *Angrezi* have very easily won *this* one.'

*

The soldiers of the 77th left the plains of Mysore under a torrent of hard monsoon rain, every fibre of their tunics soaked, and many wondering why they had gone to Mysore in the first place? All they had defeated was the treacherous passes of the Ghauts, and now they must wade through the mud and tramp up and down them again.

34

The return journey was horrific. Bullocks hauling the cannons dropped dead in the mud from exhaustion and men were forced to take their places under the harness. Baggage and supplies had to be dropped and left behind in the slough. The men's rice rations diminished, leaving them only a handful of biscuits to sustain them at the end of each tortuous day.

Boats were hired to sail them down the swollen Belliapatam River. Lachlan sat in his boat as if in a nightmare, trying to swiftly identify the corpses that swirled past, the corpses of soldiers who had drowned from capsized boats.

Lachlan began to feel sick, very sick. He was soaked to the skin and had not eaten for three days. He had lost his tent and most of his baggage on the Ghauts. He had also lost his horse that had slipped and foundered, breaking two of her legs; he had almost wept when her big eyes had pleaded with him to take out his pistol and shoot away her pain.

Back on land, Lachlan trudged with his men through miles of mud and rain until finally they came within five miles of Tellicherry on the Malabar Coast. Tellicherry was civilisation, a coastal town with well-built houses and a small British community.

Three miles from Tellicherry, Lachlan received the news that General Abercromby and all the officers of the High Command had already reached the town, and even junior officers were being offered accommodation in the houses of the British community.

His head thumping with pain, Lachlan felt too wet and dirty to resume the gilded role of an officer in the civilisation of Tellicherry, choosing instead to roll up in his camp cloak and sleep on the floor of a deserted old hut near to the main camp. Outside the hut, the jungle steamed under the heat of a new sun.

Some hours later he awoke inside his mother's comfortable home on Mull, Donald was bending over him, a hand on his brow.

'Donald?'

Delirious at seeing his brother again he attempted to raise himself, but the pain banged inside his head, his bloodshot eyes blinking in puzzlement, unable to understand why Donald's face was shrouded in fog.

'Fever,' McKenzie said, turning to the soldier standing beside him. 'Make speed an' tell Surgeon Anderson that Lieutenant Macquarie is lying in a filthy hut shiverin' and shakin' wi' fever.'

Lieutenant Dr Colin Anderson was in his twenty-seventh year, the same age as his closest friend, Lachlan Macquarie. He arrived at the double, his face white with apprehension as he examined his patient.

'Malaria,' he said finally.

McKenzie was staring hard at his lieutenant; at the dark patches under his closed eyes; his tanned skin had a grey hue, his face drenched in perspiration, and every breath he drew sounded like a strangled rasp.

McKenzie whispered. 'Will he make it?'

'Hopefully,' Dr Anderson replied. 'He is fit and strong which always helps. I've given him a large dose of quinine and mercury, as well as a few opium pills to deaden the headaches. But he is dangerously ill and could take a fatal turn for the worse. He will need a servant to look after him, day and night.'

'He's already got one,' McKenzie said stoutly. 'He's got me, hasna he?'

Dr Anderson looked dubiously at the big Scotsman who had just promoted himself from the ranks into the personal service of an officer – an enormous man, built like a bull.

'Is this simply your way of escaping the drudgery of the ranks?'

'Nae sir.' McKenzie glared. 'It's ma way of looking after ma own lieutenant until he is well and fet again. Then I'll go back to ma comrades in the ranks.'

After a pause, Dr Anderson nodded tiredly. 'Very well, I shall arrange it with Colonel Balfour.'

'Aye, do that,' McKenzie said. 'An' while you're at it, mebbe ye could arrange for a couple of coolies to come an' help me clean up this place.' He looked disdainfully around the hut. 'This will no' do for ma lieutenant. This will *no'* do at all!'

'I'll send some coolies,' Anderson said, turning to leave.

'An` blankets,' McKenzie called after him. 'He'll be needing' a few more clean blankets to keep him comfortable when the shivering gets really bad. An` water! I'll need water to keep his face freshly sponged and cool. Ye'll see to that an all, will ye?'

At the door, the young military surgeon abruptly stopped in his tracks, turning to stare at the audacious private, eyeing him up and down as if unable to believe his insolence.

'Oh – an` some tae!' McKenzie added. 'If I'm stayin' here awhile I'll need a drop of the auld life saver.'

Dr Anderson turned and thrust himself out the door before his patience and temper escaped him.

*

When the doctor returned some hours later, the interior of the hut was as clean as a corporal's kit. A kettle was boiling on a small oil stove and McKenzie was ladling a spoon of the East India Company's tea into a pot of boiling water.

'Oh, this is *much* better!' Anderson said with surprise.

'Aye.' McKenzie nodded. 'But I had to promise them two lazy coolies that I'd give `em the last of ma bescet ration before they would even make a start to help me. Will ye have a drop o' tae, sir?'

Dr Anderson shook his head and moved over to his patient. When he turned back some minutes later, he saw McKenzie sitting with a contented expression on his face as he dipped a biscuit into his tin mug of tea.

'My, my,' the doctor said dryly. 'I thought you said you had promised the last of your biscuits to the coolies!'

'Aye, I did, sir. But not until they had done one final job for me.'

'Which was?'

'The Last Post, sir. I told them to go and find the Last Post and give it a good scrub down. Make it nice and clean. And no' to come back until a corporal or sergeant had signed a chit confirming they had done so.'

McKenzie dipped another biscuit in his tea. 'I told them any soldier would tell `em where to find the Last Post.'

It was an old trick pulled on very young and raw recruits. Dr Anderson could not help smiling as he pictured the faces of the soldiers who would very kindly send the two coolies running here, there, and everywhere, in search of the Last Post – a military bugle call sounded at sunset and military funerals.

McKenzie sniffed. 'I made a guess that ye'd already paid them to do the work, sir.'

'Your guess was correct.'

'So they had a reet cheek bargaining for ma bescets as well!' McKenzie exclaimed. 'That's why I sent them to the Last Post.'

Dr Anderson turned to leave. 'Well, McKenzie, if you look after Lieutenant Macquarie as efficiently as you look after your biscuit ration, then I think we may have no fear about his safety and welfare.'

'No fear,' McKenzie agreed. 'I'll treat him like a brother.'

'You most certainly will not!' Anderson snapped in final outrage. 'You, man, will treat him like an *officer*!'

McKenzie stared at the young surgeon's furious face and, not wishing to jeopardise his new career as an officer's aide, hastily assumed a look of sublime contriteness. 'Yes, sir, like an officer, sir. I'll salute him day and night, sir. Every time he wakes up, sir.'

At the door Dr Anderson looked back at the soldier coldly, 'Damn you and your thickheaded insolence, McKenzie. I sincerely hope that when Lieutenant Macquarie gets better, he will have the good sense to boot you and your audacity back to whence you came!'

'Yes, sir.'

McKenzie's face remained complacent. Such expressions of endearment from the officers were routine.

'I'll be back at three.'

'Verra good, sir.'

*

In the week that followed McKenzie cared endlessly and tirelessly for his lieutenant while the fever raged, forcing the required doses of mercury and opium into him; finally smiling happily when he managed to spoon-feed a cup of boiled rice down his patient's throat without it coming up again.

'Och, ye'll soon be in fine fettle, sir,' McKenzie said cheerfully. 'A few more days and ye may even decide that a drop of the army's brandy would be a better medicine for ye than mercury. Aye, brandy's a gleg medicine for easing' the shivers. I'll order the brandy for ye now, sir, if ye like?'

It was an order that McKenzie had already attended to. As soon as his lieutenant had again fallen into a sleep, he slyly produced the small flat metal flask from inside his tunic, took a long drink and smacked his lips appreciatively. 'Scotland for ever!' he gushed, and downed another gulp before returning the bottle to its hiding place.

A week later Lachlan had recovered enough to move into more comfortable accommodation in Tellicherry, procured for him by Dr Anderson, in the house of an elderly official of the East India Company and his wife. And McKenzie, as his official servant, went with him.

Lachlan spent the first night luxuriating in a hot soapy bath, his mood thoughtful as he contemplated his life since he had left his home on Mull to travel to India. What had he gained since then?

Nothing but malaria.

He lay in thoughtful stillness and let his mind drift home to Scotland and his family. He thought of his mother, still working her farm, and still depending upon financial assistance from her son in India. And poor Donald, working from dawn to dusk and constantly keeping an eye on the hilltop for his brother's return.

Lachlan climbed out of the tub, dried himself swiftly, knotted the towel around his waist, and searched through his leather holdall, the only possession he had not lost on the Ghauts, and wrote a short letter to his mother.

He chose his words carefully, because as his mother was unable to read, he was forced to write to her through the medium of his Uncle Murdoch who – when he had the time – would ride over from Lochbuy to read the letter to her.

His letter was short and cheerful, telling her of the wonderful and carefree life he was enjoying in India. Then he counted what money he had. It was not much for an officer in India, but a fair amount to a Scottish widow.

He walked to the door, opened it, and rang the bell on the floor outside which brought an Indian servant rushing to serve him. 'My aide, Private McKenzie,' he said in Hindi. 'Please ask him to come at once.'

When McKenzie arrived he was surprised to find his Lieutenant sitting on the bed, dressed in only a towel. 'Och, sir! This will no' do! This will *no'* do at all! Ye've just had the fever and must keep warm after a bath. An' that is a fact!'

Lachlan held out the money. 'First thing in the morning, I want you take this money and get a bank draft, signed and guaranteed by the Army, and made out to this name. Do you know where to go?'

McKenzie shook his head. 'But it'll no' take me long to find out.'

When McKenzie had gone Lachlan added a postscript to the letter, asking his uncle to see that the draft was cashed on behalf of his mother.

Then he sat and added it up. He had nothing left. He had just given away every rupee he possessed, but somehow he felt richer for it.

*

The following morning McKenzie woke him with his breakfast and the bank draft. Lachlan sealed the draft inside the letter and ordered McKenzie to arrange for it to go in the mail on the next boat out.

An hour later he received an order to report to his commanding officer. As always, Lachlan dreaded the worst. During the last year out in the field, whenever Colonel Balfour had sent for him, it was usually to reward him with some filthy job that kept him building batteries or roads, or standing to arms throughout the night on piquet duty in the rain, while other officers lounged in their tents and complained of the hardship of running out of claret.

For some reason Balfour seemed to be testing him more than any of the other officers, but he was determined not to waste time on resentment or complaint, not even inwardly to himself, because what would be the point? The British Army and the wage it gave him was the only thing that kept his mother and his poor beloved brother from complete impoverishment, and for this reason alone, whatever Balfour heaped upon him he was determined to respond with grit and resolve.

Colonel Balfour greeted him with his usual effusiveness. 'Ah, Lieutenant Macquarie, how are you, dear boy?'

'Back in good health, sir.'

'Oh, I *do* hope so.' Balfour smiled and spoke gently. 'But now, let us get straight to the reason why I have sent for you. You did very well out there, Macquarie. We are all very pleased with you.'

Lachlan responded with the usual answer in return for praise. 'Just doing my duty, sir.'

'Of course, but you did your duty very well, Lieutenant. It must have been a tough old sweat building the roads and hauling those guns up and down the slopes, eh, what?'

'The men are to be congratulated, sir. They worked exceptionally well.'

Balfour eyed him shrewdly. 'Tell me, did any of the men under your command make complaints about going under harness in replacement for the bullocks hauling the guns? Or at any time, in any other circumstances, refuse to obey any of your orders?'

'No, sir. Every man pulled his weight as best he could. And if I may say so, each and every one was a credit to the 77th.'

'Good, good!' Balfour smiled in genuine happiness. 'Always good to hear our lads are not bad lads! In fact, General Abercromby and myself were discussing your work with the men only last evening...' Balfour's voice tailed off as he looked at a paper on the table before him. Lachlan glanced up at the ceiling in weary resignation. Here it came, the sting in the tail, another of their damned rewards.

When it came, Lachlan could only stare at Balfour in astonishment. The Command had rewarded him with a Captaincy.

*

Private McKenzie was sitting on a wooden bench outside his lieutenant's quarters, his head back and eyes closed, enjoying the warmth of the sun on his face.

'McKenzie.'

'Sir!'

McKenzie jumped up as Lachlan approached and gave him the good news. 'Lord Cornwallis has been pleased to announce that from the money paid by Tipu Sultan, he intends to pay the Army a handsome gratuity in lieu of prize money, as well as pay and allowances.'

McKenzie was astounded into incoherence. He stood staring blankly, his mouth open and his body hunched like a huge bear. Finally his senses returned and he endeavoured to speak sense. 'Eh, wha' sir? What for, what way, what did ye say?'

Lachlan repeated the news that the army was to receive a gratuity amounting to six months extra pay.

'Six months extra pay!' McKenzie exclaimed. 'Even the men?' His eyes narrowed. 'Or just the officers?'

The officers were getting an even larger gratuity, but Lachlan did not tell McKenzie that. 'Every man in the army is to be rewarded. Even you, McKenzie, even you.'

'Ye're no' jesting me now, sir?' McKenzie expostulated. 'Pay and allowances and six months extra batta on top for every man?'

'And two week's extra pay for you, McKenzie, as a personal gratuity from myself to my head servant.'

McKenzie looked around him in a searching motion, then again stared at his lieutenant uncomprehending. 'Head servant? But I'm your one and *only* servant, Lieutenant Macquarie!'

'That is true.' Lachlan nodded agreeably. 'And that is why I can afford to give you an extra *two* weeks pay, whereas poor Major Jones can only afford to give his eight servants a mere one weeks extra pay in return for being such good and faithful servants throughout this campaign.'

'Thank ye, sir. It's verra kind o' you,' McKenzie purred, his eyes dilating with exultation. 'I'm grateful to ye. I'm beholden. I'm indebted. And losh – I'm rich!' He could contain himself no longer. 'Heck, sir, for the first time in ma life – I'll be *rich!*'

'Don't get carried away, McKenzie. A private's pay, even with six month's extra on top, can hardly be described as riches. And by the way, it's no longer lieutenant, but *Captain* Macquarie.'

'Wha'? Ye mean ... ye're getting' pay an' allowances an' six months extra of a *captain's* batta? Och! Sweet Jesus! Ye'll be richer than me, sir! Rich as a rajah!'

'Oh I doubt that,' Lachlan smiled. 'Now get your senses and head in order and go and give the good news to your comrades.'

'Aye, I will, sir.'

'And tell them the 77th are shipping out first thing in the morning.'

*

At daybreak the 77th started out for home. Home being Bombay. All were relieved to breathe the sea air again as they set sail on board the *Hercules*. All were older, all were somewhat richer, and six days later all were very glad to view once more the sight of Bombay harbour, its water shimmering under the saffron glow of a sunset, just as it had done on that first day of their arrival in the East.

It seemed as if the entire British community had travelled out to greet the returning Army and welcome it home after its long absence in the field. A band played thumping military tunes and the harbour was all bustle with coming and goings from small boats.

Lachlan stood by the ship's rail gazing at the crowd. A soldier's voice rose up from the back of the deck, declaring a wish that it was the people of Glasgow welcoming them home, not those of Bombay.

For a moment Lachlan found himself thinking of the stark and eerie beauty of the western islands of Scotland: of green mountains and blue lochs and silent, tranquil glens. He saw again red deer on the crags, and an occasional golden eagle on sail above the hills. He heard the whistles of the shepherds as they brought the sheep home to pen, the calls of the drovers as they herded the longhaired Highland cattle.

But it was just a moment, one of a thousand homesick moments all soldiers knew, and minutes later he was preparing to disembark and continue his life in India.

TWO

The town of Bombay contained rows upon rows of high brown houses but few European residents, the houses being hot, closely built, with projecting upper stories over narrow streets.

The British civilian population had established their own settlement in a garden suburb two miles away, a peaceful and tranquil place dotted with pretty bungalows and handsome houses built in the European style of architecture, with the addition of a veranda or covered piazza to shade the rooms from the sun.

In the cantonments of Colaba the soldiers of the 77th sweated through exercises forced upon them by their drill-sergeant, whilst their officers relaxed in their quarters or sipped drinks on the shaded veranda of the San Souci Club.

General Sir Robert Abercromby had been promoted to the post of Governor-General of Bombay. To celebrate, he decided to hold a 'Grand Ball' at Government House.

'*You*, Captain Macquarie, have been chosen as manager of the event,' Colonel Balfour told Lachlan in a proud voice.

No, *you* have been chosen to manage it, Lachlan thought wearily, but *you* can't be bothered, so you are delegating it down to me.

'You will, of course, have the assistance of a platoon of duty aides,' Balfour added. 'And we shall want a good show. Plenty of dancing and feasting and no expense spared. Something to delight the women and give them something to write home about, eh?'

Balfour paused. 'But also ... General Abercromby has also

asked me to come up with some form of entertainment, yet I'm damned if I can think of anything. Any ideas, Captain? A young man like you should be able to come up with something exciting.'

Lachlan thought, and shook his head. 'No, sir, I can't think of anything.'

'Nothing at all? Nothing that would delight and entertain our civilian guests?' Balfour pursed his lips in disappointment, and then began to fume. 'Why is it that none of my officers are capable of coming up with a single idea of any kind?'

Because they are soldiers, not entertainers, Lachlan thought wryly. The battlefield was hardly instructive in the ways of civilian socialising. The battlefield was a place ... Lachlan's eyes became fixed and distant for a moment as a sudden idea came to him.

'How about a fireworks display, sir?'

'A fireworks display?'

'It would be very easy to arrange. And it would give our civilian guests some idea of the rocket flares and cannon explosions on the battlefield.'

'A fireworks display! Why, that's an excellent idea!' Colonel Balfour beamed. 'We are the military after all, and I'm sure General Abercrombie will approve.'

Balfour rubbed his hands together in anticipated pleasure. 'Well, I shall leave all the arrangements in your hands, Captain, while I attend to the business of choosing plenty of good claret – wonderful stuff for making an evening jolly!' He gave a chuckle of approval. 'And it will do us all good to have some time in the company of women. Too long since we have had any time to spare for women, dear boy.'

48

'Yes, sir, too long.'

'Oh, damned if I forgot – ' Balfour swatted an invisible fly, 'but being on duty on the night, Macquarie, you won't be able to dance with any of the young ladies, will you?'

'No I bloody will not, you bastard,' Lachlan thought, but his face showed only a slight smile. 'Regrettably not, sir.'

'Such a pity!' Balfour exclaimed. 'Still, duty first.'

*

The arrangements and organisation for the ball at Government House were carried out with all the precision and efficiency of a battle campaign. On the night, a guard of sepoys stood to attention around the lawns of the house while inside a battalion of uniformed native servants waited in readiness to serve.

At precisely seven o'clock the guests began to arrive in streams: officers resplendent in scarlet coats with gold loops and chains, others in the pale blue and gold of the Light Cavalry or the green of the Rifle regiments; all every bit as colourful as the ladies in their shimmering gowns of every shade and hue.

By half past seven the ball was in full swing with guests still arriving. Lachlan moved around the outskirts of the ballroom conferring with other duty-aides, occasionally pausing to speak and joke with some of his fellow officers.

As the night progressed the room became unbearably noisy with hysterically happy laughter, ladies shrieking greetings across the room and men bowing graciously in response. On every female neck and hand, Indian jewels blazed garishly. Some of the civilian gentlemen of the East India Company were almost as bejewelled as the ladies, ruby and diamond rings dazzling on both hands. Lachlan considered it all to be excessively vulgar. The room quickly became like a hothouse, the exuding odour of perfume and powder sickened him.

All in a moment, as if he was alone, the silent peace of the Scottish hills descended upon him. He had a sudden yearning to walk alone amongst trees and sit by the still waters of a silent loch again ... and just as quickly his senses cleared and the brouhaha all about him came back ... more guests were arriving, more colours and silks and feathers and jewels.

An elegant couple were being announced, 'Mr and Mrs Morley,' but it was the girl who accompanied them who caught Lachlan's attention. A tall, graceful girl, with beautiful long dark chestnut hair which was undressed and without jewels or peacock feathers. She was no more than twenty and wore a gown of watery green silk, exquisite but simple. No frills or flounces, no emerald halter round her neck or diamond tiara on her head. She looked as refreshing as a walk through the trees.

Her arms were bare and her skin golden. That surprised him, for most of the wives and daughters of the East India Company prided themselves on their milky-white skin and took every precaution to protect it.

He watched as the threesome moved down the side aisle to one of the tables, his eyes fixed on the slender figure of the girl as she sat down beside her two companions. She sat with her back straight, and she was beautiful with a dark serene beauty that was rare in the English.

'Lachlan...?'

He turned to see John Forbes, a personal friend from the civilian population of Bombay.

'Man, John, it's you! He shook his friend's hand vigorously, confused by his own sudden excitement. 'I am very glad you decided to come tonight.'

'Oh? Why so?'

'Because you might be able to do me a personal favour.'

John Forbes, an elegant man in his early forties, and a well-established banker, prided himself on knowing everything about everyone in Bombay. So Lachlan asked him: 'Do you see that girl, John? Long chestnut hair, a green dress ... sitting with an older couple.'

'Where? ... Oh, yes.' John had now picked her out in the line of tables. 'Miss Jane Jarvis. She arrived in India just a few days ago, from the West Indies. Comes from a very wealthy family on one of the islands there, but I can't remember which one.'

'The West Indies?' That explained the sunburned tan of her skin. 'Go on,' Lachlan urged.

'Well, whichever island it was, her father was Chief Justice there. He died recently and left her a very acceptable fortune.'

'So she's rich?' Lachlan was not surprised – most of the white civilians in Bombay were rich.

'Oh, yes, very rich indeed,' John replied, 'but as she is not yet twenty-one years old, only nineteen, her sister's husband, James Morley, has now assumed the role of her guardian.' He gave Lachlan a glance of warning. 'But in view of her wealth, I doubt if he would ever consider relinquishing her to any man worth less than a thousand a year sterling.'

'How much?' Lachlan looked startled.

John Forbes could not help smiling at Lachlan's shock. It was obvious he still did not fully realise the enormous wealth of British Bombay.

Lachlan's gaze focused silently on the girl sitting at the table, her eyes watching the dancers as if she was gazing at some enchanting scene. Something about her was familiar. He wondered if the island she came from was Jamaica, or perhaps Barbados. Just looking at her reminded him of the sweet air and magical nights of the Caribbean.

Resolutely, he said, 'I still want to be introduced to her.'

John Forbes shook his head. 'No point, old chum, no point. James Morley is a nabob who cares only for the company of senior staff. He would have no time for a junior captain.'

Undeterred, Lachlan straightened his scarlet jacket. 'An introduction, John, if you please.'

*

The table where James and Maria Morley were seated was directly under a swaying punkah, a length of matting pulled by a rope to make a breeze. Behind their chairs a turbaned servant stood in weary monotony pulling the punkah rope.

John Forbes approached the table and bowed low. 'Mr and Mrs Morley, Miss Jarvis, I already have your acquaintance, but may I now have the honour of introducing to you, Captain Lachlan Macquarie.'

Lachlan stepped forward and James Morley allowed three of his fingers to be shaken. He was a senior civil servant of the East India Trading Company and therefore, in his opinion, one of the Heaven-born – pure and white and blessed by God to be rich and wealthy in a land of brown-skinned heathens.

And if Captain Macquarie had been a senior officer,

Morley might have given him his entire hand to shake, but for a mere junior captain, the touch of three fingers was enough. His wife also extended three gloved fingers with a gracious inclination of her head.

John Forbes watched with eyes keen as Lachlan at last took the ungloved hand of Jane Jarvis and smiled. 'Miss Jarvis,' he said softly, 'welcome to India.'

She looked up at him with her beautiful soft brown eyes, and there it was – in her eyes too – that sudden and unexplainable light of recognition that sometimes happens between strangers.

'Thank you,' was all she said, but as John Forbes watched, into his mind came a line from an Eastern poem he had been reading earlier that evening, translated from the Persian – `Looks, the language of the eyes.'

And then she smiled, and once again John Forbes saw the Persian poet's language of the eyes ... 'Tears may speak, and so may smiles.'

A subaltern rushed up and addressed Captain Macquarie. 'Colonel Balfour's compliments, sir, and would you please report to him in the library.'

Lachlan sighed irritably, glanced sideways at John Forbes and murmured, 'Balfour – that man just delights in persecuting me.'

*

Colonel Balfour beamed with pride when everyone filed out to the lawn after supper to watch the magnificent fireworks display. Even James Morley and his wife exuded their pleasure at the entertainment, and continually said so to Colonel Balfour who stood beside them rocking happily back and forth on his heels in satisfaction, his humour at tip-top height.

So much so, that when the display was over, Balfour even wandered back into the ballroom with the Morleys, although he usually preferred the company of officers to civilians. But Mrs Maria Morley was a very attractive woman, much younger than her husband, and Balfour derived great pleasure in flattering her in a most chivalrous way, purely for the exercise of it. Still a bachelor he may be, but he *did* intend to find himself a neat little woman when he had the time, or when he returned to England, so he could not allow his charm to rust over.

Balfour was happily sipping a glass of wine, his eyes benevolently roving the dancers swirling around the ballroom, when he caught sight of Captain Macquarie dancing with a willowy young piece in green.

'Good Heavens!' he said aloud, his eyebrows pitching in that named direction.

Colonel Balfour could scarcely believe his eyes: Captain Macquarie – dancing! This was the first time he had ever known Macquarie to blatantly disregard his duty. Well, by God, he would suffer for it with a stern reprimand at the very least!

'But James...' Maria Morley was saying to her husband in a perplexed voice. 'Was it not Mr Forbes, the banker, who escorted Jane out to the fireworks display? So how is it that she is now dancing with a soldier?'

Furious, James Morley stared hard at the officer in scarlet finery guiding his young sister-in-law around the floor in a waltz. And the waltz, everyone agreed, was the most sociable dance ever invented, for it allowed a dancing couple to talk privately to each other.

Too damned private, James Morley thought as he watched the couple and wondered what the redcoat was murmuring down into Jane's upturned face.

*

Close up, Lachlan decided that Miss Jane Jarvis was not only deliciously beautiful, but also even more magical than he had imagined. In the space of the last five dances he had held her slim figure and felt her move with such a youthful and natural vitality that he now wished he could just dance away with her into the Indian moonlight.

She was also much younger in every way than she had first appeared at a distance, more innocent, her conversation devoid of any false coyness or sophisticated game playing.

She answered all his questions openly and honestly, stimulating his senses like a fresh wind after being confined in stagnant air. She told him all about the oddity of her upbringing on the island of Antigua and it was clear she was still pining for her home in the Caribbean and her Negro Mammy, Dinah, who had cared for her since birth, and whom she had been forced to leave behind.

'I wanted to buy Mammy's bond, out of my own money, and at least give her her freedom before I left,' she told him, 'but I was unable to draw even a penny from the fund my father left me. So Mammy is still bonded to the sugar estate and now that my brother owns it, he will *never* give Mammy her freedom.'

The words tumbled out breathless and anxious, as if it was something that plagued her but no one had ever listened to her before. She glanced quickly over her shoulder towards the table where her guardian was sitting, and saw him preoccupied in conversation with a senior officer.

*

'I have no wish to criticise a member of your staff, Colonel,' James Morley said to Balfour in a voice that was coldly superior, 'but I am *compelled* to say that when *I* was an officer, we would never dream of participating in any frolicking whilst on duty. Neither, I may add, would any of our officers have been capable of such effrontery as to dance with a young lady without the permission of her guardians.'

And it was that criticism alone that saved Captain Macquarie from the sternest dressing-down Balfour might have given him. And Morley's mistake had been in using the word 'officer' in such a superior way.

'Officer?' The colonel turned his face slowly to the civil servant. 'I did not realise you had served as a soldier, sir. How very interesting! You must tell me something of your campaigns. Serve long, did you? And which regiment, pray?'

James Morley flushed, realising that in his anger he had said the wrong thing to the wrong man. It was all right to boast about the days of being an officer to other civilians, but not to a professional soldier such as the colonel.

'Militia regiment in England,' he said quickly.

'Militia!' Colonel Balfour smiled his professional smile, which often covered a multitude of emotions. If there was one thing he could not stomach it was civilian males who had spent a year or two in some poxy militia regiment in some safe bolt-hole in England, then spent the rest of their lives talking as if they knew more about how to win battles than the generals of the Regular Army.

And there were many of them here in India, men who had never ploughed for months through the field in the most deplorable conditions, had never slept in wet ditches and gone hungry through loss of supplies. Men who had never risked their lives in battle or seen their comrades cut down by an enemy's cutlass or cannon-shot. Men whose `service' in the militia amounted to no more than a regular strut around the town square in a parade of regimental pomp and self-importance.

And men like that *dared* to criticise officers of the Regular Army! It made Colonel Balfour's blood boil with seething contempt, but not a glimpse of this showed through his professional smile.

'The militia,' he said amiably, 'England's home army, God bless `em. But I do think, sir, that had you elected to serve in the Regular Army, you might have found there is a very great difference between us and the militia.'

Balfour ignored Morley's blushes and spread a hand expansively towards the dance floor. 'Now consider Captain Macquarie there, a fine young man and a fine officer. No more than a boy of fifteen when he left Scotland with his regiment and crossed the Atlantic to serve in Canada and America. Ah yes, ...' Balfour smiled even more expansively as he watched the dancers, 'the militia may march with starch, but our lads have the polish.'

Uncomfortably, James Morley glanced at Balfour and wondered if he should concede defeat now, or allow the colonel the pleasure of demolishing his pride completely.

Which was what Balfour had every intention of doing. The army was a family, and all the lads in the regiment were his military sons. He spared no mercy to any civilian who dared to criticise them.

James Morley had got the message. He shrugged pettishly. 'My concern at the moment, Colonel, is that Captain Macquarie has chosen to dance with my sister-in-law without the benefit of either my own or her sister's permission.'

Colonel Balfour held up his palms and went on smiling. 'You have absolutely no need to worry! The man is an officer and a gentleman so she is in good hands. And times really *are* changing, dear fellow. Even in England a girl is now allowed to give her dances to whomever she pleases, just so long as she carries them out under the watchful eyes of her protectors. And there she is – before your eyes – safe and sound and looking as happy as a sparrow in spring.'

The Morleys looked.

Throughout the conversation the music had changed from a waltz to a quadrille and now back to a waltz and Jane was still dancing with the captain as her partner. Such behaviour for a young lady so recently entered into Bombay society was quite unacceptable.

Although Maria Morley had to admit, 'They do dance rather well together.'

'Indeed, ma'am, they do indeed!' Balfour agreed. 'But now, Mistress Morley, my dear lady, how about some more wine? Capital stuff for making an evening jolly!'

Balfour beckoned to one of the turbaned servants and commanded more wine, a twinkle of mischief in his blue eyes.

*

'Is it true what they say about Scotland? It rains there every day?'

'Aye, it does have a reputation for its morning and evening mists,' Lachlan admitted. 'Especially where I come from, Mull, one of the western islands. But between the mists the sun does occasionally shine.'

'So different to Antigua. Most of the year the island is painfully dry.' She looked at him thoughtfully. 'I think you would find the long dry days of the West Indies very strange.'

'No, no,' he assured her, 'not at all.'

She was astonished to learn that he knew the West Indies very well, having served there for two years after leaving America. She asked eager questions.

'Jamaica, mainly,' he told her, but he had also spent time on some of the Windward Islands, including Barbados.

'But not leeward to Antigua?'

He smiled regretfully. 'No, alas.'

*

James Morley saw the soldier's smile. There was no mistaking what it meant. Inwardly Morley's fury continued to rage, but he was careful not to betray it in the presence of Colonel Balfour who seemed to possess an unreasonable affection for his junior officers.

Morley gave a quick sideways glance at Balfour – a damned country squire in the gaudy lace and braid of a colonel who survived solely on the pride of being a fighting soldier. What did a man like him know about the real world outside the ridiculous camaraderie of the military? How could a man like him understand that the care of Jane and her fortune required constant vigilance. No suitor could be taken on trust, but subjected to the most thorough scrutiny.

Morley continued staring at the dance-floor where his young sister-in-law was happily dancing with her soldier . . . Macquarie? A Scot from the wilds of nowhere . . . the Scots had a reputation for being a stubborn race . . . but there was not a man in the world more stubborn than he was. And if Macquarie continued to push his luck, he would soon find that out.

THREE

The Ball had ended, all the dining and dancing over. The guests passed out of Government House into the warm night air.

'I'm holding a picnic in the gardens of my own house on Saturday,' said John Forbes. 'For just a few chums. You will come, won't you?'

Lachlan nodded inattentively. They were standing on the steps of Government House and his eyes were searching the departing crowd cheerily surging towards their carriages and tongas; but he could find no sight of Jane and her guardians.

'Cricket will be played of course. So extend the invitation to Edward Grant too, will you. Good batsman is Edward, always knows the spot. Come at noon or thereabouts, but no later than one o'clock. Are you listening to me?'

Lachlan stopped searching and looked at John. 'Aye, of course I'm listening. A picnic, on Saturday, yes, definitely.'

'And Edward Grant.'

'What about him?'

'I want you to extend my invitation to him also. I'd invite him myself but I can't find him, so will you do it for me?'

'I will,' Lachlan consented, giving up his search of the crowd. John Forbes took his leave, smiling all the way to his carriage as a sudden idea occurred to him, another favour for his young friend.

*

On Saturday, Lachlan expected to find about twenty-five

men standing or sitting around on John Forbes's green lawn, but when he and Edward Grant arrived the place was packed, inside and out. The 'picnic' was in fact a sumptuous daylong feast served continuously by a troop of servants.

And *she* was there.

She was standing on the veranda, speaking with a woman old enough to be her grandmother. She seemed ill at ease, fluttering her fan and attempting to act in the genteel and refined manner of all young white ladies in India.

As soon as she saw him her whole demeanour instantly changed – leaning over the veranda rail to speak down to him with all the excited enthusiasm of a starry-eyed girl of sixteen.

'Miss Jarvis!' the lady behind her was outraged. A moment later Maria Morley appeared, dragging her young sister away from the rail; and from then on Jane was remorselessly chaperoned.

Fortunately, James Morley had not attended. Even so, it was only due to the constant efforts of John Forbes to distract Maria Morley's attention from her sister, persuading her to step forward and watch the wonderful Edward Grant take the bat, which enabled Lachlan to snatch a short time alone with Jane.

She seemed glad to be able to confide in him again. 'Most of the women here seem to have never even *heard* of Antigua,' she whispered. 'All they talk about is England, England and dear old Blighty. Why do they call it that?'

'*Belait*,' he said smiling. 'It's the Hindi word for Britain, only very few of them can say it properly.'

'The people here are so different to Antigua,' she continued wistfully. 'No laughter or fun in any of them, just rules and regulations and decorum at all times.'

'Aye, that's the way in British Bombay,' Lachlan agreed. 'In time you'll get used to it.'

Jane shook her head in denial, then turned to him enthusiastically, 'Tell me some more about your adventures in the West Indies. Banish my homesickness, if just for a little while. Did you like it there? Or did you simply *love* it?'

Ignoring the cricket, they stood talking together for some time, until Jane clapped her hands and laughed outright, a laugh so full of humour and unrestrained that all the women turned to look at her and it seemed, extraordinarily, as if the air had suddenly chilled. Her open and natural laughter appalled them.

Aware that such behaviour was not acceptable Jane pressed her lips together and lowered her head as if in shame, but smiling at him all the while out of her laughing brown eyes.

'Jane!' Maria Morley arrived, excused herself and her sister, and ushered the heavenly young creature away.

With perfect courtesy he had stepped aside, but he watched her go, back into the protective company of the women. No, he realised, she was definitely not a young lady who would fit in well with the society of British Bombay. There was too much of the Caribbean in her ways, as untamed as Antigua ... She suddenly turned and looked over her shoulder, her dark eyes meeting his in one final smiling glance.

*

'It's not that I have anything against the man personally,' James Morley explained to Jane the following morning. 'It's simply due to the fact that Macquarie is a junior officer who possesses no wealth or private fortune of his own. A penniless captain. And he's been in India long enough to know the rules about place and position and wealth and courtship. So any interest he has thus far shown in you, m'dear, is clearly based on a desire to get his hands on your money.'

'I have no money,' Jane replied. 'You have it all.'

'I am simply *holding* it for you,' Morley insisted. 'As your brother-in-law and guardian, and as your *only* protector here in India.'

Jane looked down as a small bird danced around her feet. She was sitting in a wicker chair on the partially-screened veranda leading from her bedroom and overlooking the back garden, wearing a lacy blue robe known as a 'tea gown', her lovely chestnut hair falling long and loose around her shoulders.

'And you think ...' she said thoughtfully, 'that I need protection from Captain Macquarie?'

'I most certainly do! Don't you know that most of those soldiers only come out here to India in search of a fortune to take back to Britain? Why else would they put up with the unbearable heat? The incessant flies and the dust, the stupid natives?'

Jane was still watching the small bird thoughtfully. 'Is that why *you* came to India, James? In search of a fortune? Is that why you married my sister?'

James Morley almost choked on his breath, just as his wife Maria appeared in the open doorway from the bedroom. 'James, do let Jane finish her breakfast. She is not even dressed. It's hardly seemly for you to – '

'I was simply warning her about that soldier!' James expostulated. 'She needs to understand – '

'No *you* need to understand,' Jane said calmly, 'that I am not the slightest bit interested in that soldier. I gave him a few dances one night, that's all.'

Maria stared at her. 'You're *not* interested in him? Then why did you make such a disgrace of yourself at Mr Forbes' house yesterday? Flirting with him like a floozy!'

'I was bored,' Jane confessed tiredly. 'Bored with all the snooty women complaining about their servants, and bored with all the talk of how things are done so much better in dear old Blighty.'

'Oh, Jane,' Maria said reproachfully, 'that is not a kind or polite way to speak about the British ladies here in Bombay. And if you are not interested in Captain Macquarie, then why put us through such worry? Why didn't you just say you were not interested?'

'I might have done, if he had once entered my thoughts in the time between the two meetings, but as he didn't...' Jane shrugged carelessly. 'May I finish my breakfast now?'

'Well, thank God that's settled,' James Morley said with relief, then added firmly, 'But remember, Jane, in any future social gatherings, interested or not, I insist that you have nothing more to do with that soldier, not one word is to be spoken to him nor even a look in his direction. Is that understood? So now ...' he nodded towards her breakfast tray, 'carry on with your *chota*, carry on.'

He left the room abruptly with Maria turning to follow at his heels. A wave of outrage swirled through Jane as she felt the injustice of his edict, the restraint of her freedom to even look at any person he did not approve of.

Minutes later she saw both of them again, walking in the garden, James still prattling non-stop and Maria nodding timidly in agreement with his every word. An incongruous couple in every way, a fifty-year-old man with his twenty-four-year-old wife. He looked and acted more like Maria's father than her husband. Why on earth had she married him? Where or what was the attraction? But Maria *had* married him, and now she too was also was forced to put up with him.

She stood up and moved down the veranda, staring defiantly at the couple with her dark eyes. How dare they suggest that Lachlan Macquarie's sole interest in her was due to her wealth, or as James always called it, her *fortune*? How dare he demean Lachlan in such a way when she herself had already come to the realisation that no man in the world could be as mean or as money grabbing as her guardian.

She moved back into her bedroom, still thinking moodily. Well, if James Morley believed that he could order her in the same way he ordered his wife, then he obviously did not know her as well as he thought he did. She was a child of the Caribbean and she was not shackled with the petty prejudices of all these self-important civil servants in the East India Company. And she had not come to India to be ordered about like a slave by her odious brother-in-law.

Sitting on her bed, she slipped her hand under the pillow and withdrew the letter she had received from Lachlan Macquarie the previous evening. A smile shaped her lips as she read his words, even though she had already read the letter a dozen times. Moments later she walked over to her small desk and sat down to write a long reply, explaining in all honesty about her guardian's mandate that she was to have no further contact with him.

'Of course, there is a valid reason why they dislike all soldiers, especially young officers, and hopefully one day I

will be able to explain that reason to you, when you will then realise why it is foolish to take their dislike of you now so personally, but in the meantime ...'

Later that day, chaperoned by her trusted *Ayah*, Jane left the house for her afternoon walk, heading towards the small park of gardens where, she had told Captain Macquarie in her letter, she would be taking a stroll at four o'clock.

*

Less than a month later, James Morley felt compelled to once again enforce his rule, although he had already decided that Jane's unsuitable behaviour was not really her fault. It was all due to the fact that she had been brought up on a small, uncivilised island, where her mother had died young, and so the child was left to run wild in the care of black slaves who had spoilt her. Thank God that Maria had been sent to England for her education as a lady. Although why the same arrangement had not been made for Jane was still a mystery.

He asked Maria.

Maria shrugged. 'It was simply impossible. She was only ten years old and had become too attached to Mammy Dinah, refusing to leave her, crying and running away until Papa was forced to send me on without her.'

'And her schooling?'

'Oh yes, she was well schooled, Papa saw to that. She attended the Missionary school at St John's.'

'Well, I intended to be very mild in my remonstrations with her,' James said, 'but as she got out of going to England for her education simply because she *refused* to go, I see now that I shall have to be very firm with her indeed. She shall not be allowed to refuse *me*.'

Throughout dinner he kept his eyes fixed on Jane, but she seemed unaware of his gaze, her mind miles away, not even answering when he finally addressed her.

'Of course, Jane, I do realise this behaviour of yours is all due to your inexperience in society, but it has to stop.'

Jane finally looked at him.

'Most afternoons you go out walking, is that not so?'

'Yes, I do.'

Morley pulled the linen napkin from his neck, threw it on the table, and sat back in his chair. 'The position of white women here in India is very different to Antigua,' he said gravely. 'In British Bombay it is not considered decorous or decent for a young woman to go out walking alone.'

Jane looked surprised. 'But, James, I am never alone – I am always accompanied and chaperoned by my *Ayah*?'

'Not good enough.' James flicked his hand dismissively. 'These promenades of yours have to stop. I forbid you to go out walking unless you are accompanied by your sister; and even then, I insist that one of the male servants accompany both of you.'

Jane flushed, as though he had struck her in the face. 'But you cannot forbid ... I have a right ...'

'You have no rights! Until you are twenty-one or you marry, you are my ward. And as my ward you shall follow my rules and my advice. And do not for a moment consider *refusing* – because a refusal is something I will *not* accept. Is that understood?'

Jane glanced at Maria who quickly averted her eyes, her face as flushed as Jane's, her head lowered over her plate.

'Is that understood? James repeated.

After a long stillness, Jane finally spoke, the word coming

with a desperate effort through her stiff lips. 'Yes.'

Standing up quickly, she left the room and the house, losing herself in the shaded areas of the garden until the tears finally came, relieving her rage.

FOUR

Two months later, in the month of May, General Sir Robert Abercrombie decided to host another grand event at Government House. Sir Robert had declared that in his opinion, during a time of peace, it was very important for the British Military to show the British civilians in Bombay some sociability

'Not my opinion at all,' Sir Robert confessed to Colonel Balfour. `An order from the Commander-in-Chief, Lord Cornwallis.'

'That dear old duck,' Balfour said amiably. `He was just the same in America, constantly hosting social events for those of the American gentry who remained loyal to the British crown. Now I hear that he is constantly dining in the company of maharajas over there in Bengal.'

'Yes, well I have a few maharajas on my own guest list,' Abercrombie confided. 'It's time to build a few bridges after that business in Mysore, don't you think?'

'Oh, I do,' Balfour agreed. 'And if we can't build new bridges we can at least try to mend those that are damaged. Don't worry, Sir Robert, the night will be a sparkling success for everyone. I shall see to all the arrangements myself, just as you ask.'

*

On the night, Captain Macquarie was once again on duty, but this time, under the watchful eye of Colonel Balfour, he did not take time out to dance.

In fact, James Morley hardly saw the captain at all, and as

the night wore on he was very pleased to see Jane continually dancing with a very eligible civil servant who had made enough money in India to buy half of London if he ever decided to return there.

A very good potential marriage prospect indeed.

True, the civil servant was a lot older than Jane, a widower in his early fifties, but a woman could not have everything. After all, he himself had been a forty-eight-year-old widower when he had married Maria three years ago, and she only twenty-one. But he knew that he would never have won Maria without the wealth he had made in India. Maria's father had accepted his proposal solely on the condition that he would keep her in the rich and comfortable lifestyle to which she was accustomed. And so far, in his opinion, their marriage was working perfectly well.

But where was Maria now?

In the supper-room James Morley stood waiting by one of the rows of long buffet tables covered in dishes containing roast chicken, cutlets of lamb, curry, rice, chapatis, mutton pie and so many other dishes that made the juices in his corpulent stomach groan with impatience.

What the devil was keeping Maria and Jane? Why women took so long preening themselves up in the dressing-rooms before supper was one of the worst irritations men had to suffer. Did they have *no* consideration for a man's stomach?

Guests jostled back and forth past him and James noticed their plates were, as usual, overloaded with food. It was laughable now to recall how he had been warned before his arrival in Bombay that the humid heat of India destroyed the appetite – yet he still had to discover any evidence of that. Personally, he loved the pleasures of the table more now than he ever did, more than he had previously loved women, and almost as much as he loved wealth.

He looked again at the tables of food with a plunderer's lusty eye, but as ravenous as he was, to start tucking in before his wife arrived was simply not done.

He decided to alleviate the torture by taking a brief stroll in the gardens at the rear of Government House. The night was very clear, the cool stillness of the garden pleasantly refreshing after the heat inside which even the swishing punkahs could not relieve.

He strolled across the moonlit lawn, savouring the quiet beauty of the night, his footsteps inaudible on the evening-watered grass. He turned to the right, towards a group of flame trees, his eyes musing on the glory of tropical moonlight, when he noticed a curious scene by one of the trees that made his eyes blink in puzzlement ... Jane ... in close and intimate conversation with Captain Macquarie!

The moonlight only emphasised the white rage that milked James Morley's face as he stared at the two figures by the flame tree. And when the soldier lowered his head and kissed Jane's mouth — blasphemy hovered on Morley's lips.

But a cunning sense swiftly intervened and — No, he thought. No, it would not be him that was reduced to a quivering state of indignity as a result of outraged shouting. No, he would simply wait for them to draw apart and when Macquarie looked around and saw him standing just a few yards away, it would be him, the offender, who would have to find the babbling explanations and apologies that would be received with nothing more than his own frozen stare of contempt.

Morley waited, and waited, but the kiss was endless. He

watched in astonishment as Jane's arms moved around the soldier's body. The minutes that followed seemed incredible to him as he stood in wonder and witnessed their strange intensity. He began to feel uneasy standing there, watching two people who thought they were alone, as if all sound was blanked out, as if the contact of their bodies and lips was appeasing some hungry heathen god.

An ambiguous feeling began to replace Morley's anger, a feeling of being old, cramped, and a desperate desire to be somewhere else – anywhere else away from here.

Silently, he moved away.

Ten minutes after his own return, Jane entered the supper-room, a sudden burning colour tingeing her already flushed cheeks as she looked at the white face of her brother-in-law and the nervous tremblings of her sister.

A few minutes later the Morleys and their ward left Government House.

*

It was no less than an ambush! That was the only way Lachlan could describe James Morley's action the following morning. Minutes after he had risen and dressed and before he had even breakfasted the man had gained access to his quarters and cornered him in a tirade of angry accusations.

'I knew from the beginning that you were no better than all the other rogues in the licentious soldiery!'

Lachlan wondered briefly if he could arrest him or kill him for disturbing him so early. He spoke as mildly as he could. 'No, sir, you insult me, I am not a rogue.'

'Well you are certainly no gentleman – no matter what your old commanding officer says about you! Because if you were a *real* gentleman, you would desist in paying such particular attentions to my sister-in-law in view of all society. Since that first night your attentions have stimulated every tongue in Bombay to wag and are causing her family great distress. Do you not realise, sir, that your conduct could prevent offers of marriage being made to her!'

Morley had clearly come prepared for battle, but as Lachlan was so unprepared he decided to answer with the truth. 'It is my understanding, sir, that my conduct has done no more than secure your sister-in-law's affection.'

'And for what bally purpose, may I ask? Do you have the means of proposing marriage to her?'

'Compared with other suitors, I could not offer her – '

'Anything more than a modest competence to live on! Are you unaware of the fact that my wife's sister is not only the daughter of Antigua's late Consul, but also the younger sister of Thomas Jarvis who owns a very substantial sugar estate on that island? And although *he* is her legal guardian, *I* am her physical and moral guardian here in India. And therefore it is *my* duty to prevent her from connecting herself to one who could not support her in a respectable and comfortable lifestyle.'

'Yes, I do realise that Jane is far beyond anything I have a right to expect...' Lachlan paused, wondering why he was excusing himself to this blethering bigot who judged all men solely by their wealth and rank. Well, that may be, but there was another aspect to this situation that Morley obviously had not considered.

'Mr Morley,' he said steadily, 'I am a soldier, and therefore not a man used to making pretty speeches or flamboyant declarations of my intentions, so all I can tell you now is that Jane is the person I have been waiting to meet for all of my life, and I have reason to believe she feels the same about me.'

Morley stared. 'I beg your pardon?'

Lachlan explained it simply. 'We are in love with each other.'

Morley's face became rigid. For a long moment he fixed the captain with his frozen stare, then snapped, 'Many men find themselves becoming amorously attached to a young lady of rank and fortune, but each man soon learns that becoming amorously attached is not enough, not nearly enough. And if he ever hopes to enjoy her wifely favours, he must at least make sure he is sufficiently endowed with worldly goods and an income that would admit any proposal to be an acceptable one.'

Morley lifted the hat he had earlier flung on the table and turned to leave, without even troubling to find out exactly just how much was the captain's income, or the present amount of his worldly goods.

At the door Morley placed the hat on his head and said curtly, 'I think we understand each other now, Captain. You are expressly forbidden to have any further contact with my wife's sister, and she with you.'

When the door had closed, Lachlan remained where he was standing, motionless and thoughtful for at least a minute, before he shrugged and murmured, `But I intend to marry her, just the same.'

It was only a question of finding a way.

*

He was on duty with his company on the artillery ground at

Matoonga when the order to report came from Major Auchmuty.

'I thought I would inform you,' said Major Auchmuty, 'of a notice that will appear in tomorrow's General Orders, which is...' he looked down at a paper, 'that Captain Lachlan Macquarie of the 77th Regiment is appointed to act as Major of Brigade to His Majesty's Troops on the Coast of Malabar.'

Auchmuty looked up. `Congratulations.'

'Thank you, sir.'

Lachlan was smiling. He would still retain the rank of captain, but the appointment of Brigade-Major was a promotion, and promotion meant more money.

'Now, you are to immediately attend upon the Commander-in-Chief,' said Auchmuty, `at Colonel Balfour's request.'

*

General Sir Robert Abercromby sat behind a desk piled with papers. In the room with him were two staff officers and Colonel Balfour. Lachlan presented himself with a salute. 'Sir.'

'Captain Macquarie.' General Abercromby sat back in his chair. 'You are happy with your appointment as Major of Brigade?'

'Very much, sir.'

`Well, I simply wanted to tell you, personally, that notwithstanding the many names put before me for this appointment, I preferred you to them all.'

'Thank you, sir.' It was all Lachlan could say.

Colonel Balfour rocked back on his heels triumphantly. Such praise for one of his own, coming from the newly appointed Governor-General of British India, was high praise indeed.

'However,' said General Abercromby, 'it was not the appointment that I intended for you. Had I remained as Governor of Bombay I intended to take you onto my staff, but that idea had to be dismissed by time and circumstance due to Lord Cornwallis's imminent return to England and the short notice of my own promotion and posting to Bengal next week.'

Inwardly Lachlan felt a rush of gratitude to time and circumstance for preventing him from being given an appointment that would have landed him in Bengal, on the other side of India. The last thing he wanted to do now was leave Bombay.

'I cannot express my thanks, sir, or indeed my feelings of gratitude and obligation for such a consideration,' he replied quietly.

'Oh, my dear fellow,' declared the general with a smile. 'Any feelings of gratitude or obligation should not be directed solely to me, but to the many officers who recommended you so highly for an appointment on my staff.'

Lachlan felt somewhat dazed by this information. It appeared that his fellow officers held him in much higher esteem than Mr James Morley.

*

James Morley was not at all pleased when Captain Lachlan Macquarie paid him an early visit at his office a week later.

'Damn the man calling at this early hour,' Morley grumbled. 'Hardly had a chance to fit myself into my chair.'

He was about to give an order that Macquarie be told he was unavailable when the captain walked uninvited into the office, removed his hat, allowed Morley's servant to leave, and closed the door behind him.

It was an ambush, but this time it was Morley who was unprepared.

'I know you are a very busy man,' Lachlan said, walking forward. `So I will be brief and take up as little of your time as possible.'

'Captain Macquarie, I am only two minutes in! This is a disgraceful hour to call.'

'It is half past nine, sir. Two hours later than the time you thought fit to call on me last week.' Lachlan put a hand inside his jacket and brought out a fold of papers. 'Now, as I said, I shall be brief.'

James Morley stared at him. It was the first time he had seen Macquarie out of uniform. He wore a dark blue riding coat cut away short in the front to show a matching waistcoat, and the cloth of both, Morley noticed, was of fine quality.

Lachlan glanced at the chair beside him. 'I take it I may sit down?'

Morley was still staring. In those clothes Macquarie looked every bit a gentleman and not at all like a soldier.

Lachlan sat down. 'I have come to put forward my proposal of marriage to your sister-in-law, Miss Jane Jarvis.'

James Morley blinked vaguely, and then shook his head stubbornly. 'I have told you, Captain Macquarie, it is out of the question. How many times must you be told that Miss Jarvis is a daughter of an honourable English family on the island of Antigua and – '

'As I am a son of an honourable Scottish family on the island of Mull. And *honour*, Mr Morley, can never be bought or measured by wealth. I would be obliged if you would try to remember that.'

Morley gaped at him like an astonished trout. The man was speaking to him in a voice and tone he might use to some erring private on the parade ground.

'Now,' Lachlan continued. 'Miss Jarvis has already accepted my proposal of marriage. So in the hope that you and her family will also agree, I have listed, for your information, figures which will give you a detailed account of my finances.'

Morley waved the papers aside. 'This is a complete waste of time. Even if I were to agree, Mr Thomas Jarvis of Antigua, I can assure you, will never agree to his sister entering into a marriage contract with any man who gives the slightest suspicion of being a fortune-hunter.'

So there it was, out in the open. Morley suspected his real goal was not Jane herself, but her fortune.

'Mr Morley,' he said softly, his voice very controlled, 'I suggest you take very great care. This is the second time you have insulted me, and my tolerance does have a limit.'

He was silent for a second two, then continued, 'Six months ago I would not have considered myself in a good enough financial position to propose for the hand of a young lady such as your wife's sister, my pay as a captain then being no more than five hundred pounds a year.'

'Five hundred pounds a year!' James Morley started with surprise. He had been under the impression that Army captains earned no more than a couple of shillings a day. Or was that only in England? In the militia?

'You surprise me,' Morley said, then repeated his thought.

'I had the impression that captains earned no more than a couple of shillings a day.'

'Privates and all ranks up to NCOs earn no more than a couple of shillings a *week*,' Lachlan informed him. 'But I, sir, am a commissioned officer.'

'Five hundred pounds a year?' Morley repeated, his tone softening.

'Since then,' Lachlan continued, 'in the course of the past few months, I have been given my own company, as well as being appointed a Paymaster of the Regiment, and now I have been appointed as Major of Brigade, all of which has resulted in an increase to my annual income of over three hundred pounds a year,'

'Three hundred pounds...' Morley added it up. 'You mean... you earn eight hundred pounds a year?'

'I do.'

'Have you, perchance ... any savings?'

Lachlan shrugged. 'One thousand pounds.'

'One thousand *pounds*?' exclaimed Morley, his bug eyes almost bursting out of their sockets. 'You did say *pounds* — pure sterling? Not rupees?'

'Mr Morley, there is no need for you to keep seeking verbal confirmation of the amounts. The figures are all listed before you in detail. My pay as a Captain, Paymaster of the Regiment and Major of Brigade, adding up to a monthly income of six hundred and three rupees, or sixty-seven pounds nine shillings in sterling.'

'Quite.' Morley looked down at the paper, scrutinising the figures. 'I make it more than eight hundred pounds a year ... I make it eight hundred and *nine* pounds and eight shillings to be exact ... Ah, I see it's not a mistake, you have been exact on paper – £809. 8s.'

He looked up with a smile of approval.

Lachlan restrained the urge to spit at him. 'I am a Paymaster of the Regiment, you will recall? The British Army is not in the habit of placing its money in the hands of officers who do not know how to be exact in their figures.'

Morley blinked. 'No, of course not. I was simply surprised that you did not mention the total amount. Nine pounds and eight shillings is no trifling sum, not even when added to the annual total.'

It was then Lachlan realised that money was Morley's God, poor bastard.

'And as you can see,' Lachlan pointed to the paper, 'I have set that thousand pounds aside so that, in the event of Jane's family accepting my suit, it can be settled on her as a marriage gift. It is not a fortune, I know, but it is all I have to give her at present.'

It was a small fortune, and Morley knew it. He sat forward. 'But tell me, Captain, how did you manage to save such a large amount?'

'Most of it is my gratuity from the Mysore campaign. But I have been saving extremely hard from the first day I met Jane.'

'Indeed?' Morley now sat in utter calm, all his muscles relaxed. He clasped his hands together on the desk and studied them.

'Well, I must confess, the situation is not nearly as impossible as I originally thought. I think it very considerate of you to settle the sum of your savings on Miss Jarvis ... in the event of you being united. But I must inform you, quite candidly, that Miss Jarvis's fortune must also be settled on her alone ... in the event of you being united.'

'Mr Morley, with all due respect, I don't give a damn

about Jane's money. My feelings for her are not influenced by any mercenary motives. All I care about is the girl herself. And in the event of our being united, her own fortune can run on accumulating without my being allowed to touch even a penny of the interest of that money, which shall remain hers alone.' He stood up. 'You will inform me of the response to my proposal as soon as possible?'

'I shall discuss it with Mrs Morley, certainly. As soon as I return home.'

'You will, I hope, remember to mention it to Mrs Morley's young sister also, in view of the fact that it is her I wish to marry.'

'Naturally I shall mention it to Jane, naturally,' Morley replied in a tone of indulgence. 'But there is, um, one small matter...' he peered down at the list on his desk and turned a page, `that you, um, seem to have overlooked, Captain Macquarie.'

'Oh?'

'In the event of you being united, Miss Jarvis, you know, could not be allowed to even consider the prospect of living in officers' accommodation. The acquisition of a private house would be necessary. A house of style, elegance, and comfort – *outside* the town. No respectable lady these days could be expected to live *inside* the town. The acquisition of a country villa would be required.'

Lachlan reflected on this. `Yes, I agree, that would be the first requirement.' He withdrew a set of keys from his pocket. 'That is why I took possession of an excellent house yesterday, in a clean, airy, and undisturbed area – outside the town.'

'Well, well,' said Morley. `You have become very sure of yourself all of a sudden.'

'I have always been sure of myself, Mr Morley. It is other people in this world that often puzzle me.'

'Leased, is it? The house.'

'Yes, leased,' Lachlan replied. 'A necessity for the military, in case of future postings to elsewhere.'

'And the monthly rent? May I ask how much?'

'No.'

James Morley shuffled slightly in his seat. 'Mrs Morley will want to inspect it, you know, the house. In the event of the suit being considered, Mrs Morley will want to make sure that the house you have taken is satisfactory in every way.'

'Then I hope she will like it,' Lachlan said with a tone of finality. 'Because I know her sister will love it.'

He left then, and James Morley peered through the split-cane sunblind on the window and watched Macquarie step into the harsh sunlight where he stood for a moment untying the reins of his horse.

From the window Morley scrutinised the appearance of the tall young captain. As always Macquarie was impeccably dressed, even when in uniform, the tight-fitting blue riding jacket immaculate and perfectly tailored, the neck-cloth snowy, the black boots quietly polished – all betraying a certain fastidiousness about his grooming and clothes, unlike some of the more slovenly officers of the various regiments in Bombay.

And yet, Macquarie wore no jewellery, Morley suddenly realised. Why, every *authentic* gentleman in Bombay, whether civil or military, wore a few pieces of jewellery – a diamond cravat pin, gold and pearl fob-watch, one or two ruby rings – but Macquarie had worn no rings, no jewellery at all, save for the plain gold pin in his neck-cloth.

Morley stood reflecting.

Despite everything Macquarie had said, and despite all evidence to the contrary, he still had a sneaking suspicion that the Scot was on the trail of a fortune.

Morley narrowed his eyes as he watched the captain mount his horse. 'Well, *you* may be sure of what you want, sir,' he muttered, 'but that does not mean you will get it.'

FIVE

Private McKenzie was very sad to be dismissed as Captain Macquarie's manservant, but he understood that the matrimonial residence of an officer was no place for a raw-mannered soldier from the barracks.

'Och, I understand, sir,' McKenzie said in a subdued voice, his huge shoulders hunched, his eyes cast down. 'Ye must follow the rules and have a regiment of native servants now. Wouldna do for ye to have anythin' less. Wouldna *do* at all.'

'Don't look as if I have put a knife in your back, man. You knew you would have to return to the ranks one day.'

'Aye, and I'm happy to be goin' back to ma comrades at last, sir,' sang McKenzie in a shaky voice, on the verge of tears. 'I canna wait.'

'Here, this is for you.'

McKenzie glanced down at the money and shook his head. 'Nae, sir. It was a pleasure to serve ye. Ye've been good to me in the past, aye, good enough.'

'Take the money,' Lachlan insisted. 'It's simply a month's extra pay in gratuity, and customary for it to be given. It would cause me great dishonour if it was known that I dismissed my aide without even a rupee in gratitude.'

'Och, aweel, if it's a matter of honour...' McKenzie hesitantly took the money and then looked at Lachlan with the genuine loyalty of a devoted dog. 'But thank ye all the same, sir, thank ye. I'll spend some of it with ma comrades to toast ye and yer missis in a dram.'

Lachlan smiled. 'You know, McKenzie, not only are you

an insolent and audacious scoundrel, you are also a rather good officer's servant. I may even find myself in the unbelievable predicament of missing you.'

'Thank ye, sir. Ye have a reet nice way of putting things.' McKenzie's eye moistened, his chest heaved. 'And if ye ever need help in any way, sir, ye'll aye remember, won't ye, sir, that McKenzie's your man.'

Lachlan reflected for a moment. 'Maybe I can arrange for you to become an aide to some other officer, or some other position that's less – '

'The supply stores!' McKenzie – never one to miss a chance – instantly perked up. 'A job in the supply stores would be pukka, sir.'

'The supply stores?' Lachlan shrugged. 'Well, I'll see what I can do.'

An hour later McKenzie was sitting amongst his cronies, drinking himself into a good mood and talking incessantly. 'Lay on more drinks, Haroun!' he shouted boisterously to an Indian waiter. 'Lay on for ma gaggle of comrades here, all good lads, even if the stingy bastards are content to sit and drink all night at ma expense. Lay on, Haroun!'

He looked at the men around him with a sudden scowl. 'Why do men like the captain do it, eh? Marry themselves away? Now I've lost ma cushy job, and all because of a woman.'

'I thought you said the captain was going to get you a job in the supply stores?'

'Oh, aye!' McKenzie exclaimed, cheering instantly. 'I forgot that! The supply stores! I'll be able to help maself to all I want and not pay a brass penny for it. Lay on more drinks, Haroun! Lay on!'

Five days later, at seven o'clock in the evening, Captain Lachlan Macquarie of the 77th Regiment and Miss Jane Jarvis of Antigua were married.

The wedding took place at the house of James Morley, on the veranda, watched by scores of guests, military and civilian, who assembled on the lawn as Reverend Arnold Burrowes performed the ceremony. The guest of honour was John Forbes, the friend and banker who had first introduced the couple.

Maria Morley still looked uncertain and nervous as she gazed at her sister, looking so beautiful in a dress of white silk, and smiling so happily as she stood beside the young captain in his elegant uniform.

Maria clutched the linen handkerchief in her hand and dabbed at her eyes, but nothing could alleviate the worry that consumed her. Her sister Rachel had also married a young soldier in an elegant officer's uniform, and what a disaster that had been. It saddened Maria to even think about Rachel now, and the sight of Jane also marrying a soldier filled her with trepidation.

James Morley had also conceded defeat, deciding the marriage to be inevitable as Macquarie was so determined and Jane had continually *refused* to even consider the names of other more suitable men in Bombay, finally throwing herself at Maria's feet with the plea that she preferred Captain Macquarie to all other men in the *world*.

So what else could he do? He had done everything he possibly could. He had personally locked Jane in her room numerous times – but the bally Indian servants kept setting her free! How the rascals managed to get the door unlocked without a key was still a mystery. Oh, yes – that had been a terrible betrayal, his own servants switching their loyalty from him to Jane – and the reason why he had fired the lot of them.

Although, as he had said to Mr Tasker only yesterday, it was simply impossible to fire an Indian servant these days, because no matter what was said to them, they kept returning to their work every morning pretending to suffer from amnesia, or a lack of understanding of his English; and some – after his edict had been translated to them in Hindi – pretended to not even understand that, their own language! Scheming rascals.

As if by telepathy, one of those servants appeared before him, holding a tray of glasses of champagne. 'Sahib?'

Morley frowned at the glasses. 'Well, Maria may like it, but I hate that French fizz, too sour on the liver. Get me some gin.'

'Yes, Sahib.'

For the newly-weds and most of their guests, the evening was one to be remembered, filled with enjoyment and laughter. By midnight everyone was singing a medley of songs, chorused by all, the most popular songs being those about that small island thousands of miles across the sea, called Great Britain, from where they all originally came.

Maria Morley whispered to Jane that it was time to slip away and retire to her new home. This was a part of the wedding celebration that was treated with the utmost delicacy and decorum. No shouts of raucous laughter, no innuendoes to the bride or offers of advice to the groom, just a quiet slipping away by the bride and her chaperone, and later the groom.

In the new house, following custom to the letter, Maria

Morley stayed to see her young sister comfortably bedded, then prepared to take her leave as soon as she heard Captain Macquarie's footsteps on the veranda.

Ushering Jane's little Indian maid, Marianne, out of the room, Maria flustered over to the bed and kissed her sister farewell; then, blushing with embarrassment and unable to meet Jane's eyes, addressed her final words to the porcelain oil lamp on a small bamboo table beside the bed.

'Now remember, dear,' Maria said to the lovely blue kingfisher painted on the lamp's porcelain shade, 'one must naturally comply with one's wifely duty on one's wedding night, but after that ... well, one is occasionally allowed to have a headache, if one feels disinclined.'

'Yes, Maria, I understand.'

'I'm sure Captain Macquarie will also understand...' The lamp's shade was cream, the blue kingfisher surrounded by beautiful red and golden flowers. 'He is, after all, a gentlcmen,' Maria continued, 'well acquainted with the climate of India, and therefore must realise that the Indian heat does so often have an unfortunate tiring effect on white women.'

'Yes, Maria, I understand.'

'I'm so glad that you do, dear,' Maria said to the lamp, 'because I would be very distressed if, in the future, I was ... well, expected to discuss this aspect of your marriage with you again.'

Maria dragged her eyes from the lamp and at last spoke to Jane. 'Now, I think that is all, don't you, dear?'

'Yes, Maria.'

As soon as Maria had adjusted the mosquito net around the bed and glided swiftly out of the room, Jane sat up and smiled as she wondered what Mammy Dinah would have said if she had been the one to prepare her for her wedding night, instead of Maria?

For a moment, although it was not possible, she thought she could smell Mammy Dinah's coconut oil ... and hear her chuckles as she learned of Maria's marital advice to the kingfisher lamp. She knew just what Mammy would say – '*O my land o' sugar and molasses...*'

Such warmth and tenderness Mammy possessed, and despite her chuckles she too would have known that Maria was only trying to do her best. Dear Maria, so very prim and such a martyr to respectability, but underneath she had a kind and well-meaning heart.

Jane came out of her thoughts when, in the stillness of the night, out on the veranda, she heard Maria's flustered voice saying farewell to Captain Macquarie.

*

Lachlan helped Maria into the seat of her palanquin, and then stood and watched as the four bearers lifted it and jogged away with her, the two in front carrying their poles in one gripping fist and a flaming torch-light in the other.

At the end of the empty road that led to the house, Maria called to the bearers to halt, as Lachlan had guessed she would. Her head appeared through the curtain, she peered back towards the lighted house, seeing the figure of Captain Macquarie still leaning lazily against the veranda post. Her head seemed to nod in satisfaction. So unseemly for a gentleman to display undue haste on his wedding night.

She waved a hand in farewell.

Lachlan leisurely waved back.

She then appeared anxious to get away as quickly as

possible, ordering the bearers to hurry on. '*Jaldi! Jaldi!*'

The palanquin was lifted and carried off at a run. As soon as it was out of sight, Lachlan dropped his languid pose and turned into the house.

*

The room seemed serenely peaceful when he entered. The only light the golden glow of the lamp. The blue kingfisher, wings spread for flight, appeared surrounded by a glow of fire. Someone had put jasmine in a bowl beside the lamp and its essence filled the room. And there, at last, in his bed, was his beloved girl. He saw her through the haze of the mosquito net. She was sitting up with her hands clasped around her knees, her chestnut hair flowing loosely over her shoulders. He lifted the draping folds of the mosquito net and sat down on her side of the bed, a smile on his face.

'Well, now, Mrs Macquarie ...'

'We did it,' she said with a little smile of triumph. 'We did as we vowed and let nobody stop us.'

'We did,' he agreed, 'although, there was a time when dear old James had me very worried. Do you know, he practically told me outright that I was a fortune-hunter.'

'He told *me* outright that you were not a man but a confounded mystery.'

They looked at each other and with one accord started laughing. 'No, I'm no mystery,' he assured her. 'I'm just – as they say in Scotland – a laddie in love with his lassie.'

And that was all it took to stop her laughing. She stared at him, her dark eyes softening like mists as she whispered, 'My love ... '

*

The night was very still. The air in the room perfumed by the jasmine, fresh and soft in its fragrance. In the darkness they did not speak, but they both trembled. She kissed his mouth in a rush of throbbing tenderness. He was the first man she had ever kissed, and although she was perfectly innocent, the closeness of his body filled her with delicious warmth, setting her heart beating in a wild and joyous happiness. She loved him, she adored him, and now they were in each other's arms, at last. Then he shuddered and pulled her body closer, and in silence they left the world, conscious only of the deepening hunger of their lips.

He laid her back on the pillow and gently bared her breasts, tracing their outline with his fingertips. The movements of his hand sent a hot fire shooting through her body, making her breath come faster, and from then on she was his, to do with what he wanted, while no recollection or thought restrained the ecstasy of the night.

Next morning, a soft sunlight crept into the room, which faced east. The cane sunblind had been lifted on the window to let in the cool night air, and now without its shade, the room was brightening. All was silence and peace, the temperature sleepily warm, the scent of Persian roses floated through from the garden.

For the first time in years Lachlan had overslept. He stirred slowly, becoming conscious of the girl sleeping soundly beside him. He eased onto his elbow to look at her, remembering the night, ravished with love. He bent and kissed her softly on her mouth, then eased out of bed, careful not to wake her.

It had been almost dawn before they had finally slept, so

it would be cruel to wake her now. She was not used to waking before nine she had told him, but he had always found it impossible to sleep after sunrise.

In the dressing room he washed and dressed, deciding to take an early morning ride. He looked into the small room next to the dressing-room where Jane's little Indian maid, Marianne, was also sleeping. The poor child was only ten years old, and probably exhausted from all the wedding preparations of the day before.

Through the skylight the sun streamed brightly down the long hall. The entire house seemed to be slumbering in a golden peacefulness. Lachlan whistled quietly to himself as he strode through the silence – totally unprepared when he turned into the drawing room and found a small crowd of people standing in readiness to greet him.

He was so startled he almost tripped over his own feet. 'Where the hell did you all come from?'

In response, the line of native servants salaamed to him respectfully.

'Where did you all come from?' he asked again. 'You were not here last night.' He looked at them uncertainly. 'Were you?'

Yes, they were, in the row of servants' quarters at the back of the house, but he had not known or noticed.

A small thin Indian in a turban stepped forward and spoke for the others in rather good English. 'The Sahiba, she say for us to come at sunset.'

'Which Sahiba? Memsahib Morley?'

'No. Missy-Sahib Jarvis. She say we all needed to take care of the Sahib's house.'

Jane? ... Jane had organised all these servants?

He stared at the regiment of servants McKenzie had

predicted he would have. And the introductions began. There was a *Chowkidar* (Night Watchman) *Mali* (Gardener) *Syce* (Groom) *Dhobi* (Laundryman) *Kansamah* (Cook) *Khidmatgar* (Waiter at table) And so it went on ... By the time it came for him to be introduced to the *servants'* servants, his head was whirling. An officer he may be, but off-duty and on home ground, it seemed he was to live the life of a gentleman of ease.

At last he was allowed to take his leave, declining the offer of morning tea. No, he insisted, he did not want *chota hazri* – not breakfast – not until the Memsahib had awoken from her sleep.

*

It was a long-held custom in British Bombay that in the days immediately following a wedding, the bride and groom were obliged to hold a period of 'sitting up evenings' when well-wishers could call upon them to express their congratulations, and be lavishly entertained in return.

The weeks that followed were sheer exhaustion for Lachlan and Jane as every lady and gentleman in the settlement, not to mention a battalion of officers and their wives, called to pay their respects, which – custom declared – must be repaid by an invitation to stay for dinner if they called before five o'clock, or supper if they called later.

Five weeks after his wedding Lachlan sat down to dinner one evening and found himself joined by thirty-eight others.

'Now you understand why it was necessary to employ so many servants,' Jane whispered, looking fretfully down the veranda-table that had been designed to seat no more than twenty.

A few nights later, in the privacy of their bedroom, when the assembled supper guests that evening had numbered a mere sixteen, Lachlan looked at his wife and enquired tiredly: 'Is this entertaining *ever* going to end?

It ended for a while when they took a trip down the coast to Goa, a delayed honeymoon of ten idyllic sun-baked days spent walking or lazing on Goa's deserted and lonely white beaches and swimming in the sparkling blue waters of the Indian Ocean.

Swimwear was a thing unheard of for English ladies, so Jane swam as she had so often done since childhood in the Jarvis's secluded cove in Antigua, naked, with her chestnut hair floating loose to her waist. To Lachlan she was a glorious mate. He dived beneath her, swimming under her body then surfacing suddenly before her, kissing her wet lips in an ecstasy of passion. 'I love everything about you,' he said. 'Will you marry me?'

'Yes, yes,' she laughed, because he had said those same words to her all those months ago on the night James had seen them kissing in the garden at Government House. 'But my brother-in-law will never allow it,' she repeated, 'because he thinks you're a *rogue!*'

And then she fled from him, back under the water, her figure moving as smoothly as if she had been born under there, while his eyes gazed into the blue depths following her rapid flight.

Finally, with sighs of regret, they left the peace and freedom of Goa and returned to the bustle and noise of Bombay, just in time for the start of the Christmas social season.

*

The early months of their marriage passed like a romantic dream. But all dreamers eventually wake up.

Married only ten months, on a morning after another lavish evening of entertaining a score of guests, Lachlan faced the fact that he was nearing bankruptcy.

He had seen it coming, but had not known what to do about it. He sat at his desk and looked in despair at the list of expenses that far exceeded his income, all due to the large and costly circle of society in which they now moved in Bombay, where every family of any consequence must live in the same style and opulence as their neighbours did.

'A poor way to live,' he muttered.

The weekly liquor bill alone was astronomical in his eyes, although no more than normal in the world of British Bombay. In the past seven days alone his guests had easily seen off twelve dozen crates of Madeira, eight dozen crates of claret, six dozen brandy, ten dozen of gin, and fifty-three bottles of port. Not to mention the tons of food required each week.

Something about it all shamed him. This gluttony, this waste, this over-indulgence in every luxury while most of India was starving, and most of the people on Mull were scraping together every penny just to survive. He had made a mistake, a big mistake, trying to live the life of a rich British officer and compete with the nabobs of the East India Company.

The cost of love? The cost of making Jane as happy as he possibly could? He added it up ... and saw that he was over nine hundred pounds in debt. Just the word '*debt*' sent a chill through his heart. And that debt did not take into account the money he had already drawn to pay the lease on his mother's farm in Scotland which had been due for renewal, as well as the quarterly rent. But then he had *always* paid the rent on his mother's farm, from the age of fifteen, from the first month he had landed in America, and ever since.

He sat for hours at his desk trying to find a solution. Naively, he had hoped that as the years passed, no more than another five, he would have saved enough money to enable himself and Jane to return to Britain and establish a home in Scotland. It was a lovely vision of a future life that often occupied them in idle and happy planning: a home in the western isles, a large grey-stone house in which, Jane had already decided, every room would display a rich and beautiful Indian carpet.

Save! How could he save when every month he was spending almost three hundred rupees more than he earned?

'A hard way to get rich,' he muttered.

*

By the evening his worries were blocking off all other thoughts, but he kept them from Jane who was still suffering spates of sadness due to Maria's departure from India a few days earlier.

Maria had simply gone on a holiday to England in order to visit two other sisters there, but she would be away for almost a year, and Jane had clung to Maria as if the ship was taking her no further than the bottom of the ocean. At the end, himself and James Morley had been obliged to pull the two sisters from each other's arms in order that the ship could set sail.

James Morley ... Lachlan scowled as he thought of Jane's

irascible brother-in-law who had begun to show signs of renewed disapproval of Jane's marriage. But Maria Morley had begged Lachlan, before she sailed, to do everything possible to keep on good terms with her husband, and not to discommode him in any way, if only for the sake of dear James's liver.

Only a month after Maria's departure, Lachlan was given harsh evidence of the deplorable state of dear James's pickled old liver.

Morley stormed into the office at Army Headquarters which had been given to Lachlan upon his appointment as Major of Brigade, waving a letter in the air as he screamed: 'How dare you, sir! *How dare you!*'

The young lieutenant who had been sitting before Lachlan's desk rose to his feet and diplomatically left the room, closing the door very quietly behind him. The sound of his boots could be heard marching down the corridor as the two men looked at each other.

'Mr Morley...' Lachlan said in a carefully subdued voice, 'kindly remember that you are on military premises now, and we do not like our quiet corridors disturbed by the screaming of irate civilians.'

'Don't you dare act the supercilious staff officer with me, sir! I know what you are, Macquarie. What I always thought you were. A conniving fortune hunter! And now you've proved it by trying to get your hands on Jane's money!'

Lachlan looked at Jane's brother-in-law with a contempt he made no further effort to conceal. 'Your accusation, Mr Morley, is offensive, and I have warned you once before that my tolerance has a limit.'

Morley threw down the letter written on expensive English bond. 'There's the proof! There it is! You, sir, have made an order upon the London bankers, Messrs Francis and Gosling, to provide the money for a London-made carriage that you intend to purchase and have shipped out here to Bombay! As well as silver and plate engraved with the *Arms of Mull!*'

Calmly, Lachlan read quickly down the single sheet of paper. 'The carriage,' he said, 'was in fact ordered before our wedding by Jane, as was the request to Messrs Francis and Gosling to make payment. As soon as I learned of it, I wrote to the London carriage makers cancelling the order.'

'And the silver and plate?'

'That was also ordered by my wife, wishing as she did, to have her silver and plate adorned with the Macquarie Arms, and that I allowed to go through.'

'And who did you expect to pay for it? You are well aware that the marriage contract forbids you to touch Jane's money or any of the interest accruing from it.'

'And I have not done,' Lachlan replied in puzzlement. 'What the hell are you accusing me of? Jane has not sought to use any of her own money either, she knows she cannot do so until she is twenty-one.'

'So where did she hope to get the money for her fancy carriage then? For her silver and plate?'

'From the thousand pounds I gave to her as a wedding gift. The thousand pounds that you insisted I also deposit with Messrs Francis and Gosling. It's Jane's money to spend however she likes, and she has chosen to spend some of it on purchases for our home.'

'No, sir, you are mistaken!' Morley shook his head in vigorous protest. 'If you had taken the time to read the marriage contract carefully, you would have seen that the contract forbids her to touch even the interest on that thousand pounds.'

Lachlan looked at Morley as if unable to believe what he was hearing. 'What the bloody hell are you talking about?'

'The money you deposited with Messrs Francis and Gosling is now invested in English funds,' Morley said, 'and that sum and all accruing interest from it cannot be touched without first receiving the written *consent* of Jane's trustees, who are myself and Mr Tasker.'

'You mean ... she has no access ... even to the wedding present I gave her?'

'No – not without the written consent to Messrs Francis and Gosling of myself and Mr Tasker.'

Lachlan was silent for a moment. 'Mr Morley,' he said finally, 'I have been very fair and agreeable to all your requests, foolishly fair, I see that now. Surely you know that Jane ceased to be your ward from the day she married me. And surely you also know that in any other marriage, a wife's money and property becomes her husband's from the day of the wedding – by law.'

'Then you must recourse to the law, sir, because that's the only way you or Jane will ever get your hands on any of that money. You see, Mr Thomas Jarvis of Antigua who still holds most of Jane's money in his charge has refused to hand it over, until a guarantee is obtained from her trustees that the money will be used *only* and *solely* for the benefit of any *children* his sister may have. The care of Jane herself and all her wants and needs are your financial responsibility now.'

Morley's eyes were dark with malice. 'So you will have to meet the bill for her silver and plate yourself, won't you? Messrs Frances and Gosling won't meet it, I assure you. If you want silver engraved with the Macquarie Arms, it will have to be paid for with Macquarie money, which shouldn't present too much of a problem to a man who has no savings, and yet has been living these past months and entertaining all Bombay in the style of a man of fortune! Yes, indeed, sir, like *a man of fortune*. Or one who shortly expects to gain one.'

'So you –' Lachlan's eyes flashed, 'a pugnacious old nabob, along with that arrogant slave-owner in Antigua, still believe I only sought to marry Jane for her money?'

He looked at his brother-in-law with an expression of profound and final repugnance. 'Get out – *now!* Out of this office and out of this building!'

'I have not finished yet,' Morley shouted. 'I have more to say and I will leave when I desire and not before! I don't think it has escaped your notice, sir, that I have considerable influence around here, especially with – '

Lachlan had risen from his chair and crossed to open the door from where he beckoned to two soldiers of the 77th standing sentry down the corridor who came at the double. The soldiers looked at the captain's face and saw something his visitor had obviously not seen – Macquarie's urge to kill and his desperate struggle for control.

'Sir?'

'Escort this man out. And if he attempts to delay then lift him up and *throw* him out!'

The two sentries glanced at each other – like most soldiers they despised the civil servants, and the pleasure of throwing one out a door was a dream of pure fantasy – but if an order was given.

'Yes, sir!' They moved each side of Morley and caught an arm. 'Come along, sir.'

Outraged, Morley roared, 'By God, you'll not get away

with this, Macquarie! I shall go straight to the Governor-General about you!'

'You can go to damnation if necessary!' Lachlan replied savagely, 'Just make sure you never come near *me* again!'

'I shall go straight to General Balfour – '

'*Out! Before I kill you!*'

The two sentries moved into action, tightening their grip on Morley's arms. 'Come along, sir. Time for you to leave.'

*

It was some hours before Lachlan could inwardly muster a sufficient command of himself to set out on the journey home and break the news to Jane. But it was imperative that she should know, and without delay, that whatever arrangements *she* might wish to make to see her brother-in-law in the future, James Morley would never again be allowed to enter Lachlan Macquarie's house, nor Lachlan Macquarie's life, ever again.

She would cry her eyes out ... if only because of Maria.

And then he would have to tell her that she could not have her silver and plate, because they had no money, and were on the brink of penury.

'Oh, hell,' he said dismally.

His horse rounded the last bend onto the tree-lined avenue leading to the large and secluded white house that was his home. He frowned at the sound of hooves and wheels, checked his horse in a pause, and then turned his head in slow disbelief as a carriage sped past him with the window curtains tightly shut.

It was Morley's carriage. The restless dog had got here first!

*

At the house he heard her footsteps running along the veranda even before he had dismounted and relinquished his horse to the care of the *syce*.

He turned and looked at her speculatively, and knew the devil had done his worst. She was standing on the step waiting for him, tense and upset. He removed his hat and pushed a hand through his hair as he stepped onto the veranda.

'Lachlan!' Her voice was breathless. `Lachlan ... James has been here, he's only just left.'

'Yes, I know.' He lifted her hand and kissed it. 'Don't look so tragic, my love.'

She drew in a harsh breath. 'But, Lachlan, he *said* – '

'A whole blather of things, I'm sure, but there is no need to tell all the servants.'

Jane turned her head to see a number of the servants had gathered in a small group at the end of the veranda and were exchanging animated whispers.

'But, Lachlan – '

'Not now, not yet,' he commanded softly, and then called down the veranda to the House Steward who was the ringleader of the whisperers. 'Bappoo!'

'*Huzoor?*'

Bappoo came running, a big man with a permanent smile on his face, adjusting his loose turban before giving a salaam.

'Yes, Huzoor?' Bappoo said cheerfully.

Lachlan emitted a weary sigh, about to tell Bappoo *once again* that there was no need to call him Huzoor – *Your Honour* – but Bappoo was a law unto himself.

'Bring us tea.'

'Oh, yes, Huzoor! I bring tea in two months.'

Lachlan nodded, knowing Bappoo's English often confused minutes with months and a great deal else. 'As quickly as you can.'

*

'You see, the family's obsession with fortune-hunters, and their dislike of all soldiers, is all due to my sister Rachel,' Jane explained later. 'Rachel married a most handsome Englishman, a charming young lieutenant who had been stationed in Antigua with his regiment, and was about to return to England. His credentials were of the highest order. He came from a respectable family of wealth and rank. And away Rachel sailed with him, having brought to the marriage a very substantial dowry.'

'I think I can guess the rest,' Lachlan said tiredly.

'Well nobody else guessed. No one had the slightest suspicion that Woodward was not from a good family by any means. Papa was appalled when he discovered that Rachel had not married prosperously after all.'

'Ah,' Lachlan said, 'is this the infamous *Woodward* whose name is forbidden to be breathed, and the reason why Maria always changed the subject whenever your sister Rachel was mentioned?'

Jane nodded. 'Woodward sold his commission in the Army as soon as he returned to England. Then he lived the life of a lord on the marriage dowry and did away with the money in the space of a year on wine, women and gambling. According to James, it was rumoured that Woodward often lay a thousand pounds on the turn of one card. He lost in

104

the end, of course, lost all the money. Poor Rachel was reduced to poverty, but when Papa died he left her not one penny in case her scoundrel of a spouse got his hands on it.'

At last, Lachlan was beginning to understand. 'And James Morley and your brother in Antigua are convinced that I am another Woodward? Is that it?'

'That's it,' she replied honestly. 'James is convinced of it.'

'Damn James,' he said angrily.

*

Bappoo's face beamed like the sun when, a week later, he was told that he would not be dismissed with most of the other servants, but would accompany the Sahib and his wife to their new house.

'You will have to do a lot more work than you do now,' Lachlan told him bluntly.

'Good, good, excellent.' Bappoo looked very pleased with himself.

Lachlan studied Bappoo's smug face, knowing that Bappoo always managed to get out of doing any task he considered not to be in his unwritten contract of employment. But he liked Bappoo, if only for his pleasing manner and unwavering good humour – a precious necessity in the frugal days ahead.

'You must be willing to do whatever task is required of you, Bappoo. Even if it is outside the role for which you were originally engaged as House Steward. It will no longer be acceptable for you to refuse to lift even a water-jar from the garden because you are the "House" steward, or because of your often-repeated excuse that you are "no strong and have bad back."'

He looked wryly at the huge brown man who appeared as strong as a Moor barbarian, dressed in voluminous white muslin pantaloons, embroidered waistcoat, and white turban.

'You must be willing and able to do all things asked of you, Bappoo. Are you agreeable to that?'

'Oh yes, Huzoor, yes, yes, by Jove! Your unworthy servant agree to be father and mother, son and daughter, sun and moon, cloud and rain, and all things pukka desired by the Captain-sahib and his lady Mem.'

'If you just carry out your normal day-to-day duties, that will be enough.'

'For the Captain-sahib and his Memsahib,' Bappoo spread his hands expansively, 'Bappoo also agrees to do enough. Yes, *enough!*' And still smiling happily, Bappoo raised his fist and shouted the words that all Englishmen seemed to shout when they agreed with something. '*Hear! Hear!*'

*

By the end of the week the Macquaries had removed to their new house, which was smaller, and half the rent of their bridal home. They brought with them only a handful of essential servants including Bappoo and Jane's eleven-year old little Indian maid, Marianne.

Without even a pause for reflection, Jane had accepted her reduced circumstances without a word of complaint, declaring proudly that no amount of money could compensate for character, and as her brother in Antigua and her brother-in-law in Bombay had obviously become a pair of *ill-natured* characters, she would have no further contact with either of them.

She would also show them, she declared, that the Macquaries could manage very well without that *beastly* money which had caused so much trouble. And then, like a pioneering Englishwoman, rather than a pampered white child from Antigua, she set about arranging her new establishment on the system of English modesty instead of Eastern luxury. She took charge of all household expenses and viewed all prices with a careful eye.

She discovered that an entire lamb cost three rupees, whereas five rupees bought only a mound of cheese. She had never realised that cheese was a luxury, but it was, so cheese would have to go!

Madeira – two rupees a bottle – but English claret demanded sixty-five rupees a dozen. Now there was a saving! Her pen dashed claret from the list with all the nonchalance of a fan wiping away a fly.

'Madeira will grace our dining-table well enough,' she said to Lachlan, who could not help admiring her efforts at ruthless economy, bearing in mind that her life hitherto had been rich and plenty.

But Jane showed no signs of missing her former luxuries, and instead of the usual ornate carriage behind a prancing team of four, she seemed quite happy to travel in and around Bombay in a modest gig, behind a solitary old white horse which, she insisted, possessed the '*sweetest*' nature, and was much better than any other horse she had known.

*

Meanwhile, James Morley, still ranting biliously about a certain staff officer, decided to quit Bombay for a time and follow his wife to England where he could ensure that she spent not one penny of *his* money on English purchases for her sister Jane. Oh yes, he knew all about the number of 'small items' that Jane had asked Maria to purchase for her in London.

Jane was beset with worry when she heard of James's departure to England. 'He will give Maria the most distorted account of it all,' she said anxiously to Lachlan over dinner. 'And even though I have written to Maria and explained everything in great detail, when James arrives with his version of events, I'm sure Maria will not know who or what to believe.'

She snatched up an orange and began peeling it with shaking hands. 'And then there's my other two sisters in England ... I wrote telling them all about my gallant officer and what a wonderful husband you are, but I fear James will convince them that you are merely another ne'er-do-well.'

Her hands went still over the orange. 'Oh, Lachlan ... James seems to detest you so much, I think it quite probable he will spend his first weeks in England doing nothing else but complaining about you.'

Lachlan shrugged, unconcerned. 'I shouldn't worry,' he advised her wryly. 'From what I have observed of dear James, I think it quite probable that he will fret himself to death before he even reaches England.'

SIX

The silver and china adorned with the *Macquarie Arms* arrived from England.

Jane's delight was so great, Lachlan knew it would be cruel to suggest sending them back. But he did, just the same.

'We can't, Lachlan. Oh we *can't* send them back!' Jane moved a finger lovingly over the engraving of the Macquarie Arms. 'They can't be re-sellable, can they? Not with the Macquarie Arms on every piece.'

That was a very valid point.

She stood clutching a silver salver to her breast, staring at him, her eyes stilled in a desperate plea. Suddenly he knew he had no choice, no choice at all No matter how much his heart quailed at the prospect, he would have to go to his bankers and take out a loan at the current astronomical rate of twelve per cent interest.

'Can we keep it, Lachlan? *Please!* Can't you find a way of paying for them, somehow?'

'For you, my sweet Jane,' he said in all truth, 'I would do *almost* anything.'

*

'Four thousand rupees!'

Jane stared at the banker's draft that had just been handed to her by John Forbes. Slowly she turned and handed the bank draft to Lachlan.

'But why?' Jane said in amazement, turning back to John Forbes, 'why should the old brigadier leave anything to me?'

John Forbes smiled. 'Because he had a sincere affection for you, Jane. It seems you were very gracious and kind to him once, at a party. And that is why he left you this gift in his Will.'

Left her a hundred rupees at the most, Lachlan thought, studying the draft in his hand, not four thousand – the *exact* amount they needed immediately, and the *exact* amount he had applied to borrow from his bankers only yesterday.

But now it had arrived as a gift.

Lachlan looked at his banker and saw that John Forbes was avoiding his eyes.

'You will stay to dinner, John?' Jane asked.

'No, Jane dear, thank you, but my nephew Charles has arrived from England and will be expecting me to dine with him. And anyway,' Forbes added with a small laugh, 'since your wedding I have dined so often at the Macquaries' table I think you both must be well and truly sick of me by now.'

'Never in a lifetime, John!' Jane declared honestly. 'Come tomorrow evening? Bring Charles with you.'

'Very well, we'd be delighted.' John Forbes glanced at Lachlan who was still looking down at the draft. 'Now, if you will forgive me, I really must be off.'

Lachlan laid down the draft and turned to perform the courtesy of seeing him out. He walked with John Forbes down the veranda and onto the drive where his palanquin and bearers waited for him.

'A generous man, the brigadier,' Lachlan murmured.

'Yes, a dear old thing,' Forbes agreed. 'But then, you know, yourself and Jane have many friends in Bombay, Lachlan, many friends.'

That was the problem. They had too many friends in Bombay.

'It's strange, just the same,' Lachlan said softly, 'that the amount of his bequest should be the same as I applied to borrow.'

'Is it?' Forbes's eyes looked vague for a moment. 'Yes, I suppose it is, now you mention it. Strange that.' He looked round sharply. 'Does this mean you will no longer need to borrow the money?'

Flinching inwardly, Lachlan answered through dry lips. 'No, I don't suppose I will.'

'No? Are we to be deprived of the interest? Oh dear!' John Forbes shook his head as he climbed into his palanquin. 'Still, I suppose the old brigadier was only doing his best without any desire to put us out of business.'

When his bearer had closed the door, John Forbes extended his hand through the window. Lachlan reached to clasp it in farewell. 'Goodbye, my friend,' Forbes said lightly. 'See you tomorrow evening, all being well.'

Lachlan nodded. 'All being well.'

He stood with a set face and watched the palanquin carried out of sight. Would he ever know the truth of it? But if the money had come from John Forbes's own pocket and not the brigadier's account, then one could only admire John's clever and delicate way of doing it – a personal gift to Jane, left to her in a Will by a dead officer whose estate the bank had been settling.

Bunkum!

Not for one minute did he believe the four thousand rupees had come from the brigadier's estate.

Lachlan turned back to the house, riven by a humiliation that John Forbes had done his utmost to avoid.

*

The money paid for the silver and plate, but what was left did little to help Lachlan honour his debts. He began to yearn an escape from this life of Eastern luxury. And yet, in comparison to the rest of Bombay society, he and Jane were living a life of Scottish frugality.

Like many another career-minded officer, he rode out to the country every morning before breakfast to keep himself strong and healthy. As he cantered along he thought of the daily routine of most other gentlemen in British Bombay, and wondered what his mother, a virtuous and hard working Scot, would think if she knew of the life here?

He decided she would probably faint if she knew that a gentleman in Bombay steps out of his bed each morning to find a servant holding his clothes: one servant held his breeches, another his shirt, another his waistcoat, and so on and so on, and these were all put upon his body without the slightest effort on his part.

The gentlemen is then seated in a chair while a servant washes and shaves his face and combs his hair; and while this is being done, a house servant places a cup of tea in one hand, and the hookah servant places the hookah smoking tube in his other hand. And all that before he has even left his dressing room.

'*My Goad, but that's sinful, Lachlan, sinful!*' Yes, that's what his mother would say. His father, on the other hand, if he had been alive, would slowly have shaken his tired head and refused to believe it.

And these gentleman, almost all attached to the East India Company – the *Civil Dogs* – as so many of the soldiers secretly called them, were amassing great fortunes in India by hook or by crook but which they simply called '*trading*'.

And when the nabob has finished his lucrative day's

trading, usually by one o'clock, and usually making as much money for himself as for the East India Company, a sedan chair and bearers wait to carry him home before the sun gets too hot. And once home his servants are waiting to remove his waistcoat, his shirt, his breeches, and the afternoon is devoted to a nice relaxing sleep, in preparation for the pleasures of the evening socialising.

There were those few, of course, who sought respite from the boredom of such long hot idle Indian days and nights by exciting themselves with an occasional smoke of opium – *very expensive* – but not for the Civil Dogs, considering the opium monopoly was held by the East India Company.

Under the shade of a huge banyan tree, Lachlan turned his horse and sat looking up at the canopy of soft green leaves above his head ... Even now, after four years in India, he still felt a tremendous awe for the magnitude of a single banyan tree, its many trunks swelling in all directions from the parent trunk of the tree, so that a banyan was a grove in itself, in which an entire company of soldiers could lie down and sleep with room to spare.

Mynah, mynah, mynah ... He turned his head and looked up at the mynah bird chatting cheekily down to him. He smiled, saluted, and rode on, cantering back at an easy pace, his mind returning to the world of British Bombay and the gentlemen who lived in it.

To give them their due, many were rich and lazy, but no servant could wish for a more clement master than a British master. The lazy British nabob may insist on his every need being catered for, but if one of his native serving tribe suffered sorrow, or difficulties of any kind, then he became the very fount of human kindness and compassion, and any real distress of a servant was rarely pleaded in vain.

And the native women of India, at least, had reason to be grateful to the British, for the custom of *sutti* – a widow being forced to burn herself alive with the corpse of her dead husband – was strictly forbidden in all districts ruled by the British, yet still widely practised in those states ruled by the maharajahs.

But it was as *friends* that the British nabobs truly excelled and became such a problem. In the private world of personal friendships the British regarded themselves as one large and friendly family, although poor relations were sternly frowned upon as letting the home side down and often ostracised. Military officers were *very* acceptable as friends, as long as they were up to snuff and good entertaining, but common soldiers were merely rowdies to be avoided at all cost.

And it was in this world of opulence, where generosity, comfort, and *unlimited* hospitality were the order of the day, that Lachlan watched his debts rising and rising, and saw no way out, no way at all.

Until, at the end of May, the new Commander-in-Chief of the Army in Bombay, General Balfour, sent an urgent summons to Captain Macquarie to report to him at once.

Balfour! Lachlan found himself thinking wryly about his old commanding officer as he walked towards the general's office at Headquarters. Balfour had long ago found the perfect solution to living in peace and escaping the expense and extravagance of Bombay society – he lived on a cruiser way out in the harbour – sailing back and forth from the cruiser in a small masoolah boat every day.

'It's very far out,' a Company nabob had said in a disgruntled tone to Balfour one day at the docks. 'Your boat, Colonel, it's very far out. I must say, your removal from the shore will make it very difficult for people to drop in on you at evening time, as is the custom here in Bombay.'

'Drop in?' Balfour had cried. 'My dear man, there is my boat on the beautiful blue ocean and anyone may drop in whenever they wish!'

General Balfour was staring at a map on the wall when Lachlan was shown in. He looked round and exclaimed in surprise, 'Captain Macquarie – why, you're just the man I was hoping to see!'

Lachlan saluted the old humbug. 'You sent for me, sir?'

'Did I? Oh yes, I think I did … but first, before we get down to the tedium of official business, tell me…' Balfour's face became paternal, his tone gentle, 'how are you enjoying married life in Bombay?'

Lachlan knew Balfour was merely humouring him. Instantly he became wary.

Balfour smiled. 'Happy are you?'

'Like you, sir, I would be happier on a boat.'

'A boat, dear boy?' Balfour seemed astonished at the answer. 'You would prefer to be on a boat – away from Bombay society?' He swatted at a fly above his eyes. 'What an absolutely *splendid* coincidence, in view of the circumstances…'

*

Lachlan raced home to Jane and sped into the house, grinning with joy. He swung her up in his arms while she laughed and demanded to know the reason.

'I'm leaving Bombay! My company and most of the 77th are being shipped out of Bombay within a month. No more playing the rich man! No more being the elegantly clad staff officer! I'm changing my coat, Jane, and going back to soldiering.'

'When? Where?'

'To a military station five hundred miles away, down the Malabar coast, at Calicut, a little south of Tellicherry.'

Jane stood very still, holding on to his arms as if dizzy. He was being sent back into the field, and leaving her alone in Bombay.

'For how long?' she asked.

'A year, two years - who knows with the Army? All that matters is you and I will be getting away from all the artificiality and ridiculous expense of Bombay!'

'You mean ... I can come too?'

'Of course you're coming too!' He smiled at her expression. 'I go nowhere without you – except into a battle area. And we'll take Bappoo with us. And Marianne.'

'Marianne and Bappoo!' She threw herself into his arms, kissing his face with little tender kisses as if he had given her some extraordinary pleasure.

He breathed in her perfume and allowed it to go straight to his head, deciding that the only thing he wanted to do now was to take her immediately to their bedroom and revel in his good news and her – and why not? It was the afternoon, the hottest time of the day.

'I must go and tell Marianne,' she said excitedly, drawing back.

'Afterwards,' he said, smiling as he took her hand and led her out of the room and down the hallway. 'After a bit of play in the games room.'

*

Afterwards, Jane opened dark-fringed eyes as if she had been drugged. She moved her body slowly, and then lay for a time in lassitude. The sun was burning on the roof but the heat did not affect her. Coming from a hot country she was more acclimatised to these hot afternoons than he would ever be.

Finally, she gazed thoughtfully at the ceiling and began to ask questions about the new life ahead of them. Would Major Oakes's wife be going? She liked Mrs Oakes. And Mrs Stirling? Was she going? And Mrs Shaw?

Her thoughts stirred her into movement. She sat up and shook out the heavy waves of her long hair, then settled herself happily against the pile of pillows covered in a cool yellow satin, and her questions continued. How far from the town of Calicut was the military station?

He did not answer. She turned her face to look at him and saw that his eyes were closed. She shook his shoulder roughly. 'Well?'

'Well, there is one wee little thing I forgot to tell you, Jane,' he murmured. 'You will be the only officer's wife on the station.'

She half rose on the pillows then dropped back again, as if the breath had been knocked out of her. For a long moment she lay staring at the ceiling, then she blurted out in a wail, 'I'm to be thrown amongst the wolves! A whole regiment of them!'

He stirred himself at last to drag himself up to kiss her bare shoulder and humour her with an easy smile.

'As a company commander's wife you will be treated like a queen. And the 77th are a fine bunch of lads,' he added. 'The best in India.'

*

A few days later, in the cantonments of Colaba, a company of that fine bunch of lads was lined to attention on the parade ground in preparation for being put through their drill.

The fact that their company commander had specially ridden over to watch them, accompanied by two lieutenants, did not disturb them in the least. They liked Captain Macquarie, thought him a good skin and one of the few pukka officers in the regiment. Not like some of the others who had too many airs and graces and strutted around like generals. But Captain Macquarie was down to earth and always ready to fight for his men if he thought any complaint against them unjustified.

The sun was getting higher and promised another day of swelter. Everyone was now watching for clouds and counting the days to the arrival of the monsoon, which usually reached Bombay in mid-June, bringing with it the blessed coolness that everyone craved.

On the parade ground, Captain Macquarie stood to the side with his officers and nodded to the drill-sergeant to commence.

Sergeant McGinnis wheeled round to face the men, opened his mouth as wide as a whale's and began barking out a series of commands that went on for almost an hour.

The sergeant finally called a halt.

The men, red-faced and panting like blown cattle, looked to their company commander who had been watching them throughout, hoping desperately that he would give Sergeant McGinnis the signal that would allow them to fall out.

They saw him looking at them thoughtfully, and then he

beckoned to Sergeant McGinnis who marched over to him. He spoke very quietly to the sergeant, occasionally glancing in the direction of the men. Then he spoke to Lieutenant Lacey, who nodded and strolled towards the men with a supercilious smirk on his face. Lacey, they had decided, was just another one of those officers who had all the airs and graces of an exiled prince.

The men groaned when they learned there was to be no falling out, but a display of their firing skills.

Lieutenant Lacey organised the drill, lining the men into ranks. Captain Macquarie watched carefully as the men loaded and fired their fifty-six inch long muskets, the bullets zapping towards the target boards lined against the end wall, loaded and fired, loaded and fired, three rounds a man.

When the noise on the parade ground finally died down and the smoke had settled, the 'best in India' were ordered back into lines.

Only then did Captain Macquarie walk over and give them his opinion of their performance.

'As soldiers, nothing but your cleanliness deserves praise. All your movements were slovenly executed. Your firing was neither close nor regular. Your discipline and strength has gone to the devil. You are slack and slow and out of condition and have obviously had life a bit too easy since returning from Mysore. So I think a few changes are in order.'

He looked at Sergeant McGinnis. 'The men must be shaped up and returned to a high standard, Sergeant. Allow them to cool off for fifteen minutes, then get them working again and keep them sweating for at least another hour. After that it will be two hours of drill morning and evening. Parades three times a day, sunrise, noon and sunset. And musket practice twice a day until we leave Bombay.'

The men stared at him, appalled.

Lachlan understood their outrage, but as their company commander the responsibility for the lives of these men had been entrusted to him, and if they were being moved down the coast to go into battle, as he suspected they were, then the best way to help them survive was to make sure they were fighting-fit and ready for anything.

And there was another matter he was forced to make them consider. 'I do understand,' he said, 'that boredom is the curse of peacetime soldiering. And nowhere moreso than here in India where a soldier has little to do outside routine than carouse in brothels, indulge in drunkenness, and smoke opium.'

His eyes moved along the lines in an expression that said he had more than a suspicion that a few of them were freely indulging in the latter.

'But any soldier found to be in possession of opium will suffer the severest punishment the Army can give him. You have all seen the effects of opium on the Indian armies. In battle it inspires a false courage that leads to a short period of brutal frenzy followed by staggering imbecility.'

Sergeant McGinnis's face was puce with shame as he listened to the captain addressing the men slowly and distinctly with a determined edge to his voice.

'You will drill until you can all march on the parade ground as one man, in perfect synchronisation. You will have musket practice until you can load and refire three rounds inside one minute and not three. You will, if nothing else, be a credit to this regiment of the British Army.'

He turned away, leaving the sergeant to dismiss the men who stood staring after him as he strode from the parade ground with his junior officers.

'Bloody Breda! Whoever said he was pukka?'

'Aye, well ... I reckon there's something brewing.'

'*Silence! Shut your blethering gobs!*' Sergeant McGinnis had come out of his shock and shame and was glaring at the men like a demon on fire.

'Ye lazy shower o' buggers! Ye couldn't even *pretend* to be soldiers, could ye? Ye couldn't help out a poor old sarge who's always been good to ye. Oh, God! I wish I was dead! Dead and no longer in charge of ye sods! Almost six years in Hindooo land – and where's it got me? I'll never make Regimental Sergeant-Major now!'

Emotion cracked his roaring voice. 'Well if my career's ruined I'm taking ye lot with me! Ye needn't worry about drills or anything else because I'm not going to give them to ye! I'm going to do what the captain should've done – I'm going to get one of the regiment's cannons – and then I'm going to blow ye all to buggery!'

He looked at the men with a sudden clearness, and saw them all regarding him with patient eyes. They all knew his bark was far worse than his bite.

*

Colaba was one of the small islands very close to the shore of Bombay and linked to the mainland by a causeway over which pedestrians and carriages could travel. Every day Lachlan rode out to spend most of his time in the cantonments of Colaba watching the men of his company in training.

Other company captains had heard of Macquarie's lecture and how he was reported to be now leaning very hard on his men. Not to be outdone, they quickly followed suit.

For four weeks the men trained, the men drilled, the men sweltered.

And still no sign of the monsoon.

Three days before the end of June, General Balfour and a brigade of staff officers, together with Major Whitelocke, the new commandant of the Calicut forces, had the pleasure of watching the companies of the 77th's first Battalion marching on parade with superb synchronisation, all commands being followed with a snap and precision that was breathtaking.

Balfour was a vision of happiness as Major Whitelocke praised the 77th's '*magnificent*' soldierly performance

'Yes, yes,' Balfour agreed happily. 'The best in India.'

The following day the 77th sailed out of Bombay harbour, just as the monsoon arrived, and the rains fell.

SEVEN

'Rain!'

The soldiers of the 77th stood on the deck of the *Endeavour* holding up their smiling faces to what had been a furnace of a sky. The monsoon had arrived at last.

For six days Jane groaned in her cabin as the ship rolled on its way down the Malabar Coast. Whenever the drumming of the rain eased she could hear the cheerful voices of the men, and sometimes the voices of women.

All 'official' wives of soldiers were allowed to travel with the Army when a regiment was moved to a new settlement, especially in India where the girls would have been rejected by their own people for marrying out of their caste.

Aboard the ship the soldiers' wives were housed apart from the men and rarely strayed from their own privacy below decks. But on arrival at Calicut, two weeks after leaving Bombay, Jane at last saw the small group of Indian girls that some of the soldiers had fallen in love with and married; delicate and beautiful girls with slender limbs, soft features, eyes black and serene, and not one could be over the age of eighteen.

Jane thought them all very young, although she herself was only twenty-one.

'Where do the soldiers meet these girls?' she asked Lachlan in a curious whisper, then gave a slow 'Ohhh, I see,' when he explained that some were servant girls who had been lured out of their caste by the twinkle in a British blue eye – but most were *Daughters of Music* – dancing girls who, under the care of their respective *duennas* were hired to dance at European entertainments, but often escaped their *duennas* to some moonlight garden to hear more of the romantic whispers of a lonely soldier.

Dancing girls! Jane looked at them now, and understood their grace. Everything about them was graceful, and all salaamed shyly to the only 'Memsahib' on the ship.

Jane smiled and salaamed back; and then turned and looked towards the coconut palms and white beaches of Calicut.

*

The military station at Calicut was four miles along the coast from the town. It was composed of a series of palm-thatched huts formed into streets, shaded by coconut trees. Some distance up a small hill beyond the huts were the officers' bungalows, bordered by banyan and jacaranda trees. Lachlan and Jane found their bungalow to be the best of all, having a large bedroom, and surrounded by a beautiful garden.

Jane explored her new surroundings. The veranda completely encircled the house and as she walked around it she could see high beautiful hills in the background, green dappled country at each side, and from her front door, the blue sea could be seen in the distance.

'We're going to be happy here,' she told Lachlan.

And she was right, for thus began the happiest period of their lives; and it was in that quiet and peaceful military oasis in Calicut that Jane Macquarie truly fell in love with India, and Lachlan fell even more in love with Jane.

*

Every day the rain fell, filling the air with the smells of wet earth, rejuvenating the land, refreshing the spirit. Hot winds blew through the night, calming almost to a breeze by morning. But the southwest monsoon was passing away from the coast of Malabar and travelling north-eastwards where it would finally exhaust itself.

By September the rainy season was almost over and the inhabitants of Calicut faced nine months of guaranteed sunshine.

The first friend Jane had made on her arrival was a mama-monkey who had taken up residence in a tree behind the house, at the far edge of the garden. She had a cute, cheeky face, and was very noisy as she chattered to her tiny offspring, instructing him in the art of jumping from branch to branch.

As soon as the mama-monkey saw Jane she paused, and sat for while looking at the girl with curious eyes, scratching her ear lazily and appearing irresolute as to how to respond. Then, after a chatter with herself, she decided to ignore the human, turning her face away in an arrogant manner and carried on with her parental instructions.

Jane nicknamed her 'Fawn' because of her colour. Day after day she watched Fawn teaching her young progeny, swinging from branch to branch herself and showing him how it was done; cuddling and kissing him when he was timid, encouraging him with cheerful chatter, then beating him angrily when he refused to budge.

These beating sessions always ended with Fawn sitting with a hairy hand to her brow and directing at Jane a hail of chatter about what Jane could only suppose to be the difficulties of parenthood.

Flowers being the delight of all Indian maidens, Jane's

little maid, Marianne, ensured that a basket of freshly gathered flowers, collected in the cool of the morning, refreshed the Macquaries' dining table from breakfast until supper. And never once did they lie down to sleep without the exotic fragrance of a bowl of some richly scented flowers by their bed.

The only real entertaining they did now was on a Sunday, when Jane, being the only officer's wife on the station, welcomed all the other officers to dine throughout the day at the Macquaries' table.

Sunday became the one day in the week when the house was lively and full. Their fare was a mixture of West and East: chickens, which were plentiful in Malabar, lamb, vegetables, curries and an abundance of rice platters dressed in a delicately oriental manner. The long leisurely meal always ended with the ritual of sipping a glass of milk, for all had learned from their first week in India that a glass of milk sipped slowly destroyed all evidence of spices on the breath and refreshed the mouth.

Friday evenings were always spent at the Brigadier's house, sampling what Jane called `his sad stew.' Although the Brigadier invariably cheered them up later by singing songs to them in his beautiful tenor voice.

Life was good, very good. Although Fawn – Jane's monkey friend – was becoming far too familiar and cheeky, Lachlan decided one day when himself and Jane returned from an early morning walk to find Fawn sitting languidly amidst the cushions of Lachlan's favourite cane chair and guzzling a bottle of his favourite beer imported by the Army from England.

All his stern commands to Fawn, ordering her outside to her own abode, went unheeded. She shook her head stubbornly and guzzled on.

Bappoo was called.

Bappoo arrived, smiling and cheerful as ever, but as soon as he saw Fawn he let out a shout and clapped his hands angrily.

Fawn sprang off the chair and scurried out of the house, but not before she had managed to grab a handful of nuts from a bowl on a small sidetable.

As time went by, Fawn and her little monkey were often to be found lounging on the veranda of the house as if they owned it – Fawn lolling back on one of the cane chairs chattering to herself while her son, more daring now, swung on the wooden rail of the veranda or hopped on to the roof to sit and stare at the sea.

Only the house itself was banned to Fawn: the usual wire netting covered the windows to keep her and all other monkeys out. Yet all of Fawn's days were spent seeking cunning ways to get inside for more beer.

Fawn's new-found taste for beer was so lustful that whenever Lachlan sat on the veranda leisurely drinking a bottle, she would attempt to seduce it from him by sitting with her mouth pursed in the shape of a kiss, clicking at him lovingly.

When this ceremony of devotion failed to move him, she would run away angrily and a short time later he would find himself and the veranda being pelted with coconuts from the advantage of a high tree.

The third time Fawn had done this, Lachlan had been so furious he had lifted the coconuts and pelted them back, and by some fluke had hit her and knocked her from the tree, with no real injury. After that she proved a coward when fighting the white man, and now only pelted handfuls of dust.

But mainly she preferred to purse her lips and click at him passionately, until he eventually lost patience and handed the bottle over. In this way she always succeeded in getting the second half of any bottle of beer he was foolish enough to drink on the veranda.

*

Fawn was not the only friend Jane made in Calicut. Accompanied by Marianne she often wandered down to the huts in the coconut groves and discovered that all the Hindu girls were as attentive to bathing and cleanliness as Marianne, for to the Hindus, purity of the body is connected with purity of the soul. They washed themselves every morning in scented water from special water-jars that were filled from the river in the evening and scattered flowers on the surface from which the fragrance was seeped during the overnight marinade.

They also took great care to keep themselves as attractive as possible. Their dress was simple, saris of the softest shades and silks draped around their slender bodies. All wore at least one pearl in their ears, and coloured bangles adorned their wrists and ankles; but it was the rings they wore on their fingers that fascinated Jane the most.

All wore one particular large ring on the middle finger which looked like a glistening silver stone, but was actually a mirror, enabling them to continually check their faces and ensure that no smudge of dust or dirt had blemished their clean olive skins. And so fascinated was Jane with this very clever ring, that one Hindu girl shyly took the ring off her own finger and offered it to the young Memsahib.

Jane flushed crimson, 'Oh, please, no, I couldn't accept, it would deprive you!' But the expression on the other girls' faces told her it would be a great insult if she refused.

Marianne whispered to Jane the Eastern proverb: 'Presents are the hand of friendship.'

'Ruchira be very happy,' the girl said shyly, holding out the ring.

Jane smiled and took the ring, slipped it on her finger, held it up and admired herself in its mirror, then declared it to be the *sweetest* gift she had ever been given and would treasure it always.

All the Hindu girls were laughing now. At first they had been frightened of the young Memsahib, for it was not the Sahibs that looked down on the native people of Hindustan with a prejudiced eye, it was the *Mem-logs* – the white women.

But not this white woman – she stayed mainly in the officers' quarters as was her place, but she was also happy to venture down to the married quarters when the men were away doing their morning drills to speak to their wives in a broken fashion, she knowing some of their language, and they knowing some of hers.

As the months passed and the weather grew very dry again, Jane often watched the Hindu girls as they went about their lives of serene domesticity, cheerfully cleaning out their huts in the morning, singing as they prepared their food on small fires outside their huts in the evening, and obviously making love with their men at night, for some who had not been pregnant on arrival very soon were.

In turn the Hindu girls watched the young Memsahib going about *her* life, and were both shocked and charmed to see her fitting into the life at Calicut in her own way, refusing to recline in languor like most Mems, but regularly setting off beside the Captain-Sahib, carrying her own knapsack and happily roughing it as a soldier's wife.

The men liked her, too. They usually couldn't bear the officers' wives, regarding their high-nosed snobbery with sneering disdain. But Jane's 'bonnie' personality and unfailing good humour had made her a great favourite with them all.

The Macquaries' bungalow was perched on the side of a small hill. Often in the late afternoons Jane would stand on the veranda and look out to sea, then over the sun-drenched station of Calicut and think how relaxed and friendly it all was. Even the officers had discarded their scarlet coats to stamp around in high boots, white breeches and white shirts with the sleeves carelessly rolled up.

In the evenings the sun would still be blazing, but low in the sky and reddening the light. Then Jane would lean over the veranda rail watching Lachlan's white-clothed figure coming up the path through the green brilliance of the trees, and she would smile and run down to meet him.

The nights were starry and hot, and those soldiers who were single regularly ventured into the town four miles away for the pleasure of flirting with the dancing girls that could be found in every town in southern India.

Nearly every night the songs of the soldiers could be heard drifting from the isolated military settlement in Calicut, tankards of beer were drunk regularly, but not a whiff of opium could be sniffed.

At the end of nine months their simple style of living had enabled Lachlan to pay off most of his debts. So much so, that he was able to write to John Forbes

*From our economical mode of living
since we came down the coast, I have
nearly cleared off all my debts; and
by going on in the same course for a
few months longer, I shall not owe
one single anna to anyone.*

But while the inhabitants of the military station at Calicut peacefully spent their days in the sun; thousands of miles away on the cold continent of Europe, a short dark-haired soldier stood by a window in a grey-stone chateau staring gravely out at the garden, thinking about India. His name was Napoleon Bonaparte.

'Liberte! Egalite! Fraternite!' The drums of revolution that had first sounded in Paris in 1789 were now resounding throughout most of Europe. Louis XVI was dead. His Austrian queen, Marie-Antoinette was dead. All of the French aristocracy and most of the old order were dead. Even the butcher Robespierre was dead. And the French drums were still beating, through Belgium, the Netherlands, everywhere. *'Vive la Republique!' 'Vive la Revolution!'*

They marched as conquerors. Armies upon armies of French soldiers in blue uniforms with red facings, challenging the whole of Europe to join them. *'Drive out your tyrants! Let France protect you!'*

In Spain the King trembled on his throne. In Amsterdam the Dutch Revolutionary Committee issued a proclamation to a cheering crowd: *'Brave citizens! By the mighty aid of the French Republic, you have cast off the tyranny that oppressed you! You are free of the Stadtholder! You are free! You are equal!'*

The Prince of Orange fled to England where he begged his

royal relatives to help him. The French, he was sure, intended not only to conquer Europe, but the world.

To the British Prime Minister, William Pitt, the Stadtholder gasped out his fears about losing the Dutch territories in India. Already it was known that the Dutch in Cochin, having heard of the rage of their people at home against the Stadtholder, were preparing to throw in their lot with Napoleon if he came to India. He begged the British Prime Minister to protect the Dutch possessions in India and hold them in trust until the French had been defeated.

William Pitt had seen it coming. As soon as the Dutch Revolutionary Committee had been formed, he had been convinced the unhappy subjects of the Stadtholder would eventually join in an alliance with the French. And that was one of the reasons why various regiments of the British Army had been moved from the cities to strategic posts around India. The British had always wanted the lucrative Dutch trading territories in India. And now, it seemed, France wanted them too.

William Pitt smiled. Britain's fight for possession of the Dutch territories in India was about to begin.

*

Four months later a ship carrying orders from the War Office in London arrived in Bombay.

General Balfour fumed as he read the Prime Minister's instructions, which had been delivered to him personally by Colonel Petrie.

'War! I have no problem with war – if it comes to that.' Balfour said furiously. 'But how in blazes can I order an army of men out into the field in lashing rain! At the very least most of the gunpowder will get soaked and become useless!'

For a moment Colonel Petrie could not answer, due to his confusion. Outside the sun was blazing and the temperature was unbearably hot. He gestured to the window. 'But, General, the weather is – '

'About to change!' Balfour snapped. 'But coming from London you wouldn't know anything about that, would you? Well the first thing you will learn about India, Colonel Petrie, is that we move with the weather – and right now we are awaiting a *monsoon*.'

*

Down the coast in Calicut, everyone was feeling irritable with the continuing fierce heat. Jane fanned herself moodily and opened the buttons of her bodice. 'Even Antigua was never this hot,' she said to Marianne. 'Look – ' she pointed to the mahogany dresser, 'it's so hot even the furniture is perspiring.'

'No, no, Mem-Jane, the furniture is showing polish.' Marianne giggled. 'This morning I polish, and now you see the shine, not heat.'

Jane smiled at the girl's giggles, and then sighed. 'So where is the monsoon?'

'The monsoon it comes ...' Marianne moved over to the window, `very soon. One day, two days, very soon.'

The monsoon arrived three days later. Everyone revelled in the rain. The soldiers whooped, the women laughed. In the bazaars of the town merchants and coolies began to dance.

Wet, cool, beautiful rain. Life-giving rain! Now the drying

rivers would be replenished, the wells would fill, and the crops would grow abundantly. *Rejoice!* The sound of conches blasted over the land. *Rejoice!* The monsoon has arrived.

A troupe of young Indian males, hoping to earn a few rupees, cheerfully skipped the four miles from the town of Calicut out to the military station where they began to dance for the soldiers. The soldiers cheered them on as they leapt and gyrated down the streets of the huts, their supple brown bodies covered only in white loincloths. In a dancing line they moved to the beat of the clapping soldiers and the drumming of the rain, singing a song that sounded like a rhapsody of vowels.

'Ho! Hi! Hu! Ha!'

The arrival of the monsoon was a time for celebration, for the rains meant more to India than a banishment of the annual dread of drought and famine. It was a time when man sat back and looked at the glistening beauty of the earth. A time for both the land and man's refreshment after the leaden apathy of the heat. A time for nourishment of the spirit in the exhilarating cool winds that came with the rain. A time when all felt younger, healthier, stronger; reborn.

The monsoon was also the time for love, for steamy and smouldering passion, when all India believed that earth and rain joined in a kind of lovemaking, uniting and procreating, and during the monsoon season there truly was a soft and vibrant sensuousness in the Indian air.

For the first three weeks of the rainy season Lachlan and Jane found it impossible to venture outside the house at all. A solid wall of water crashed around the bungalow in a non-stop torrential downpour. But apart from this inconvenience, and the pounding of the rain, the days spent within their enforced seclusion was as blissful as Eden.

With all duties suspended, no fixed hours, no callers, they were free to select their pleasures according to their inclinations. To read books. To drink wine. To make an even deeper discovery of each other through long and relaxed conversations sitting on the window-seat looking out at the warm rain. To smile and tease each other. To make love in every desirable way that pleasure suggested, however the mood took them; the mood was the thing, the atmosphere perfect.

They slept late and were not awakened by the sun. The God of Rain ruled and made the days short and the nights long.

Then the rain began to ease. Sometimes it stopped for a few hours, or even an entire day when the air would steam in the heat of the sun. On days of light rainfall some of the officers came to call, spending the afternoons sitting on the veranda drinking wine and conversing while gazing at the wet garden.

Only the Brigadier seemed to find displeasure with the monsoon. 'Damn me but I hate all this rain,' he said glumly. 'The weather in this country is shocking. First the dry heat of the hot season, now the damp heat of the rainy season. It fills me full of gloom. What about you, Macquarie?'

Lachlan looked at the raindrops glistening like crystals on the green leaves of the trees and gave a sigh of perfect contentment. 'Well, sir, at times like this, we must console ourselves with what the Hindus say: "What does it matter if we are unhappy, as long as we are all unhappy together."'

The Brigadier thought about it, and then looked at Jane who immediately fixed an unhappy expression on her face. 'Yes, I think there may be something in that,' he said, his mood brightening.

He turned on his seat to look behind him at Lieutenant Lacey who was lolling in a hammock, covertly studying the love positions of the *Kama Sutra* inside the covers of a more sober book, *The Rules and Regulations for the Formation, Exercises, and Movements of His Majesty's Forces.* More commonly known by the officers as *"Stuff every Redcoat should know."*

'You feel miserable too, eh Lacey?' the Brigadier asked. 'With all this rain, what?'

Lieutenant Lacey was thinking about the beautiful young harlot he had met in the town of Calicut and who was now his exclusive and regular playmate, and whom he would be seeing later.

'I feel it won't be long before I find myself going completely out of my mind, sir,' Lacey replied, without lifting his eyes from the book.

The Brigadier cheered up immensely – there was nothing quite so uplifting as knowing others felt even more miserable than oneself. He reached for his wineglass and said cheerfully, 'Still, we mustn't grumble.'

'*This is physically impossible ...*' Lacey mouthed the words silently to Lachlan while holding up the Rule Book behind the Brigadier's back, showing him an illustration within the *Kama Sutra*.

'I'll not quarrel with that,' Lachlan said, smiling at the Brigadier. 'More wine, sir?'

*

By mid-August all were refreshed and ready for a long spell of sun again. And with the sun, came Colonel Petrie.

As soon as he had settled into his quarters, Petrie summoned all officers to his house and read out the order from the War Office and the Prime Minister – to prepare to take possession of the Dutch settlement of Cochin.

'The Dutch in Cochin are declaring themselves allies of the French and no longer subject to the Stadtholder.' Colonel Petrie's contempt was obvious. 'Governor Van Spall and his army may open the gates of the Cochin fortress and receive us as friends,' he continued. 'But if they don't, we are ordered to attempt negotiations in a friendly manner, and if the Dutch *still* refuse to be reasonable, we are to move in and reclaim Cochin in the name of the Prince of Orange.'

Colonel Petrie looked directly at Captain Macquarie, and as soon as he spoke Lachlan knew that Petrie had received his orders directly from General Balfour.

'The rest of the combatants will travel to Cochin by ship, but you, Captain Macquarie, will take the overland route with your company, and bring with you the regiment's nine-pounder cannon.'

'Yes, sir.'

Lachlan's face remained expressionless while inwardly wishing he could strangle General Balfour. For all other combatants it would be a two-day cruise by ship down the coast to Cochin. But for Captain Macquarie and his company – twelve days of marching over land and rivers in the dust and heat, hauling supplies and a ton weight of cannon.

Why did Balfour do it? Lachlan wondered. Why did the old bastard always single him out for preferential persecution?

Jane was devastated when she heard the news. They had never been parted since the day of their marriage and just the thought of Lachlan leaving her and going into the danger of battle was simply beyond her contemplation. And Cochin was over one hundred miles down the coast from Calicut.

She pleaded to be allowed to go with him, as a soldier's wife, willing to share all the hardships of a soldier's life in the tented field.

When she began to pack her things, Lachlan had to grab the clothes out of her hand and stop her. 'You must stop this!' he warned her. 'I am a soldier, not a fool! Only a fool would allow his wife to accompany him into a possible battle area.'

'But that's *unfair!*' she cried distractedly. 'Even the battle area will be swamped with female camp followers! Cochin will be full of them!'

'Yes, well, most of the female camp followers are prostitutes who go there at their own risk. The Army claims no responsibility for them. But you are my wife and my responsibility. And that, my dear Jane, is a very different matter.'

He refused to even consider it.

Two days later they prepared to say farewell. He stood looking ruefully into her mournful eyes, then bent and kissed her mournful mouth. 'I'll write a letter to you every day,' he promised. 'And every day I'll send a native letter-carrier speeding back to Calicut with it.'

She rested her face on his scarlet jacket. 'I love you.'

'I love you too.' Words were pointless. He kissed her once more, and then turned out of the house.

A small force had been left in control of the station. As Lachlan mounted his horse he spoke quietly to Bappoo. 'I can trust her to your protection, Bappoo?'

Bappoo nodded his head loyally. 'I protect her with my life, Huzoor.'

And so the soldiers moved out, past the station guards, towards the town of Calicut. From the veranda Jane watched them go, the men marching in columns and the officers mounted on chargers.

Then Jane turned her head and saw the small group of Indian girls standing together, all looking as lost and afraid as she felt.

She took a deep breath, squared her shoulders, and began the walk down to join them. As the only officer's wife on the station, it was her duty to cheer the other women and keep their spirits up.

EIGHT

In 1635 the Portuguese had built the coastal settlement and Fortress of Cochin, then lost it in battle to the British. Thirty years later the Dutch came along and drove the British out, and since then the Dutch had held Cochin for over a hundred years.

But now the British were back.

Upon arrival at Cochin, after a twelve-day march, Captain Macquarie's company received an order to pitch tents and make camp near the Mattancherri Gate of the Fortress, although every officer had been offered quarters in the houses of Mattancheri itself, inhabited principally by Jews.

Unlike the other inhabitants, the Jews of Cochin did not reside within the fortressed town, but about a mile distant outside the walls. Mattancherri was situated on the banks of the Cochin River, contained two synagogues, a cluster of lovely houses with beautiful gardens, and a Hindu Palace only a hundred yards distant from one of the synagogues. In Mattancheri the Jews and the Hindus had always lived in harmony.

Lachlan found he was to be billeted in the house of a Dutch Jew named Mr Francis Wredé, a wealthy man of property who was loyal to the Stadtholder.

'Oh, yes, Jews from Holland and many other parts of Europe are all intermingled here in our little Hebrew colony in Cochin,' said Mr Wredé as he showed Lachlan around his home, a large and beautiful house with an open pavilion at the back, overlooking a garden adorned with fountains and every kind of eastern flower.

Lachlan's pleasure in his new quarters was magnified by the discovery that two of his favourite friends were also lodged there, Dr Colin Anderson and Captain Edward Grant, both of whom had sailed directly from Bombay a few weeks earlier.

Captain Grant waited until they had sat down to dinner before he briefed Lachlan on the current state of affairs in Cochin.

'A siege is inevitable now,' Grant said in a resigned tone. 'When we first arrived a communication was sent to Governor Van Spall, informing him that the British had been ordered to take possession of all the Dutch settlements in India in order to prevent them being seized by the French, and that was why we were here – to take possession of Cochin in the name of the Prince of Orange.'

Grant reached across the table for the salt. 'So what did Van Spall do? And what has he done ever since? He vacillates and vacillates and appears to have no idea what to do. Proposals have been going back and forth for over a week and still Van Spall can't decide whether to surrender Cochin or fight it out. And we on our part can do nothing until the artillery ship arrives from Bombay. So Van Spall's dithering is proving a great help to us.'

'What's happened to the artillery ship?' Lachlan asked. 'Does anyone know?'

'It apparently ran into some difficulty near the coast of Goa, but now it's reported to be on its way.'

'How many men do the Dutch have?'

'Almost a thousand regulars, and even more irregulars.'

'That many?'

'Yes,' Grant smiled, 'but the poor darlings haven't fought a battle for over a hundred years, have they?'

Later Mr Wredé joined them and suggested they take their wine out to the veranda overlooking the garden at the back of the house. Francis Wredé proved to be a kind and gentle-mannered man who was devoting all his time and money to the translation of the history of the Malabar Jews into Low Dutch.

On the veranda, tea was served in small porcelain cups placed on silver saucers, while Mr Wredé conversed companionably with the three officers. Lachlan was very surprised to learn that Jews had lived in India since the fifth century.

'Oh yes, the first Cochin Jews originally came from Babylon.' Mr Wredé was delighted at Lachlan's interest. 'Captives of Nebuchadnezzar,' he continued, 'held as slaves until some miraculously escaped and fled here to Hindustan. Other Jews, of course, fled to Europe. We are a people scattered all over the face of the earth. But wherever you may find us – ' Wredé spread his hands and smiled, `we are all the sons of Abraham.'

It was pleasant, sitting in the cool evening air, listening to the gentle voice of their host telling them the history of his scattered people, their cruel bondage in Egypt, their days in the wilderness, and the reign of King Solomon.

Soothed into a warm relaxation, his eyes on the rippling fountain in the centre of the musky garden, Lachlan heard of the wealth and power and greatness of Solomon. 'A king who surpassed all other kings on the earth, until, alas, Solomon forgot the lessons of his youth and in his old age built altars, not to the God of Israel, but to the strange Gods of his wives.'

The mention of wives jolted Lachlan out of his lassitude. Very politely he interrupted his host and asked if a *halcarra* could be procured to carry a letter for him that night.

'Of course,' Mr Wredé agreed graciously.

And while Lachlan went to his room and dashed off a hasty letter to Jane, and while Mr Wredé went to procure a letter-carrier, Dr Anderson and Captain Grant remained seated in the cool evening air debating their own views on King Solomon, the author of the 'Song of Songs.'

'He liked his women, Solomon, that's for sure,' Anderson murmured.

Captain Grant sat thoughtful. 'The only bits of Solomon's Song that I remember are the bits the Theology Master always left out ... *'Your breasts are like clusters of the vine, and your kisses like the best wine that goes down smoothly, gliding over lips and teeth...'*

Grant lifted his glass and sipped, gazing thoughtfully at the evening sky. 'Breasts like clusters of the vine, eh? I suppose he must have been referring to her dusky nipples, saying they were like purple grapes, what?'

He looked at Anderson for his opinion, but Anderson was laughing. He liked Captain Grant, an exceptionally handsome young man, and one of the many English officers attached to the 77th.

Captain Grant continued gazing at the sky, now streaked with the gold of a setting sun. 'Everything about the East is sensual,' he murmured. 'No wonder Englishmen are never quite the same when they return home.'

He turned his head and grinned slyly at Anderson. 'I wonder what Macquarie will think when he gets a look at those erotic Hindu frescos all over the walls in the Mattancheri Palace, eh? A Scot from puritan stock as he is, as *you* are. Shall I tell him how you almost collapsed when you saw the paintings?'

143

'Swooned, is the better word.' Anderson laughed. 'And I shouldn't worry about Macquarie. He has his own little love-nest and seems very happy in it.'

'What?' Grant regarded him with disbelief. 'Don't tell me the man is still in love with his wife?'

`My dear Edward, surprising as it may seem to you, the Macquaries positively dote on each other.'

'Dote? Really? Even him?'

'He's besotted.'

'Poor man ... and married now how long? Two years? Three years?'

'More or less.' Anderson smiled. 'She's very nice, you know. And loyal. She left Bombay and came down to live with him on the station at Calicut. And no other officer's wife did that.'

Captain Grant was silent for a few seconds. 'Lucky Macquarie, eh? I must confess I'm a bit jealous of the *doting*. It's such a long time since I had any. Not since Nanny wept all over me the day I was packed off to Eton.'

Anderson was laughing again. 'Edward, you were born a fool.'

'That was my father's opinion too, alas.' Grant stretched his legs and languidly gazed over the garden.

'No, I tell a lie,' he admitted. 'The very last female who doted over me was a young golden-haired beauty named Hannah. She and I spent one lovely summer hidden for most of the time in a field of buttercups in Berkshire. An unforgettable summer that was. We were very young, of course, but she doted over me wonderfully. Then I was sent up to College, and a few months later I discovered that her father had quickly married her off to a doctor in Cornwall, while I had been wasting my time writing long love-letters to her from Oxford.'

'Why did he do that?'

'God knows. I still often wonder. Out of the blue, completely out of the blue, her father sent me a packet containing all my letters unopened, and a curt note informing me that his daughter was now married, and expecting a child.'

He sighed wistfully. 'Sweet Hannah ... funny how it's the sweet ones we soldiers never seem able to forget. Even now, when I sleep with Eastern beauties, no matter what they say their names are, I always call them Hannah.'

Anderson looked at him with a shrewd curiosity. 'Sounds as if you might still be in love with her?'

Grant was silent for a long moment. 'There is that possibility, yes.'

*

At the front of the house, Lachlan was placing his letter to Jane into the hands of a *halcarra*, watching it being slipped inside a secret fold of the youth's shabby garment, then with a brief salaam he started off on his journey to Calicut.

'They are a strange people, the halcarras,' Mr Wredé murmured as they both stood watching the youth run off, 'very poor, but lightningly swift on their feet. I suppose that's why they are usually employed as flying messengers and letter-carriers.'

'I wonder how they manage to run so far so quickly?' Lachlan said. 'Most are so thin, and the only nourishment they seem to take with them on their long journey is a handful of rice and a small flask for water.'

Mr Wredé looked at him curiously. 'You don't know what

else the halcarra runner always takes to help him ease the boredom of his long journey?'

'No.'

'Opium.'

'Ah.' Lachlan was about to say that half of India seemed to be addicted to opium, then realised he would only be stating the obvious.

*

Three weeks later, Governor Van Spall finally made up his mind. On behalf of himself and his Council, he sent Colonel Petrie a very clear and decisive answer for the Prince of Orange and his relative on the English throne. He was positively determined not to admit a British garrison into the Fortress of Cochin, but on the contrary to defend Cochin to the last extremity.

War was, more or less, declared.

And Colonel Petrie found himself unable to do a thing about it, because the artillery ship containing the guns for the siege had still not arrived.

The British remained encamped around the walls of Cochin, but the Dutch democrats made no attack. In the end the British were convinced the Dutch had lost their nerve, and the Dutch in turn were convinced they had called the British bluff.

The British remained in position, while the Dutch stood on the walls of the fort and jeered at them – until the day the beleaguered artillery ship carrying the British guns finally arrived at Cochin.

Lachlan was sitting on the veranda with Mr Wredé, learning more about the history of the Tribe of Manasseh, when a tornado of fire ripped into the sky over Cochin and a deafening explosion crashed through the air.

'*Gevalt!*' Mr Wredé cried. 'What is that?'

'The new allies of Napoleon,' Lachlan replied. He could see the blossoming black smoke about half a mile distant.

Now aware of the arrival of the British guns, the Dutch had jumped to attack before the emplacements for the eighteen-pounder British guns could be completed. All British officers raced back to their positions. Colonel Petrie sent for Captain Macquarie whose nine-pounder cannon had long been emplaced in position near the Mattancheri Gate, only five hundred yards from the walls.

Lachlan learned that although he and his men were the last to arrive in Cochin, they were to be the first to go into action.

Colonel Petrie gave him his orders straight and brief. `Your orders, Captain Macquarie, are to return fire on the Fort with your nine-pounder. You must distract the attention of the enemy and divert his fire until the other emplacements are completed and our guns can be positioned to bombard the walls. In short – keep the bastards occupied and diverted from our main breaching battery. '

'I'll do my best, sir.'

Colonel Petrie raised a brow. 'A soldier's best, Captain, is the very *least* we expect of him.'

'We're to be the bloody suicide squad!' Macquarie's men reacted furiously when he told them what was required of them.

But a short time later, Colonel Petrie was pleased to see Macquarie's nine-pounder cannon slamming back on its wheels as it opened fire, sending a huge ball of roundshot pounding through the air to explode inside the walls of the Fortress of Cochin.

Under cover of clouding smoke, green-coated skirmishers from the Rifle Regiments had run swiftly forward and were now lying flat in the elephant grass in a skirmishing chain. Their job was to keep any enemy skirmishers away from the vulnerable cannon crew, but all knew that if an enemy ball hummed over their heads and managed to hit the gun itself, the gun would explode and the crew and its officer would be blown to pieces.

Behind them Macquarie's gun-team were frantically clearing the barrel ready for the next shot, ramming the bag of gunpowder in the breech, followed by the ball of roundshot.

'Ready, sir.'

Lachlan gave the elevating screw another twist, pointed the gun himself, then stepped back a pace and gave the order. 'Fire!'

The firer touched his smoking portfire to the quill, which flashed down flame to the gunpowder charge. All hurled themselves away from the gun's recoil as it banged out its contents, bucked on its wheels, and crashed back yards from where it had started. Again the ball exploded inside the walls of Cochin.

'Reload!'

The weight of the gun was rumbled forward, and again the spongeman dipped his wad of fleece into a bucket of water, ramming the wet wad down the barrel to clear it of any scraps of burning powder before reloading. Again Macquarie aimed the gun himself, as he did every time it fired.

The Dutch responded as hoped, turning every gun they

could towards the British post near the Mattancheri Gate, opening fire with a volley of poorly directed shots, throwing up heaps of earth and dust over British faces but not a man was wounded.

'Reload!'

It went on for hours into the night as the Dutch kept up a barrage of fire on the British entrenchment near the Mattancheri Gate, trying to knock out the gun; while under cover of the darkness the rest of the army completed their batteries around the other walls, ignoring the noise of shells in the air, although most gave an occasional murmur of gratitude to the officer of the nine-pounder and his team at the Mattancherri side who were keeping the enemy occupied and taking all the punishment.

By dawn a cloud of dust and smoke had settled over Mattancheri, and a wavering Mr Wredé made his way through the smoke and noise and finally found Captain Macquarie, his face and uniform muddied by earth and dust.

'Captain Macquarie,' Mr Wredé looked at the smoke and dust stains on the captain's face, and enquired solicitously, 'How are you and your men?'

'Fine sir, just fine.' Lachlan assured him. 'Every shot we've fired has gone inside their walls, but for all their bombardment not one of theirs has managed to hit us. Quite close on occasions, but no hits. And we hear our skirmishers are doing a fine job.'

'That is good, that is good, you are all well, thank God. But Captain ... ' Mr Wredé clasped his hands together in a beseeching way, 'you must stop.'

'Stop?' Lachlan peered at him in puzzlement. 'Stop what, Mr Wredé?'

149

'Stop provoking the rebels with your gunfire and making them fire back at you. The people...' Mr Wredé gestured a hand back towards the houses, 'are becoming very distressed.'

Lachlan half smiled. 'Mr Wredé, we cannot stop just because the people are disturbed by the noise. Now, please, I must ask you to go back home, sir.'

'But that is what I am trying to tell you, Captain Macquarie. If you do not stop provoking them, I will soon have no home to go back to. The rebels may have been very bad at hitting the target of you and your men, but they have been very good at hitting the houses of the Jews.'

'What?' Lachlan glanced back in the direction of the houses. 'Anyone killed?'

'No, no person killed, thank God. Many with small wounds. Cuts and bleedings. But the houses...' Wredé gestured with his hands to depict walls falling down.

Captain Grant came riding onto the scene. 'What's going on, Macquarie? Why has your cannon stopped? Are you in trouble?'

'No, not us, but the poor sons of Abraham are suffering a wholesale loss of their houses. Fortunately there have been no deaths, but we must consider their safety.'

Captain Grant dismounted and tied his horse to a tree. 'Well, our batteries are completed and we're ready for them now. Marvellous work done this night by the working parties, bloody marvellous!' Grant grinned at Lachlan. `I've been ordered to relieve you and give you a rest.'

Lachlan turned to Mr Wredé. 'You must leave this area immediately, sir. All I can do is contact Colonel Petrie and see what arrangements can be made for the protection of the Jews.'

'Thank you,' Mr Wredé said graciously. 'You are most kind.'

'Now go, quickly.'

Mr Wredé scurried off.

'You go also,' Grant urged, 'and leave the Dutch darlings to me.'

Lachlan threw him a vague salute and walked tiredly away, glad that his night shift was over. He had walked only a few yards when an explosion of noise blasted the air and a fountain of earth and dust swished around his ears. Fragments of dirt flew into his eyes making them stream with blinding tears.

He whipped out his linen handkerchief and stood for a second or two rubbing at his eyes, then looked back towards the gun and saw the figure of Captain Grant lying on the ground, the shoulder of his tunic discolouring with blood.

Two heartbeats later every British gun on the completed batteries opened fire, slamming their shells towards the Dutch walls in an eruption of smoke and flames that seemed to rock the earth.

Lachlan ran back to Grant who was staggering to his feet and looking around him, blinking in stunned puzzlement.

'Edward ... how bad are you hurt?'

'I was hit from behind!' Grant cried furiously, his right hand moving to his left shoulder where blood began seeping through his fingers. 'From behind, I say! A damned foul!'

Lachlan examined the injury and saw that Grant had not suffered a direct hit from the enemy, but had been struck from behind through the shoulder by a flying roof-slate from one of the houses of the Jews. The force of the blow had sent Grant sprawling, and part of the slate was still lodged in his blood-soaked shoulder.

Lachlan immediately called two of his men and arranged for Grant to be helped away to the surgeon's tent, then shouted more orders to the corporal in charge of the gun. Seconds later he had swung up onto Grant's horse, slashing back his heels and galloping out of the smoke towards Nynheen Point where Colonel Petrie was sitting on his horse between two mounted staff officers, watching proceedings through his spy-glass.

Petrie turned his head curiously as Captain Macquarie approached and slid his horse to a stop.

'Permission to order the Jews into the safety of the synagogues, sir?'

'Why?'

'They are suffering a major loss of their homes and their lives are in danger. The synagogues offer better protection, sir.'

'Very well.' Colonel Petrie nodded. 'But first, as you have come at a very opportune moment, and as you are mounted, I wonder if you would be so kind as to deliver some rather important instructions, verbally, to Major Wiseman?'

Lachlan rode back as fast as he could with instructions to Major Wiseman, who was very busy at his battery demolishing the northwest bastion of the Fort. He delivered the verbal instructions, then stayed for a short time to watch the British eighteen-pounders throwing out their fire, the gun teams working like slaves, their officers keeping up continuous commands of 'Fire! Back! Reload!'

Delaying no longer, he rode back to his own post where he ordered a detachment of men to take command of Mattancheri and escort all civilians into the synagogues. He then resumed command of the gun.

At sunset, accepting defeat, the enemy began beating out

the *chamade*. The White Flag of Surrender slowly rose and fluttered over the South-West Bastion of the Fort.

The British guns ceased.

The gates of the Fortress finally opened. The rebels marched out and piled their arms in surrender.

Capitulations were signed that night. The British officially took control of the Dutch settlement of Cochin, and all roads leading to it.

*

The following morning Lachlan and Colin Anderson took a stroll through the bazaar within the city walls where business had resumed as if no battle had taken place. The streets, although piled here and there with rubble, were clamorous and colourful with merchants calling out in high-pitched voices to the brightly clad Indian citizens of Cochin who jostled and haggled over prices. All paused to look at the two red-coated officers who walked idly amongst them – two of the new masters – two of the British.

'A shawl, I think,' Lachlan murmured, his eye caught by a blue shawl hanging on a merchant's stand, thinking it would make a nice present for Jane. He had just moved to lift down the shawl when he heard the crack of a whip.

He turned his head sharply, and heard people laughing. The whip cracked again, definitely a whip. More laughing.

'What's that?' Both men stood looking to where a crowd were gathered near the Mattancheri Gate.

'Some short of show, I think,' Anderson said, as the whip cracked to more laughter. 'Probably trained monkeys dressed up in scarlet uniforms and turning cartwheels to the sound of the whip – just like that other lot back there.'

Lachlan shrugged and turned back to the blue shawl. Within seconds the merchant had brought his attention to another shawl that hung at the back of the tent where no thieving hand could snatch at it. This particular shawl had come from Kashmir, the merchant said. It was woven in all the colours and shades of the sun, from red to amber to gold, in one of the most delicate fabrics of silky wool ever woven on a loom.

It was beautiful, and perfect for Jane.

'From Kashmir,' the merchant said. 'From the Paradise of Nations, where Akbar and all the imperial princes lived.' The litany went on for some minutes and ended with the price, 'Three hundred rupees.'

Lachlan stared at the merchant in astonishment, then glanced again at the shawl, thinking of Jane's chestnut hair which could also shine with the gold and amber lights of the sun ... and ten days ago she had spent her twenty-third birthday all alone in Calicut.

Without further hesitation he bought the article of luxury from Kashmir, the Paradise of Nations.

The merchant salaamed and smiled, his dark eyes dancing with delight. The *Angrezi* officer had paid five times more for the shawl than a Dutchman ever would.

The two soldiers strolled on towards the crowd gathered at the Mattancherri Gate where all the whipping was taking place, their faces sardonic as they prepared to see the show of red-coated monkeys doing their tricks at the hand of a Dutch trainer.

But it was no troop of monkeys the Dutch trainer was whipping – it was a small, naked, brown-skinned boy of seven or eight years of age. His hands were tied behind his back and he was struggling like a wild cat at the end of a thick rope tied around his waist. The whip flicking under his feet made him jump and howl in a parody of a dance.

The Dutchman was sitting on a box with his back against the wall. He was very fat and very drunk and laughed hysterically as he held the rope in one hand and the whip in the other – enjoying himself so much that he was caught by surprise when Lachlan's hand closed about the wrist holding the whip, twisting it savagely.

The Dutchman yelped in startled pain and let the whip fall onto the dust.

'*Vah!*' the Dutchman exclaimed; then a mixture of emotions compounded of rage, and contempt crossed his face as his inebriated gaze took in the red-coated uniform.

'Ah!' he said scornfully. 'It is von of the mighty British!' He tugged his wrist free and looked around at the crowd who were watching with renewed interest. He suddenly let out a drunken giggling laugh and shouted in amusement at the crowd. 'The British, they come, to make Cochin safe for the Stadtholder. So safe, the Stadtholder vill never see Cochin again! The British take – the British keep! Never give back!'

He threw back his head and laughed hysterically at the stupidity of the Prince of Orange, but Lachlan's eyes were on the struggling boy.

'You!' His fist thumped the shoulder of the laughing Dutchman. 'What the hell are you doing to this boy?'

'Him?' the Dutchman tugged hard on the rope and brought the boy stumbling towards him. 'He is mine.'

'Yours? What do you mean he is yours? Is he your servant? And you treat a servant like that? Put him on public show, naked, and whip him for public amusement.'

The Dutchman looked at the crowd with a humorous

155

expression, then smiled fatly and spread out a hand in a gesture of resignation. 'The people must see the quality of the goods before they buy.'

'Buy? The boy is for sale?'

Colin Anderson, who had been in Cochin longer and knew more of the trade of the settlement than Macquarie did, muttered towards Lachlan's ear. 'The man is a slave-trader, for God's sake!'

'He is beautiful, is he not,' the slave-trader said, grabbing the boy's jaw and jerking up his head. 'Beautiful black-eyed boy, but light-skinned, yes? Father's skin vas light.' He reeled off the boy's pedigree. 'Boy now nine years. Mother from Morocco, taken as slave and sold as concubine to royal son of maharaja in palace at Surat. Mother fifteen when boy born, prince seventeen. Good stock. Young seed. Both parents very beautiful.'

The Dutchman grinned slyly at the British officer. 'Englishmen like beautiful boys to play with. You vant to buy'

'You son of a scorpion!' Lachlan snatched up the whip and angrily flicked a lash at the wooden box under the Dutchman. 'How would you like it, mynheer, if I made *you* do a little dancing?'

'Lachlan – ' Anderson caught his arm warningly, but the wide-eyed boy had jerked his face free of the Dutchman's sweating hand and threw himself at Lachlan's feet.

'Sahib, I be good servant!'

A Mussulman of Arabic appearance standing on the inner edge of the crowd stepped forward and spoke angrily to the slave-trader while throwing hostile glances at the British officer.

The slave-trader turned his inebriated gaze to the

Redcoat, glanced at the lowered whip, and then smiled fatly. 'The Mussulman vants to buy,' he said. `First he come and say he pay thirty rupees, then thirty-five, then forty. Now he say he pay forty-five rupees for beautiful boy.'

'*Sahib!*' the boy cried, clawing at Lachlan's boots while glancing in terror at the Mussulman. '*Sahib! I be good servant!*'

'You can have the boy, British,' the slave-trader said to Lachlan, 'for eighty-five rupees.'

'Boy no good for the noble Sahib,' the Mussulman said quickly. 'Sahib want good Hindu or good Mussulman for servant, but this boy – ' he made a contemptuous gesture, `this boy is *kutch-nay!* He is nothing! His mother was slave in palace at Surat then thrown away, no good. She then slave to Dutch Sahib in Cochin for few years, but die. Mother weak, lazy, no good servant, no good, like boy.'

'Then why do *you* want to buy him?' Lachlan demanded. He glanced down at the boy who was staring up at him with terrified, desperate eyes, an innocent child being brutalised and bartered like a whipped pup.

'Eighty-five rupees,' the Dutchman said. 'Who pays? Who buys?' He looked from the Mussulman to the Redcoat.

'Fifty-five rupees,' the Mussulman said. 'No more. Boy worth ten. I pay fifty-five.'

'*Saahib!*' the boy wailed. '*Saaahib!*'

'Sixty rupees,' the Mussulman added quickly, 'Sixty rupees I pay.'

'Now he say he pay sixty!' The slave-trader smiled at the Redcoat. 'You can afford to pay more? Eighty-five rupees?'

Of a sudden Lachlan nodded, his decision made. Colin Anderson hastily caught his arm. 'Lachlan, are you mad? Surely you're not going to buy the boy?'

'From this bloated pig's bladder? No I'm not going to *buy* the boy.' He snapped out his pistol and jammed the barrel into the Dutchman's head, flicking back the hammer. 'I'm going to *take* him. Right now. Hand over the rope, or I'll blow your drink-sodden brains out!'

The slave-trader was too shocked to answer, his head pressed back against the wall, his eyes quivering with fright as his quivering hand loosened its grip on the rope. Lachlan snatched it and began to back away, taking the boy with him. He watched the crowd of staring eyes and knew none of them would dare to challenge him. Taking a man's property without payment was against the law, but all knew that the British ruled Cochin now, and the British were the law.

*

That same afternoon Lachlan was back at work, and then found himself on duty for five long days consecutively, in command of a detachment of the 77th on duty inside the Fort.

Almost collapsing from want of rest, he was finally relieved from his five day command, but only in order to discharge his duty as a Paymaster of the Regiment, and give the soldiers their pay.

'Put an extra few rupees in, Captain!' a bright young spark shouted as Lachlan sat at a fold-table under a tree and began paying the lines of soldiers.

Lachlan smiled a polite response, but the foolish young soldier, standing halfway down the line, made the mistake of becoming more familiar and bold. 'I mean, Captain,' he said with a laugh, 'all you officers will be getting a nice rich reward for taking Cochin, won't you?'

'Take that soldier's name, Sergeant,' Macquarie said, without looking up.

'But, Captain!' the soldier argued, 'I was only saying – '

'Don't you *dare* argue with me. Take his name again, Sergeant.'

'Oh bugger me for speaking!' the soldier muttered.

Lachlan put down his pen and looked directly at Sergeant McGinnis. 'How many times is that now, Sergeant?'

'Three times, sir. He's answered ye back three times.'

'Then this afternoon, Sergeant, let him take three hours of double-drill or whatever other punishment you think fitting.'

The soldier almost collapsed; involuntarily his mouth opened again but was stopped by the soldier behind him who hissed impatiently. 'Shut up Berwick, or I'll stuff a mango in your gob! Some of us are waiting to be paid.'

Sergeant McGinnis looked severely at Berwick who had come out to India with a new detachment of soldiers, and had been sent down to Calicut only a few months previously. Berwick was a likable lad, but very cheeky, and reputed to be hopelessly in love with the captain's wife of all people, Mrs Jane Macquarie.

The Sergeant muttered in an undertone, 'Ye, my laddie, are even more stupid than I gave ye credit for.'

'What's to be my punishment, Sarge?' Berwick quavered, almost in tears. 'Not double-drill, Sarge, please! I'll do anything, but not three hours double-drill!'

Sergeant McGinnis regarded him with a look of lofty rectitude. 'And why not?' he demanded. 'If I say ye'll spend three hours running round the parade-ground under full pack, then ye will!'

'But Sarge – '

'No whining, Berwick, no whining if ye please. We don't like whining lads in this regiment. And I hope them's not tears I see in your eyes! If they are tears, then ye know the punishment – a collection to buy ye a baby's rattle!'

Berwick's eyes blinked rapidly as he jerked up his chin.

Sergeant McGinnis clasped his hands behind his back, did a slow strut up to the top of the line, about-turned, and strutted back down again. He paused, and stood looking sideways at Berwick, eyes narrowed thoughtfully.

'Not three hours drill,' he said finally, in a more gentle tone. `Not for ye, Berwick. It's been a good campaign and so I'm going to be kind to ye.'

'Thanks, Sarge.'

'So, this afternoon, Berwick, I want ye to spend your time writing three letters to your friends back home on the subject of – "Why I joined the Army."'

The soldier behind Berwick spluttered.

'And when ye have written them,' the Sergeant continued, 'I want ye to write a last letter, addressed to the Commander-in-Chief, on the subject of – "How I learned not to be cheeky and argue with an officer who has just done a five-day spell of duty and is badly fatigued and in need of a rest, but can't have one because he has to spend a further day paying out wages to the men which includes cheeky young buggers and good soldiers alike!"'

Berwick was staring, while the soldiers in front and behind him were endeavouring to control their shaking bodies.

'I couldn't write all that, Sarge!'

'And why not?'

'I never learned writing.'

Captain Macquarie glanced up as a number of soldiers down the line erupted into laughter, and Sergeant McGinnis looked up at the sky as if wishing he was dead.

*

At last it came, the time to leave. Captain Macquarie paid off the casual servants and coolies who had joined his company on the march overland from Calicut, and gave them all an extra few rupees to carry them home to Tanore or Paniani or wherever they had been hired along the way to Cochin. Their service with the British Army was no longer needed. A regular garrison was now installed at Cochin under the command of Colonel Petrie, and everyone else was leaving the tented field and going home to base at Calicut or Bombay.

In order to prevent the fortune-tellers, the conjurers, the cooks and horse-keepers, the boot-shiners and silversmiths, and all the other trades that made up the camp-followers, and especially the prostitutes, from swarming after the soldiers and their pay, a ship had arrived to take the 77th back to Calicut by sea, and was due to leave in three days time.

Lachlan couldn't wait that long.

He went to the extravagance of hiring a pattamar boat and two nights later he was back at Calicut, arriving there in bright tropical moonlight.

He had left his horse at Cochin to be transported on the troop-ship. Arriving at Calicut he hired a horse and was soon speeding a further four miles up the coast to the British station and Jane.

In the quietness of the military settlement, the sound of

his horse had been heard from a half a mile away. He briefly acknowledged the sentries with a touch of his hat as he rode past them, slowing his speed as his horse picked its way up the narrow path towards the officers' bungalows.

Turning his head sideways, he murmured over his shoulder, 'Almost home.'

'Yes, Sahib,' whispered the boy sitting behind him.

As he neared the house he heard footsteps running along the veranda ... and there she was, his beloved girl. He smiled and swung down to her.

*

Bappo, Marianne, and the other household servants seemed almost as excited as Jane to see Lachlan again. None seemed to notice the small boy sitting motionlessly in the darkness above the horse, until Lachlan turned back and lifted him down.

The boy was now dressed decently and wore a small dark blue turban on his head. 'This is George,' Lachlan said, leading him into the light on the veranda. 'A new addition to our household.'

Jane stared at the boy. Her hands rested on his shoulders as she looked into his face. 'Oh, he's beautiful!' she exclaimed.

The boy smiled back at her happily.

'And so *sweet!*' Jane added.

Lachlan nodded. 'I had a suspicion that's what you would say.'

'But why – '

'Not now, he said. 'Let's get this wee laddie some food and off to bed and then I'll tell you everything.'

As soon as George had been taken off to the servants' quarters, the questions poured out of her. Had he eaten? What? Good gracious! He had not eaten since that morning!

Lachlan insisted that he was not hungry, but she would have none of it. He *must* eat! And immediately!

Bappoo agreed with her, clapping his hands for the two household servants to see to the Captain-Sahib's food.

While he ate, Jane sat at his left hand and continued to ply him with eager questions, which he attempted to answer between mouthfuls of food.

He told her about the conquest of Cochin, which had been won with only two deaths on the British side.

He told her about the slave-trader and the Mussulman, and how the boy seemed to have no proper name as his mother had always called him her 'Prince' because his ancestors were kings. And that had given Edward Grant the idea of calling the boy George, after King George, which the boy had liked very much – although he had to be persuaded that he could *not* be called 'King George' but simply George.

He told her about the Jews of Mattancheri and Mr. Wrede. The only thing he did not tell her about was the night he had been invited by Colonel Petrie to join his staff on an official visit to the Hindu Palace of Mattancheri.

The Hindus didn't seem to care which set of Europeans ruled them, so long as their customs and religious practices were not interfered with. Although they accepted the British with more resignation than they did the Dutch, because it had been predicted by the Brahmins that the British would rule India for not less than one hundred years before the sword could be raised against all *feringhis* in a war for Hind to rule herself.

He didn't tell her that on arrival at the Hindu Palace of

Mattancheri, the British officers were all graciously welcomed and, once luxuriously seated in a chamber of silk cushions, dishes of opium had been handed round to them in the same easy manner that snuff or tobacco is offered in England; although she would not have been too surprised at that.

He didn't tell her because of her questioning and curious mind, and if he had once in conversation led her through the doors of the Hindu palace, erotic frescos painted on every wall and ceiling, she would want to know everything – absolutely *everything* – in true Jane style.

And how could he tell her about the black-eyed, bare-breasted, dancing girls who had later been brought into the all-male chamber for their entertainment. Young beauties of considerable personal charms who had danced before them, bells jingling on their ankles and wrists, expressing with every movement of their hands and hips all the delights of passion and pleasure that all lovers know and which needed no translation or language.

He suddenly laid down his fork, took a drink of his wine, then rose and pushed back his chair.

Jane frowned at his unfinished plate. 'Where are you going?' she asked.

'Bed,' he said with a brief smile. 'And so are you.'

NINE

Jane's maternal instinct, which was growing stronger every day, was now being poured over George, the little Cochin boy whom she had taken to with a strange sense of possession, mothering him in the same loving way that Mammy Dinah had mothered her.

George's initial attachment to Lachlan had now transferred completely to Jane whom he had fallen head over heels in love with, literally; for his favourite trick was doing spinning cartwheels from one end of the garden to the other when his happiness overcame him.

And George's greatest happiness came when Jane decided he must possess more than one name, and gave to him her own maiden name of Jarvis, even going so far as to write to her lawyers instructing a legal deed to that effect.

From that day on, George, a proud boy, insisted that he was always called by his two names of George Jarvis, and not just George.

Bappoo was appalled at the behaviour of his mistress. He thought it disgraceful that this boy – this *slave* boy – should be treated almost like the son of a sahib and not like a servant, which is what he was, a rascally servant.

'Yes, by God, by Jove, my dear!' Bappoo admonished George severely. 'You unworthy of name George *Jarvees*. You only rascally servant! You son of slave!'

`My father was a prince and my ancestors were kings!' George answered proudly, then ran behind Bappoo and cheekily tugged hard on his baggy pantaloons.

A moment later Lachlan stepped into the garden to be

met with the astonishing sight of Bappoo's enormous bare brown backside as he bent to pull up his pantaloons – gasping out a hail of Hindi curses against the slave boy and every member of his ancestry.

Lachlan listened with a straight face to Bappoo's angry complaints about the boy, but only until he was forced to excuse himself and stride back into the house, ostensibly to find George, but really to find a safe haven where he could throw himself onto the cushioned sofa beside Jane and laugh and laugh until she thought his hysterical laughing must be the result of an oncoming bout of heat-fever.

'You spoil that boy, he told her in the end, wiping the tears from his eyes. 'Soon he will think he is the *Burra-Sahib* and will be telling us all what to do.'

'He deserves a little spoiling.' Jane moved closer to him on the sofa and slipped an arm across his waist. 'I want a child of my own, Lachlan,' she said quietly. `A child that is half you and half me.'

He looked at her wryly. 'I should hope so.'

'*Our* child,' she whispered. 'That's all I want, Lachlan, nothing more. I don't even ask for two or three. I would be ecstatic with even one.'

She gazed at him seriously. 'Why has it not happened yet? Why am I still not pregnant? Do you think there could be something wrong with me?'

He could only look back at her and wonder. He had tried not to notice the months and years passing without a sign of Jane becoming pregnant, but he had told himself it did not matter. He would prefer her without a child to another woman who might give him a brood. He had not married her for the purpose of breeding children, just as he had not married her for her money. And now it seemed that what he had not sought, he was not to gain.

'What if we never have a child,' she said anxiously. 'Some couples never do.'

He sat thoughtful, not knowing how to answer her. She seemed to be waiting for him to speak, and when he did not, she confessed that for a long time now she had been secretly pining for a child, secretly *longing* to add to their marriage with the start of a family.

'Why secretly?' he asked.

'Because I think...' she said in a breaking voice, 'after all this time there *must* be something wrong with me, and we will *never* have a baby of our own.' Slow silent tears began to roll down her cheeks.

He pulled her against his chest and held her tightly. She held him as desperately. It was a mystery that united them, a shared bewilderment.

'*Kooie-hai!*'

They broke apart and stared at the small figure of George Jarvis standing in the doorway with hands joined in a humble salaam as he apologised most profusely for his bad behaviour to the noble and honourable Bappoo – who was standing smugly behind him with arms folded like a Moor king.

'*Bugger off!*' Lachlan snapped.

The two turned and fled like terrified children.

TEN

Throughout his young life George had always believed that the world began in Surat, and ended in Cochin; and when the Captain-Sahib had taken him on another boat journey, lasting two days and two nights, to this place called Calicut, he believed he had reached the very edge of the world.

And he liked it here. He was so happy here. But now Mem-Jane was saying he must go on a boat again to some place even farther away, and he would have to stay on the boat for *five* days.

'No, no, I not go,' George wailed. 'The boat fall off edge of world and I die!' His agitation was so great that Jane had to hug him tightly for a long time, assuring him that the boat would not fall off any edge and he would be very safe, before his body finally stopped trembling and his tears ceased.

She drew back and looked into his beautiful black eyes. 'Have you never heard of Bombay?'

George shook his head.

'Well, Bombay is where the British Sahibs have their headquarters. Would they do that if it was not a safe place? Would I be going on the same boat if it was not safe? Would the Captain-Sahib?'

Jane smiled at the sudden change of expression on George's face as he asked, 'The Captain-Sahib go on boat too?'

'Yes, George, we are all going, Bappoo and Marianne too. But it is for just a short time, no more than a few weeks, and then we will return here to Calicut.'

George's faith in his safety on the boat was restored, but

still his heart feared something else. 'The Captain-Sahib –
he no sell me there?'

A great gush of sadness swept through Jane, and for
moment she could not speak. Her eyes remained fixed on
him very seriously as she said slowly, 'No, George, we will
never sell you to anyone, in any place. You are one of our
household now, one of my children. That is why I gave you
my own name of Jarvis. And I give you my promise that I
will never allow anyone to harm you, or take you away from
me. Do you understand that?'

George looked back at her with eyes like burning lights.
He did understand, and her promise to him sounded like a
promise from Heaven itself.

'I promise you,' she repeated.

George was so overcome with joy he fell to the ground
and began covering her shoes in small kisses of gratitude.
She smiled and was about to reach down and pull him to his
feet when the sudden scud of footsteps in the hallway made
them both turn to look towards the open doorway as
Bappoo appeared, breathless and furious.

'You rascally son of slave! Where you hide my new
turban?'

George let out a yelp of laughter and sped across the
room and past Bappoo like a flash of lightening.

'*Now I kill you!*' Bappoo yelled, and bundled after him.

Next morning, as they boarded the ship in time to catch
the early tide, Jane noticed that Bappoo's head was adorned
in a bright red turban, instead of the usual white one. He
looked as proud as a peacock. She smiled at him. 'You found
it then, Bappoo, your new turban?'

Bappoo heaved a despairing sigh and waved his hand
vaguely in the direction of George Jarvis. 'Slave boy very

wicked, Mem-Jane, slave boy naughty naughty. I tell him you sell him to nabob in Bombay and get the Captain-Sahib's rupees back!'

'The Captain-Sahib *not* pay!' George said indignantly. 'He *take* me – with gun!' He raised his hand and pointed an invisible gun at Bappoo. 'Like this!'

'*Chut!*' Bappoo almost exploded with laughter. 'Son of Prince, name of English king, now no pay when sold!' Still laughing, Bappoo turned to his mistress. 'Slave boy crazy, Mem-Jane, he tell lies every day. Captain-Sahib must sell him in Bombay to a nabob with a big stick.'

Jane was about to protest and severely admonish Bappoo, but her attention was distracted as Lachlan arrived, the last to step on board. As soon as he appeared George ran over to him and tugged at his coat. 'Why we go Bombay?'

'Business,' Lachlan answered, 'just military business, George.' He had received orders to return to Bombay for a meeting at headquarters, but he didn't know the reason for the meeting. 'Oh, and Christmas,' he added, smiling at Jane. 'As we will be there over Christmas, we might as well enjoy it.'

*

British Bombay was just as they had left it, teeming with life and people and parties every night. As soon as they arrived they were welcomed to stay at the home of Major and Mrs Oakes. The first week whirled by as Bombay society came out to welcome them back. Every afternoon British matrons came with their daughters to drink tea with Jane and hear all the news about Calicut and Cochin.

'No negotiations about it this time, dear boy,' Major

Oakes was saying to Lachlan. 'This time we're going straight in.'

Lachlan was not listening. He was watching Jane sitting amongst the women with a baby cuddled in her arms, hugging and petting it, and then holding it in the crook of her arm and tinkling a rattle over its face.

The scene saddened him, reminding him of Jane's genuine love of children, and her desperate longing for a child.

'Oh yes!' Major Oakes nodded emphatically. 'The French won't know a ruddy thing about it until it's too late. They may now have possession of Mauritius, but they won't get Ceylon.'

'No,' Lachlan agreed absently.

'Still, the outcome of these things is never absolutely certain.' Oakes downed a gulp of his wine. 'So we may as well make a good bash of Christmas before we go.'

Christmas was a round of suppers and parties at various houses. John Forbes was very pleased with Lachlan. Not only had he paid off all his debts, but also his share of the prize money for reclaiming Cochin on behalf of the Stadtholder had left him with a sizable sum of money in Forbes's bank.

'Aye, but there's still one debt I haven't yet paid,' Lachlan told him, and then arranged for John to draw up a bank draft and send it to his Uncle Murdoch in Scotland, in repayment of his education fees.

'That should finally shut him up,' Lachlan grinned. 'Now he'll have to find something else to blether about.'

*

171

Three days after Christmas, Jane confessed she was not feeling so good. A feeling of tiredness consumed her. She had lost her appetite, found it hard to sleep, and even her high spirits became very low. Lachlan had never seen her looking so woebegone.

The doctor could find nothing wrong with her, but suggested that she be encouraged to drink plenty of warm buffalo milk to put energy back into her bones.

'It's Bombay,' Jane said wearily to Lachlan. 'I need to get out of the noise of Bombay. Can we soon go back to Calicut?'

Well, no, they could not, and then Lachlan very nervously told Jane the news he had learned upon his arrival in Bombay, but which he had put off telling her until after Christmas. 'On the third of January, I will have to leave you again ... for service in Ceylon.'

'Ceylon?' Jane was devastated. Ceylon was a Dutch island beyond the southern tip of India. 'Why must you go to Ceylon?'

'Because the Dutch Governor of Ceylon has become as rebellious as Van Spall of Cochin, and as friendly with the French. The British cannot allow the French to gain a foothold in Ceylon.'

'How long will you be gone?'

'Hopefully, just a few months,'

'A few *months* – again?'

She wept and begged him not to go. 'You don't have to go,' she insisted. 'You have your duty as Major of Brigade to use as an excuse not to go! You could use that as a reasonable excuse, couldn't you?'

'No!' He looked at her as if shocked that she could even suggest such a thing. She had been a soldier's wife long enough to know better.

'My duty as Major of Brigade may satisfy *you* as a reasonable excuse for trying to get out of going, but it would not satisfy the malicious world. You would have them say I used a glorified administration job as an excuse to escape going into battle? They would say I was a coward, bewitched by my wife.'

'I don't care what they say, I only know I cannot survive your absence a second time.'

He turned away from her, hopelessly trapped between love and duty and honour. And the last, once lost, could never be regained. Honour was the code of the gentleman. Honour was what made a soldier march bravely into battle even though he was inwardly shaking with fear. Honour was essential to a man, and even moreso to a man who was also a soldier.'

'It's a matter of honour,' he said finally. 'I must go.'

'Then let me go with you,' she pleaded. 'You know I'm no wilting flower. You know I could share all the hardships of a soldier's life during a campaign. You *know* I could!'

He turned to look at her, and saw how drawn and pale she looked.

No, she could not.

In the days that followed nothing could console her. The nearer the time came to his departure, the more often she lay down on her bed morosely and refused to eat. On the night before he left, he stayed awake with her until the dawn came.

It was time to leave, and suddenly Jane's arms were tight about his neck, but he talked to her, softly and reassuringly, and she relented.

He got out of bed and began to hurriedly pull on his clothes. She listened to the sound of buttons clicking and leather creaking.

'I should come and see you off,' she said.

'No, get some sleep.'

He bent and kissed her, then said seriously: 'Now listen, I am leaving you in the good care of Mrs Oakes, with friends all around you, and I have bought you a very good milk cow from Surat for your own personal supply. So by the time I come back I shall expect to find you in good health and high spirits again.'

He turned down the wick on the bedside lamp, leaving her in a grey darkness more conducive for sleep.

'And Lachlan. . .' she said.

'Yes,' he was at the door.

'Do you still love me?'

'Yes,' he answered simply, and went out the door.

*

Colombo, the main port of Ceylon, fell to the British in a campaign that lasted less than two days. But the cost to the British had been the deaths of one ensign and eighteen men.

Jane received a letter from Lachlan informing her of the surrender, frowning prodigiously as she read on:

> *Now that Colombo has fallen, I have been entrusted by Colonel Petrie to command a detachment that is to take possession of the fortress of Point de Galle, ninety miles south of Colombo ...*

Jane suddenly felt sick, but she had been feeling so very sick of late, unable to do much more than lie on her bed and sleep or read. The words of the letter blurred before her eyes, the nausea was rising in her again, the blood draining out of her face.

She called out, 'Marianne!'

Marianne arrived, as dainty as a flower, her hands joined in a salaam.

'Marianne, tell Mrs Oakes I need her. Tell her I need a doctor.'

'Oh, oh, you art sick? You art sick!' Instead of running for help Marianne threw herself at Jane in a clinging embrace and began to cry.

George Jarvis, who had heard Jane's call of distress to Marianne, came running into the room, all eyes and fear. Marianne sobbed to him, 'Mem-Jane is sick!'

'Are you, Jane?' Mrs Oakes had entered the room, crossing quickly to place a hand on Jane's forehead. 'You do feel quite hot. Is it the nausea again?'

The nauseous sensation was passing. Jane drew in a deep breath and slowly exhaled, a pale smile on her face as she looked at Mrs Oakes. 'I'm fine now, not sick, well I am a bit sick, but only because I'm pregnant.'

'Pregnant? Really? Are you sure?'

Jane nodded. 'I suspected it when the doctor suggested lots of warm buffalo milk. I think he suspected it too, but he wasn't sure, but now *I* am certain!'

Mrs Oakes smiled at the expression on Jane's face. 'Oh, Jane dear, I'm so happy for you.'

*

Lachlan had been at Point de Galle for less than a month when he received a letter from the Commander-in-Chief,

General Balfour, informing him of his promotion to major. He was given no time to relish his promotion because in the same post he also received a letter from Dr Kerr in Bombay, stating that he felt Captain Macquarie should be informed that Mrs Macquarie had been in a very delicate state of health for some weeks and, if possible, his return might be beneficial to her.

Lachlan knew that Dr Kerr would not make such a request unless the situation justified it.

He requested immediate leave from duty. As soon as he received it, he covered the ninety miles ride to Colombo inside forty-eight hours. His Indian *syce* had ridden on ahead to find out if any ships bound for Bombay were in port.

He was about two miles from the town of Colombo, on a lonely road, when his *syce* came riding back towards him holding out another letter. Lachlan snatched it, was about to shove it inside his tunic pocket, when he recognised Jane's handwriting.

He dismounted, and sat on a small stone boulder near a tree at the side of the road, opened the letter and began to read, and as he did all his anxiety faded away as she told him that despite the doctor's worries, her health was much improved now.

'*And also,*' she wrote, '*not only is my health improved, but I also have every reason to believe that I will soon be making you a happy, happy father.*'

Lachlan was so surprised, and so delighted, he jumped to his feet and gave a soldiers whoop of joyful victory.

The *syce* was standing and staring at him in fright. 'He is mad,' he muttered nervously to the horses. 'The Captain-Sahib is struck with the madness!'

In the East, madness is both respected and feared, for one so afflicted is believed to have been struck by God and therefore under divine protection. But too close contact and others could also be afflicted by the same madness.

Moving behind his horse's rump, the *syce* peeped nervously round a haunch and watched the Captain-Sahib move towards his horse, then spin round and sit down on the boulder again, reading the letter again, kissing the pages and laughing, as if the contents were beyond his belief.

'It is *dewanee* – the madness,' the *syce* whispered. 'Allah has struck the *Angrezi!*'

Finally Lachlan rose and pushed the letter inside his tunic, a faint, abstracted smile on his face as he looked round for his *syce*, then spied him hiding behind the horse.

'Why are you hiding back there?'

The *syce* slowly came out and bowed towards Lachlan with hands joined in a terrified salaam. 'Praise Allah!' he wailed, eyes rolling in his head like a frightened mule. 'The Captain-Sahib hast been charmed by Allah into madness and laughter.'

'Allah and a woman,' Lachlan grinned as he mounted his horse, and then rode at speed towards Colombo, with his *syce* following at a safe distance behind him.

*

In the officers' mess at Colombo he was toasted with congratulations all round as he announced his good news. Colin Anderson clapped him on the back. 'Becoming a major and a father, eh? I'm very happy for you.'

Lachlan grinned. 'I'm very happy for me too.'

The following morning he boarded a British ship bound

for Bombay. On May 6th she anchored in Bombay Harbour, after being delayed by more than a week due to the violent winds that had struck the Malabar Coast. This time Lachlan had been away from Jane for four months.

No delay, no delay. Lachlan would not pause to converse with anyone as he mounted a fresh horse and rode at speed out to the country beyond the town of Bombay where he found Mrs Oakes taking tea on the veranda of her house, in the company of Dr Kerr.

Both seemed to stagger to their feet in a very untidy way when he approached and dismounted. Mrs Oakes laid down the cake-dainty she had been holding and put a hand to her heart.

'Oh dear!' Mrs Oakes murmured as the returning husband took a jump up onto the veranda and kissed her hand in greeting, smiling at her like a happy adventurer who has at last found his treasure. 'Oh dear!'

'My dear sir,' Dr Kerr said, but Lachlan would have none of it. 'Not yet, Dr Kerr. We can discuss buffalo milk and the necessity for plenty of rest and all that later. But now, if you will excuse me, I urgently need to see my wife.'

'Captain Macquarie – '

'Oh, it's now Major Macquarie,' Lachlan said with a grin.

'*Major* Macquarie,' Dr Kerr said firmly, 'I really must insist that I be allowed to speak to you before you speak to your wife.'

Lachlan looked at Dr Kerr, then at Mrs Oakes, at the two faces, one to the other, and slowly realised that something was wrong. Something was wrong with Jane.

'She fancies she is pregnant,' Dr Kerr said in a soft ¬mpassionate voice as the two men walked slowly down ¬afy avenue leading away from the house. 'But she is not, I can assure you most sorrowfully of that. The child she is convinced she is carrying, is nothing more than a delusion of her own wishful thinking.'

Lachlan remained silent.

'The sadness,' Dr Kerr continued softly, 'is that she is positive in her heart and mind that she *is* pregnant, and when you go in to see her, you will not find a happier mother-to-be in the whole world.'

Mynah, mynah, mynah . . . Lachlan glanced up at the irritating myna bird and exhaled a long breath, feeling a curious sensation in his chest, half pain, half numbness, as if someone had slyly slipped a knife under his ribs and rent a thin crack down his heart.

'Poor Jane,' he said softly.

He looked around him. The sun shone, the flowers bloomed, and the mingling odours of India haunted the air. Above him the green branches of a banyan tree interlocked to form a canopy in which birds frolicked and a tawny monkey busily flew from branch to branch with a baby on her back. It seemed as if Nature, in all her lustiness, was happily mocking him, mocking them both.

'Just one little baby, that's all she wants,' he said. 'And why is that too much to ask?'

'Life can be very unfair,' Dr Kerr murmured.

'But to be reduced to this pathetic state,' Lachlan continued, 'imagining bouts of sickness and having fainting spells. She fainted every day in the week before I left Bombay. Did you know that? Yes, every day. I even began to wonder myself if she might be pregnant, but I dared not allow myself to ask. Now it seems it was all a product of her imagination.'

'Oh no, you are quite wrong,' Dr Kerr said. 'Her sickne

is very real, so are the weak spells. I did not say this to you in my letter asking you to return from Ceylon, but I must say it to you now.'

It was eerily silent.

Lachlan looked around him. Something in his head had stopped. Every sound in the whole world seemed to have stopped . . . he glanced up at the silent mynah bird as if wondering if he was having one of those dreams where everyone is speaking but no sound is heard.

He smiled slightly. Yes, that was it. He was still on board his ship, asleep in his cabin, having a nightmare.

He shook himself, and then looked at Dr Kerr with a twist of a dubious smile on his lips. 'What did you say?'

'Jane is gravely ill,' Dr Kerr repeated quietly. 'I can no longer guarantee her life.'

ELEVEN

Jane was beaming with a happiness that nothing could spoil, cheerfully making plans for the life of her child and unaware that her own life was in danger. She unwrapped a beautiful silver rattle she had bought and tinkled it in Lachlan's face. 'Isn't it *sweet*?'

'Sweet,' he agreed, speaking with a palpable effort and managing a smile.

She laughed, unaware of the trembling of his hand as he pushed back a dark curl from her brow.

'And now we can go back to Calicut?' she asked

'Well ...'

A sea voyage, the doctor had recommended. A voyage of fresh sea air, and a holiday in a different and invigorating setting, might restore her.

'Maybe not back to Calicut,' he said. 'At least, not for a while.'

'Oh, *why*?' She sat up on the sofa padded with cushions and stared at him in disappointment. Indeed, his entire attitude since his return yesterday had been very disappointing to say the least. Not over the moon about the baby, as she had expected, but inattentive, tired, abstracted.

'I need a holiday,' he said, looking into the pale face of his wife. Her frailness and pallor had shocked him on his return. She herself did not seem to notice it because it had come upon her in imperceptible degrees, day by day, and the reason she had lost pounds in weight, she believed, was simply due to the bouts of early morning sickness she had suffered.

'It's the baby,' she had assured him. 'Mrs Oakes says many women lose weight in the early months.'

'I need a holiday,' he said again, 'and after the Colombo and Galle campaigns, I have been granted leave to take one.'

Jane was staring at him, studying his face with concern. 'You are ill ... oh my poor darling!' Her own selfishness assailed her. 'While I have been lying here resting like the Queen of Sheba, you have been marching and fighting and suffering all the hardships of a soldier. Yes, you *must* have a holiday,' she insisted, holding his hand in tight determination. 'A holiday somewhere peaceful and relaxing and away from the Army. So where shall we go?'

Somewhere in the tropics, the doctor had said. No place cold or damp. Somewhere like India in the region of the tropics, but different and new and full of exciting sights for her to see and enjoy, after a voyage of healthy sea air.

'Scotland,' she said suddenly. 'Why don't we go to Scotland? Wouldn't it be just wonderful if our child was born in Scotland, and I could meet your mother at last.'

'No, not Scotland,' he said, 'not yet. The Atlantic can be very cold and choppy. And apart from that, the voyages there and back would take six to eight months before we spent even a day there. My holiday leave is only for six months.'

'Take as long as you need, dear boy!' General Balfour had said compassionately. *'If a holiday will help Jane to recover, then have whatever time it takes to get her well again. She's an Army wife, after all. Must look after our own.'*

Lachlan stood up and moved over to a cane bookcase by the wall where Major Oakes' military books lined every shelf. He searched for an Atlas, found one, and brought it back to her.

'You choose,' he said. 'I honestly don't care where I go as long as I can enjoy a long and relaxing sea voyage with plenty of fresh air. Choose some place you would really enjoy seeing.'

The whole time she sat studying the Atlas, Lachlan stood by the window watching her. She turned page after page of the Atlas and seemed to be carefully studying each one. Then she turned another page and instantly her demeanour changed. She looked up at him, eyes sparkling.

'China,' she said. 'Oh, Lachlan, I have always wanted to see China, haven't you?'

China was in the tropics.

'Always,' he said.

*

Nine days later, on the 17th May, they boarded the *Cambridge* and set sail for Macao, a peninsula of the China coast, south of the tropic of Cancer.

Bappoo, Marianne, and George Jarvis went with them, full of both fear and excitement at going out of India and seeing another part of the world.

'Chin people small,' Bappoo said authoritatively to George Jarvis, 'but very wise.' He pointed to his brain. 'Very wise.'

'How you know?' George asked curiously.

'Ship captain's servant tell me. He say Chin people very wise – but speak all time to confuse us.' Bappoo pointed a warning finger at George and said cunningly, 'So! – we no let Chin people confuse us!'

'Confucius!' Jane said smiling. 'I think, Bappoo, you will

183

find that the captain's servant was talking about Confucius, a Chinese philosopher of ancient times.'

'*Chut!*' Bappoo looked shame-faced as George peeled out a laugh and Lachlan restrained one.

After only a week on the sea Jane's spirits rose and the lovely blushing colour came back to her cheeks. Lachlan could actually see her recovery happening before his eyes.

After three weeks on the sea he wrote a letter each to Colin Anderson and John Forbes, eager to give his friends `*pleasing accounts of my Angel's improving health.*'

Captain Lestock Wilson was the master of the *Cambridge*, and as they sailed across the Indian Ocean towards the South China Sea, Jane won his approval with her good humour. Most of the women Captain Forbes had sailed with had spent all their time complaining in a weak and whining way, but young Mrs Macquarie was brave and hearty and always happy to sit up at night for dinner in the captain's cabin. She was very beautiful, very pleasant, and there was a wit in her conversation which rendered her truly fascinating in his eyes.

'What is supposed to be wrong with her?' Captain Wilson quietly asked Lachlan one day, while Jane was sitting in her cabin busily writing a list of the names of all the children of her friends for whom she wanted to buy toys and presents in Macao.

Lachlan shrugged. 'The medical profession of Bombay is primitive, to say the least. They don't seem to have the slightest idea of what is wrong with anyone who is sick, and so they prescribe quinine and mercury for all. And buffalo milk, of course.'

'Have you ever had malaria?' Wilson asked.

'Unfortunately, yes.'

'I've had every fever including malaria.' Wilson held up his two hands. 'And I would need more than the fingers on these hands to count all the times I've been told I was at the door of death.' He boomed a laugh. 'And look at me now – still hale and hearty!'

'It's terrible, just the same,' Lachlan said, 'the fright that doctors often give to people.'

'Well, your fellow did at least recommend a sea voyage which is proving the correct remedy. What else did he recommend?'

'Plenty of red wine...'

'Oh, wonderful!' Captain Wilson laughed, topping up their two glasses with more red wine.

'Red wine,' Lachlan repeated, 'mixed with spices.'

'Ugh! That doctor must want to make her sick again to keep up his fees!'

'Mercury...'

'Naturally!' Wilson grinned. 'Where would we be without good old mercury, eh? It doesn't do you a damned bit of good but it eventually burns the mouth off you just for spite.'

'And three daily doses of tincture of yellow bark.'

'Yellow bark? That's a new one! What is that for?'

Lachlan shrugged. 'Well, of course, Jane thinks all this medicine is to dispel her weakness and make her strong for carrying the baby.'

Lestock Wilson sat still. Now that was the sad part. The poor girl convincing herself she was pregnant. He said: 'When are you going to disillusion her, and tell her what the doctor said – that she has made a very big mistake?'

Lachlan sat back and sighed. `I'm not going to tell her anything, or believe anything that Dr Kerr has said. He's made mistakes before. If she's not pregnant, then in time she will realise that for herself. All I believe now is the evidence I see before my own eyes, that she seems well and full of health again.'

Lestock Wilson lifted his glass and grinned. 'She looks healthier than both of us!'

*

Always one for rising early, Lachlan often went up on deck as the morning watch was relieved, the most peaceful time of the day. The sea and winds were calm and the ship simply ghosted along at no more than four knots an hour. One morning Jane joined him at the deck rail with a smile. He was surprised to see her up so early.

'A beautiful day ahead, I think,' she murmured.

Lachlan followed her gaze. The sea and the sky were very blue, the sun rising into a red dawn. At peaceful times like this he wished he were a poet. He looked into her face and smiled to see her looking so well.

'And *what* is amusing you now?' she asked.

He lifted her hand from the rail and kissed it, then held it against his cheek as he stared out to sea. Her returning health had given a life-spring to his soul. With Jane he had discovered there is a kind of love so true, so perfect, that just the thought of its end was enough to break the heart utterly. He could not have borne it, and now he would not have to. Thank God the doctor had been right about the sea voyage.

But then, he reflected, he should have known it was not in Jane's nature to go under at the first sign of sickness. It was her nature to be courageous and happy. And there was nothing mentally wrong with her. No imbalance that he could detect. So maybe she *was* pregnant. Yes, maybe she was ... after all, she would know whether she was pregnant or not better than any doctor.

He turned to look at her and asked softly, 'How is the future young general?'

She smiled and put a hand on her stomach. 'Very well behaved. Not making me feel sick anymore.'

'You truly feel well again?'

She nodded. 'Yes.'

'You do look well.'

'So do you,' she observed, for he was the one she believed to have been ill. Both had spent weeks worrying about the other's health, and now both were very relieved.

And suddenly, as he looked at her, Lachlan was convinced that Jane *was* pregnant. That *she* was right and the doctor wrong. Women knew these things before ever consulting a doctor. His hand moved to join hers on her stomach, and it did feel roundly swelled; the familiar flatness he had known for years was gone.

'How many months pregnant are you?' he asked.

'Five,' she answered.

'And when did you know for sure?'

'When three months had passed, just before I wrote to you.' She was looking at him strangely. 'I have told you all this before, Lachlan.'

'Yes,' he said with a sigh, 'but I was not listening before.'

'Thank you very much! I think I'll go back to bed.'

He caught her in his arms and held her, and with her he held the fullness of his life. And once again he felt the excitement and happiness he had felt that day in Ceylon, on the road from Point de Galle to Colombo, the day he had read Jane's letter telling him she was going to make him a happy, happy father.

'I love you,' he whispered, and kissed her on the eyes, the mouth, and the forehead, his lips covering her with love, until presently she put her hands to his face and kissed him back.

'Is that what you came on deck to see?' he said suddenly, looking beyond her.

'What?' She turned her head and stared. 'Where?'

He pointed to a small black peak far into the distance. 'China, on the horizon.'

She turned and gripped the rail in excitement.

'Are you going back to bed,' he asked at length.

'No, I'm wide awake now.' She linked her arm through his and they remained together, standing by the deck rail in the warm morning sun, looking towards China.

*

At daybreak on the 2nd of July, the *Cambridge* reached Macao. Captain Wilson sent word to prepare to disembark into a small boat that would take them into the harbour. The voyage from Bombay had taken six weeks.

All through the previous night a gale had blown against them, and now Lachlan watched Jane eating a hearty breakfast and wondered how she could possibly eat a thing with the ship rocking and lurching.

She had risen at daybreak and packed all her clothes and trunks herself, leaving Marianne with nothing to do but keep George Jarvis company as he ran on deck, staring in wild excitement at the packed and busy harbour of Macao. Bappoo stood behind them, reprimanding them severely for their unruly noise, whilst trying himself not to jiggle with excitement.

'Bappoo – why all boats have eyes painted on front?' asked George Jarvis.

Bappoo didn't know. All three stared at the hundreds of small Chinese junks tossing about in Macao harbour with a large eye painted on each side of their bow.

'Why all boats have eyes painted on front,' Captain-Sahib?' George asked later when Lachlan came on deck.

Lachlan didn't know either, but he came up with a possibility. 'So the boats can see where they are going?'

'Yes, by God, by Jove!' Bappoo cried exultantly. 'That is what!' And George Jarvis let out another shout of delighted laughter - Bappoo knew nothing, but Lachlan-Sahib knew everything.

'Boats have eyes to see where going,' George said to Marianne, and Marianne nodded and giggled at the cleverness of the Chin people.

An hour later the baggage, children, and Bappoo were all packed with Lachlan and Jane into the large Chinese junk that was to take them through Macao's outer harbour to the inner harbour, where they finally disembarked after a further two hours on the water, the wind and tide both being against them.

Captain Wilson travelled ashore with them, and as they set foot on land he was amazed to see that the person who did not seem in the least fatigued from sitting so long in the windy boat was young Mrs Macquarie. He watched her as she stepped ashore, looking wonderfully strong and in high spirits as she rallied everyone to the exciting time ahead in China.

She was young, he thought, and how indomitable were the young. She had recovered from her illness and proved the doctor wrong. Good girl. And since she had spoken to him of her child, he too was now certain that under the masking folds of her skirts she was carrying a baby for her husband. Lucky man.

And the face she now turned on Macao – a city built on seven hills around the harbour – was so full of excited anticipation that Captain Wilson saw in her all the beauty of youth that knows no complaints and no tiredness.

He looked at Lachlan. And the Major – how old was he? Thirty? Thirty-one? And he too seemed full of youth as he helped the sick-looking little Indian girl ashore.

Captain Wilson slapped Lachlan on the back. 'So! Here we are, my friend! In Macao – the opium gateway into China.'

'Opium!' Lachlan stared at him in dismay. 'Here, too?'

'Everywhere in the East. clever men make a fortune from it, stupid men are destroyed by it.' Wilson shrugged. 'Bright silver and slow death bargaining daily with each other. That, my friend, is the opium trade.'

'Every ounce of it should be dumped in the sea,' Lachlan said with disdain.

Captain Wilson had to smile. 'I suspect you do not know that it was the *British* who first brought opium from India to China, and sold it at a colossal profit. There are many rich families in England whose wealth comes from the sale of Bengal opium, and thousands of opium addicts left behind in China.'

Lachlan looked at him, taken aback. He had always believed it was the British who were trying to stop the opium trade in India, not making a wholesale profit from *exporting* it to China.

Wilson nodded. 'Only this year, the Emperor Tao Tuang

issued an edict banning the drug. But all that will do is make it more expensive for the Chinese addict and keep the pirates in business. The traders of the Honourable East India Company will now *smuggle* the opium into China, and the Co-Hong merchants in Canton will simply corrupt their own Chinese officials with bribes and pay-offs and the trade will go on as before. But now...' Lestock Wilson smiled, 'you are on holiday, so no more talk of opium.'

He moved to Jane and turned her to look east. 'Over there, my lady, less than forty miles away, is Hong Kong.'

Jane was only interested in Macao – one of the main trading centres of the East, teeming with life and noise and running rickshaws pulled by men with hair worn in long black pigtails. She couldn't wait to get into the thick of it, but first they must rest and dine and take possession of the house they had rented.

It was for that purpose Lachlan looked around him searchingly until he saw a very obvious-looking Englishman pushing his way through the streams of coolies working on the waterfront.

As he was out of uniform and dressed elegantly civilian, the Englishman looked uncertainly at Lachlan. 'Major Macquarie?'

'Yes, sir.' Lachlan shook hands with the man. 'Mr David Reid?'

'At your service,' Reid replied with a smile; and the introductions began.

'My wife, Mrs Jane Macquarie.'

Mr Reid seemed delighted at Jane's pretty youth. He bowed over her hand. 'Mrs Macquarie, what a singular pleasure it is to welcome you to Macao.'

Lachlan continued the introductions. 'Captain Lestock

Wilson, our voyage master ... Bappoo, Marianne, George.'

Mr Reid bore patiently with the last three – one was not usually introduced to servants.

'I have some disappointing news for you, I'm afraid, Major,' Reid said. 'In accordance with the letters I received from both yourself and Mr John Forbes which, I hasten to say, I received only two days ago, I have succeeded in renting a house for you in a clean and airy part of Macao, quite near my own, actually, with a good view of the sea. But unfortunately the house is without furniture and the new furnishings will not be completed until tomorrow.'

'So what do we do until then?' Lachlan asked.

'Stay with me, of course. Be delighted to have you! There are not many of us British here in Macao, so it's always good to see a new face. The place is overrun with Chinese of course. Not to mention the Portuguese! They own Macao, you know? The Portuguese.'

Lachlan was feeling distinctly uncomfortable due to the fact that he had invited Captain Wilson, now a friend, and whose ultimate destination was Canton, to bide a while and spend a few days in Macao with himself and Jane, in the hospitality of their own house.

'You will come along too, will you, Captain Wilson?' said Reid, solving the problem. 'Be delighted to have you. The more the merrier!' Reid smiled merrily. 'As I say, always a joy for us exiles in the British factory to have some more of our own amongst us. Now then, Mrs Macquarie dear, shall we be off?'

Jane was scooped away into a waiting rickshaw and the rest left to follow in other rickshaws.

Their stay in Mr Reid's house lasted not one day, but two days and two nights; and throughout they had no time to venture into the town and markets of Macao because every British resident of Macao's small trading post of the East India Company, responsible for the export of tea and silk, called to pay their compliments to Major and Mrs Macquarie.

Jane found herself sitting until almost midnight, eating sweets and talking animatedly to Mrs Beale and Mrs Drummond about the European fashions of Bombay, which were at least two years behind London.

Lachlan and Jane's bedroom in Mr Reid's house, they were pleased to discover, had eastern windows, facing the rise of the sun.

'The best sun is the morning sun,' Lachlan had often said, and Jane had always agreed with him, because in India and Antigua, only the morning sun was soft and mild with a gentle radiance that warmly awakened a room and its occupants to a new day.

They awoke on the third morning to see the golden rays creeping through the louvered shutters. Jane stretched her body luxuriously in anticipation of a new day that promised to be the best so far. 'This morning, we move to our own house,' she said. 'And this afternoon we go into Macao to buy some presents.'

Lachlan freed the arm that was deadened from her sleeping on it, and blinked at the clock. 'It's not yet six.'

'That early? *Oh my land...*' She rolled onto her side and dived under the silk sheet like a young porpoise, and went back to sleep.

At seven o'clock a Chinese servant whispered into the room with a tray of early morning tea and whispered out again.

By ten o'clock they had moved into their own house, a

two-storey stone villa built in the Portuguese style, with Chinese long windows and a sloped attic roof.

A low stone balustrade surrounded the shaded terrace that opened onto the front garden, the sunny path lined with ornamental stone urns filled with green foliage and plants of large round flowers, all of the same genus, varying only in their colours, a beautiful mixture of red, pink, and white.

'The peony,' said Captain Wilson, bending to touch a bloom. 'The flower of China.'

When they entered the house, Lachlan and Jane were very touched to discover it had been partly furnished by the tiny colony of British people in Macao, who had insisted on filling it with extra little items of English oak and English china and lace in order to make them feel more comfortable during their stay in this foreign land.

'Don't they know that you have come from living years in India and not direct from Britain?' Captain Wilson asked in a tone of puzzlement.

'They know we come from India,' Lachlan replied, 'from a *British* part of India. But there is nothing British here in Macao. This house is rather nice, don't you think?'

'Yes, yes indeed.'

The house was spacious and comfortable with a lovely view over the harbour. 'And the cool sea breeze will be delightful during these summer nights,' Wilson said.

Jane adored the house, but as soon as they were installed and the baggage had been unpacked, she pleaded with Captain Wilson who happily agreed to be their guide and escort them around Macao.

Travelling in rickshaws, he took them first, *away* from the town, up to see the temple of Kun Iam Tong, which was more a series of temples within beautiful pavilions. They passed through the ornate entrance to the dim interior of the first Prayer Hall that flickered with candles, the air heavy with the fragrance of burning joss sticks, and where they found three Buddhas staring at them steadfastly.

'Each represents the past, present, and future,' Lestock said, and then took them on to the second hall, within an open courtyard, to meet the Buddha of Longevity.

Jane was entranced as they climbed the steps to the various pavilions, linked by paths, each a little garden secluded within itself. It was like another world, drenched in tranquillity and the fragrance of flowers. Without demur she allowed Lachlan to kiss her under the 'Sweetheart Tree' – two ancient banyans with roots and branches intertwined, symbolising true love.

She bent to admire the trees gnarled old trunks, which must have been there for – 'How long?'

Lestock Wilson shrugged. 'The temple has been here at least two hundred years, so I suppose the tree has too.'

Then it was time to leave the serenity of the temple gardens and venture down to the noisy streets of the town where Jane was eager to spend Lachlan's money buying presents for all their friends back in India.

'And Mammy Dinah in Antigua,' Jane said, as they strolled through the busy streets filled with Chinese hawkers, craftsmen, peasants, and merchants. 'Something beautiful from China for Dinah.'

'*From China for Dinah...*' sang George Jarvis as he skipped along, slyly pulling the long black pigtails of Chinamen as they passed, then looking innocent when heads turned.

Jane was in raptures at the beautiful merchandise for sale

in Macao. Here was some of the most exquisite art and craftsmanship she had ever seen. Her first purchase was a Chinese robe of blue silk embroidered in red peonies; then a beautiful clock set in jade, followed by a silk shawl for Dinah.

They returned to the house that evening laden with purchases and presents, and found two Chinese servants in residence and waiting for them, having been employed that day on their behalf by Mr Reid.

A married couple, the two Chinese bowed graciously, and a short time later they beckoned to Lachlan, Jane and Captain Wilson to come into the dining-room where a beautiful table had been laid out, dressed with small bowls of miniature white orchid blossoms and circlets of white jasmine. The rest of the table was covered in steaming dishes of rice and all kinds of Cantonese food.

'Delicious!' Jane said, eating a forkful of shrimp rice, while Lachlan and Lestock Wilson sampled spicy prawns and had to agree that the standard of cooking was superb.

In the servants' quarters, Bappoo found himself with a whole Canton duck all to himself, which he held in both hands and continually pointed, between bites, at George Jarvis.

'You rascally son of slave!' he said severely. 'You no pull Chin people's hair tomorrow!'

'No, Bappoo,' George said, and then let out a giggle of laughter because one Chin man had blamed Bappoo for pulling his pigtail. And when Bappoo had lifted his big fist threateningly over the head of the small Chin man, the Chin man had not even blinked as he reached for a particular point in Bappoo's wrist and twisted it in a way that left Bappoo gasping in pain, his surprised eyes standing out like huge black dates on glistening white saucers.

'Chin men very clever,' George said, sending up another bout of laughter that rang all the way through to Lachlan and Jane and Captain Forbes who all smiled, because the boy's laughter was very infectious.

'He's a brat,' Lachlan said. 'Sometimes I wish I had left him in Cochin.'

'How long will you stay in Macao?' asked Lestock Wilson.

Lachlan glanced at Jane. 'Six weeks, at the most. Then we must return to India in time for the baby to be born. When do you leave for Canton?'

'One more day in Macao, after that I must leave.'

Jane had been struggling with a fruit pancake and now gave up, feeling too full. 'Where will you stay in Canton?'

'In my own house,' Lestock replied. 'I've had a home in Canton for many years now. And if you two have six weeks to spare, then you must come and spend at least two of them with me in Canton. It is worth the journey. And my house is very charming, up in the hills.'

Another shout of laughter rang through to them. Lestock Wilson grinned. 'You can even bring the laughing little Cochin brat with you!'

*

Later, when they were alone, Lachlan and Jane decided to delay going to bed for a while longer. Lighting a candle, they left their bedroom and climbed the stairs to the sloping attic of the house. One wall was comprised solely of large leaded squares of glass, which gave a lovely moonlight view of the harbour.

They looked around, seeing there was no furniture in the

197

attic save for one small bamboo table and an old ornate armchair, placed together by the window, as if some previous occupant had often sat up here alone, staring out at the harbour.

Lachlan set the candle on the small table and they stood quiet for a moment watching the bright sails of the junks on the dark water.

Then he took her hand, sat down in the armchair and she sat down on his lap, her arm moving companionably round his neck as she settled herself against him like a kitten in a basket. She then gazed out at the sea with her cheek pressed against his, and he gazed with her.

'How pretty the harbour looks with all the colourful lights of the lanterns,' she said. 'And the little dots of lights bobbing up and down on the junks. Would you like to live on a boat?'

'We did, for six weeks,' he reminded her. 'On the boat that brought us here.'

'Oh yes, I forgot ... but travelling in a boat is very different to living in one.'

'All one and the same, I suppose, to a sailor.'

She giggled softly.

'Are you happy, Jane?'

'Yes, happy, very happy.' She slipped out of his arms and sat forward, staring at the dark line where the land ended and the glistening water began. After a long silence she said in a low voice, 'Isn't it wonderful to know that we are really here, in China, the largest empire in the world.'

It was true, now that he thought about it, China *was* the largest empire of them all, and Macao was just a pebble on its shore.

He looked at her as she stared at the harbour, at the

Chinese robe of blue silk which she had bought that day and changed into, at the tumble of hair which moved in light glints and dark shadows in the candlelight. Oh yes, she was happy tonight. Did anything else matter?

His eyes moved back to the waters of the harbour and he felt a great welling of peace seep through him, a satisfied contentment that had something to do with her excitement and delight in Macao, a romantic and strangely genteel place, despite the busyness of its streets in daytime and the cargoes of opium smuggled into its harbour by night.

She lay back quietly against him. Time passed unnoticed. The moon made a silver river on the surface of the dark water.

She stirred and put her hand in his. 'We did so many lovely things today,' she said softly. 'Seeing so many strange and exotic sights. Buying this beautiful robe and all those sweet presents; then that superb dinner waiting for us. So many lovely things.'

She turned towards him and smiled sleepily. 'Tell me that you love me.'

'I love you.'

The room was tranquil with silence, filled with the salty scent of the ocean that gently lapped its waves against the boats in the harbour. She studied his face thoughtfully and he returned her gaze, both isolated in a world that had no space for anyone else.

She tightened her arms about his neck and he felt the touch of her warm mouth as she kissed him lovingly and endlessly, until the dying candle finally quivered and spluttered in a thin smoke of extinction and left them in darkness.

He put his hands under her arms and gently lifted her to

her feet, taking her hand and leading her through the shadows to the door. It was time to leave the dark attic and the view of the harbour. Time to light a candle in the bedroom below. So many lovely things today, but now came sleep and the night.

*

The night ached with an excess of tenderness and unspoken expressions of love. The night was also the moons, brightly glowing, and moving slowly in a sky of crowding stars.

Peacefully, the stars began to dim in the moon's afterglow. Then the night ceased, and the house became still in the long silence that spread over the sleeping junks and seven hills of Macao: until, once more, the sun began to rise in the east.

TWELVE

The following day Lestock Wilson escorted them on a tour of the town of Macao itself. All the streets were very narrow, and those that had names were in Portuguese.

Outside doorways, venerable old Chinese men sat at small tables playing a game of mah-jong, and never batted an eyelid if they had a foreign audience. Not even when George Jarvis peered curiously over their shoulders as they rattled the mah-jong pieces did their concentration waver from the game. Only once did a white-haired sage glance up as the foreign group strolled on, and that was simply because he had felt a tug on his pigtail.

'The Chinese are inveterate gamblers,' Lestock said. 'They will gamble on anything, but a game of mah jong is their daily favourite.'

He then took them up one of Macao's seven hills to the beautiful Church of Sao Paulo, a monument to the Jesuit missionaries who had succeeded in getting into China long before the traders.

The flight of stone steps up to the church seemed endless. Jane stood between her husband and Lestock Wilson, laughing as each held her hand and the three mounted and counted the steps in unison, '... twenty-three, twenty-four...'

Behind them George Jarvis and Marianne did the same, skipping up the steps without knowing how to count.

Bappoo merely followed in a weary succession of puffs, pausing every so often to mop his face with the scarf of his turban. Why the disciples of the Nazarene had to build their temples so high up was beyond his understanding. And he said so, to George Jarvis.

'Where other?' George said intelligently, pointing to the hills all around Macao.

The three leaders had reached the top step. '*Seventy!*'

Lestock Wilson was panting slightly. 'They say the higher the climb to the church, the more the spirit is uplifted. But I don't know if I agree.'

Marianne and George, and, finally, Bappoo, remained standing at a distance while Lachlan and Jane stood looking up at the magnificent facade of Sao Paulo.

'Some say it is a sermon in stone,' Lestock said. 'See, all the carvings record all the important events in Christianity ... the dove at the very top, that is the Holy Spirit. Beneath, on the second tier, Jesus, surrounded by the sun, moon and stars. Beneath Jesus, the angels ... as I say, a sermon in stone.'

They entered the dim interior, talking softly as they walked over the magnificent mosaic floor. 'One of the first missionaries of the Jesuit Order to reach China,' said Lestock, 'was St Francis Xavier. It was he who found Macao for the Jesuits.'

'But he is buried in India,' Lachlan said.

Surprised, Lestock turned. 'In India?'

'Yes, at Goa. Jane and I went there on a short voyage not long after we were married. We saw his tomb, Francis Xavier's, and dined with some of the Jesuit priests. Their mode of living was so sparse it was almost mediaeval.'

When they had stepped outside again into the sunlight, Lestock continued, 'I have a great respect for the Jesuits, especially here in Macao. Their interests have conflicted frequently with the Portuguese officials here. The officials are always at war with the priests, and the priests with them. There was a time when the Portuguese government tried to banish all forms of Chinese traditions here in Macao, especially Ancestor Worship and Family Cult, condemning the practice as a heresy. But the Jesuits fought them all the way, insisting – as they still do – that these traditions are a secular rite of the Chinese and do not go against the spirit of Christianity.'

They began the descent of the steps and then paused for tea down in the town, in a small teahouse named *Casa de cha*: after which Jane was again busy in the markets choosing more gifts with the help of Marianne and George.

And then, as on the previous evening, on this final evening of Lestock Wilson's' stay at their house, a beautiful dinner was waiting for them, prepared and served by the Chinese couple.

Later the three strolled down to take a moonlight walk near the harbour. 'I love Maçao,' Jane said dreamily. 'It is just as I imagined China to be. The rickshaws and the lanterns and the serenity of the Chinese.'

'Would you like to live here?' Lachlan asked.

'No, not live,' she said swiftly. 'India is home to me now. Calicut is the only place I want to live.'

Lachlan had to agree. Calicut was their own little heaven amidst the coconut trees, and suddenly he found himself looking forward to their return there.

'But tonight, Lachlan,' she said softly, 'I am very tired and have a great longing to go to my bed.'

He looked at her, and suddenly realised she had been leaning very heavily on his arm. 'My love ... why did you not say?'

'I was having too much fun! But the sight-seeing and buying we have done would exhaust any woman, never mind one who is expecting a baby.'

'Then you will not walk a step further.' He caught her about the waist and scooped her up into his arms and began to carry her.

She laughingly protested, but he would not let her down. Finally she put her arms around his neck and relaxed in his arms. Every so often, as he carried her back towards their house, he paused to kiss her, and she allowed him to do so quite peacefully.

Following them, Lestock Wilson knew they had forgotten him completely, but he did not mind. He had come to love them both. And when they came to visit him in Canton the situation would be more equal, for there he had his own woman: a Chinese girl who was as beautiful as a lotus flower.

*

Next morning Jane was so tired she was unable to do more than sit in an easy chair on the terrace and gaze out towards the sea. A paleness had returned to her face and she felt very weak. 'I'm pregnant and I overtired myself, that's all,' she assured Lachlan with a pat and a smile. 'In future I will try to take it more easy.'

They decided to have a day of rest, just sitting in easy chairs on the terrace, both reading the books they had brought with them. In the evening Jane declined dinner, preferring instead to take a tray of tea in their bedroom and prepare for an early night.

David Reid had come to call. Lachlan was obliged to dine with him.

David Reid had noticed the anxious look in Lachlan's eyes as they sat down to dine. 'Mrs Macquarie's indisposition is 'nothing serious, I hope? Feeling ill, is she?'

'She is tired,' Lachlan said.

'Not like her to be indisposed,' Reid persisted glumly. 'Full of sparkle usually.' He began spooning rice onto his plate. 'I said it to old Beale just this morning. Like milky water most of the women who come here, but young Mrs Macquarie, bubbling and sparkling – pure champagne!'

'Yes.'Lachlan smiled as he helped himself to rice.

'She ain't likely to remain ill for long is she?'

'No, no, she is pregnant and needs to rest, that's all.'

'I say, is that somebody wailing? Sounds like it to me. Would you say that was somebody wailing, Major?'

It was Marianne calling to Lachlan that he must come to her mistress at once. 'Come, come!' she wailed from the doorway. 'Mem-Jane sick! Mem-Jane need you!'

He ran to their room and found Jane half-lying on the bed, a look of utter shock on her face, her breathing coming in hard gasps as if she had been running. 'I can't stand,' she gasped. 'Lachlan ... my legs, I can't stand!'

He tried to steady her but her legs were too weak to hold her weight. The nausea in her stomach was making her feel sick. She looked at him whitely. 'I think I'm losing the baby.'

'I'll get a doctor,' he said, and heard himself stammering. But she had begun to sob and moan in pain. 'Oh, Lachlan, there's a great heat burning all through me ...'

'I'll get a doctor,' he said again. 'I'll be back in just a few minutes. A servant ... send him...'

David Reid had already sent George Jarvis running for the doctor.

*

205

When Dr Duncan arrived Jane was in bed, feeling a lot easier, and looking much more composed. 'But the heat,' she said faintly, 'I can still feel this burning heat...'

Dr Duncan was Scottish and very efficient, as well as kind and fatherly in manner. He made up a negus of red wine and spices and sat by her bedside as she drank it, speaking to her in a soothing and questioning way, until she sighed and relaxed and agreed that the mixture was indeed giving her relief from the burning pain.

Dr Duncan's face registered satisfaction. He urged her now to drink a cup of hot milk, in which he had slipped a measure of laudanum. The drug swiftly took effect, her eyes dulled over, and within minutes she was sleeping soundly.

'In the morning she will find she can walk again,' Dr Duncan said quietly, his back to Lachlan as he took a bottle from his medical bag. 'Although, she will still feel very weak. Now, I shall leave you this bottle of spices to be mixed with red wine whenever she feels the burning heat again and needs relief.'

'Red wine and spices?' Lachlan ushered Marianne out of the room and glared at the doctor. 'Is that all you intend to give her? Red wine and spices!'

Dr Duncan buckled the fastenings on his bag. 'I do not think it advisable to give her any other medicine. The mixture of wine and spices has given her relief so far, and will continue to give her relief.'

'From what?'

Dr Duncan half turned his head and looked at the girl in the bed. 'The burning heat she feels, is, of course, due to the onset of a fever.'

'She is not having a miscarriage then?'

'Miscarriage?' Dr Duncan turned and stared at him. 'Mr

Macquarie, pray forgive me, but in my letter from Dr Kerr I was led to believe that you understood the true state of your wife's health.'

'She *is* pregnant,' Lachlan snapped. 'She says she is pregnant, and has never once varied in that conviction. And I believe *her* — not Dr Kerr. My wife, Dr Duncan, *is* pregnant.'

'She is also dying, Mr Macquarie, and I sincerely apologise for not realising that you did not fully understand that.'

For a long moment all the noise in the world seemed to have stopped again ... the silent blade of the knife was back, slipping under his ribs, preparing to rip through his heart. Then, once more, he heard the doctor speaking to him, but from somewhere very far away.

'So hard for a doctor to say these things ... not the smallest hope of recovery, not now the fever has come on ... beyond the help of any medicinal aid ... Cannot live for more than a few months, maybe even weeks ... She has no idea, of course ... thinks all is due to pregnancy ... no point in alarming her...'

His pain was devouring him, but he held it back, concentrating only on Jane as he went through the following days, living in a hell of smiles and lies.

She rose the following morning and insisted on leaving her bed for breakfast, agreed to take it very easy, and sat for most of the morning in an easy chair reading.

Later she walked with him in the garden, regaining her strength and some of her humour, speaking to him of their child, their return to Calicut, their future, and the presents she had still not bought for some of their friends' children. In a day or two, perhaps, they would again go into Macao, could they?

He agreed, and she smiled, but there was no colour in her face.

In the evening they sat side by side on the warm terrace, their hands held together, listening to the noise of the harbour, comfortable with each other, as they had always been comfortable with each other, and never so much with anyone else. He rarely left her side, always to be found sitting beside her like a devoted husband, but then he had always been that.

Five days after Dr Duncan's visit he awoke just before dawn to find Jane sitting up in bed.

'What is it?'

'The pain,' she gasped, 'the burning pain ...'

He quickly got out of bed and fumbled in the half-dark to light a candle, and then reached for the mixture of wine and spices that was already prepared. He handed her the glass. 'Drink this, it will relieve you.'

He helped her hold the glass to her mouth but after a few sips she was sobbing with the pain. 'Drink more,' he said. 'Drink more!'

Obediently she did as she was told, wiping the tears from her eyes as he laid the glass aside and settled her back against the pillows. He began to pull on his clothes. 'I'll send for Dr Duncan.'

When he had reached the door she called him back. 'Lachlan!'

He turned.

'Don't leave me,' she pleaded. Her face looked very frightened and very pale against the loosened chestnut hair that tumbled about her. Her bare arms and shoulders in the white petticoat had changed from golden to a pale ivory.

He came back to the bed and took her face in his hands. 'In a moment I'll be back, my angel. I promise you, I'll be back.'

When he returned her pain had gone, but she was still shaking with fright at the thought of losing her baby. 'Hold me, Lachlan,' she whispered.

He sat on the bed and held her, cradling her shaking body against his chest, comforting and soothing, until her trembling ceased. It had become his habit, ever since he had returned from Ceylon and known she was sick, known she was expecting a baby, this urge to cradle her, protect her, give her anything she wanted, anything that would make her happy.

'Lachlan,' she whispered.

'Yes.'

'Last night I was dreaming of Calicut, of that blissful little place, and in my dream all I wanted to do was get back there. Can we go back? Not in four weeks, but sooner?'

He squeezed his eyes shut against her plea. He was not taking her back to Calicut. He had already made his plans to take her to Scotland, to Edinburgh, where there were good doctors, the best doctors in the world.

'In just a few days,' he said, 'an English ship is due at Macao. We will be on it. In just a few days we will leave here.'

'Oh Lachlan,' she said softly, 'you're so good to me, so good ...'

The last words had trailed away into a whisper. After a time he wondered if she had fallen asleep. He bent to look into her face, and as he did a sudden pounding began to shake his heart. Her hand had gone limp in his own, he stared at it, squeezed it hard.

'Jane?'

The pounding of his heart and the roaring in his head was like a thousand battering bells as a quaking terror swept over him. `Jane,' he said, shaking her. 'Jane ... Jane!' Her head fell back from his shoulder, her eyes closed, her lips parted.

He stared at her in bewildered disbelief. The doctor had said months, enough time to get her to England or Scotland. Maybe weeks. But that had been only five *days* ago!

'Jane!' he cried frantically. 'Oh God, oh, Christ ... *Jane!*' Again he shook her in terrified denial. *'Jane!'*

But then it came to him, finally, that Jane had died in his arms. Snatched from him without warning.

He stared at her lifeless face, and felt the agonising pain of his heart breaking.

THIRTEEN

'Those whom the Gods love die young.'

It was the only complete sentence Marianne had managed to utter amidst hours of sobbing incoherently at the bedside of her mistress.

'What is written, is written,' Bappoo whispered, wiping a hand over his wet face.

By noon the house was packed with visitors from the British factory. Mrs Beale whispered tearfully to Dr Duncan. 'She never did say to us her age. Do you know it, Dr Duncan?'

The doctor consulted a paper in his hand. 'She was aged twenty-three years and nine months.'

So young. And the poor girl had lived for only twelve days after arriving in Macao. Yet all noticed the bereaved husband looked very calm in his sorrow and sudden loss; unaware that he was seeing nothing, hearing nothing, and thinking nothing, lost in the pit of a dark and agonising hell.

*

Later that afternoon he was standing alone by the bedroom window, when, from behind him in the room, a few words spoken in broken English broke through the sound barrier of his calmness.

He turned his head to see the speaker – it was the kind-eyed Portuguese woman, Mrs Beale's personal maid, who had come to dress Jane for burial. His own Chinese housekeeper was assisting her, and she had paused to repeat to her mistress something the Chinese woman had said.

'What did she say?' Lachlan asked Mrs Beale. 'What did the Chinese woman say to your maid?'

Mrs Beale dabbed at her eyes. 'You may tell him, Carlota.'

Carlota glanced at the Chinese woman, then turned to Lachlan and flapped the air with her hands. 'She say...'

He listened with sharp attentiveness as Carlota explained in a mixture of English and Portuguese that the Chinese have a way of preserving the body so that it remained sweet and incorruptible for many years, and the Chinese woman had said that such was the way of this beautiful young lady who should now be preserved, sweet and incorruptible.

'Yes! She is right,' he said huskily. 'Ask her to arrange it at once.'

The Chinese woman looked at him, and seemed to understand him. '*Gwai*,' she warned.

'Costa many monies, O senhor!' Carlota said.

'Have it done as she says it can be done!' Lachlan snapped.

By that night the specially constructed Chinese coffin had been delivered, worked on by a team of expert craftsmen. And later still, the small tribe of Chinese women had finished their art of everlasting purity, and bowed to him graciously.

'*Joi gin*,' each whispered as they left the room, leaving him alone with Jane who lay sweet and incorruptible inside a beautiful lead and silver casket lined in white silk, looking as if she was simply in a peaceful sleep.

He drew up a chair and sat to look at her. He spent hours just looking at her. In the darkest hour of the night Marianne gently touched his hand, but it was George Jarvis who whispered to him: 'You sleep now, my father.'

When he gave no sign of hearing, both children sat down

at his feet and accompanied him in his silent vigil.

Was happiness truly such a fleeting thing? he asked himself. Were the Gods truly jealous of those on earth who possessed it? '*Paradise*,' someone had said in ancient times, '*is a place which lies in the East.*' And he knew now that place was in India. Calicut had been his Garden of Eden, where the sun had set and the moon had risen over a house and garden basking in happiness and where there had been no pain or gloom or sin.

And within the dark mists of his silent torment he felt he was dying himself, as the nightmare went on.

*

'She was a heretic! Both of you – *heretics!* She will not be buried in Holy Ground.'

Lachlan stared in shock at the Portuguese official. 'But the priest said – '

'The priest is a *Jesuit!* All Jesuits think they are above the law of the Portuguese government in Macao. Take heed, Britisher, there is no cemetery here for heretics. And any Jesuit priest found to have assisted at the burial of a heretic will pay with his own death. Who is this priest? What is his name?'

For a long time the two men stood staring at each other in silence.

At last Lachlan slowly turned and walked out of the dim office, pausing at the door to look back for a moment, speak a few words, then closed the door quietly behind him.

The Portuguese official turned to the window and watched him as he left the building and walked into the sunny square of Largo do Senado, watching until the

Britisher was out of sight, his eyes troubled and his heart beating with a vague fear, for never had a man looked at him with such black hatred, and still his parting words trembled in the air.

'*May God damn your soul in Hell for all eternity!*'

*

The gentlemen of the British factory looked at each other in silence, and then gazed at him compassionately. His wife had been dead four days now, and they were sure he had not slept. His face had a worn pallor and there were deep shadows under his eyes.

'I think you still do not understand,' said Mr James Drummond gravely. 'When the Portuguese say your wife cannot be buried in Catholic soil, they mean the whole of Macao, within the city walls. Outside the walls is Chinese territory, but she cannot be buried there. The Chinese do not allow other religions to desecrate their soil either.'

'So where then, *in God's holy name*, can I bury my wife?'

'We have no religious minister here,' said Mr Reid, `and never have had one. There are too few of us to warrant one being sent, you see. In the past Protestants *have* been buried in the Catholic grounds, but only by those priests who are prepared to risk their lives in so doing. The only place left, and where a number of other Protestants have been buried, is in that small strip of neutral territory beneath the city walls.'

'But that neutral ground is not consecrated ground, is it?'
'Well, no.'
'Then it is not *good* enough!'
'I'm sorry.' Mr Reid was startled at the savagery in

Lachlan's voice. 'I'm sorry ... but does it really matter where a body is buried? I know you are a good man, but I'm sure God will – '

'No, sir!' Lachlan pointed towards the room where Jane lay. '*She* was a *good* girl! An *angel*. All her principles were good and kind. And she will not be buried under some filthy dust outside the city walls of Macao!'

After a silence, Mr Beale said quietly, 'There is another place, up on the empty hills."

Lachlan looked at him. 'But you said that was Chinese territory.'

'Yes, yes, it is, but...' An idea had come to Mr Beale and he sat forward as he voiced it. 'Perhaps we could take her up there in secret, during the night, and with all of us helping, perhaps we could bury her on the hills and get away before morning without the Chinese knowing anything about it.'

He looked questioningly at Lachlan to see his reaction, but Lachlan's mind was miles away. 'Well?' said Mr Beale. 'Do you think it worth a try, to take her up to the hills under cover of the night?'

'No,' said Lachlan, coming out of his thoughts. 'No, she will not be buried anywhere in China. There will be no hole in the dark burial for my wife.'

An idea had come to him too – the best idea of all, and he could not understand why he had not thought of it before. He said incredulously: 'Why did I even consider leaving my angel alone in this foreign and hostile place? I will take her back with me to India.'

'What? Good gracious! I say, dear boy, are you mad?

The small British group looked at him as if he was indeed mad.

'All the way back to India!'

'My dear man, are you not getting this whole business out of proportion? In the end what does it really matter? The whole world is one big graveyard.'

But Lachlan was suddenly and stubbornly resolved to taking Jane back with him to India. That night, for the first time, he lay down to sleep with a small measure of peace; but the nightmare went on.

*

The Chinese officials refused to allow him to take the coffin out of the country.

The government of Macao, Lachlan began to realise, was not a simple matter to comprehend. The Chinese ruled, and the Portuguese ruled, depending on which door you happened to step through. Officially, Macao was ruled by the Chinese under a Portuguese administration. And the Chinese refused him permission to take his wife aboard a ship.

Slowly he was beginning to understand that here in Macao he had enemies all around him – not because of his religion – but because he was *British*.

The Portuguese hated the British because they had stolen nearly all the valuable land and rich trading posts they had founded in India. Even Bombay – *Bom Baìa* – the Good Bay, had belonged to the Portuguese, before the British swept in.

The Chinese hated the British because twenty-four years earlier, in 1773, the British had unloaded a thousand chests of Bengal opium in Canton, and were still managing by corrupt and illicit methods to unload thousands of chests of the addictive 'foreign mud' every year, in return for China's precious tea.

It did not seem to matter to these Western barbarians that, every year, more and more Chinese addicts were needed to keep up the demand for Indian opium in order to supply the British nation's craving for tea.

And China's tea was not the only thing the Western barbarians wanted. In the past there had been a number of Anglo-Dutch attempts to move into China and drain it of its riches. The first invasion attempt had been at Macao, but the Portuguese had joined the Chinese in fighting them off.

Since then, under the guise of legitimate trade, the British had practically taken over Canton, and now had their greedy eyes on the superior harbour of Hong Kong.

For almost a century the Chinese had been noting the activities of the British all over the world, and they had no intention of allowing the British to carve up China in the same way they had sliced up India.

The Chinese Mandarins and Portuguese officials had no charity to spare for the bereaved husband, not the smallest drop of mercy, because he was one of the opium-smuggling, land-grabbing British.

But even if he had found a way around the solid steel of Chinese officialdom and managed, somehow, by bribery or some other means, to get permission from the Chinese government to leave with Jane, he quickly learned that there was still no way he could take her out of Macao, because of the superstitions of the ordinary Chinese themselves. Their spiritual beliefs would not allow them to carry a coffin on their sampans and junks. Macao's inner harbour was simply not deep enough for a heavy sea-going vessel, and without a sampan or junk, there was no way he could get out to sea to board a ship.

He had managed, with the help of his friends, to secure a passage on an English ship that was lying at the mouth of the outer harbour, but when he arrived at the waterfront, and the junk sailors saw his cargo, they waved their hands angrily and refused to take him.

For hours he beseeched and offered bribes, in a position to do nothing else, but all in vain. Daybreak found him sitting on a box at the waterfront, numb and sick and swamped in exhaustion, surrounded by all his rejected cargo, a huge Moor servant, two Indian children, and a young wife in a coffin.

Together he and Bappoo lifted the beautiful lead and silver casket. There was nowhere else to go, but back to the house.

*

For sixteen days he stayed within the house without once venturing outside the door or allowing anyone to enter and give him the consolation of their company.

On the seventeenth day he allowed his worried friends from the British factory to enter, but the experiment failed. Worn by weeks of solitude, and desolate for his wife, their conversation seemed pointless and trivial to him. His attention kept wandering, their words drifting unheard.

His lack of sleep, personal grief, and sabotage from all directions had led him into a state of vague disorientation. The casket, which had been closed and screwed down forever within days of Jane's death, now took on an unreal aspect in his eyes. It contained something belonging to Jane, something precious left in his care, but not Jane herself.

As he stood at night, alone in the glass attic flickering with light and shadow, gazing out to the harbour, he felt Jane's presence at his side, soothing him, and time became meaningless. All the urgency left him as day followed day when he watched the sun rise through the eastern window of his bedroom, and later set into the sea as he sat on the terrace.

He did not realise that his every movement was being watched by George Jarvis who silently followed him everywhere and squatted unobtrusively in a corner of the veranda, keeping a steadfast eye upon him, and later reporting in whispers to Marianne and Bappoo, when Bappoo would rub a big hand over his face and sigh and sigh, but voiced no judgement.

All the laughter had died in George. The eyes in his beautiful ten-year-old face were now grave. In the space of a few weeks George had matured years. The sudden loss of his beloved mistress, who had given him her own name, had wounded him far more than his years of being a slave.

Now George spent his days looking at the man whom he thought of reverently as 'Father' and whom he loved passionately, watching him like a guardian angel and wondering how many more days Lachlan-Sahib would be content to stay here listening to echoes and gazing at memories.

Why did they stay here? Where nobody wanted them. Why did Lachlan-Sahib not look for a way back to Hindustan? And if there was no way, why did he not look to Heaven and ask Allah to show him a way?

The harbour below them was sinking into a silence as the sun began to set like a huge blood orange down into the far horizon of the sea, but George's eyes were turned up to the sky, his young mind questioning. Why all religions fight, when there was no God of one tribe but God of whole universe.

*

The letter came one week later, at the end of August.

As Lachlan read it, the clouds of his memory cleared and he wondered how he could have completely forgotten his friend?

The following day he was up at sunrise, dressed and preparing for a journey, leaving instructions with Bappoo, Marianne and George, and even running as far as David Reid's house to request him to keep an eye on his house and servants and his beloved Jane while he was away.

David Reid nodded his head and assured him that he could rely on it. `Rely on it most assuredly, dear boy.'

Reid watched him running away, in a devil of a hurry, and sighed and turned back indoors to his wife and said yet again that Macquarie's situation was no longer tragic, it was positively shocking!

When Lachlan returned to his own house he found George Jarvis eagerly waiting for him.

'Where we go?' George asked.

'Not we, George, just me. I am going alone.'

George's face fell, then his eyes narrowed suspiciously. 'Where you go?'

'Canton.'

*

Lestock Wilson was so shocked he had to flop into a chair

when Lachlan arrived alone at Canton and explained the reason for Jane's absence.

'But why—' Lestock made an effort to clear the lump in his throat. 'Why did you not send word to me?'

Lachlan shook his head vaguely. 'I didn't think. I haven't really been thinking straight at all.'

'Yes, yes, I can imagine.' Lestock rose to his feet and headed for a bottle of wine.

The two men sat for hours talking. Lestock looked at his friend, pitying him, but Lachlan spoke calmly, as if there was no real feeling in him, as if all that had happened had happened to somebody else.

'Stay here for a few weeks,' Lestock suggested. 'I'll not be sailing again until the spring. And you need not worry about having to put on a social face for visitors from the Canton English factory. Most of my friends here are Chinese. So we will allow no callers and you can rest and live just as you please.'

'Thank you, but I have not come to Canton for a holiday.' Lachlan suppressed a wincing smile. 'I have come for your advice on a way of getting out of China.'

Lestock shrugged. 'Most of the Chinese are polite, quiet and good people, you know. But they do have their superstitions which only another Chinese really understands.'

He poured more wine. 'Tomorrow I shall introduce you to a good friend of mine named Chinqua. A nice young man. Speaks fairly good English and is very clever, very smart. You will like him. He may be able to help us in finding a way around the superstitions of the sampan and junk sailors.'

'But will he be able to sort out the Chinese officials?'

'Ah, now, no. They are a very different kettle of

fornicating fish.'

'So what about a ship? We will need an English ship bound for Bengal or Bombay. It *has* to be an English ship. The French are our enemies. The Portuguese and Dutch can no longer be trusted. And the Chinese are forbidden under penalty of death to sail out of China.'

'The problem is a difficult one, I don't deny,' Lestock said with a worried frown on his face, standing up as a Chinese girl signalled to him that supper was ready. 'But all we can do,' he said, 'is take each day as it comes, and see what happens to drift into harbour.'

*

As they dined, Lestock slyly watched Lachlan's eyes to see if he noticed the exquisite beauty of the Chinese girl who served them, but as time moved on he realised that Lachlan had not noticed her at all.

There had been no more talk that night after supper, for Lachlan was very tired. He was still asleep the following morning when Lestock Wilson set out to find his friend Chinqua.

Lachlan awoke when a soft hand gently touched his cheek. He opened his eyes slowly and looked into the face of a girl, a beautiful Chinese girl with a flower in her long black hair, bending over him, with a soft smile on her lips.

'*Jo san,*' she said softly. '*Nei ho ma?*'

He sat up slowly, weary in body and spirit, and gave her a shadowed smile of apology. 'I don't speak Cantonese.'

'*Cha?*' she said, and handed him a small saucer and cup of steaming tea.

'Thank you,' he said, and when she continued to stand

and watch him, he looked into her face and said it again, 'Thank you.'

'*M goi*,' she said with a smile, and in a blink had glided out of the room.

By the time Lachlan had washed and dressed, Lestock Wilson had returned with his friend Chinqua.

Lachlan took an immediate liking to the strong-looking young Chinese man who came towards him with an easy athletic stride and wearing a genuine smile of friendship.

'*Jo san*,' Chinqua said in greeting, and then throwing up his hands in apology, spoke in English. 'Your friend, my friend,' he gestured to Lestock Wilson, 'he tell me of your sorrow. I know not how to help you, but I try.'

The three immediately sat down to discuss Lachlan's situation. They spent hours and then days discussing the various problems, but even Chinqua could find no obvious solution. In the end, he, too, was of the opinion that Lachlan must take each day patiently and wait to see if an English ship drifted in to Canton's harbour.

One month later Lachlan returned to Macao, no nearer to leaving China than before, for no ship at all had drifted into Canton's harbour.

*

The gentleman of the British factory came to see him, but still he resolutely refused to bury his wife in the neutral strip of unconsecrated ground and leave China without her.

And now, familiar with the obsessive determination that had sprung to life in Lachlan Macquarie's character, the British group gave up their argument and made no further protest.

Lachlan hired an interpreter. Day after day he approached the Chinese officials for permission to take his wife out of the country, but they had their laws and would not allow the slightest deviation from any of them.

Finally, due to his dogged persistence, they agreed to take further consultation and look into the matter, which resulted in many meetings and many questions from the mandarins who looked at him silently and without expression when he admitted that, Yes, he was a soldier, a British soldier. Yes, an officer, of the rank of major.

'But I am here as a civilian!' he insisted. 'Tell them!' He turned angry eyes on his interpreter. 'Tell them I am here as a civilian who wants to take his wife out of Macao and never come back!'

But as the meetings went on, he realised that all the Chinese officials were doing was tying him up even tighter in knots of red tape.

FOURTEEN

A month had passed since his return from Canton. Nothing had been achieved and nothing had changed, except his silent face now had a worn pallor and showed even deeper lines of strain. The Portuguese officials still scorned him, and the Chinese Mandarins continued to ignore him.

Every day was now a torture for him, and he could see that the long days imprisoned in this place, with no end in sight, was also becoming a torture for Bappoo and the two children.

In the first week of November, he returned from a desolate evening walk along the waterfront to find Bappoo waiting for him at the door of the house, telling him there was a visitor waiting to see him.

'A visitor?' Lachlan assumed it was one of the gentlemen from the English factory. He frowned at Bappoo. 'Which one?'

'He only say he from Canton. But, Sahib ...' Bappoo clutched his arm with a whisper of warning, 'He a Chin man'

Lachlan entered the house and stared in amazement at the young man who came towards him with that easy athletic stride of his.

'Chinqua!'

'May the Gods bear witness to the turn in tide of your fortune,' Chinqua said, smiling.

'Chinqua, oh, man, am I glad to see you!'

'Bearer of good news always welcome, heya?' Chinqua held out a letter addressed in Lestock Wilson's hand.

After the traditional greetings had been exchanged, and

while the traveller sat down to refreshment, Lachlan read the letter from Lestock Wilson.

It was brief and to the point: There was an English ship, the Sarah, bound for Bombay and leaving Canton on the 10th of the month. The Sarah was mastered by a Captain McIntosh, who on hearing of Lachlan's situation had readily offered a passage to himself and family, but in view of the restrictions of the Chinese government, Lachlan would have to find a way of meeting him at the mouth of the Pearl River and board the ship there.

Lachlan looked up from the letter and met Chinqua's calm gaze. 'Do you know what this says?'

Chinqua nodded. 'The winds of favour and fate have blown English ship into harbour.'

'But to get to the ship means a long journey up the Canton River, with my wife, my servants, my baggage – and not one sampan or junk willing to take us – not at any price!'

Chinqua calmly laid down his rice bowl and smiled. 'That is why Chinqua come to help you, heya?'

The following night, under cover of darkness, Lachlan and his precious coffin, his servants, and his baggage were being loaded into a spacious junk, followed by Chinqua who spoke in quiet but rapid Cantonese to the boatmen, urging them to be off.

Incredulously to Lachlan, other junk owners had come forward and offered to take them, but Chinqua had shaken his head in apology.

And now, as the lopsided junk made its silent passage up the dark reaches of the Pearl River, Lachlan could not believe the tide of fate had finally turned and he was truly getting out of China.

'Chinqua,' he said in quiet admiration, 'you're not just clever, you're a bally genius! How did you do it? Persuade the boatmen to take us so willingly?'

Chinqua smiled his calm smile and threw a glance at the junk-master who was standing astride the bowsprit with his back to them.

'In the beginning,' Chinqua confessed in a low voice, 'it was a problem to which I find no answer when starting my journey from Canton with the letter. But I find the answer in Macao itself, because Macao's true name is A-Ma-Gao, which means "Bay of A-Ma".'

Chinqua glanced at the junk-master, and then continued. 'Chinese legend say A-Ma was poor girl seeking to travel. Rich junk owners refused to take her because she cannot pay, but a fisherman, a poor but kind disciple of Buddha, he agree to take girl. And as soon as A-Ma steps in his boat, the winds of a storm blew and roared like a dragon. The storm wrecked all junks on river – except boat carrying A-Ma. When fisherman's boat reached land, the girl vanished like smoke before fisherman's eyes. The people then said A-Ma was a goddess of the sea and protector of all kind seafarers. They built A-Ma temple in her name, and land where she last seen is now called A-Ma-Gao... Macao.'

'But how did that help ...' Lachlan stared at him. 'Chinqua, you didn't ... you didn't infer that Jane may be a goddess?'

'She your goddess,' Chinqua said calmly. 'This journey up river speaks truth of it.'

Just in time Lachlan checked his startled objection. Chinqua had sought a way to help him, at no advantage to himself, and to repay Chinqua now with a stern rebuke would not only be impolite, it would be disgusting.

'I not say she goddess,' Chinqua explained. 'I speak only of A-Ma and how no junk or sampan would take her, and then I look up at the wind and contemplate in silence.'

Lachlan had to smile.

Chinqua motioned his head in the direction of the junk-master. 'Look at him,' he whispered with a smile. 'See how proud he stands, heya?'

Lachlan turned his gaze to the junk-master who indeed made a very proud figurehead in the moonlight as he stood astride the bowsprit, one hand on hip and head held high.

'When he return to Macao,' said Chinqua, 'he think all junks be wrecked by storm, but not his.'

Lachlan shook his head, and Chinqua grinned. 'No sorrow, no guilt, no need. Junk-master get good joss from Heaven in other way.'

They spoke a little more, then both settled into an easy silence as the lopsided vessel yawned up the dark river through the long night and Lachlan eventually laid his head down on one of the cushions and went into a deep sleep in which for once he did not dream.

When he eventually awoke it was to the bright yellow light of the morning sun, and the sight of the ship the Sarah, waiting for them at the outreaches of Canton's harbour.

'Oh, thank God!' Lachlan whispered.

'Ya Allah!' George Jarvis shouted, jumping up and punching his fist at the sky.

Marianne and Bappoo simply smiled in tired relief: the lopsided junk had been very uncomfortable and Bappoo was sure he would be listing to one side for days.

*

Two hours later, the Macquarie entourage were standing on the strong deck of the Sarah, waving farewell to the junk-master who had already turned back towards Macao, standing now at the stern and bowing to them deeply and graciously.

Then they all turned to look at Chinqua, who was grinning and waving from a small sampan that would take him home to Canton.

Lachlan gazed fondly at the noble-hearted young man who had taken the time to help the friend of a friend and would take no reward, simply because China was his land and its people were good if not always its government, and at the end of a day and a life, friendship was more valuable than gold.

FIFTEEN

India, at last.

As soon as the *Sarah* anchored in Bombay harbour it was surrounded by a number of small boats, one of which took a message ashore to John Forbes.

John Forbes, a practical man, immediately took charge of everything. He insisted that Lachlan stay for a while at his house where he could be in the company of friends, yet still have peace and privacy.

On the second morning after his arrival in Bombay, Lachlan faced the task of arranging the delivery of all the little toys and presents that Jane had bought in Macao for the children of their friends. Throughout the day ladies all over Bombay opened their door to the call of '*Kooee-hai!*' from George Jarvis, who handed over parcels with short notes, all of which more or less said the same: '*Some toys for little Anne and a Chinese fan for yourself – from Jane and Lachlan Macquarie.*'

The four-year-old son of Mrs Oakes received a boxful of toys. The wife of Jane's doctor, Mrs Kerr, received a breakfast set of china. Mrs Coggan, Mrs Scott – the deliveries of Jane's gifts went on. The poor girl had spent her time in Macao buying presents for them all, and now they couldn't even thank her.

Then, in the cool of the evening of the third day after their return, the funeral of Jane Macquarie finally took place.

The whole of British Bombay turned out to walk in the train of the sweet and amiable twenty-three year old girl who had been born in Antigua, married in India, and died in

China. Her coffin, covered in white jasmine, was solemnly pall-beared to Bombay Cemetery by six senior officers of the 77th Regiment.

John Forbes, the man who had first introduced the couple less than five years earlier, walked as chief mourner beside Lachlan who seemed to be moving within a dream. Despite all the people around him, he seemed so alone. His behaviour was impeccable, no outward signs of grief, but his responses were not quite in tune with life, slightly abstracted from what was happening around him, as if people were saying things to him that he couldn't quite hear.

But then, none of them yet knew of his experiences in China, or of the nightmare that began that summer dawn of the 15th July in Macao. And with the dawn of each new day since then, his life without Jane became harder to deal with, impossibly hard since his return to India.

China had been alien and hostile, but India was now a reflecting mirror for every memory of her. Wherever he looked, he saw only her absence. The long empty years of his future stretched before him like an arid and lonely wilderness.

To John Forbes, with whom he lived, it was the most dreadful study of grief after bereavement he had ever witnessed, and helplessly so, because Lachlan would not even allow himself to be consoled. He stood apart, walked alone, convinced there was no consolation, not for him. Without Jane he was emotionally dead, spiritually dead, and only the dead can comfort the dead.

He spent the days in solitude of lonely walks, or in the horse rides he took into the country. Often he rode out to their first home, their bridal home, and in his mind he saw her again in full health and youth, saw her face, her smiling eyes, heard her questioning and laughing voice. And in these times she became the light that banished the darkness in his life.

But it came only in flashes, and when his mind returned from that distant place where no one could reach him, to the desolate world in which he now lived, his memories only made his grief worse.

He tried to reason with himself. He had loved a girl and he had lost her. As simple as that. But there was a real and constant physical pain in the region of his heart that nothing could alleviate. In the rare times he slept his sleep was troubled, full of images and voices from the past.

It was easier not to sleep at all, nor to eat. He wanted nothing, asked for nothing, and longed to feel nothing. All he wanted was Jane back in the world and back in his life, but he knew that was as impossible as trying to tie a ribbon around the sun.

John Forbes became so worried he sought the private advice of Dr Kerr, who declared it all to be 'A tragedy,' and then demanded, 'Describe to me the symptoms of Major Macquarie's state of mind.'

Upon hearing the symptoms Dr Kerr shook his head and again declared it all to be 'A tragedy,' then insisted he visit the patient immediately.

'No, no!' John said swiftly. `He stays in my house because we are friends. He trusts me implicitly. I would hate him to know that I have been discussing him behind his back.'

'My dear Forbes, I get the impression he would not care if you stuck a knife in his back. The man *needs* the help of a doctor!'

'I know, I know,' said John with impatience, 'but he won't have one! So I thought, perhaps, some form of medicine that could be slipped in his tea?'

'You do realise that Macquarie is quite ill?'

John nodded sadly.

'Oh yes!' Dr Kerr said emphatically. 'I suspected it at the funeral. And now my diagnosis has been confirmed by a letter I received only last evening from Dr Duncan in Macao. Shocking. Quite shocking. Enough to make any man crack. Did you know that he had to smuggle his wife's coffin onto a junk in the dead of night and sail God knows how far up the Canton River in order to board a ship back to Bombay?'

'No, I did not know that.'

'And that was four months after his wife had died. *Four months!* And during all that time he refused to bury her, refused to return to India without her, refused to lay her down in unconsecrated ground. No, some kind of madness took possession of Macquarie in Macao, a madness that kept him going for those four months and the voyage back. But now that his purpose is accomplished, his life has collapsed. Has he spoken to you much about his sojourn in China?'

'He never speaks about China at all.'

'The problem is,' Dr Kerr looked bleak, 'there is so little a doctor can do in cases like this. This is something he must come through on his own. But as for medicinal healing, the only medicine we have for pain of any kind, is opium.'

'Well he won't take that!' John exclaimed. 'He's seen the terrible effects it's had on too many other soldiers. He has often said he would prefer to shoot himself and be done with it than degenerate into eventual death from opium.'

Dr Kerr assumed a tolerant expression, and said in the professional tones of a doctor: 'In the treatment of illness, in the deadening of pain, if used carefully, in measured and restricted doses, opium is the greatest narcotic discovery the world of medicine has known for centuries. It is the money-baggers that have abused it and earned it such a vile reputation! *Any* drug, taken habitually and in unrestricted dosage, becomes addictive and destructive.'

'He won't have it,' John said stubbornly. 'He won't have opium under any circumstances. And knowing how he feels about it, I could not, in all conscience, give it to him secretly in his drinks.'

'But he needs sleep, you say? And sleep is a great healer. How about laudanum? Would your conscience allow you to slip a few drops of laudanum in his drink at night in order to help him sleep?'

'Why, yes ... I had quite forgotten about laudanum. Nearly everyone I know has used that at some time or another in sickness.' John brightened. 'If it will help him to sleep I'd have no qualms about slipping him a few drops of laudanum.'

'Oh, good! So we *can* help our poor friend after all!' Dr Kerr exclaimed with relief, and then moved to his medicine cabinet, lifted down bottles and sighed wearily to himself as he made up a measure of laudanum, which was mainly opium prepared for use as a sedative.

Dr Kerr came back to John Forbes carrying two bottles. 'I am also giving you a tonic mixture to encourage his appetite. Slip it in his drink in the morning. I suggest very strong tea. This small bottle is the laudanum. Five drops at night. I suggest a glass of the richest wine or even a small glass of brandy. No more than four or five nights, mind you. Then every second night until the bottle is empty. The supply I have given you is a restricted dose.'

*

Unbeknown to Lachlan, he began to take Dr Kerr's medicine every morning. He even unwittingly took the laudanum in a glass of wine each night and began to sleep long and deeply. And as the days passed, his physical recovery began.

He was even beginning to smile naturally, and converse with friends again. Finally he decided he was well enough to face the world. He insisted he had imposed too long on John's hospitality and wanted to leave.

John would not allow him to leave. 'Not yet, not until we have sorted out what you are going to do with your life now and in the future.'

'The man is a soldier!' General Balfour said to John Forbes. 'The sooner he gets back into uniform and back to soldiering, the sooner he will be fit again. Macquarie loves the Army. Always has done. Meat and drink to the man.'

Balfour looked down at a paper on his desk. 'Now then, after eight years of continuous service in India, he was given a years leave. There is still a month or so of that left, but I think we should get him back to work as soon as possible. I'll give him just a couple more days, then I'll have him recalled.'

On the day Lachlan received the order to return to his duties at Headquarters, he also received a visit from a man named Mr Phineas Hall, a lawyer.

'Major Macquarie?' said Mr Hall as he held out his hand. 'I was most distressed to hear of your wife's death. A most charming girl.

'You knew her?' Lachlan looked at John Forbes then stared again at the lawyer. 'You met Jane? When?'

'Oh, not long after you were married, when she came to me to draw up her Will. It seems there was some dispute about money between you and her family.'

'She made a Will?' Again Lachlan looked at John Forbes, but John clearly was as surprised as Lachlan.

Mr Hall accepted the chair offered and sat down behind John Forbes's desk, then laid a leather folder on top from which he drew out a sheaf of documents. 'The Will is quite short,' he said, 'so I shall take up as little of your time as possible.' He put on his spectacles, lifted a document, and began to read:

'I, Jane Jarvis Macquarie, being in sound health of mind and body...'

When he had finished reading, Mr Hall looked up and peered over his spectacles at Lachlan who had gone white around the lips. 'It is a very short Will,' Mr Hall said. 'Quite the shortest I have ever drawn.'

It was indeed a short Will, in which Jane had bequeathed to Lachlan Macquarie, her lawful husband, and his heirs for ever, the sum of her fortune held in English funds and in Antigua, should she predecease him.

Mr Hall turned a page and looked at Lachlan.

Lachlan looked back at him with tear-dimmed eyes. The money! He had forgotten all about Jane's money. And what damned bloody use was it now? The one person who should have benefited from Jane's money, was Jane.

'There is a codicil,' said Mr Hall, 'in which she requests that should she predecease her husband, she trusts him to expend every effort and as much money as is necessary to buy the bond and freedom of her Negro Mammy, Dinah, in Antigua. She also expresses a wish that five other named slaves in Antigua be bought their freedom.'

Mr Hall looked up. 'The codicil, however, is signed but not witnessed, and therefore not legal. So you are not bound to adhere to it. Other than that...' Mr Hall smiled, 'you are now quite a wealthy man.'

'Her brother in Antigua ... her trustees...'

'Have all been dealt with,' Mr Hall assured him. 'I made very sure of that before coming to see you. Mr Thomas Jarvis relinquished charge of his sister's money, which became hers by legal right on her twenty-first birthday. Now the entire sum, and all the interest accruing therefrom, is safely lodged in your name at the bank of Messrs Francis and Gosling in London, and you may draw the entire sum if you wish, whenever you wish, without the prior *consent* of any second party.'

Mr Hall reached for his leather folder. 'In accordance with your late wife's wishes, and by legal right, her money is now yours.'

*

Money was also the subject of a discussion in a house far away in a small and rainy country miles across the sea.

James Morley, who was still in London, was sitting by the fire in the drawing room of his house at 27 Wimpole Street, angrily shaking out the pages of his newspaper and complaining biliously. 'Now we'll see if I was right or wrong! Now we will see all the spending! Damn me if Macquarie don't go through the lot in a year – just like that blackguard Woodward!'

'Oh, *really*, James!' Maria said wearily, almost at the end of her patience as she clutched a copy of Daniel Defoe's *Robinson Crusoe*, endeavouring to keep a firm grip on the book and herself. 'Lachlan Macquarie is not in the least like Woodward. Not in the least!'

'You wouldn't think so, would you? Because he gulled you with his charm just as he did your poor sister.' Morley unstoppered a decanter of brandy at his side. 'Well, Macquarie should be happy now. He's finally got what he married her for – her money.'

Maria's temper finally snapped. 'I'm just about *sick* of all this petty viciousness about Lachlan,' she cried savagely. 'If you just knew, James, if you just *knew*...'

She stopped her mouth in time, for James knew nothing of the letter she had received from Lachlan, a very long letter that spoke of nothing else but Jane. And with the letter he had forwarded the assortment of lovely presents Jane had bought for her in Macao, the presents that James could not be told about, because they were bought with the money of Lachlan Macquarie, the nobody from nowhere whom James had grown comfortably accustomed to hating and maligning.

Suddenly, a great weariness overcame Maria. Her heart still grieved for Jane and in Lachlan's letter she had found solace, and gratitude, because his letter had contained a detailed account of everything he believed Maria would want to know.

She had immediately written back to him, a long letter full of tenderness and consolation, ending with a plea for him to maintain a regular correspondence with her. And Maria now knew, without a shadow of doubt, that Lachlan had truly loved Jane. And having to listen to James's constant sniping was becoming unbearable. She looked across at her stubborn and irascible husband.

'Oh, James,' she said, 'if only you knew...'

'I know this, my dear ...' There was a pause as brandy gurgled down James's throat. 'Now Macquarie has finally got his hands on Jane's money, there will be no stopping him. He'll spend it faster than the Prince of Wales.'

'Truly, James, I sometimes think Jane was right about you. On occasions you can be a very *stupid* man!'

James lowered his newspaper and gaped at her.

'Has it never occurred to you,' Maria asked, 'that you might be terribly, terribly wrong?'

'*Wrong*?' James's voice came out much too high. Never before had Maria dared to criticise or answer him rudely. Never before today. And now she was making a habit of it!

'And what, may I ask, might I be terribly, terribly *wrong* about?'

'About Lachlan Macquarie. *Wrong*, James, about him and Jane's money.'

'Oh, no!' James was having none of that silly nonsense. 'Oh, no! Whatever else I might or might not be wrong about, Madam, I am not wrong about Lachlan Macquarie!'

In the pettishness of his anger, James had spilled his brandy. He pulled a handkerchief from his pocket and mopped furiously at the stains on his waistcoat. 'Now look what you've made me do!' he accused. 'If you hadn't been so bally awkward about your precious brother-in-law, I wouldn't have been reduced to shaking with anger and spilling my brandy!' He threw the wet handkerchief onto the floor like a spoiled child, and then lifted the glass to his lips, where it paused.

'Stupid, am I? Is that what Jane said? Well, we all know where she got that opinion from, don't we? If Lachlan Macquarie said red was green Jane would agree as if God had spoken. Don't interrupt! You seem to forget that I have friends on the board of the banking house of Messrs Francis and Gosling. And I'll wager that before six months is out,

Messrs Francis and Gosling will be receiving drawings on that money that will leave them staggering!'

SIXTEEN

On Sunday evening John Forbes was sitting in the garden reading a book of Persian poetry, occasionally looking up to gaze at the sunset, when Lachlan appeared and sat down on the bench beside him, his face thoughtful.

`I 've been thinking,' he said quietly.

John smiled. 'You've been doing little else since the day the lawyer left.'

'About Jane's money, yes,'

'It is *your* money now. So what are you going to do with it? Leave it in London with Francis and Gosling? Or have it transferred over here?'

'Into your bank?'

'Of course into our bank.'

'Well I do have a lot of my own money deposited in your bank already, but I'm going to need a lot more than that now, and as soon as possible. If we were to make arrangements immediately for part of the money in London to be sent over to your bank, could you advance me as much as I may need now, even before the London money arrives? At your standard rate of interest, of course.'

'My goodness ...' John looked astonished, `*more* than the amount already deposited with us? What on earth do you intend to spend it on?'

'Quite a few things, but I wish to get it all done quickly, before I return to active service.'

'If time is short,' John closed his book, 'we can see to the documentation for the transfer tonight if you wish.'

'And I will need quite a few bank drafts.'

'Very well.' John stood to turn indoors. 'We shall work on them together. Have you drawn up a list?'

'Yes.'

'Then I shall draw up the bank drafts tonight and have them authorised tomorrow.'

*

The first gift of money was sent to Mammy Dinah in Antigua, together with the beautiful silk shawl Jane had chosen for her in Macao. In the same post he also sent a letter to Thomas Jarvis, requesting to buy Dinah's freedom, for which he was prepared to pay any price.

The second bank draft went to Jane's impoverished sister in England, Rachel Woodward, together with a trust deed that would see Rachel generously provided for over a period of ten years.

Individual amounts of money were also sent to various cousins on the island of Mull, for the purpose of educating their daughters as well as their sons. An annual allowance was settled on his mother and brother Donald for life. The lease and rent of the farm at Oskamull would remain his responsibility. A one-off payment was sent to his Uncle Murdoch, but it was his mother and Donald that concerned Lachlan the most.

In the accompanying letter he urged Murdoch to command his mother to abstain from all laborious work and to attend more to her own ease and comfort. The money he had settled on her would relieve her of all financial worries, so she should now consider employing at least one servant to help her in the house, and at least one male servant to help Donald with any heavy work on the farm.

When the letter to Murdoch was finished, he sat for a long moment staring in front of him with a thoughtful frown. His concern about his own mother had caused him to remember something Jane had once said to him in a worried voice about Mammy Dinah. *'She's becoming a little infirm now, her knees are very stiff, yet she has to work from morning till night.'*

He abruptly lifted the pen and began writing another letter to Thomas Jarvis, reminding him of Dinah's advancing age, and urging him, *'in all humanity and compassion,'* to grant Dinah her freedom, *'to allow the poor woman to spend her final years in some degree of ease and retirement.'*

*

To Lachlan's surprise, and in a shorter time than he had expected, he received a reply from the lawyers of Thomas Jarvis in Antigua.

Dinah's freedom, and that of the five other named slaves in Antigua, was formally and legally granted. Sums of money were then sent to the lawyers for all six, enough to allow them to buy their own homes and become financially independent, without the need to recourse to 'unpaid slave labour' with anyone on the island again.

Finally, Lachlan turned his attention to Jane's little Indian maid, Marianne. He was at a loss to know what to do with her. Marianne was now almost fifteen, an age when most Indian girls were married and preparing for motherhood.

Since returning to his duties at Headquarters he had leased a house on the Ramparts in Bombay, in which he now lived with Marianne, George Jarvis, Bappoo and a few other household servants. Only one person was missing from his usual happy household, and without her, Marianne had no role to play.

What was he to do with Marianne?

As Lachlan studied Marianne, he noticed for the first time that she was very pretty, with that small oval face so popular in India. Indeed, everything about her was small and delicate and dainty. He watched her move gracefully around the house and garden, dressed in her colourful saris with a billowing gauze veil hanging from her head. She was, he realised, the perfect picture of India's idea of beauty. And let loose in the world she would be swiftly snatched up by a Maharaja or European as a concubine.

What should he do with Marianne? She had no family, having been abandoned long ago by her starving mother who had sold her for the price of a bowl of rice. But that was India, the darker side of India, where if the yearly crop failed and famine set in, the people were driven by starvation to seaports like Cochin or Bombay where a mother could sell her daughter into slavery for the price of a bowl of rice, and a father could sell his wife and all his children for fifty rupees.

Marianne had been sold at the age of four. Since then she had been sold numerous times as a servant to various families, the British residents of Bombay being liable to move on every few years.

Marianne's last household had been that of the Morleys, but Maria Morley had asked no price when she passed the girl on. She had simply given Marianne to Jane as a wedding gift.

He had two options, the first of which might appeal to

244

Marianne herself. Firstly, he could try and arrange for her to be married to some respectable and personable Indian male, for which he would supply the bride dowry.

But then, he realised, no respectable Indian male would agree to marry a Hindu girl who lived out of her caste and had spent most of her life as an *Angrezi* slave. She would be considered unclean, unworthy, fit only for work as a servant or a concubine, but never a wife.

And somehow, as he thought about it even longer, he had an uneasy feeling that bestowing Marianne with a dowry in order to secure a speedy marriage to an Indian of the lower castes was not what Jane would have wanted.

A second option remained. He could arrange for Marianne to go into service with yet another British military household, or the household of a British nabob of the East India Company.

No – not with a nabob! So many of them had their own little *zenana* quarter of concubines hidden away somewhere at the back of the house, under the guise of `servants' quarters. And poor little Marianne – just the thought of some fat, over-curried nabob touching the child filled him with revulsion. And she *was* just a child. He knew he would never forgive himself if she were unwittingly placed into bad hands or with anyone that would use her ill.

Finally, he decided to discuss the situation with Marianne herself.

She came into the room in answer to his summons and greeted him with the familiar salaam of `Namaste,' palm joined to palm.

He bade her to sit down.

In one graceful movement she dropped into a lotus posture on the carpet. She wore a peacock-blue silk tunic over fitted pyjamas crinkled at the ankles. Her flimsy veil slipped from her head and slid down to settle around her shoulders, but she made no move to return it to its former position. Her dark eyes were riveted to his face.

He started by speaking to her casually, conversationally, but she was shy with him and smiled demurely without answering, her small rosebud mouth pursed coyly like two crimson petals.

He persisted speaking casually, because he knew her so well, knew all her little ways. He talked to her about Britain, knowing how much she loved hearing about *Belait*. He poured himself a glass of brandy and listened to her giggling as he told her about the Grand Gala Balls in London where men in white stockings and ladies in enormous gowns danced in couples all night long. She shook her head in laughter and refused to believe it.

Why dance themselves and not pay others to do it for them, she wanted to know. In Hind, no people of any worth or consequence danced themselves. If dancing was needed for entertainment, then dancing girls were hired to do it! She found it very amusing that the people of *Belait* had servants to do their cooking and cleaning and serving, but when it came to the evening entertainment, they had to do all the dancing themselves!

'*Kyo?*'

He confessed he didn't know why.

She thought it hilariously funny, and presently she was laughing and chattering. He then brought the conversation back to India, and asked her what would *she* like to do now? There was no longer a mistress in his house for her to serve. Would she like to go to another English lady? Would she like to be married to a young Indian male? Whatever *she* wanted, he assured her, is what he would try to arrange for her.

Marianne said nothing. Lachlan watched her dark eyes widen until they looked huge in her small face.

'Well?' he asked.

She bowed her head and sat very still. The length of the silence became oppressive. He had to repeat the question. 'What would you like to do?'

Slowly her head lifted and her dark satin eyes regarded him nervously. 'I like to go to English school,' she whispered.

Astonished, he stared at her. 'You want to go to England?'

'No, no, stay in Hindustan, but go to English school.'

'The English school in Bombay?'

'She nodded tensely.

He sat looking at her. My God – it was the best solution of all!

'Yes,' he said slowly. 'Yes, I think Jane would like that.'

'I think too,' Marianne whispered.

The days that followed found him arranging for Marianne to be boarded at the English school in Bombay and educated and cared for at his expense.

Two weeks later Marianne was all packed and ready to leave. She could not, of course, be housed in that part of the school reserved for the daughters of Europeans, but in a wing that housed the half-caste daughters of soldiers and officials who had married Indian women, and were termed under the category of 'mixed blood.'

Now the time for departure had come, Marianne looked nervous and apprehensive. Lachlan assured her that he would keep in constant touch with her. She must write to him often, in Hindi at first, but then, hopefully, in perfect

English. He had also arranged with her schoolmistress that he be sent correspondence every week to inform him of her progress and welfare.

Then, finally, he handed her an important-looking legal document that was sealed with red wax. In his other hand he held an identical document.

'This one I will give to your schoolmistress, Marianne, but the other you must keep safely yourself. Both are documents which confirm that you are perfectly free, and nobody's servant or slave.'

Her lips quivered, she attempted to control them, bowing her head and keeping it bowed.

'But as a free person,' he said, 'you are required by law to have more than one name. So I have given you the name of Marianne Jarvis. Is that acceptable to you?'

'Yes, my father,' Marianne whispered. Her head stayed bowed as she knelt down and went to the trouble of unstrapping her box and unpacking all the clothes she had so carefully packed, removing each item one by one until she could hide the document at the very bottom, as if it was some valuable treasure.

George Jarvis, who stood watching her return the clothes to the box, fully understood why Marianne had handled the document as if it was priceless. It was, after all, a certificate from her employer and guardian – the Major-Sahib Macquarie of the British Army and British Raj – and who in all Hind would *dare* to harm her on seeing that!

But George himself was feeling very frightened, his eyes over-bright and nervous. He realised that Marianne was speaking shyly to him, saying she was sorry they all must part now, so sorry.

'I too,' George whispered. 'I sorry we all part, too.'

Under normal circumstances, a Hindu girl would never mix freely with a Muslim boy, but Marianne had never lived the life of a true Hindu. From too early an age she had grown up with the *Angrezi*. Nearly all her life had been spent with the Mems in their houses, and George now spent all his time with the Sahibs of the Army. Neither truly fitted into any race anymore. Both had been sold as slaves, and both would still be slaves, if it were not for the kindness of Lachlan-Sahib whom they both loved and whom they referred to as 'Father' in the respectful tradition of reverence as used in the East, and not the paternal tradition of the West.

'Shall we go? Don't forget to say goodbye to Bappoo.' Lachlan walked over to the waiting Tonga while Marianne moved to stand before Bappoo with hands joined in a salaam and whispering a shaky farewell.

Bappoo sighed, smiled, sighed again, and wiped a big hand over his face as if he too felt sad at saying farewell to the little Hindu girl. Then, with a sudden smile he broke all traditions and patted Marianne affectionately on the cheek.

'*Khudaa haafiz,*' he said tenderly. God protect you.

Lachlan sat beside Marianne in the Tonga. As it drove away her eyes filled with tears and she turned back, waving tearfully to George and Bappoo.

George Jarvis stood with hand raised, feeling sick with terror. He knew it was his turn next to be either sold off, or sent away.

But George's turn never came. As the days passed into weeks and then months his constant presence at the side of Major Macquarie seemed to be taken for granted.

And two years later, in 1801, when the British Prime Minister decided that the French must now be driven out of

249

Egypt in order to protect the British possessions in India, Lachlan and the 77th Regiment sailed out Bombay, destined for the Port of Suez, and George Jarvis went with them.

SEVENTEEN

After an absence of fifteen months, and after scoring a triumphant victory against the French Army at Alexandria, a huge welcoming crowd gathered at Bombay harbour as the British troop ships returned from Egypt.

Disembarking with George Jarvis into a masoolah boat which cruised swiftly towards the dockside, Lachlan saw a number of friendly faces waiting to greet him: John Forbes, Colin Anderson – and there also was the huge bulk of Corporal McKenzie, furiously shouting to the jostling crowds of coolies, ordering them to stand back.

'Stand back, ye bastards, stand back!'

From his seat in the masoolah boat, Lachlan found himself eyeing McKenzie with suspicion, thinking to himself sarcastically, 'Well, his voice is still loud enough,'

McKenzie – upon hearing of the Egypt campaign – had immediately suffered a heart attack, and had been declared unfit for the gruelling march of the desert, escaping orders to prepare for battle, on the grounds of ill health.

Lachlan had doubted the veracity of McKenzie's heart-attack, certain that the big Jock was faking it all the way, but he had let it go, deciding that McKenzie would be more of a hindrance than a help out in the desert. His complaints alone would be enough to kill any officer unfortunate enough to be in charge of him.

As soon as the boat reached the shore McKenzie was the first to reach down and give Lachlan a hefty hand ashore.

'Welcome back, sir, steady on yer feet now, safe and sound on dry land again. Every day I was fearful for ye in that desert, sir, certain ye might suffer the death o' sunstroke.'

Lachlan looked at him wryly. 'Still, I see *you* have recovered fine and well, McKenzie. In fact, I don't think I have ever seen you looking so hale and *hearty.*'

McKenzie, suddenly remembering his heart attack, knew what the major was hinting, and immediately changed his demeanour.

'Och, no, sir, it's just me puttin' on a brave face to welcome ye back,' he said wearily. 'I'm not fet for much, as ye can surely see. The truth is, sir, I'm a done man.'

Lachlan might have said more if Colin Anderson had not touched him on the shoulder then, and from there on he was greeted with handshake after handshake from his fellow officers.

'*Bappoo! Bappoo! Assalaam alaikum!*' George Jarvis shouted excitedly, breaking into a run, pushing through the crowds until he reached Bappoo who hugged him like a young brother home from the war.

'*George Jarvees!*' Bappoo, in his voluminous pantaloons and a new green turban, jiggled and laughed like an hysterical child. '*Vaalaikum salaam!*'

Still laughing, they pulled back and stared at each other for signs of change, but only George had changed; he was at least three inches taller, and now that he was almost seventeen, he was showing signs of approaching manhood.

'*Aappaa kyaa haal hai?*' Bappoo asked eagerly.

'*Shukriiyaa, mai Thiik hui.*' George shrugged nonchalantly. He was well, fine, excellent, he assured Bappoo.

The crowds of soldiers and coolies on the docks began to thin, baggage was carried off, and officers subsided into palanquins or tongas and were jogged away in the direction of the fort.

Lachlan and his entourage ended up at John Forbes's house where an extravagant dinner was served. The talk centred on Egypt and the French, and finally the recent Treaty between Britain and France.

When dinner was over, and while conversation buzzed, General Balfour slipped Lachlan a military dispatch. 'I could have waited and given this to you tomorrow, dear boy, but I wanted you to have it as soon as possible.'

Curiously, Lachlan unfolded and read the letter which was from London, from Colonel Brownrigg, informing him that His Majesty was graciously pleased to appoint him to the rank of Lieutenant-Colonel.

Balfour was at his happiest, as he always was when something good happened to one of his own. 'Well done, dear boy,' he said, blue eyes crinkling, enjoying Macquarie's surprise. 'Good news, eh what?'

Lachlan smiled. 'Very good news.'

'Splendid! This calls for more claret I think. More claret, Gupta!' Balfour called gaily to the *khidmatgar* by the table. He called all the Indian servants Gupta if he didn't know their name, but he was ever courteous. 'More wine, Gupta, if you please.'

*

In the servants' quarters at the back of the house, Bappoo was sitting cross-legged on the floor, opposite George Jarvis. George had finished eating but Bappoo was still tucking into a huge dish of spicy meatballs and yellow rice.

Throughout the meal Bappoo had listened silently to

everything George Jarvis had told him about Egypt, occasionally nodding his head in understanding as he ate his food without pause and with relish.

At last, Bappoo paused in his eating, took a long drink of sherbet, smacked his lips, then looked keenly at George Jarvis and asked the most important question of all – the only thing he wanted to know about Egypt.

'*Khaanaa kaisaa lagaa?*'

George sighed, and told Bappoo that the food was not good at all. And even when it was almost good, it was nowhere near as good as the food in India. *Cus-cus* was all the Arabs seemed to eat. Bowls of *cus-cus* – a grain that was tasteless and not spicy like pilau rice.

Bappoo was smiling, no longer envious. 'Oh well,' he said happily, reaching for more rice, 'it was written then, by a kind God, that I not chosen to go to Egypt and left here to take care of Lachlan-Sahib's house.'

George assured Bappoo that if he *had* been chosen to go to Egypt he would surely have died during the Army's ten-day march across the burning desert.

'From Suez we were forced to march for ten days across the desert to the Nile,' George explained. 'For ten days, Bappoo, all that was required of us was to suffer. Such barrenness! Such solitude! All of us so tired, staring at a scenery that never changed.'

'Bad, bad ...' Bappoo kept eating.

'A flat open plain without one palm tree for shade from the sun,' George continued, 'and no living creatures – not even a lizard or a serpent – the usual creatures of the desert, not one did we see. Even the birds hated that desert, Bappoo, in all ten days of the long march, no bird did we see flying above. Not even a *vulture*.'

'Good! No vultures! Vultures are bad birds,' Bappoo said carelessly, not totally believing George's dramatic tale.

George knew what Bappoo was thinking, but every word he had said was true. After marching forty miles from Suez and then twenty miles into the basin of the desert, all their water had gone, and not a sign of a well. No water to drink, and no water to cook the rice.

And the *heat!*

Even the suffocating heat of India in the hot season could never compare to the blinding dry heat of the silent desert. But the torture of the heat was nothing to the craving thirst, a gravelly thirst so painful some of the soldiers began to cry just to lick their own tears.

There was even a time when George thought he might die from the thirst, until he remembered an old Arab trick taught to him in his childhood by his mother from Morocco – to carry a small stone in the mouth to keep the tongue moist when thirst was bad. Quickly he had searched for a stone, and found one, and passed the trick on. Within hours every soldier was searching for his stone, and even if it did not quench the thirst, it greatly helped to ease the mouth from dryness.

Two days later they had found the first of only two wells on that hundred-mile passage across the Egyptian desert; but by then, the desert had claimed three dead soldiers from the 77th.

'For two long days, Bappoo,' George said in all truth, 'I have no water, no food. For two days all I have in my mouth is a small stone to suck.'

'A *stone!*' Bappoo stared at George in horror, and then slowly his face moved into a disbelieving smile.

'*Chut!*' said Bappoo, and threw back his head and roared

with laughter, delighted with life and even more delighted with George Jarvis who, in the past, had tried to convince him that he was *not* a rascally son of slave, but the son of a prince and a descendant of kings! And even now George was *still* making up his funny and fanciful tales.

'*Accha!*' Bappoo reached across to slap George's shoulder in laughing praise. 'Very good!'

*

It was dark when Lachlan returned to his own house. He found a packet of letters from England awaiting him. He left them where they lay, too tired to read them now; plenty of time tomorrow to find out what was happening in the world outside the East.

As always, he awoke before daybreak. The *chik* sunblind had been raised and the air was still cool from the night. He got out of bed and pulled on a robe. The rest of the house was still sleeping. He collected his letters, found himself a glass of mango juice, then returned to his room and propped himself against the pillows to read his letters.

The first was from Lestock Wilson, bearing an unusual address, *Jerusalem Cafe, London*, and was seven months out of date. He read the letter with pleasure, smiling as he turned the pages.

The second letter was from Maria Morley. He read it with interest. She had written him ten letters in all, and in each her expressions of affection for him grew less inhibited. 'My dear, *dear* Lachlan.' She longed to see India again.

Finally, he opened the last letter of the batch. This one was from Scotland, from his Uncle Murdoch. His breath expulsed sharply as he read it – his brother Donald had died

– a short illness, a quiet and peaceful death.

The Chinese clock on the sidetable ticked noisily in the silence. Poor Donald ... all his years of waiting and watching the hill for his brother's return had been in vain.

Lachlan's sorrow welled around a sharp stab of guilt. His preoccupation with Jane over the years had relegated Donald to that distant part of his life which no longer existed. He felt sorry, painfully sorry, that he had neglected to care for his quiet and forlorn brother beyond the assistance of money. His sorrow swiftly changed to anger – anger at himself. But it was too late, much too late, to try and make amends now.

He moved off the bed and sat in the cane armchair by the window, staring at the sky already bereft of stars in the silver dawn. Soon he saw the first far-off glimmer in the eastern sky, watched the pale rays rise higher and become stronger until the morning sun swept over the trees and streamed through the window.

There was a jingle of crockery at the door.

'*Chota hazri*, Huzoor,' Bappoo said cheerfully behind him, laying down the morning tray of tea and fruit. 'I leave here on table by bed.'

After a pause, Bappoo exclaimed in a bright chatty mood. 'Oh yes, good show, you read now all letters from your Blighty. Now you happy! Yes? No?'

Lachlan did not stir nor answer. He was engrossed in thoughts of home ... his home in the West.

PART TWO

SCOTLAND

And not by eastern windows only,
When daylight comes, comes in the light,
In front, the sun climbs slow, how slowly,
But westward , look, the land is bright!

EIGHTEEN

In the west of Scotland, on the island of Mull, the Laird of Lochbuy was becoming much too passionately engrossed in his daily shoots of the black grouse and tawny hare – when he was not deer-hunting – to have much time left for riding from Lochbuy over to the farm of his elder sister at Oskamull to read to her the letters that came with affectionate regularity from her son in India.

Murdoch knew he owed a huge debt to Lachlan, who had come to his rescue two years earlier when Murdoch found himself facing bankruptcy and the moneylenders were preparing to move in and seize his estate lands.

Lachlan had immediately responded to his plea for help by sending a bank draft from India for the enormous sum of ten thousand pounds, rendering Murdoch solvent again, with money in the bank, and all the loans paid off. And Lachlan, too, was now also a landowner, having bought ten thousand acres of land and estates in Mull from the Duke of Argyll.

Murdoch knew he also had a duty to his ageing sister who depended on him to ride over upon immediate receipt of the letters from India, but the old girl did gang on at times, insisting he read the letters over and over, and always resulting in the same lament:

'I mustna be angry with him for staying away so long, must I, Murdoch? He's a good son, aye. But, Murdoch – ' she would wail in the end, `poor Donald never did, but I must, oh! I must see Lachlan again before I die.'

And there was little chance of that! As far as Murdoch

could see, Lachlan Macquarie had no intention of ever leaving India.

And so, while the black cocks were strutting and the hares were running, the Laird of Lochbuy was greatly relieved when his wife's younger sister, Elizabeth Campbell, who was staying with them at Lochbuy House, very kindly offered to take the letters from India over to Oskamull and read them to Mrs Macquarie.

Nevertheless, as pleased as he was, Murdoch was visibly shocked when Elizabeth insisted on doing the journey by sea, around the island, with only the boat's crew for company.

'Murdoch, you know well that I'll come to no harm with Ivor and Jamie,' Elizabeth laughed as the boat rowed away.

Murdoch gave a long sigh before glancing sideways at his wife. 'Maggie,' he said, in the tone he always used when voicing his reservations about her youngest sister, 'I know I should not say this, Maggie, but betimes yon Elizabeth attacks life with an almost masculine vitality that's indecent. Aye, indecent. It's a large vice for a female to be too independent. What makes her so? Would it be a fault in her upbringing, do ye think? All that schooling?'

Margaret opened her lips to protest in her sister's defence, but before she could say a word Murdoch continued, 'Elizabeth should never have been allowed to go to school in England. Big mistake! Edinburgh would have turned her out far better.'

*

Elizabeth had her own reasons for wanting to make the journey to Oskamull. Now twenty-four years of age, she had never forgotten the young man who had been her first love, her only heartbreak. And when she ventured out to the farmhouse at Oskamull to read his letter to his mother, it was the same young man she saw in her mind, as if he had not aged a day in the years that had passed.

Having arrived at Oskamull, Elizabeth's eyes moved round the parlour of the farmhouse, surprised at its lack of grandeur when Mrs Macquarie's son was reputed to be a rich man now with ten thousand acres of land and estates on Mull – yet here was his mother without even one servant in her house.

Elizabeth's eyes went to the comfortable though antiquated furnishings, surprised at the spotlessness of everything, the wood on tables and cupboards sparkling with polish; not a sign of clutter or dust anywhere, and yet the old lady did all the cleaning herself.

Mrs Macquarie was making her own covert inspection of the girl, noting her natural open-air type of beauty and her lovely copper-gold hair, wondering why Elizabeth had offered to perform this service. The Campbells of Airds were relatives of course, but very distantly so, apart from Margaret Campbell who had married Murdoch years ago and since then had given him nine children.

But then, Mrs Macquarie thought, Margaret Campbell Maclaine was a simple and homely type of lassie who adored children, but was barely educated, whereas her younger sister, Elizabeth, was a young lady of refinement who had been educated and finished at a school in Hammersmith in England. A young lady who must surely have better things to do than travel the long journey from Lochbuy to Oskamull just to sit and read letters to an old woman.

Bereft of a servant, simply because she had always

refused to have one, Mrs Macquarie prepared the tea herself.

Elizabeth immediately offered to help her.

As they moved around each other they began to converse. Mrs Macquarie discovered that Elizabeth possessed a down-to-earth unfussy personality, which she liked. Before long a warm and genuine rapport developed between the two women.

They talked of each other's families.

'Aye,' Mrs Macquarie answered Elizabeth, 'My dear husband died from pluerotic fever, due I think, from all his early mornings out fishing in all weathers, and then working as a kelper over on Ulva. He loved that island, aye, truly loved it. And so he is now buried there. She nodded towards the window. 'From that window ye can gaze straight across the water to Ulva.'

Elizabeth spoke of her own family, of her father, Sir John Campbell, who had died and left the estate at Airds, encumbered by debts, to her brother John, in whose house and under whose care she still lived.

'But now that John is married,' Elizabeth said, 'I don't feel quite at home at Airds as I used to do.'

'Aye, ye were the lady of the house after your father died, I suppose,' said Mrs Macquarie. 'But when another woman moves in as mistress of the home you were born and reared in, it takes some getting used to.'

Mrs Macquarie opened a drawer in the dresser and took out a plain but snow-white tablecloth that she spread over the table. 'Is that why ye spend so much time with your sister at Lochbuy?' she asked Elizabeth.

'Perhaps. But even at Lochbuy,' Elizabeth admitted, 'I sometimes feel like the spare spinster sister.'

Mrs Macquarie looked at her, puzzling as to why such a nice-looking young woman should still be unmarried.

The kettle was steaming. Elizabeth bent and swung it aside, and then added another peat brick to the fire. 'What I would really like to do,' she said, 'is find some useful employment.'

'What? Employment?' Mrs Macquarie stared at her with eyes horrified. 'Oh, I doona think that would be a good thing at all!' she blurted. 'A gentle-bred young lady like ye! Oh no, Elizabeth! And I doona think your brother at Airds would ever allow ye to work on a farm?'

'Work on a farm?' Elizabeth laughed. 'I wouldn't know how.'

'Ye were only jesting me then?' Mrs Macquarie looked relieved. 'Aye well, I'm verra glad you feel ye can jest with me, Elizabeth. I take it as a compliment.' She nodded her head and smiled.

Elizabeth had not been joking, she had been considering the idea of becoming a teacher, but she let the matter drop when Mrs Macquarie said eagerly, 'But now, Elizabeth, ye've had such a journey ye'll surely be glad to get some food inside ye. Come sit ye down, and I'll let ye be the one to send up a prayer before we eat.'

Elizabeth knew that poor Mrs Macquarie was bursting to know what was in her son's letter, but this pleasure she would not allow herself until Elizabeth's welcome, after her journey, had been attended to with true Highland hospitality.

They sat down to a tea of a small chicken and fresh vegetables in a thick tasty broth, followed by fresh bannocks and oatcakes kept hot by the hob, all delicious, and all made by Mrs Macquarie's own hand.

Then, with a lovely fire glowing, the two women moved to the hearth and Elizabeth opened the letter from India.

Mrs Macquarie listened intently and without interruption as Elizabeth read aloud to her.

When Elizabeth had finished reading, Mrs Macquarie sat with her brow furrowed as she ruminated on her son's words. 'He seems cheerful,' she said. 'Verra cheerful.'

'Yes,' Elizabeth agreed.

'Too cheerful.' Mrs Macquarie sat in meditative thought. 'Ye know the way people sometimes put on a show of cheerfulness because it's expected of them? Well that's what I think he's doing in that letter.'

Elizabeth couldn't see it. She looked quizzically at the letter, then at Mrs Macquarie. 'Why do you think that?'

'I think he's verra lonely meself. I think he wants to come home.'

Elizabeth looked at her with dubious misgiving. 'I see no evidence of that in his writing.'

Again Mrs Macquarie sat silent in reflective thought, and then blinked her eyes. 'Aye, that's true ... Maybe I'm hearing things written between the lines that are nae there at all.' She sighed heavily. 'Aye, I suppose it's just the yearns of maternal love ... an old woman craving for the sight of her long-lost son again. Murdoch is right. He'll no' come back from his beloved India. Not in my lifetime. So I must try to forget him, I must, aye.'

Elizabeth looked at the grieving old lady with pity. 'Perhaps,' she said, 'perhaps if you were to write to him, through Murdoch, reminding him of his duties to his family at home – '

'Oh! I couldna do that! It wouldna do at all! It would serve only resentment.' Mrs Macquarie shook her head.

'Nae, I couldna force him with reproaches. If he wants to bide in India then let him bide. But if he wants to come home to Scotland, then let him come willingly, or not at all.'

*

The thoughts of his home in the West had stayed with him. Through August and September he had allowed them to toy around in his mind; and by October the thoughts had developed into an uncomfortable yearning. A yearning to see the morning mists over the hills of Scotland again; to see his mother again; to see the beautiful islands of Mull and Ulva, and all his cousins and kin again.

At the end of October he confessed to General Balfour that he was having serious thoughts about returning home.

'Indeed?' The confession seemed not only to have surprised Balfour, but also upset him. They were dining at the San Souci Club, sitting on the shaded veranda, overlooking the lawns.

Lachlan said quietly. 'It's been eleven years since I left home for India, and since then I have never once gone back.'

Balfour knew, only too well, the truth of that. For a long moment he was oddly silent, then he said in a slow voice, 'Well ... I suppose your wish to return is quite reasonable, after such a long absence.'

Balfour sipped his drink. 'I won't stand in your way. If you wish to transfer to a regiment in England or Scotland, I shall of course recommend your request to the Commander-in-Chief.'

'Thank you.'

Again Balfour was oddly silent. A *khidmatgar* appeared to clear the table. It was only after he had cleared it and moved away that Balfour suddenly blurted, 'You know you *do* surprise me, I must say! I thought that you, of all people, Macquarie, had no intentions of ever deserting India.'

'I'm not *deserting* India.'

'Yes you are.'

Balfour shook his head as if the whole business was a great disappointment to him. 'Of course, I quite understand you wishing to see your mother, but I've always thought that since Jane – '

'My mother is old,' Lachlan said, 'almost seventy years old now. And while she is still alive, and before she dies, I would like to see her again.'

'Yes, yes...' Balfour squinted thoughtfully at his glass. 'Is that the only reason you wish to return?'

'No, I have several reasons. But mainly I just have a soldier's natural longing to return home.'

'After such a long absence it is, I suppose, reasonable,' Balfour said again, then sat gazing silently over the lawns, his blue eyes thoughtful.

Eventually, Balfour stirred and sighed heavily. 'Yes, well, to be honest, I *do* know what you mean. Somewhat coincidentally ... I have been having a little itch to see the old country again myself.'

*

By the end of December Lachlan's passage to England was booked, his baggage packed, his household arrangements completed, and new employment for his servants secured. He had, during the various parties of the Christmas season, made his farewells to his friends.

Now came the last farewell.

Jane's grave was enclosed in its own private little garden in Bombay's British cemetery, a very lovely and peaceful spot, surrounded by white-stuccoed walls. An oasis of fragrant and warm serenity with Persian roses planted around the inner walls of the garden. Beside it a kikar tree was drooping with scented yellow blossoms.

Inside the garden Lachlan sat down on a small wooden bench, while at the arched entrance George Jarvis sat in a cross-legged lotus position and waited in silence. He waited for hours, keeping watch like a young guardian angel, just as he had done in Macao.

But in Macao, George recalled, Lachlan had been paralysed in mind and soul with a dark and terrible grief, a blindness that saw no tomorrow. And there had been a thousand sad and lonely tomorrows in the long years since then, before the dawning of acceptance.

Now, as George silently watched Lachlan's face, he saw a man lost in tranquil thought and nostalgic dreams.

Now, George thought, now he has learned that what is written is written. Now he has learned the wisdom of the East.

A little gust of soft wind blew through the warm silence of the garden, carrying with it a vapour of salt air from the sea. Lachlan looked up and saw that the sun was preparing to dip towards the horizon.

It was time to go.

He made no move, not until the reflected glow of the sunset had turned the white walls around the garden into a muted pink. And even then, he waited until the glow faded, and the birds in the kikar tree stopped their flutterings and singing and settled down to rest.

*

In Bombay harbour, on the morning of 6th January, the *Sir Edward Hughes*, a coppered and fast-sailing Indiaman, complete with round-house and a balcony over her stern, prepared to set sail.

Bappoo, who was now employed in the household of John Forbes, wept profusely as he hugged George Jarvis tightly, and said farewell.

'*Khudaa hafiz*,' Bappoo sobbed. God protect you.

George straightened and took a deep breath. '*Khudaa hafiz*, Bappoo,' he said quietly, defying tears, then abruptly turned towards the small-boat.

The crowds on the dockside watched the stream of boats carrying their passengers out to the ship from where, only a minute after they had boarded, Bappoo saw the figure of young George Jarvis waving to him excitedly.

Bappoo sighed, and wiped a big hand over his wet face, knowing that for George Jarvis this journey to *Belait* was not a sad departure, but a glorious adventure.

Lachlan was also waving to the distant crowd. All his friends, British and Indian, had come to wave him farewell. Many had given him letters for their families at home.

In his portmanteau he also had a list of addresses given to him by those soldiers who were unable to read or write, Scottish lads who knew that during his journey through Scotland to the Isle of Mull he would pass near their homes, and pleaded with him to call on their parents, to say they were well and doing fine.

'Ma mither, sir,' one lad had said, `ma mither will near swoon at havin' ma commanding officer call at the house – home from India. But she'll be reet pleased if ye do. Ma fayther too! Och, sir, I canne tell ye! It'll make them sleep happy for many a moon!'

The *Sir Edward Hughes,* under a cloud of white sail, began to cruise out of the harbour of Bombay. A roar of farewells rose up from the dockside and hands waved frantically.

George Jarvis waved back, but Lachlan stood without moving, just looking – looking back on the land where so many sons of Britannia had come in the past, where so many British men, and women too, had chosen to end their days.

Looking back to the land where he had spent so many Indian summers; looking back at the happiest period of his whole life.

Later, much later, when the sun had set and the moon had risen, India was gone from view... vanished into the darkness and distance.

*

Three months later Elizabeth Campbell came rushing into Mrs Macquarie's parlour waving a letter. 'He's coming home! He's booked his passage on a ship that leaves Bombay on the 6th of January.'

Mrs Macquarie, her heart palpitating, regarded Elizabeth in stunned silence ... then she reached out and clasped the girl's arm as if she was going to fall.

'Sixth of January – what year?'

'This year.'

'But it's March now.'

'Yes!' Elizabeth laughed. 'So he's already on the sea. In just a couple of months he will be in Scotland.'

In the months that followed more letters came: from Cape Town, from St Helena, from Portsmouth, from London.

''No' long now!' Mrs Macquarie said excitedly, and like Elizabeth who was just as excited, the old lady was visualising in her mind the return of the same twenty-five-year old lieutenant who had walked away from her all those years ago.

'There'll be no more letters,' Mrs Macquarie said to Elizabeth as she poured the tea. 'But ye'll still come and visit me, Elizabeth hennie, won't ye?'

'I will,' Elizabeth promised.

They waited eagerly for the return of the wanderer, but by the close of summer – months after his arrival in England – there was still no sign of him.

His letters explained the reason. His arrival in London in May had coincided with the breakdown of the Peace Treaty of Amiens. Britain was again at war with France. The War Office had cancelled all leave. He had been assigned immediately to the post of Adjutant-General on the staff of the London District, under the personal command of Lord Harrington.

From then on his letters were all about the military world of London. The Commander-in-Chief of the Army, the Duke of York, had sent for him in order to discuss at length the state of the regiments in India.

As his time in London moved into the autumn, and his letters still spoke of his longing to return to Mull as soon as it was possible to obtain leave, a social note crept into his letters. He had dined with Lord Harrington and the Prince of Wales. He had been given a week's leave in July, but as it was too short a time to travel to Scotland, he had instead escorted Maria Morley on a week's excursion to Cheltenham and Gloucester.

Maria's husband, James he explained, had died six months earlier. And under such circumstances, he found it impossible to refuse the grieving widow's request to escort her to Cheltenham.

'Maria Morley,' said Mrs Macquarie to Elizabeth. 'That's his dead wife's sister.'

Elizabeth waited curiously to see if his letters contained any more references to this newly widowed Maria Morley.

By Christmas, Mrs Macquarie had given up hope of her son ever returning to Mull. 'He'll no' be coming home in my lifetime,' she said quietly, blinking her eyes. 'I lost him to the Army when he was a laddie of fifteen and they've had him ever since. And aye, that's the truth.'

Once again Elizabeth looked at the grieving old lady with pity. 'It's an uncommon mild day for December,' she said. 'Shall we take a little stroll?'

Mrs Macquarie cast a fond eye on Elizabeth Campbell. 'You're as bonnie as a daughter to me at times, Elizabeth hennie. Aye, let's take a wee stroll.'

*

In January Elizabeth returned to her home at Airds on the mainland. Three months later, in April, she travelled over to Mull and spent another few days with Mrs Macquarie.

'No sign of the wanderer yet?' Elizabeth asked.

Mrs Macquarie shook her head gloomily. 'His last letter is there. Murdoch brought it over and read it to me.' She pointed to the dresser. 'Do you want to read it?'

Elizabeth did. She scanned through the pages that told

only of his military life in London at the War Office.

The two women moved outdoors to the warm spring sunshine. 'He'll be home soon, I'm sure,' Elizabeth said as they strolled down to the seashore opposite Ulva.

Mrs Macquarie shook her head again. 'The Duke of York is the villain. Won't give any officer leave of absence at all. Every day they're expecting an attack from across the Channel.'

They had reached the land's edge, and stood to gaze across the water to Ulva's shore where a number of boatmen were hauling in nets of seaweed to be dried and burned into kelp, which would then be taken to the mainland for the manufacture of soap and glass.

Mrs Macquarie blinked her eyes. 'D`ye know, Elizabeth, that it takes twenty tons of seaweed to make one ton of kelp.'

Elizabeth nodded.

'And all that carrying and drying and cutting and burning first.' Mrs Macquarie sighed. 'It's a hard way to make a living.'

Elizabeth stood gazing across at the green and basalt landscape of Ulva, an island of tranquil splendour and rare beauty where red deer sat under the shade of pine trees, lazily watching seals from the Atlantic playing near Ulva's shore.

In the three days that followed, the two women took ambling strolls together down to the shore to stare across at the Ulvan kelpers at their labour.

On the fourth day Elizabeth was surprised to find a small rowing boat moored on Mull's side of the shore, and looked around for the owner ... not a soul in sight!

She waved and called across the water to the Ulvan

kelpers, but they misunderstood her, and merely waved back in greeting.

Mrs Macquarie was too stunned to protest when Elizabeth bundled her into the boat, whipped off the rope, then got in herself and swiftly and expertly inserted the oars inside their catches.

'*Elizabeth!*' Mrs Macquarie finally screamed when Elizabeth applied her strength to the oars and the boat began to move.

'*Elizabeth!*' Mrs Macquarie cried again. 'What are ye doing! A gentle-bred lady like ye handling a boat! I've never been across this water except when taken by a man!'

Elizabeth laughed as gleefully as a schoolgirl. 'And if you were drowning, would you take my hand in rescue – or wait for a man?'

'This is no time for riddles!' Mrs Macquarie replied, and then began to relax slightly as the boat skimmed swiftly and smoothly across the water towards Ulva. Elizabeth was clearly an expert at this.

When the boat reached Ulva, the staring kelpers let out sighs of relief, which turned into a loud cheer when Elizabeth stepped ashore.

Elizabeth turned to Mrs Macquarie and unleashed an excited girlish smile. 'Now then, shall we go adventuring?'

Mrs Macquarie had to smile back, in bewilderment. Elizabeth was treating her as if they were both schoolgirls.

'Is it up to the Laird of Ulva's house you want to go, Elizabeth?' she asked uncertainly.

'No,' said Elizabeth, 'but it has occurred to me these last few days while we were gazing across at Ulva, that *you* might like to visit Kilvechewan.'

'Kilvechewan?'

Mrs Macquarie stared at Elizabeth, seeing her with new eyes. 'Fancy you thinking of Kilvechewan,' she said, then smiled at the girl from Airds with deep fondness. 'Aye, Elizabeth, a visit to Kilvechewan would be a real treat.'

Elizabeth harboured no regret at her suggestion, even though the walk up to Kilvechewan took four hours. Both women were Highlanders and took the journey in their stride, engrossed in the wildlife of the small woods and moorlands, pausing here and there to talk with crofters when Mrs Macquarie enjoyed a succession of short rests and caught up on all the gossip.

And then, finally, at Kilvechewan, the old woman stood gazing thoughtfully at her husband's grave, which now also contained Donald.

'My husband was a good man,' Mrs Macquarie said quietly. 'The Macleans of Torloisk might be the lords of Mull, but I didna marry a pauper when I married a Macquarie, I married a gentleman. Aye, I did.'

She looked at the girl. 'Did ye know, Elizabeth, that the first people to settle on Ulva were Nordic Vikings?'

Elizabeth nodded.

Mrs Macquaric suddenly chuckled. 'I remember my man telling me that when the first Vikings arrived in their longboats at Ulva, they sent a scout ashore to see who was here, and how the land lay. The scout wandered over the island which was completely deserted of all human habitation, then returned to the shore, shouting, "*Ullamh dha!*" That's Viking for "Nobody home."'

The walk back seemed twice as long, and so tiring that poor Mrs Macquarie let out a sigh of ecstatic relief when she reached the lonely little rowing boat. It had been morning when they rowed across from Mull, and now it was sunset.

All the kelpers had gone to their homes, the shore deserted.

Mrs Macquarie yawned tiredly as Elizabeth lifted an oar and pushed the boat away from the rocks, too tired and too full of gratitude to make any objection when the girl from Airds delayed the homeward journey even longer, by pausing halfway across the Sound to rest on her oars ... gazing dreamily at the sunset.

From the western horizon the sun's purple and orange rays glinted like coloured glass on the sheen of the water. Only the seagulls flapping and screaming overhead disturbed the warm still evening.

Mrs Macquarie watched Elizabeth's face and smiled to herself, knowing now that her first instinct about the girl had been right. Underneath all that sensibleness and no-nonsense practicality, Elizabeth had a heart of gold.

And moments later, when Elizabeth dipped the oars and continued rowing gently, Mrs Macquarie heaved a sigh of inward satisfaction. There were so many frauds in this world, so many people who took you in with their falseness and insincerity; so it was a good feeling to know that her own sense and judgement was not completely gone, and her first instinct about Elizabeth Campbell had proved to be a sound one.

The following day Elizabeth decided that although Mrs Macquarie's house was as clean as a new pin, it was foolish for it to be bereft of the charm and colour of fresh flowers when the hills and banks were smothered in wild spring blooms.

As they ambled back from the shore to the house, she paused here and there to collect handfuls of wild blue hyacinths, mixing in a few sprigs of golden gorse.

Back in the house, without waiting to remove her hat and

while Mrs Macquarie made tea, Elizabeth divided the colourful array of flowers into two bowls, placing one on the table and the other on the window ledge.

And it was then, as she sat on the window-seat arranging the flowers, Elizabeth saw a carriage on the crest of the eastern hill, slowly winding its way down the narrow road ... She peered curiously ... was the carriage coming here? Or passing on to the McLean's farm at Lagganulva?

'Mrs Macquarie dear,' she said hesitantly, 'there seems to be a carriage coming this way.'

'A carriage? Now who may that be? Would it be Murdoch coming from Lochbuy do ye think?'

'I doubt it,' Elizabeth replied. 'He usually prefers to take the short cut by horse through the hills from Lochbuy to Rossall.'

Mrs Macquarie joined Elizabeth at the window, peering until the carriage came to a halt on the road down by the wall that marked the farm's boundary.

The carriage door opened and the occupant stepped out, and the two women at the window simply gaped when they saw him ... a beautifully handsome and tall young man of about eighteen years, dressed exquisitely in a suit of royal blue with pure white silk at his neck. His skin was light brown, his hair short and as black as coal. He walked up to the driver and spoke a few words to him, and every move of his body was as graceful as his clothes.

Elizabeth gasped – he was stunning – a prince straight out of the *Arabian Tales*.

Mrs Macquarie blinked at the strangest sight she had ever seen in this primitive region – a brown-skinned young man. 'My God!' she cried. 'It's an Indian prince in English dress! He musta come looking for Lachlan! And he no' here!'

She got all in a fluster and began to shake, running to the door, then running back again 'Will he speak English do ye think, Elizabeth? Will he want to speak to me, Elizabeth?'

Elizabeth rose from the window-seat and said helpfully: 'Shall I go out to greet him?'

'Aye, hennie, aye!' Mrs Macquarie was running towards the stairs to her bedroom. 'Ye go out and keep him talking, Elizabeth, while I go up and put on my best shawl and bonnet!'

When Elizabeth stepped out of the house and walked down to the wall with a confident air, George Jarvis turned his head, surprised at the sight of her.

George had been expecting an old woman who lived alone, not this tall and attractive young lady with a long-legged stride. She wore a dark-green riding habit with yellow lace at the cuffs and throat. On her head she wore a three cornered green hat which crowned a sheen of bronze curling hair which fell around her shoulders.

Elizabeth smiled, about to hold out her hand in greeting – then stopped dead when a second occupant stepped out of the carriage, still hastily jotting down something in what appeared to be a small journal or diary, which he then closed, shoved inside an inner breast pocket of his jacket, and looked round.

Elizabeth stood mute as Lachlan's eyes met hers, lingered quizzically on her for a moment, as if wondering who she was – then at the sound of a woman's incoherent cry, looked beyond her to the house where an old woman stood at the door staring in disbelief.

George Jarvis exchanged a fixed look with Elizabeth, and she immediately understood what he was silently asking of her.

They both remained standing by the carriage as Lachlan Macquarie walked towards his mother.

Like a startled victim of the ague, Mrs Macquarie stared at her son with a tremor of shaking and blinking eyes, barely recognising him as he walked the gravel path round the sheep field.

This new Lachlan Macquarie was a strikingly elegant man, older than the son she remembered, wearing a blue cloak flaring back from his shoulders to reveal a perfectly tailored jacket of expensive navy broadcloth. And his skin – oh, she had not expected his skin to be that colour – as brown as a man who had spent too long in the sun.

She stared at the man coming towards her. Was it he? Her eyes, old and moist and blue, blinked as if she feared that either her sight or her imagination might be playing wishful tricks on her.

He was standing before her now, looking into her startled eyes and smiling. He said softly, 'Hello, Mother.'

And her poor old heart nearly burst.

She collapsed into his arms and clung to him, overcome by the excess of her emotions as tears of joy coursed down her face. Aye, it was he ... her youngest son ... Lachlan ... home to her at last.

NINETEEN

'Ye'll note,' said the builder, pointing to various points around the spacious parlour, 'that we've done all the repairs ye asked for, sir. I hope they're to your satisfaction.'

Lachlan made a quick inspection, and then looked at his mother. 'I'm satisfied, are you?'

'Me?' She could say no more, confused by her emotions, so she simply nodded her head a few times before shooting a quick glance at Elizabeth's expressionless face. She had begged the girl to stay with her and keep her company while these strange workmen were in and around her home, taking no comfort from Lachlan's assurances that all were from Mull, and all could be trusted.

'And the rest of the alterations?' the builder asked. 'How soon do ye want us to start on them?'

Again Lachlan looked at his mother, who simply gazed glumly at Elizabeth, seeking her help.

'As soon and as quickly as possible.' Elizabeth smiled at Mrs Macquarie. 'These things need to be done, and while the air outside is fresh and warm we can take some nice long walks and get away from the noise.'

Mrs Macquarie looked as if her best friend had just cruelly betrayed her, but again she simply nodded and said meekly, 'Aye, that's a grand suggestion, Elizabeth, a grand suggestion.'

In the stress of her mind, Elizabeth felt divided between pangs of great sympathy for Mrs Macquarie, as well as feeling a practical support for her son who was finally attending to all the repairs and alterations to the house that should have been done years ago.

Yet she could not help feeling sorry for the old lady whose quiet life was now being so disturbed. At first Mrs Macquarie had been braced and fortified by the unexpected joy of her son's arrival, but now the strain was beginning to show. She had not been prepared, and neither had Elizabeth, for the staggering energy that Lachlan had brought with him to Scotland, and which showed no signs of abating.

Later, when Lachlan and the workman went outside, Elizabeth followed them out. She said clumsily, 'Mr Macquarie ... although I, personally, am very happy to see the work being done at last, is it necessary for *everything* to be done this summer?'

He paused, gazed at her in thought, and shrugged. 'Yes, haste is necessary, because I have only a few months leave at the most, and that's only if I am not recalled tomorrow or next week or next month.' He nodded upwards. 'And that roof won't last another winter.'

Elizabeth turned and looked up at the roof, and saw that it was indeed in a very bad state. 'Oh goodness, yes, a heavy rainfall and your mother would be drowned in her bed.'

'I'm glad you understand. Perhaps you could explain that to my mother, more successfully than myself?'

Elizabeth nodded, excusing herself with a faintly shamed smile.

*

The gloom in Mrs Macquarie's eyes always receded whenever her son came to call, replaced by a bright and eager smile. 'I'm so thankful for him coming here,' she said to Elizabeth one afternoon. 'Oh, aye ... thankful as can be. But, to be honest with ye, all the work he had done to my house, I did resent it, didn't I, Elizabeth hennie?'

Elizabeth was not listening, reclining in the rocking-chair by the parlour window, unconscious of her surroundings and her mind lingering somewhere in the far distance, her blue eyes seeing something that occasionally made her mouth shape into a small smile.

'And to be fair to him,' Mrs Macquarie continued, 'he *did* want me to leave here and go stay with him at the Inn at Callachally, even before the work started, to get me away from all the disorder, didn't he, Elizabeth?'

Still no answer came; and Mrs Macquarie found herself wondering about all the new furniture and drapes and carpets that Lachlan had ordered from Edinburgh.

'It's no' necessary, is it, Elizabeth hen?'

At last Mrs Macquarie realised she had been speaking to only herself. She turned round in her chair by the fire and stared at the girl. 'Elizabeth hennie?' she said loudly. 'Have ye dozed off?'

Like a sleeper aroused, Elizabeth looked around, recollected herself and smiled. 'No, no, I was listening to you.'

'And ye agree with me? Whatna way to waste money, eh?'

As Elizabeth had not heard a word and so could not grasp the significance of the question, she responded agreeably, 'Yes, it's foolish to waste money,' then quickly stood and moved over to the dresser and opened a drawer to lift out the tablecloth. 'Shall I prepare the table for tea?'

'Tea?' Mrs Macquarie shot a glance at the mantel clock. 'Elizabeth, it's only ten minutes past three! I've no' even put the chicken in the pot.'

Elizabeth paused, then with a glance at the clock continued lifting plates from the shelf of the dresser. 'I may as well get it done,' she said mildly, 'and then I can start mixing the flour and oats for the bannocks ... it's no trouble.'

When Lachlan arrived a short time later, he looked at the table set up for the evening meal. 'Are we not a bit early today?' he asked his mother curiously. 'I have only come for five minutes, not for dinner.'

Elizabeth began to needlessly move everything around on the table until her hands suddenly lifted the beautifully ornate china teapot in the centre. 'It's just my excuse to take another look at this beautiful teapot,' she said, smiling. 'I've never seen one so beautiful.'

'That's one of the presents Lachlan brought me from India,' Mrs Macquarie put in proudly. 'In Bombay, ye got it, didn't ye, son?'

The teapot had been bought for his mother by Jane in Macao, but he deflected the question by asking Elizabeth if she often cooked for his mother.

'Oh, aye, she does,' Mrs Macquarie answered for Elizabeth. 'I keep telling her that a gentle-bred young lady like herself should no' be doing any kind of cooking at all'

'Nor should a gentle-bred lady like you,' Lachlan replied. 'Remember, you were brought up in Lochbuy, with servants attending to your every need. If you had been allowed to inherit – '

'Och, I couldna have inherited Lochbuy, and well ye know it!' Mrs Macquarie said impatiently. 'I may have been the eldest, but I was still only a woman.'

'A woman who should not be still cooking her own meals and doing household chores at seventy. Will you behave yourself, Mother, and allow me to arrange things for you.'

A short time later, after he had left, Mrs Macquarie looked apprehensively at Elizabeth. 'What d'ye think he means – arrange things for me?'

Elizabeth smiled. 'He is just trying to be kind.'

The following day, two local girls were employed as maids, and one of Lachlan's cousins had agreed to give up his job as a kelper and take over complete control of the farm.

'But, Lachlan!' his mother cried anxiously. 'What am *I* to do?'

'Sit back and rest.'

When she protested he railed her teasingly. 'It was you who brought me back from India. So you owe it to me to live for another twenty years at least, and live *comfortably*. And you could do, if you stop wearing yourself out with work and take life a little easier.'

Elizabeth voiced her agreement: 'He's right. You do need help, especially when you are here alone. Some times, when I arrive from Lochbuy, you're worn so fine you look about to drop.'

Lachlan smiled in appreciation of her support. 'There, you see? Even Miss Campbell agrees with me.'

Then he was gone again, and in the days that followed, in the company of George Jarvis, he rode over the ten thousand acres of land he now owned on Mull. He had bought the lands of Callachally, Gruline, Bentella, and Kilbeg. His Scottish home, he had decided would be built on the land at Callachally, because it was right beside the beautiful River of Mull.

He even discussed his plans with Elizabeth, and found her suggestions very helpful and intelligent.

'Do you intend to live here on a regular basis, then?' she

asked him one day as they rode their horses over the land of Callachally.

He sat for a moment in silence, contemplating the land around him. 'Yes, I plan to live here, one day.'

Elizabeth unaccountably found herself thinking of Maria Morley. 'Do you have plans to marry again?'

'Me? Marry?' His eyes and voice warmed with sudden amusement. 'I am too old an Indian to marry again.'

'You are not old, and you are not an Indian!' she said indignantly. 'You have merely reached your prime I would say, and eleven years in India does not take away the fact that you are Scottish.'

He shrugged. 'Yes, well, India does leave its mark on a man, you know. So many in the military return home pretending to hate India, then spend all their days seeking out the company of fellow Anglo-Indians returned from service there. And many, in the end, do go back.'

'Will you?'

'Perhaps. I honestly don't know. I'm employed by the Army and so must go wherever its commanders please to send me. And their pleasure at the moment seems to be that I should remain on the staff in London.'

'And your servant ... the young Indian? He must surely find Britain a strange and cold place? Will he not wish to return to his family in India someday?'

'George is not a servant.' Lachlan turned his horse around. 'And *I* am his family, Miss Campbell.'

*

After escorting Elizabeth home, Lachlan rode back to the Inn at Callachally where he and George Jarvis were lodged.

George was surprised to see him back before evening. 'I thought you said you stay all day with your mother?' George said in almost perfect English.

'No, George, I suddenly remembered an urgent matter that concerns you. Your education, as a matter of fact.'

George's dark eyes flashed. 'I do all my education in London! For one whole year! There is nothing more I can learn! I know everything!'

Lachlan smiled. 'You may think you do, George, but you don't. Not by a long shot. So I'm sending you to a school in Edinburgh.'

'How long?'

'A year.'

George smiled persuasively. 'Three months?'

'A year.'

'Yes, yes, I go for six months,' George agreed.

'A year,' Lachlan said firmly. 'You need another year at least.'

George knew it was pointless to argue. When it came to schooling Lachlan could be as strict as he was on the parade ground. He lowered his eyes and sighed.

'Yes, my father.'

*

Lachlan's plans to build his house at Callachally were thwarted when he discovered that an adjoining strip of land was still under lease to a Dr Donald McLean for a further nineteen years.

'A lease is a lease, Mr Macquarie,' said McLean stubbornly. 'And it was the Duke of Argyll who sold me the lease.'

'But I bought the land from the Duke of Argyll,' Lachlan replied. 'So this land is now mine.'

'Just so, just so, but this particular strip of your land is legally leased to me. And as I say, a lease is a lease.'

Lachlan was forced to fall back on his second choice of site, and chose Gruline.

*

Elizabeth ventured out with him again on horseback and thought Gruline an even better selection than Callachally. The site was south of the valley, by a lovely fishing stream that ran into Loch Ba. All around were fine woods; and above Gruline the green and purple sweep of Ben More towered in mountainous beauty.

'And Ulva is only a *kooee-hai* away across Loch Na Keal,' Lachlan said as they dismounted.

'What do those words mean?' Elizabeth asked curiously. 'George Jarvis used them almost every time he called at your mother's house.'

'In Hindi the words are *koi hai*, which means, "Is anybody there?"' Lachlan explained. 'Nobody ever knocks on a door in India. As soon as they approach the veranda of a house they simply call out "*kooee-hai*" and a servant appears. George Jarvis has never quite lost the habit. My only hope is that he doesn't use it whenever he knocks on the master's door at his school in Edinburgh, as he continually did at his school in London.'

They both laughed.

Still curious, Elizabeth asked, 'And where did he get the very English name of George Jarvis?'

'From my wife,' he replied quietly 'Her maiden name was

Jarvis.'

'Oh,' Elizabeth said, wishing she had not asked. Her mind ran riot looking for a change of subject, but her curiosity and mouth ran on the same subject. 'And how ... how did George come to be in your care?'

For a moment he did not answer, but when he did, the strangeness of his words shocked her. 'I stole him, Miss Campbell, from a slave-trader in Cochin.'

*

By the end of August the improvements to his mother's farmhouse were finished, the new furniture installed. 'Now you really will be more comfortable,' Lachlan told her.

Mrs Macquarie wanted to cry at the loss of her old friendly furniture. These new pieces were like strangers, grand swanky strangers, and she felt very shabby in their presence, least of all comfortable. But she said nothing and pretended to be very pleased, knowing he was only doing his best, trying to make up to her for all her years of frugality.

'And I've arranged with the stores in Tobermory to supply you with all the wines and groceries you will need, and the bills sent to me.'

'Wines...' his mother simply gaped, but minutes later he was gone again, seeing to business, meeting with the carpenters and stonemasons to discuss the plans he had drawn for the building of his own house at Gruline. It was to be of a traditional Georgian design in grey stone, spacious an elegant, but nothing ostentatious or baronial.

'I would like it ready for my return next summer. Is that possible?'

The builders agreed it could be done. 'But Mr Macquarie,'

said the stonemason, 'do you not think it's time you had this estate of yours registered? A new owner of a new estate usually means a new name.'

Lachlan was well aware of that. He had already arranged for the Writer of the Signet to come to from Edinburgh to Mull for the registration.

'And a new registration usually means a party,' grinned one of the carpenters. 'A party for all the tenants given by the new Laird.'

Lachlan smiled. He was well aware of that also.

*

The party was a big one. A huge tent had been erected on the site of the house and the weather stayed fine for the outdoor jamboree which was attended by the Maclaines, Macleans, Mackinnons and Campbells, old and young kinsmen, drovers, farmers and tenants, all determined to enjoy the party in true Highland style.

Eventually a silence was called for, tankards and glasses were filled in readiness for the toast. It was time for the new Laird to officially name his estate. 'Speech!' the tenants shouted. 'Speech from the new Laird.'

Elizabeth Campbell sat beside Mrs Macquarie who seemed overcome with pride as her son rose to address the gathering. At his side stood the Writer to the Signet who would register the title in Edinburgh.

'Today...' Lachlan began slowly, 'is a very special day for me. Because today I can at last make true a promise I made to myself before leaving India, a promise that the name of my beloved wife would be kept alive in the family of Macquarie into which she married. So in honour of the memory of Jane Jarvis Macquarie, I name these lands and estate ... Jarvisfield.'

The tenants cheered as the new name of their estate echoed over the land: 'Jarvisfield!'

*

Amidst the noise and the music that followed, no one noticed the change in Elizabeth Campbell who sat in silence throughout the ensuing conversations, lost in her own thoughts, occasionally flushing a deep red as if some angry or self-condemning thought had struck her.

The following day Elizabeth returned to Lochbuy, and there she made the decision to leave Scotland far behind her and take a carriage to London where she intended to build a new life for herself.

A life in London full of fun and dancing all night long, Elizabeth decided. She had spent years being good and helpful and everyone's sensible friend, and look where it had got her – ignored! She may as well go to London and simply *swoooon* helplessly into a delicate faint whenever she desired to attract a man.

She dragged out her trunk, hauled it into the centre of her bedroom and kicked it open, all her natural composure completely deserting her.

She had made an utter *fool* of herself!

For almost four months she had practically thrown herself at a man who had not the decency to notice. Just as he had not noticed her all those years ago when he worked at Lochbuy before leaving for India!! A man who was still in love with his dead wife! A man who had not, after all, returned to the British Isles to start life afresh, but simply to perpetuate the name of his beloved wife in Scotland!

She began to pack her clothes, hurt and smouldering, her mind racing. Her brother John had been right about those officers who returned from India, men who were used to their women wearing jewels and exotic scents and languishing in luxury all day long. And all of them, men and women alike, being waited upon by a tribe of cosseting Indian servants who attended to their every need and spoiled them like children.

'*Yaaa!*' She flung clothes in the trunk and yearned to scream out her contempt. She now knew all about Jane Jarvis Macquarie and hated her – hated her type. A pampered rich miss from the West Indian Islands who had owned her own slaves and inherited a fortune from her English papa.

So how could *she*, Elizabeth Campbell, the daughter of a poor West Highland Laird who had left nothing but debts, ever compete with someone like that?

And then she remembered that Jane Jarvis Macquarie was dead. And had died very young. Younger than she herself was now.

She sat down on the bed and wiped an angry tear from her eye, ashamed and horrified at her thoughts. She knew nothing about that poor unfortunate girl, nothing at all.

TWENTY

From the day Elizabeth arrived at her house in London, Henrietta Campbell knew the poor girl was still suffering from neglect. A terrible neglect which Elizabeth had tried to brave as cheerfully as possible from her earliest days. Her mother had died not long after her birth and from then on Elizabeth had been left to scramble her own way up through childhood with the assistance of a few daft servants and her sister Margaret who, at that time, was little more than a child herself.

Like many fathers, John Campbell had shown little interest in his daughters, all his pride being reserved solely for his precious son and namesake, the heir to his estate. On a number of occasions during her visits to Scotland, Henrietta had attempted to advise her brother to be more mindful of his daughters, and he had tried, but the relief on his face when Margaret was married off to Murdoch Maclaine of Lochbuy was shamefully visible.

Within months of Margaret's marriage, Elizabeth had been sent packing to a Finishing School for Young Ladies in Hammersmith. A place where the daughters of England's finest fathers were housed and instructed in the role of becoming England's finest future wives and mothers. A place where even the teachers found little prestige was to be gained from devoting much time or affection to a somewhat *gauche* thirteen-year-old girl from the remote wilds of Scotland.

Henrietta's main regret was that she had not been informed of Elizabeth's removal down to Hammersmith until six months after the girl had been sent there. A situation she had rectified immediately by ordering her carriage to be made ready to take her across London, a short journey of five or six miles.

Henrietta still often smiled with amusement whenever she remembered those first few minutes after her arrival at the school. Her carriage, with its gold crest on the doors, and two footmen standing to attention on the back ledge, was enough to bring a gaggle of servants running out in attendance.

The headmistress soon followed, red-faced with surprise. 'Why, Lady Breadlebane! Oh my, to what do we owe this delightful honour!'

'Any honour from my visit is owed to my niece.'

'Your niece?'

'Yes, my niece, Miss Elizabeth Campbell. I hope you are taking very good care of her? Now please bring her to me at once.'

Henrietta was not shown into the Visitors Room, but into the Headmistress's own pleasant parlour where Elizabeth arrived some minutes later, a faint blush on her cheeks and pushing a wisp of hair out of her eyes.

The first few tense minutes were a trial for both of them, but as soon as tea had been laid out and the headmistress had departed, Elizabeth's stiffness softened into enjoyment, overflowing with questions about the world outside, to which Henrietta had all the answers.

Henrietta's friendship and fondness for the girl ripened from that day. As the months and years passed Elizabeth spent every Sunday and all her holidays at Henrietta's home in Wigmore Street, until, reaching the age of eighteen and perfectly finished in all her schooling, she had been summoned back to the estate at Airds, to keep house for her father and brother.

*

A year or so after her return to Scotland, Henrietta remembered, Elizabeth had received a very good proposal of marriage from a gentleman with his own estate just north of Edinburgh, but as soon as her father had approved the match, Elizabeth had fled down to London.

'Oh, Henrietta, he's ancient and wheezy and as stiff as an old gander!' Elizabeth had explained breathlessly. `I would spend all my time expecting him to die at any minute.'

'Then marry him for his money,' Henrietta advised practically. 'Because once he is dead, believe me, you will find yourself surrounded by many handsome *young* men eager to marry a young widow with her own fortune, You will be able to take your pick.'

'I'd prefer to take poison!'

Some years later, another offer of marriage was proposed, this time from a young man reported to be very handsome, of good breeding, reasonable wealth, and destined for a career in politics.

'What's the matter with this one?' Henrietta had asked impatiently upon Elizabeth's unexpected arrival back in London. 'What's to do now? He's young, isn't he? Got all the requirements – and even destined for a high career in Parliament!'

'But he's got no *heart!*' Elizabeth had wailed. 'And even worse, he's got no *brain!* No intellect, no mind of his own at all!'

'It's you that's got no sense in your head,' Henrietta had

retorted grumpily. 'And what's more, when it comes to men, you're simply too self-willed. You'll have to change that.'

*

'Shall I light the candles?'

Henrietta came out her memories, opened her eyes, blinked, and looked up at Elizabeth. 'Yes, dear ... oh goodness, my mind was miles away. Where's that Ginny? She should have been in to do the candles by now.'

Elizabeth shrugged, lit a taper from the fire and moved from one candelabrum to another ... and after a short interval the candles burned up brightly, lighting the room. 'Ah, that's better.' Henrietta yawned. 'Now dear, let's get back to our conversation.'

Elizabeth sat down and lifted her sewing. 'Which one?'

'The same conversation we've been having for two weeks now. Are you *sure* it was not another marriage proposal that sent you running down here this time?'

Elizabeth sighed. 'I'm sure.'

'Well, I know you are not dishonest, although sometimes you can be very evasive, but there must be something wrong. I can tell these things. No man involved? You are sure?'

'Yes.'

'Then we must get one involved,' Henrietta decided, 'and I know just the man who may be able to help us. But first, Elizabeth, we really *must* attend to your clothing. When was the last time you had a new gown?'

'Gown?' Elizabeth half laughed. 'I don't believe I have ever worn a *gown*.'

'Exactly my point, but riding habits and plain dresses are

not the mode here in London, dear. Not if you wish to mix in the best of circles. So tomorrow we must rectify that and go shopping.' Henrietta pressed her palms together firmly, enthusiasm brightening her face. 'Tomorrow, Elizabeth, I am going to *spoil* you!'

Elizabeth woke at dawn. She hurriedly washed and struggled into her clothes. She had packed her small trunk the night before and now she wondered if she could successfully slip out of the house by way of the servants' hall in order to catch the early-morning Mail Coach back to Scotland.

It was a sneaky and shameful thing to do, but Henrietta had become infuriating – older and grumpier and *infuriating*. Ever since the death of Elizabeth's father, three years earlier, Henrietta believed the only path to Elizabeth's life-long security was the acquisition of a husband.

Brushing her hair, she reflected that all Henrietta's intentions were good, and all from the heart; always ready to give a helping hand or send a letter of advice, and her home was always open with a warm welcome.

And yet ... here was Henrietta's self-willed ungrateful niece preparing to slip out of the house ... without a word of thank-you or farewell.

Elizabeth thoughtfully sat down on the edge of the bed. Whichever way she looked at it, leaving now in this secretive way was a devious and dishonourable thing to do, she realised, no matter how urgent the need. And the deep hurt and offence that Henrietta would feel was not to be contemplated.

No, no, Elizabeth decided, she could not do it. She could not hurt Henrietta, now or ever. She would have to go the shops and allow herself to be dressed up like a pretty doll or a desperate debutante in search of a husband.

*

London itself, with its glamour in every shop window, was very seductive. Henrietta insisted they began their fashion hunting in Bond Street, and then eagerly and happily set about turning Elizabeth into one of the best-dressed women in London. By the end of the day Elizabeth found herself the owner of two beautiful gowns and seven very chic day and evening dresses.

Later that evening, once dinner was over, Henrietta continued her plans. 'Now,' she said, 'I want you to pop upstairs and change into one of your new dresses, dear. You see, earlier today I sent a note over to a dear friend of mine inviting him to drop in tonight if he can. He knows so many men he could introduce you – '

'I'm sorry,' Elizabeth interrupted, `I'm sorry, Henrietta, but I would rather die than have some stranger – '

'*Stranger?*' Henrietta put down her wineglass. 'Don't be ridiculous! I would never involve any stranger in our business. He is a relative of mine, although a very distant one, I grant you, seeing as he has spent most of his life in foreign climes. And *you* must know him too, Elizabeth. Surely you must have met him at least once during all those visits of yours to Lochbuy? Was he not at Margaret's marriage to his uncle?' Henrietta thought back. 'No, I believe he had gone to India by then.'

'India? Surely you don't mean ... Lachlan Macquarie?' Elizabeth's face had paled.

'Yes, dearest Lachlan, he and I have become great friends since his posting to the War Office. Well, in truth, he's more

298

friendly with my son, seeing as they both served in India.' Henrietta paused, then continued thoughtfully, `Now that I think of it ... not only am I related in some way to his mother, but as my niece Margaret – *your* sister – is married to *his* uncle, then that makes him a relative of yours also, Elizabeth. A cousin of some sort.'

Elizabeth was seriously regretting her decision earlier that morning not to offend Henrietta by slipping out to catch the Mail Coach back to Scotland.

'Is he ... is he back in London then?'

'Recalled about a week ago. Duke of York in one of his panics again. That man drives me mad.' Henrietta motioned to the footman to come and lift back her chair. 'Come along, Elizabeth,' she said rising. 'You need to change into one of your new dresses, and I need to change my wig – this new one is too tight and very uncomfortable.'

*

An hour later, in the drawing room, the moment Elizabeth dreaded finally came, yet Lachlan greeted her as friendly and as casually as if he had seen her only yesterday.

He moved to a chair and accepted a glass of wine. 'Henrietta tells me you are planning to settle in London for the autumn.'

'I have no plans.' Elizabeth hesitated, lowered her eyes. 'Nothing definite.'

'Poor Elizabeth!' Henrietta lamented to him, the baby-curls of her copper-brown wig dancing as she shook her head sadly. 'Poor Elizabeth now has an entire new wardrobe of beautiful dresses, but has absolutely nowhere to go in them, no man to escort her.'

Elizabeth's face crimsoned with embarrassment. She sat staring at her aunt as if wishing the world would instantly end.

'Lachlan, you must take her into society and introduce her to some of your officer friends,' Henrietta said bluntly. 'Become her chaperone. Would you do that for me?'

Lachlan glanced at Elizabeth with some surprise. 'Of course, if that is what Elizabeth wishes.'

'Oh *goody!*' Henrietta smiled in gratitude. 'Now Elizabeth might meet a possible husband, if *you* can help her to find one. Twenty-five is far too old for a girl to be unmarried.' She looked at her niece. 'Well, Elizabeth, will you allow Lachlan to escort you out and introduce you to some of his friends?'

Elizabeth's embarrassment had paralysed her. She sat with head bowed, her china teacup rattling in the saucer which she held with shaking hands.

'She wants to say yes but she's too coy, aren't you dear?' her aunt said helpfully.

After a silence Henrietta persisted louder. 'You would love cousin Lachlan to introduce you to his friends – all those handsome officers – wouldn't you, dear?'

The teaspoon on Elizabeth's saucer rattled to the floor. She bent to retrieve it, bringing her nose closer to the spot of carpet where the cat usually left his hairs, and she responded to the third – 'wouldn't you, dear?' with a paroxysm of sneezing, her head nodding convulsively.

Henrietta clapped her hands triumphantly. 'There – she said yes!'

A short time later, Elizabeth excused herself, pleading a headache and walking very carefully to the door, certain she was about to collapse at any moment with shame and humiliation, turning into the hall and groping with her hand for the oak banister. By the time she reached her room she had made her decision – yes, it would definitely be the Mail Coach first thing in the morning, whether it hurt Henrietta or not. Especially as Henrietta, despite her good intentions, had embarrassed her so completely tonight by treating her like some pitiable spinster.

The following morning she woke late, no doubt due to her fitful sleep during the night. She also felt very tired, probably due to all the shopping she had done the day before. She lay in bed listening to the sound of movements throughout the house. All the staff were up, going about their business in preparation for breakfast. She glanced at the clock – too late to catch the Mail Coach now.

She decided to lie in bed a little longer and think some more about her situation. Through the chinks of the curtains she could see the day had started with a bright autumnal sunshine. Turning languidly towards the window she stretched her limbs and after a long period in thought, concluded that she had two choices. Either she could continue to feel humiliated by having a chaperone forced upon her like some dismal spinster – or she could turn her back on the dark shadows of her own resentment and instead choose to enjoy it all and have some *fun* for a change.

TWENTY-ONE

Lachlan was an easy chaperone, friendly and relaxed and always ready to allow her to choose where they should go. On the second evening she chose to go to a play at the theatre, simply because Murdoch had often said that all plays were spawned by the devil. When she imitated Murdoch's dour scowl, Lachlan laughed out loud.

The weeks that followed were the most hectic Elizabeth had ever known. He took her to the Lord Mayor's Ball and introduced her to a number of suitable gentlemen. He escorted her to the Queen's levee where Elizabeth saw some of the most glamorous women in the world.

At least three times a week he took her somewhere, always introducing her to officers and gentleman, many of who immediately sent their cards to Wigmore Street the following morning. Elizabeth always managed to quickly hide the cards before her aunt could see them, and then in the evening she presented a woeful face and a shake of her head to Lachlan when he casually asked if any calling cards had arrived.

It was baffling. Lachlan couldn't understand it. A number of his fellow-officers, all eligible, had seemed charmed at the sight of her. Maybe it was her rather cool manner that put them off? If only she was as pleasant with them as she usually was with him.

'It's because I find I am quite at ease in your company,' Elizabeth explained over supper, 'which I seldom am with people I don't know well.'

The social whirl went on up to and including the

Christmas season. He took her to the ballet *Achilles et Deidamia* and again introduced her to a number of eligible young men. They went to the theatre to see Mrs Siddons and Charles Kemble in *The Tragedy of Pizarro* and enjoyed themselves so much he forgot to introduce Elizabeth to anyone; just as he forgot when he took her to hear the great Grassini warbling at the heights of her voice in *La vergine de sole*.

'But you must *remind* him, dear,' Henrietta said. 'We must get you a husband somehow.'

And then came the greatest event in any Scottish calendar, the Hogmanay Ball on New Year's Eve. In the drawing room at Wigmore Street, Elizabeth presented herself to her aunt. 'How do I look?'

Henrietta gasped at the sight of Elizabeth in her new pale gold silk gown, which contrasted magnificently with the burnished bronze of Elizabeth's hair. It was of the new *young* style of silk gowns, not voluminous, but slimly-draped and elegant

'Oh, Elizabeth, you look divine!' Henrietta exclaimed. 'A vision of bronze and gold ... beautiful and just *divine!*'

Elizabeth smiled her relief.

At the sound of a knock on the front door brass, Henrietta said quickly, 'Now remember, dear, you must make every effort to capture a general or even a captain tonight. Dear cousin Lachlan simply cannot understand why no calling cards have arrived. And neither can I.'

'Maybe Scottish girls are not in vogue this season,' Elizabeth murmured.

'Nonsense! Scottish girls are always in vogue!' Henrietta Campbell replied crisply.

A maid showed Lachlan into the drawing room. He stared

at Elizabeth, and then smiled in approval. 'They'll be queuing in lines to dance with you.'

It was a military ball, held in Chelsea, and Elizabeth was indeed besieged by young officers requesting a dance. The wine flowed extravagantly and Elizabeth drank her fill, accepting as many dances as she could, determined to enjoy Hogmanay in true Scottish style – while `dear cousin Lachlan' spent his time within a group of male friends which included his favourite officer who had returned home from India, General Balfour.

The next time Elizabeth caught sight of Lachlan he was waltzing with a very plump and blowsy dark-haired woman in a gown of startling red, who kept waving her plump arms in the air and gesticulating animatedly as she danced and talked at the same time.

Elizabeth suddenly realised her own partner was speaking to her. She turned her face to him – a jovial major with a pleasant smile, but very fat, tightly buttoned in a coat of the brightest red with loops of straining gold braid.

The major was paying her a compliment, she realised. She smiled, about to reply, when suddenly a female voice cried out in a high, delighted shrill: *'BENNIE!'*

Elizabeth quickly glanced over her shoulder to see Lachlan and his partner only a few feet away, and the blowsy plump woman in red was staring with mouth open at the portly major.

Elizabeth's eardrum almost popped with the resulting roar. *'ROXIE!'*

Dancers swirled by as the two rotunds in red stood and stared at each other with ecstatic joy.

'Bennie! I didna know *you* would be here tonight!'

'Well – fire all my guns – Roxie Carmichael! My, but

you're a bonnier sight than ever ye were, Roxie!'

'Oh, Bennie! Sakes alive! You always did say such lovely things to my own wee self!'

'Dash it all, Roxie, but you're still a devil of a draw to a man!'

Elizabeth peeked at Lachlan from under a flutter of eyelashes and smiled with an exaggerated simper. 'You will dance with me at least *once* tonight, won't you, Colonel Macquarie?'

'Miss Campbell, I will be happy to dance with you anytime,' Lachlan replied, curving the chattering Roxie towards the chattering Bennie with one arm and sliding the other round Elizabeth's waist. 'How about now?' he said, leading her away in a swift turn.

They danced very close together, their hands clasped. Lachlan smiled as he looked down into her face. 'I think you're a little intoxicated, Elizabeth, I've never seen you so sunny and unrestrained.'

'Sunny? Oh, it must be due to the gold colour of my gown,' she laughed. 'And the wine too, of course, but it *is* Hogmanay!'

They had only covered one circuit of the floor when the music stopped and the waltz was over. Before Elizabeth could even blink Captain John Buchanan was across the floor. 'I believe this is my dance now, Miss Campbell.'

Lachlan smiled and pressed her fingers affectionately before moving aside, and left them to carry on, crossing the floor towards General Balfour and his friends, past Bennie and Roxie who were still standing wheezing reminiscences, the lack of musical accompaniment not troubling them at all.

Captain Buchanan claimed three more dances before

Elizabeth could escape him, straight into the arms of General Balfour who led her very gracefully through a contredanse, then imperiously escorted her off the dance floor where she was immediately claimed by a young lieutenant who shyly led her back again.

Elizabeth wished she had not accepted the lieutenant who proceeded to blush at every word she said, and danced like a rabbit.

'Lieutenant Kellyson, Lieutenant *Kellyson*,' Elizabeth hissed in painful indignation, 'that again was my foot you hopped on!'

The lieutenant blushed self-consciously. 'Oh p-please, Miss Campbell, call me F-Freddie.'

An hour later, all music and dancing ceased as the time arrived for the bells to ring in the New Year. Everyone stood in anticipated silence as the lone piper in a kilt played a beautiful tune, and then all joined in the counting as the chimes rang out the old year, and the room erupted with a roar of cheers and endless shouts of 'Happy New Year!'

The success of the evening, and its enjoyment, surpassed all of Elizabeth's expectations. Between the dances with her various partners, Lachlan had escorted her to the dining room to find them refreshment, and on their return they had sat at one of the small tables drinking wine and watching the dancers, exchanging humorous comments, until another gallant arrived to claim a dance from her. It had been a wonderful evening, glittering and glamorous, and she had enjoyed every minute of it.

The lamps suddenly flared up, brightening the ballroom. It was late, and the tired and happy crowd began saying their farewells, dispersing to brave the coldness of the night.

'Time to go, Macquarie!' General Balfour called from the

doorway. 'Time to return to our hammocks!'

*

The night was cold and clear and the stars gleamed like diamonds. At Wigmore Street, Lachlan sprang out of the carriage and escorted Elizabeth to her door. As soon as the maid opened it, he again pressed her fingers affectionately and wished her a 'Happy New Year,' and then he turned down the steps and was gone.

Elizabeth stood watching the carriage as it slowly moved off, but it was only the old general who poked his head through the window and looked back, as if suddenly remembering he had not said farewell, calling back to her: 'Happy New Year, Miss um, um ... what?' His head disappeared for a second then re-emerged. 'Oh yes – *Campbell!* Happy New Year, Miss Campbell! Cheerio!'

*

On the journey home General Balfour became talkative. 'Frankly, Macquarie, I am inclined to agree with my friend General Stuart, it's high time you married again.'

Lachlan glanced at Balfour who smiled and cocked a twinkling blue eye 'Miss Campbell looks quite suitable, what? She's a nice-looking young woman.'

'She is, sir.'

'And she appears quite sound and reliable as well as charming. That's the kind of woman you want, sound and reliable.' Balfour pulled a face. 'Not like that Italian Countess who had her eye on me tonight! She may have been a lady, but I got the distinct impression she was going to ask me for a loan.'

Lachlan smiled disbelievingly.

'Not that I have anything against Italian Countesses,' Balfour explained, 'but three dead husbands hardly makes her trustworthy, eh what?'

The carriage slowed to a stop. Lachlan sprang out and held the door for Balfour. `Here we are, sir.'

Balfour remained seated, his face thoughtful. 'She gave me her card and invited me to call on her at home tomorrow, for afternoon tea ... but no, I'm sure it's for a loan.'

'And what makes you think that, sir?'

'Her non-stop talk about rubies and emeralds and all the other fine jewels we officers can pick up so cheaply in India, not to mention the handfuls we receive in prize money. Oh, she knew all about it. And you must remember, such things can make a man very attractive to a woman. '

'Then maybe it's more than just a loan she is looking for,' Lachlan grinned. 'Maybe it's *you* that should give some consideration to the subject of marriage.'

'God forbid,' Balfour said as he climbed out. 'I'm off to Perth first thing in the morning. The carriage is arriving at six. Hardly worth my while going to bed, eh what?'

'Goodnight, sir.'

'Goodnight, dear boy.'

Later, upon entering his own quarters, Lachlan was surprised to find his manservant still up, waiting for him. 'What is it, Joseph?' he asked.

'This dispatch, sir. It came just after you left this evening. It's marked urgent.'

Lachlan threw down his cape and ripped open the dispatch. He read the contents quickly, and then read them again more slowly, a frown on his face. He looked around, nodding to his servant. 'You may go to bed now, Joseph.'

'Thank you, sir. Goodnight.'

Lachlan poured himself a glass of brandy, and sat down in an armchair thinking about the content of the dispatch, hardly able to believe it. That old humbug Balfour – the man was incapable of talking straight about anything! All the time they had spent in each other's company tonight at the Ball, and then during the carriage journey home – all that nonsense about the Italian Countess looking for a loan. Yet not a word about *this!*

Lachlan read the dispatch again, informing him of his immediate posting to Perth in Scotland – and to ensure that the arrival of himself and his commanding officer in Perth could be effected as speedily as possible, a carriage to convey them to Scotland would arrive the following morning at six.

'Hardly worth my while going to bed, eh what?' he mimicked Balfour as he pulled out his portmanteau and began to pack.

When the carriage arrived just after six, General Balfour was already seated comfortably inside. Lachlan climbed into the carriage, sat on the seat opposite and glared at him. 'Why did you not give me any warning of this last night? And why does it have to be *me?*'

'You? I had no idea it would be *you* accompanying me to Perth.' Balfour gave him a wonderfully innocent stare. 'No idea at all.'

'Come, sir, the command would not assign you without informing you of the name of your staff officer. They would have told you that days ago.'

'No ... well, perhaps they might have suggested a few

names ... but none that I can recall.'

None that Balfour would accept, Lachlan thought. None that he was sure he could persecute with his favouritism. 'Did you request me, sir?'

'Request you?' Balfour smiled with withering suavity. 'My dear boy, of course I did not presume to request you.' He shifted into a more comfortable position on his seat. 'But, um ... well ... now that you mention it, I do seem to recall my pointing out your years of experience in India. So it must have been the Commander-in-Chief who decided that you would be a most suitable candidate for the job in hand.'

'My experience in India? Are we being posted back there?'

'Unfortunately not – well, not immediately.' Balfour relaxed back on his pillow, 'But our knowledge of India is urgently needed now, because the soldiers stationed in Perthshire are about to embark on some extensive training, and their officers need our wise and experienced guidance ... before they all depart for Bombay.'

*

There had been no time to write a letter, so when Lachlan's manservant called at the house in Wigmore Street later that day, the message he verbally conveyed to Henrietta Campbell was that Colonel Macquarie had left London due to his urgent posting elsewhere.

'Where elsewhere?' Henrietta asked.

Joseph had no idea, other than Colonel Macquarie had received an urgent dispatch, which required him to leave before dawn.

Elizabeth was so dumbfounded when Henrietta told her,

she remained speechless for many long minutes as she tried to take it in. The `elsewhere' was India, she concluded. It had to be India. Didn't he say General Balfour was already pining to go back there.

'Oh dear, I shall miss his visits,' Henrietta said sadly. 'And you, Elizabeth, have lost your escort.'

When Elizabeth made no reply, Henrietta said gently, `Elizabeth, you are a very lovely young woman, so I'm sure we will get you a suitable man very soon, one that will make you a very good husband.'

'But I don't *want* a husband,' Elizabeth responded angrily. 'To be honest, I have always been more interested in finding suitable and fulfilling employment.'

'Employment?' Henrietta almost sprang out of her chair. 'Elizabeth, are you forgetting that you are a first cousin to my son, the Earl of Breadlebane. What will people think if they hear that his young female cousin had to resort to seeking employment? And he'll be coming home in a few months, you know that.'

Elizabeth nodded, but she was suddenly determined. 'Then I will have to ensure that whatever employment I secure will not in any way disgrace him.'

TWENTY-TWO

Two months passed before Lachlan was granted any leave from his duties in Perth. During that time he had managed to get away and spend a day with George Jarvis in Edinburgh, but now that he had been granted seven days leave, he had decided to return to Mull to visit his mother.

Heavy rain poured down as his carriage rolled west, splattering against the windows. The journey was only seventy-five miles to Oban, yet the hours dragged dismally for Lachlan, unable to write a letter or read a book due to the furious jolting of the carriage. He was sure the axle on one of the wheels must be loose, but if he made the driver halt to check each wheel in the pouring rain, the delay could take hours and he wanted to reach Oban in time to catch the evening ferry.

He sat watching the rain batter against the windows, obscuring any view. Hours of silent thought was not his choice, he preferred his mind to be active and occupied. He made a fresh attempt to read his book, but it was simply impossible.

For a time he allowed himself to worry about George Jarvis and what George's future should hold. Marianne was now a teacher of mixed-race children at Bombay's English school and she wrote to him often in perfect English ... which reminded him of the two letters he had written to Elizabeth Campbell since his departure from London, but so far she had not replied. He stopped thinking and let his gaze travel into the distance. The rain had eased and he could see the wetness of the hills.

When they reached Oban he warned the driver, 'You

should check those wheels. I think the axle is loose on at least one of them.'

The ferry crossing was smooth, the rain had stopped. He finally reached Lochbuy and ran up the steps, feeling so hungry now that all he could think about was the enjoyment of a good supper.

Murdoch greeted him with a woeful face. 'Margaret is up in her bed,' he said. 'She's been up there all day, crying herself sick, and who can blame her? I always said that young sister of hers was a strange one.'

'Who, Elizabeth?'

'Aye, Miss Elizabeth, who else? Margaret feared that all Elizabeth's gallivanting down in that sinful London might turn her into some Englishman's trollop, but this – this is a hundred times worse in Maggie's opinion.'

'Worse? What is?' Lachlan asked, perplexed. 'Murdoch, what are you talking about?'

'Let's eat,' said Murdoch, leading the way into the dining room. 'I canna get my poor Maggie to eat a thing, so there's plenty.'

Lachlan took his seat, watching silently as two maids carried dishes to the table and began to serve. When they had left the room he looked questioningly at Murdoch. `So? What's all the distress about Elizabeth?'

Murdoch took a mouthful of food, and then shrugged with some annoyance. 'Miss Elizabeth has decided to become a Missionary teacher. Oh aye, it's all signed up and sealed. She's been learning and preparing for over a month, and now her passage is already booked and stamped to sail away next week.'

Lachlan stared at his uncle in astonishment.

'Aye, that was my reaction too, same as yours,

dumbfounded!' Murdoch lifted his glass. 'But, I tell ye, it's nearly killed my poor Maggie. She sent a letter over to Airds to her brother John asking him to try and stop Elizabeth, but I don't think he will be able to stop her either. No, from as far back as I can remember, Miss Elizabeth's behaviour has always been ill-judged and obstinate.'

'Where is she sailing to?'

'China.'

Lachlan slowly put down his knife. 'China?'

'Aye, China, as God is above us, China – to the very end of the earth she's going. So mebbe now you'll understand why her poor sister is crying herself into a sickness upstairs. Their father would never have allowed this to happen, never. Especially as it's not even to a Presbyterian Mission she's going, but one run by a group of them English Evangelists.'

Lachlan did not answer, hardly knowing what to say. If Elizabeth was determined to do this, then Murdoch was right, nobody could stop her. The depth of his own shock and disappointment surprised him. He looked down at his plate and realised he had not eaten a thing, nor did he feel like doing so, his appetite completely vanished.

'China ...' he finally murmured. 'Why?'

Murdoch shrugged. 'Why anything with Elizabeth? I've never understood the girl myself.'

'But why *China* of all places?' Lachlan persisted. 'The Chinese offer no welcome to Westerners, missionaries or otherwise, as the Jesuits have already found.'

Murdoch sighed, and gave up on his food, rising from his chair. 'I'd better go up to see how my poor Maggie is doing. This business has knocked her down flat.'

Lachlan was glad when Murdoch left him to join

Margaret. It gave him time alone, quiet and solitary, to try and give his thoughts some semblance of order. Elizabeth's decision was not the only surprise tonight, but also Murdoch's genuine concern for his wife.

In theory, he reflected, the union of Murdoch and Margaret should have been doomed from the start, based as it was on convenience. But reality had proved the marriage a great success, with husband and wife appearing to grow fonder of each other with every passing year, not to mention their production to date of eleven children.

And then he thought of Elizabeth. She was nice and she was fun, especially during their time together in London, but in truth he had always liked her. Yet he knew she was tired of the life she had been living and constantly yearned for new places and fresh experiences ... but if she believed that *China* was the solution, then she had been very ill advised.

China ... the place of his torment ... his thoughts went back to his own past for some long minutes, until the memories and the feelings within him made him feel physically sick

Later, in the darkness of his bedroom, he slept badly, dreaming of cold-eyed Chinese Mandarins who despised the British, their nightmarish images distorted beyond all reality.

He was glad to wake up, glad to see the morning light. He sprang out of bed, all his actions hurried. The previous night he had not known what to think or to do, but now he did know. Despite all his own persuasions to the contrary, he knew that one other solution was possible. At least it was worth a try.

The sound of his boots running down the stairs must

have awakened Murdoch. He had reached the front door of the house when Murdoch came lolloping down the stairs and into the hall calling after him, oddly comical-looking in his nightshirt.

`Where are you off to at this hour?' Murdoch asked.

'To London.'

'London?'

'I can't let her go to China, Murdoch. I have to try and stop her.'

'So why are ye going to London then?'

'Because that's where she's living, isn't it? At Wigmore Street.'

'Och no! She's been here in Mull for the last two days, saying her farewells to all of us. Didn't I tell ye how she left poor Maggie in such a bad state.'

'Yes, but you didn't tell me she was here on the island!' Lachlan snapped impatiently. 'So where is she now?'

'She left here yesterday to go over to say farewell to your mother. If you leave now you'll likely catch her before she leaves to come back here. But mind, she's planning to catch the evening ferry.'

Moments later Murdoch was back in his bedroom, standing by the window and watching Lachlan ride away at speed in the direction of Rossall. Margaret had clambered out of bed to stand and watch also.

Murdoch murmured, 'Do you think he'll be able to stop her, Maggie, when we couldna?'

Margaret's hand wiped at the tears on her red-blotched face. 'I couldna say, dear, but one thing I do know. Mebbe no one else in this world is capable of stopping Elizabeth, but *he* might. She was madly in love with him once, when she was about thirteen or so.'

*

The journey through the woods and tracks of Rossall to Oskamull took him longer than he had expected, due to the wetness of the ground from the rain the day before. Finally he reached the road leading down to the farm, his heart beating faster as he approached his old home.

His mother and Elizabeth were in the kitchen when he entered, seated at the table, their breakfast over.

'Lachlan!' His mother's smile was delighted. 'I'd no word ye were coming!'

He walked over to kiss his mother's cheek. 'Are you well?'

'Aye, I'm well. A trifle under the weather mebbe ... and so sad to hear Elizabeth is leaving us.'

Elizabeth had risen from her seat. Lachlan was alarmed to see the change in her. Her lustrous hair was severely scraped back into a knot and she wore a black dress of the kind worn by servants.

'My God, you even *look* like a Missionary,' he said. 'What's happened to you, Elizabeth? What's making you do this fanatical thing?'

Elizabeth turned to leave the room, but he caught her arm. 'I can't let you go,' he insisted, 'not to China.'

She wrenched away from him and put her hand to her head, as if trying to think. 'This is unfair,' she said. 'And this is certainly none of your business.'

'I've been to China. I know what it's like there. And it's definitely not a place for you.'

Mrs Macquarie rose to support him. 'Oh, I agree, verra likely it's no' the place for ye, Elizabeth.'

'So where *is* the place for me, in your opinions?' Elizabeth demanded angrily. She turned furious blue eyes on Lachlan.

'And is that why you came rushing over here at this early hour, to convey to me your downright disapproval of my journey to China?'

'No, not entirely, but can you please calm yourself down and allow us to talk about this. You're not catching the ferry until this evening, so you do have some time to spare, if you're willing to grant it.'

'It would be poor of you not to – spare him some of your time, I mean,' Mrs Macquarie said quickly. 'Maybe just a wee bit, Elizabeth hennie?'

Elizabeth sighed. 'Oh, very well. '

'So, now,' said Mrs Macquarie, moving towards the door. 'I think I'll take a wee stroll down to the shore and see how the kelpers are doing.'

When she had left the room, Elizabeth turned away from him. 'Just say whatever it is you want to say.'

'Elizabeth, why you are doing this? You were never obsessed with religion before.'

She spun round, cut to the quick. 'How dare you say that? I've always been a devout Presbyterian.'

'Then why are you going to China with a group of English evangelists?'

Confounded, she stared at him. Then her hand went to her head again and she stood in a dull pause. 'Oh, what does it *matter*,' she blurted out. 'And why should it matter to *you*? You're not my dutiful chaperone any more. '

'Marry me,' he said gently.

'What?' She stared at him, her eyes unbelieving, then accusing him bitterly. 'Is this yet another of your kind gestures?'

'No, just a simple and sincere request.'

'To marry you?'

'If you would be so kind.'

'But *why*?' She was pale now, quite distraught. 'It's inexcusable to make such a request when you have no feelings of that kind for me. Or do you think, like Henrietta, that I cannot live anywhere in this world without a *husband*!'

'I think' – he took a quick breath – `that I do have feelings of that kind for you ... it hurts me to realise that now. I never thought I could, or would, feel much affection for any woman again, but there are so many things I like about you, Elizabeth ...'

'Such as?' she interrupted bluntly. 'What are these many things you like about me? Please enlighten me? Go on.'

He smiled faintly. 'Do you think I came prepared with a list?'

'I don't know what to think,' she admitted.

He paused, then with simple frankness. 'The proposal is mine, Elizabeth, the answer is yours.'

Elizabeth was so dazed and confused she could not take it in. She sat down and put her face in her hands. 'Oh, I don't know ... I feel as if a hammer has struck my head ... my decision to go was made with such certainty ... I need time to think ... oh, this is so *unfair*!'

TWENTY-THREE

Dark clouds hung over the grounds of George Jarvis's school in Edinburgh. Lachlan felt his anxiety increasing as he walked slowly up the drive to the main door. He glanced up at the clouds, heavy with rain, and hoped that George would understand.

Minutes later he was standing in the hall of the school, his eyes moving over the numerous portraits of former Deans without seeing them, his mind preoccupied with the task ahead. He now faced a crisis of decision about George Jarvis, just as he had once done with Marianne.

At last a student appeared, listened to his request, nodded agreeably, and then led him up a flight of stairs to a long corridor where he silently indicated a dark mahogany door.

George Jarvis answered his knock with a smile of surprise, but instantly he sensed something was wrong and his smile faded. 'What is wrong?' he asked.

'Nothing,' Lachlan replied, walking into the room. 'I'm sorry to drop in on you like this without warning.'

'No, no, do not apologise for coming,' George said. 'You know I am always happy to see you.' He gestured to a leather armchair for Lachlan to sit down. 'Let me get you something to drink. Some hot tea?'

Lachlan shook his head and remained standing, silently looking around the room, realising that George had been working hard before his arrival, his desk covered in open books. 'I see I have interrupted your studies,' he said.

'It is a welcome interruption.' George sighed. `It's all so

boring, and I already know it all.'

Lachlan smiled. 'You know it all?'

'Yes,' George replied simply. 'Everything they teach me I have already learned in London. It is all very easy.'

'Then why do I continue to pay such high fees for your education here?'

'Yes, why?' George queried. 'I wonder that also.'

Lachlan turned towards the window and saw the clouds had broken into a heavy rain. Of course George was very intelligent, he knew that. And according to his Masters he had always worked very hard at his studies, determined to acquire a sound education. But getting George Jarvis to admit to that was impossible. Even as a boy he could never be persuaded to pretend he liked anyone or anything he disliked.

But George was no longer a boy, a fact that had become clear to Lachlan after his return from London. He had not seen George for almost six months and only then, visiting him here in Edinburgh, did he see the change, and realised that George Jarvis was now a very different young man to the one who had arrived in England almost three years earlier.

George had always been graceful in manner and handsome in looks, in a very *Eastern* way, but now everything about him was westernised. His black hair was as straight as silk, cut short in what Bappoo would call `the new *Angrezi* fashion'.

In Britain, George Jarvis had changed from a native to a foreigner, a brown boy in a school of whites. Perhaps it had been cruel to place him at such risk of racial prejudice, but George had quickly proved in London, and also here in Scotland, that he could take very good care of himself.

There were those, of course, who would forever damn George for the colour of his skin, but George had found a way of dealing with that type. He rarely got offended, preferring to laugh at them. But if bullies did persist in taking their prejudice beyond words, they soon learned to their cost that George Jarvis had not grown up in the slave trade, and then in a world of hardened soldiers, without learning something about self-defence. In the end, though, it was George's own personality that had eventually won him many friends.

So what was he to do now about George Jarvis, the young man? What would be best for him?

Lachlan sighed, knowing the answer. George was an Arabic-Indian. He had been born in India and spent most of his life in India. So perhaps it would be best if George returned to India.

'I think I would like some tea,' he said, needing more time to think. 'Will you arrange it, George.'

'Of course.' George agreed. 'I am your servant.'

'No, George, you are *not* my servant.'

'Then what am I?' George said offhandedly.

Lachlan turned back to the window, pretending to look at the rain. In memory he saw again the small slave-boy he had taken from Cochin. The boy Jane had loved on sight. Since then the boy had become a part of his life, a part of his heart. More like a son than anything else. God knew it would break his heart to part with George Jarvis, but it was for the best.

George said quietly, 'Before I arrange your tea, first tell me how you are? What you have been doing, and why you have come here now?'

Lachlan told him about Elizabeth and their forthcoming

marriage. George did not seem in the least surprised. He said, 'She will be happy now. And for you, it is time for you to be happy again also.'

'What about you, George?' Lachlan asked. 'It's also now time to decide your future. Have you given any thought to what you would like to do?'

George looked at him silently for a long moment. 'Have you?'

'Have I what?'

'Given any thought to what you would like me to do.'

'It's not a matter of what *I* would like, I'm asking what *you* would like to do?'

Lachlan's anxiety was turning to anger. George *knew* what he was trying to say, and how *hard* it was for him to say it, yet George was refusing to help him.

'You do know, George, that once I marry, I can never again return to India. Not even if the Army wishes it. Not with another wife at my side. I could not do that now, and never again, ... go back to India.'

George's dark eyes were expressionless. 'But now you want *me* to go back to India.'

'No, no, I don't *want* you to go back. I'm just trying to decide what is best for you, in the long term. You have an education now. The opportunities are numerous, and I will see that you are financially secure.'

George's face remained expressionless.

'You know that you would be *happier* in India, George. India is where you belong, and have always belonged. There is no need for you to stay here in Britain because you feel some duty to me. And the truth is, George, I think we both know that once you leave this school, life here in the West may be very hard for you, not only in Scotland but in

England too. People will be prejudiced against you, and you won't be able to deal with the entire world as easily as you have done in school. But in India ... with your education and financial security, we both know how you would be treated ... like a prince.'

George smiled in a way that hurt Lachlan with a memory of times past. The boy had always insisted he was the son of a prince, and if he returned now to India he would surely be treated like one.

George turned and sat down in the chair behind his desk. He opened a drawer in the desk and took out a book. 'In my school,' he said, 'in London, and also here in Edinburgh ... they made me read their Bible.'

Lachlan hadn't known that, but it was hardly a surprise. He should have realised they would consider it their duty to convert the heathen.

'There was one story in their Bible that I liked very much,' George said. 'I read it many times. ... especially a little story of two women. Naomi and Ruth. Do you know it?'

'Yes, vaguely, but I can't remember it. Why?'

George opened the book in his hands and began to search until he found the right page. 'The Book of Ruth,' he said finally, and Lachlan realised the book he was holding was a Bible.

'It tells of a famine in the land of Moab,' George continued. 'Naomi's husband and two sons died in the famine. One of these dead sons was the husband of Ruth. So both women are left alone with only each other. Naomi had great love for her daughter-in-law, but wanted to return to her own country of Judah. So she said to Ruth, "Go back now to your people. May God give love to you, as you have given love to the dead and to me. Go back now, to your people and your gods."'

Lachlan turned back to the window, deeply hurt.

'But Ruth said, "Ask me not to leave you, or stop me from following you. For where you go I will go. Your people will be my people. And your God will be my God. Where you die, I will die, and there also will I be buried." And when Naomi saw that Ruth was determined to stay with her, she said no more.'

George closed the book.

A long silence fell within the room. Lachlan stared out at the rain, realising this was the day that George Jarvis had always feared, and had prepared himself to fight it by using a story from the Bible to explain his feelings: that no amount of money could influence his choice, and no degree of racial prejudice would frighten him.

Lachlan felt a thickness in his throat, and an emotion of sheer relief. Thank God the decision had finally been made – and made by George – not him. His own decision would have been wrong, and too painful for both of them, he knew that now.

He turned round. 'Are you sure that's what you really want, George? To stay here with me in Britain, no matter what?'

George nodded. 'Britain or anywhere else.'

Lachlan finally sat down in the leather armchair and sighed. 'I really do feel in need of that hot tea now. Will you bring it, George?'

George Jarvis smiled. 'Yes, my father.'

TWENTY-FOUR

Mrs Macquarie awoke at dawn and creaked out of bed slowly, feeling a bit shaky, but after a glass of buttermilk and an oatcake she walked it off by rambling down to the shore's edge and watching the kelpers for a time, and then her eyes moved away from the kelpers to gaze out towards the old grey sea.

Hours later she returned to the house to be greeted by her maid Morag, a little girl of only seventeen, who immediately scolded her for getting up before her and seeing to her own breakfast.

'Ye canna be doing for yourself no more, Mrs Macquarie. Ye have to remember that you're very old an' very feeble an' that's why I'm here to look after ye.'

She was not really that old, in her own opinion, and definitely not feeble. No, there was plenty of life in her yet. But Morag was tiresomely young and tiresomely tactless and she would have to ask Lachlan to please, *please* replace her with someone a wee bit older.

She glanced at the clock, surprised to see it was ten minutes to eleven. She must have spent longer down by the shore than she had realised.

'I need to tidy meself up,' she said to Morag, and then she had moved eagerly up the short shallow stairs to her bedroom where she smoothed her hair and straightened her collar, before donning her best bonnet, and reaching for her finest shawl to wrap around her shoulders.

'I'm away out again,' she told Morag.

The sun had risen over Oskamull hours earlier, bright

and warming, lighting the ridge of the grey path down to the farm.

Mrs Macquarie sat on a stone boulder by the edge of the field and gazed towards the eastern hill, just as Donald had done so many times in the past, waiting and watching.

She had decided it would be more peaceful to wait for Lachlan outside the house, outside in the fresh air and silence, where she could sit and think of all the changes that had taken place during the past year. And aye, it had been a gleg year, a wonderful year, starting with Lachlan's marriage to Elizabeth, and then with each visit seeing the gradual change in him, the gradual change in Elizabeth, both looking more and more relaxed in each other's company, as if they had stopped being awkward and strange with each other, and had quickly become very close friends.

She sat very still, her neck curved in lassitude, listening to the occasional bleating of the sheep as she smiled while remembering how much she had liked Elizabeth, and how she not been at all surprised when, only eleven months after the wedding, Elizabeth had given birth to a healthy baby girl.

The sound of wheels ... she looked up. Her heart jumped when at last she saw the horse and carriage coming down the grey road. Aye, it was Murdoch's carriage to be sure, but she hoped to God that Murdoch himself was not in it.

She stood up and hurried forward, and in the hustle and bustle of excitedly greeting her visitors, she felt a profound relief that nobody from Lochbuy had come with them. No, it was just Lachlan and Elizabeth and their two-month old baby daughter whom they had brought to meet her grandmother.

Surprisingly, it was Lachlan who carried the bundle

containing the child, holding it protectively while Elizabeth fussed with the driver, asking him to lift out her 'baby bag'.

Mrs Macquarie felt a melting of her bones as she looked into the tiny face of her first grandchild, a child with bright blue eyes and wisps of golden hair. 'Bye, but she's bonnie ...' she said slowly. 'Oh, I didna expect her to be so bonnie ...' and as she lifted her hand to touch the tiny face, tears of joy began streaming down her own weather-beaten cheeks.

*

The Christening was to take place the following afternoon, with everyone from Lochbuy travelling to Oskamull for the occasion, including Reverend McBride who would ride over from Tobermory. His mother would not be forced to travel long journeys anymore, Lachlan had decided, so everyone else must get into their carriages or up on their horses and make the journey instead.

'And ye say the McLeans of Lagganulva are coming in the morning to prepare all the food?' Mrs Macquarie said to Elizabeth. 'Bye, that's kind of them. They were always good cooking women, the McLean's. And arc thcy happy to do it, Elizabeth?'

'Very happy,' Elizabeth assured her. 'In fact, from the tone of their letter in reply to mine, I believe they would have felt very insulted if we had asked anyone else.'

'Ah, that's good to know ...' Mrs Macquarie sat for a long moment looking down at her hands in her lap, trying to remember another question she wanted to ask, and then it came to her and she looked up. 'And who's to be the godfather?'

'George Jarvis.' Lachlan carefully placed his daughter into

her travelling crib. 'George will be a fine godfather.'

'George?' Mrs Macquarie looked at Elizabeth. 'Not Murdoch? I thought Murdoch woulda insisted on being the godfather.'

'Well, yes, he did insist,' Lachlan replied, 'but Murdoch has nine children of his own to care for; and if, in the future, he was ever called upon to give his godfatherly help to my child, he would probably turn that help into an outstanding debt, but George will be very different in that respect.'

Elizabeth smiled. 'George simply adores her. Every move she makes seems to fascinate him, every little cry and he goes running. From the day she was born George has always referred to her as his "little sister"`.

'Aye, oh aye ...' Mrs Macquarie nodded. 'George is a fine young man ... and a kind one.'

*

Later that afternoon, while she sat on the window-seat cradling her sleeping granddaughter, Mrs Macquarie watched through the window as Lachlan and Elizabeth took a stroll down to the shore, their manner of happy companionship heightening her own feelings of joy. The two were talking and laughing together, and then Elizabeth suddenly gave a little skip as if she was delighted to be going down to the water and breathing in the sea air.

She smiled to herself ... Elizabeth looked so fine and fit and not at all like a woman who had recently given birth.

And Lachlan ... well, he had travelled a long way to reach this time of love and happiness in his life ... not as passionate as his love for the first girl, she supposed, but aye, it was a new kind of love she saw in his face now when he looked at Elizabeth, more calm and contented, as if all the scattered threads of his life over the years had finally knitted together back here in Scotland in a pattern of stability and completion ... Aye, for him now, there would be no slipping back into the past. His new love for Elizabeth, and his adoration of this wee child in her arms, would ensure that.

She came out of her thoughts and continued watching as the two figures, hand in hand, dwindled into the distance and disappeared down the grass-edged path towards the calm waters of the old grey sea.

AUTHOR'S NOTE

In Macao, (Macau) the first Protestant Cemetery was finally established in 1821 by the British East India Company.

THE FAR HORIZON

In this sequel to *BY EASTERN WINDOWS* George Jarvis is now a young man, and with him we travel to a wilderness on the other side of the world and witness the rise to greatness of Lachlan Macquarie who, with extraordinary intelligence and a deep compassion for the inhabitants, turned a neglected convict colony into a country, and named it Australia.

New South Wales, a convict colony peopled with characters from all walks of life, and all places in the British Isles, who find themselves banished to the Antipodes for crimes often no greater than fishing in a neighbour's stream, or pilfering a strip of ribbon from their mistress's sewing basket.

And it is amongst these unlucky people that George Jarvis meets the girl of his dreams, and teaches her about the goodness of life.

Also by Gretta Curran Browne

The Liberty Trilogy

TREAD SOFTLY ON MY DREAMS

FIRE ON THE HILL

A WORLD APART

*

GHOSTS IN SUNLIGHT
(Contemporary Thriller)

ORDINARY DECENT CRIMINAL
(Novel of Fim starring Kevin Spacey)

RELATIVE STRANGERS
(TV Series Tie-in starring Brenda Fricker)

*

The Macquarie Series

BY EASTERN WINDOWS

THE FAR HORIZON

JARVISFIELD

www.grettacurranbrowne.com

22732822R00188

Printed in Great Britain
by Amazon